Books by C A Farlow

The Nexus Series

A Quantum Convergence
Book 1

A Quantum Uncertainty
Book 2

A Quantum Singularity
Book 3

Buzz for *A Quantum Singularity*
Book Three of The Nexus Series

2020 GCLS Awards: Finalist, Best Science Fiction/Fantasy Novel
Golden Crown Literary Society

2021 BookAuthority.org: Named one of the 13 Best New
Singularity eBooks To Read in 2021

"Fantastic world-building, colorful characters, alternate realities, magic, science, and telepathy between humans, wolves, and horses! Who could ask for anything more?" —*MB Panichi, author of* **Saving Morgan** *and other award-winning science fiction novels*

"This book 3 was wonderful. It tied up all the lose strings of the previous two books. It brought a proper ending to this trilogy. This was a wonderful series. This was a great addition to my collection of sci-fi books. Thank you for a great travel through the universe." —*A Delighted Kindle Customer*

Buzz for *A Quantum Uncertainty*
Book Two of The Nexus Series

2017 Rainbow Awards: Winner,
Cate Culpepper Award for Best Paranormal Romance

2017 Rainbow Awards: Best Lesbian
Book of the Year, Tenth Place tie

"SciFi through the fresh eyes of a real science person! The story is well-written and reflects some cutting-edge scientific applications of theories suggested as much as a century ago. The characters are a bit self-conscious but likeable. The science is presented in a clear and compelling manner and the SciFi angles are clever and creative. The writing overall is approachable and entertaining." —*Elise Rolle, Rainbow Awards*

"Loved this second book into this unique trilogy. Another cliff hanger that makes you anxious the read book three. CA Farlow does an excellent job at creating this world, with all the ins and out of any society."
—*A Happy Kindle Customer*

"Watching the bond and love deepen between Alex and Lauren as they weeded out corruption in the months leading to their wedding was wonderful. Experiencing their honeymoon and Lauren's reunion with her friends was also pure joy, but the stinger to lead into book 3 tore my heart from my chest as roughly as it could. I hope the finale isn't too far away." —*DefinitelyNotARabbit Review*

Buzz for *A Quantum Convergence*
Book One of The Nexus Series

2016 Rainbow Awards: 3rd Place Lesbian Sci-Fi/Futuristic
2016 Rainbow Awards: 3rd Place Lesbian Debut Novel
2016 Golden Crown Society Awards: Finalist, Best Debut Novel
2018 The Lesbian Review: Named to Top 100 Best Lesbian Books List

"Okay, I'm ready to gush about this one. There isn't anything I can say I didn't like . . . I couldn't put the book down, and if you're into sci-fi or fantasy, you won't be sorry if you pick it up." —*Inked Rainbow Reads*

"Fascinating! This was a wonderful story, full of drama and love. The characters were full-bodied and the story grabbed and dragged you along on the tips of your toes from beginning to end. A fascinating read."
—*Skip Maslan, Goodreads*

"This is a great book for sci-fi lovers, and probably some fantasy lovers, as well. Also, anyone who loves a romance with fated mates or soulmates would find this interesting. The book drew me in quickly and had me turning pages, always wanting to see what came next. Farlow has also left some interesting threads dangling at the end, making me want to read the second book as soon as it comes out to see where she takes Alex and Lauren next." —*The Lesbian Review*

"I also liked a lot how fantasy elements were well-placed into the story to give the plot an edge that other sci-fi don't have. I will wait impatiently for the next book." —*Elisa Rolle, Rainbow Awards*

A Quantum Singularity

Book Three
The Nexus Series

C A Farlow

LAUNCHPOINT
PRESS

2021

ISBN: 978-1-63304-225-4
Ebook: 978-1-63304-226-1

Editing: JZ
Formatting: Patty Schramm
Cover: Lorelei

Launch Point Press
Portland, Oregon

Foreword

For the Second Edition

Where does science fiction end and science begin? This boundary is fluid, as ongoing scientific research and discovery evolve. Sometimes, science fiction is the driving force, providing insight into the future. Where would we be without our smartphones? These marvelous devices have origins in Star Trek communicators. Thank you, Gene Roddenberry.

This story makes use of some of the most recent discoveries in physics and chemistry. Gravitational waves were first postulated by Henri Poincaré in 1905. Albert Einstein predicted their existence with his special theory of relativity in 1916. However, gravitational waves were not discovered until September 2015. In that month, the Advanced LIGO Detector arrays in Washington State and Louisiana detected them. Since that date, many more have been detected.

In May 2019, a photo was taken of S02, a gigantic blue star, as it swept past Sagittarius A, the supermassive black hole at the center of our Milky Way galaxy. Light from S02 was stretched by the gravitational forces created by this supermassive black hole and the color of the star shifted from blue to red, as predicted by Einstein's theory of special relativity. Experimental proof of a theory proposed more than a hundred years ago.

Quantum computing using entangled pairs of photons is in use today. Quantum communications is at the cusp of applied application. A quantum message has been sent between two places on Earth and from low orbit satellites to a point on Earth. Quantum devices, using Einstein's "spooky actions at a distance" will make digital privacy an impenetrable fortress in the near future. In 2019, physicists at the University of Glasgow School of Physics and Astronomy captured a photo of a pair of entangled photons. A picture worth a thousand words or in this instance—a thousand equations.

Molecular weaving and the basis for Terran analyzer gel are recent examples of applied science generated from theoretical research noted in today's scientific journals. Nanites are now used to deliver medication directly to tumors, rather than treating the entire body and to address superfund site cleanup. The origin of the moon and its anorthosite exterior are real, as proven by the rock samples brought back by the *Apollo* astronauts. Quantum loop gravity and the existence of parallel realities are still in their theoretical infancy.

The Comin bioweapon deployed against Terra Prime is based on the theory our DNA contains relic fragments inherited from ancient viral infections. These ancient retro-viral leftovers which the Comin used to impact the current generation of Terrans, is now being researched by the veterinarians in Australia and their work with koalas. An inherited retroviral change in koala DNA is causing cancer in the present generation. These endogenous retroviral changes were previously thought to be 'junk' DNA which caused no change in the current generation, but now are identified as precursors of chlamydia, an HIV-AIDs-like infection, and other cancers changing future koala generations risks to these diseases.

This book is named *A Quantum Singularity* in honor of Albert Einstein and his postulation of the existence of black holes and singularities—the immensely dense bits of matter—which exist at the center of black holes. And in honor of Steven Hawkins, whose seminal work in cosmology helped refine our thoughts on black holes, including the difference between stellar black holes and supermassive black holes. Until March 29, 2019, black holes were still highly theoretical, and in fact, there were physicists who argued vehemently against their existence. However, on that day in March, a photo of a supermassive black hole in the center of the M87 galaxy was taken. These denizens of the universe exist and again, Albert Einstein and his theory of general relativity are proven from experimental and actual evidence.

One of the events in this book, which occur on Terra, deals with the bloom of *Cypripedium reginae* or the Queen's Lady Slipper orchids. These rare, beautiful, solitary flowers do exist in the northern reaches of North America. Their delicate white and pink blossoms are so rare they are protected by Canadian law.

As in Book One and Two, readers interested in learning more about the science and scientific theories used as the basis for this science fiction novel are encouraged to explore further. The author has provided a reading list at the end for their personal indulgence.

Though the persons inhabiting this tale and the existence of parallel realities and faster-than-light travel are creations of the author's imagination, the geographic places and most of the scientific concepts used do exist in Earth's reality—as are the environmental and health challenges planet Earth shares with the Comin Homeworld.

CA Farlow
July 2021

Acknowledgments

An author owes much to all who touch her work: up close, as the editor reviews the plot and themes and point-of-view conflicts; the beta-reader who believes in the author and gladly reads her work with enthusiasm and a keen eye; even closer still are the proofreaders who look for and corrects things that auto-correct and the author's weary gaze misses. Further off a publisher paves the way with introductions and advertising and recommendations to various reviewers. Furthest away yet closest to the author's heart are her readers. You keep the author focused, energized, and motivated.

I thank all the readers who embraced *A Quantum Convergence* and *A Quantum Uncertainty,* who have waited patiently for this final installment of the trilogy and those who sent words of question and encouragement to me. And a special thanks to those who took the time to review *AQC* and *AQU* and post their thoughts on the various sites. Each and every review is taken to heart, listened to, and appreciated. It kept me going, gave me the strength to top every hurdle life and the third volume threw up.

Lori and the wonderful staff at Launch Point Press for reissuing this series. Thank you for believing in Lauren and Alex and their world.

Jodi, as always, this book is better from your review. Your input is invaluable, and I treasure our friendship.

Lorelei, graphic designer, you provide a wonderful picture of our journey.

Author's Note About Appendices

PLEASE NOTE: The back of the book contains information to help readers understand and navigate the special world of this novel. There you will find:

- List of the characters and their roles
- Pronunciation guide
- The Thirteen Clans of Terra
- List of Terran Clan Ships
- List of books to learn more about the science in this series

Dedication

Life has a way of inserting itself at the most inopportune times, as it did for me over the last two years. I apologize for the tardiness of this work and thank my readers for their patience.

This book is for the readers who've enjoyed taking this journey with Lauren and Alex and have been patient enough to wait for the conclusion.

And

For all the furkids who touch our lives and provide us poor humans with undying, unconditional love.

Starbuck, 13 May 2003 to 24 June 2018—I love you Boo-ba-Doo.
Aonwyn, 11 November 2000 to 23 April 2020—I love you Aonie-Bon.

Dedication of the Nexus Series

The scope of work needed to produce this series would not be possible without the support of my very best friend and mate, J.P. I thank you for all you do, all you sacrificed and suffered, all you give to me each and every day. Your contributions made these three books what they are.

Prologue
We begin where we ended . . .
Book Two: The Epilogue

The howl of wolves and the scream of horses shattered the pristine wilderness and echoed off the surrounding granite peaks as blue lightning streaked from the nexus membrane, blackening the snow-covered ground around the small group of Terrans and their animal companions. Robert McLaran dropped to one knee, his head hanging, black hair draping over his shoulders and his scream joined the cacophony of the animals. The ground shook with tremors and boulders cascaded down the tallis slopes surrounding the nexus cave as psi-energy tore through the roots of the granite peaks. Lauren dropped to the ground in semi-consciousness as her soul was torn asunder.

"What's happening?" Susan yelled and ran to Lauren, reaching out to cover her kneeling form and protect her from the falling rocks.

Làireach answered her bondmate's question. *"Alex is gone. I can no longer feel her across the nexus. She is lost in the quantum tubula."*

"No. Not again. No—" Lauren's cry tore through the basin. Her pain engulfed the companions adding to the flood of psi-energy being released from the nexus. A flood of memories crashed over Lauren. She was back in the Keep, kneeling in a snow-covered courtyard. The silence within her soul was deafening and she screamed through their bond, trying desperately to reach Alex. She was forcibly evicted again, just like that winter's morning. Sent away. Banished. Alone. Her heart and soul bled.

Newkirk staggered to his feet and grabbed Lauren up off her knees, lifting her into the air. He shook her hard by the shoulders, as her feet dangled above the ground.

"Lauren," he screamed at her.

She slowly raised her head and looked into his eyes.

"You must not succumb to the void. Fight it. Fight it hard. Alex needs you."

Lauren felt herself nod, but she was disembodied, numb, standing outside the moment, watching the action from a different perspective.

"Reach out. Find Alex. Pull her back."

Lauren knew she nodded again.

"You can do this. Your bond is strong enough."

As Newkirk placed her back on the ground, Lauren slowly stood to her full height and began to gather her strength.

"Find your bondmate. Do it now, Consort!" Newkirk screamed again.

Raising her arms to the blue sky above, Lauren closed her eyes. She focused her psychic energy and began to search this reality and across the quantum tubula to Earth's reality. Her strength began to flag. Then, Lauren ripped strength from each of the others. Sharon and Susan collapsed. Làireach squealed and dropped to her knees as her bondmate lost consciousness but Lauren did not stop.

More, I need more. And then Lauren felt her, but she was far away, moving at a tremendous speed. *"Alex, there you are. I have you."*

Nothing.

"Alex! Our bond can overcome this distance. You must help me complete the connection."

Nothing again. Lauren screamed, raising her head to the bright afternoon sky. She spun on her heel, aligning her body in the direction her soul's other half was traveling. *"Alex, I need you! Now and forever! I am yours and you are mine. Hear me!"*

"I hear you," a pain-laced whisper answered Lauren's shout.

"Where are you?"

A pause, then another whisper, *"I do not know, but I feel her. She is near."* Lauren felt Alex gather her strength and then their bond snapped fully into place and hummed with their combined strength. A command followed, and each of the companions bowed their heads as their queen spoke. *"You will follow your Co-Ruler. She will lead Terra. You will honor and obey her. For Terra, for always."*

Part One

The Search

*Be alone, that is the secret
of invention; be alone, that
is when ideas are born.*

~Nikola Tesla

Chapter One
Council Chamber, The Keep, Terra

Molten, boiling anger raged through Lauren like lava spewed from a volcano. Her anger threatened to consume her. Never had she been this angry. The edges of her vision tinted red as the Terran council continued to fight over Alex's kidnapping. The circular granite chamber rang with their shouts. *How can these fools not see what's before them? How can they argue at a time like this? This is the time for action, for working together, not fighting among ourselves.* Lauren thought as the maelstrom of the Council continued to build.

She wanted to join their argument and scream at them to listen, but she knew she couldn't. Lauren was now the fifteenth Ruler of Terra and knew she must act accordingly. Alex set the example of behavior before her. Alex used diplomacy based on inclusiveness, listening, and negotiation. Suddenly, Lauren realized she wasn't Alex. Nor was the situation anything this council had dealt with before. Even their escape from Terra Prime and the subsequent journey across the Milky Way galaxy to find Terra couldn't compare. Lauren realized she couldn't join the fight or demand action. Nor could she hide behind Alex's strength of position and power, as she had as Co-Ruler and Consort.

This thought spurred others. She was Ruler now and she must assert her right-to-rule. She must lead as she sees fit, not worry about what Alex would do. There wasn't time for second-guessing herself.

Alex was gone. Again. The large, ornately carved ironwood chair next to her own was empty. Lauren's only salvation was the tenuous connection she still felt with Alex. She had no idea how she was able to feel Alex through their bond. Gwenhwyfach stole Alex out of the nexus and spirited her away on the *Dubh Mogairle*. Now, the giant Clan Cador ship was racing away from Terra to an unknown destination.

Lauren clung to the nanometer-thin filament of pure psi-energy connecting her to her bondmate. It stretched across the intragalactic distance to where Alex was held captive. *Will the connection hold?* She didn't know. *Will I survive if the filament breaks?* She knew she wouldn't. *Will I be able to follow it to find Alex?* She was certain she would. Paramount to everything else was getting Alex back. If the Terrans were to survive, she must rescue her love. For Lauren to survive, she must reunite their souls, torn asunder by Alex's kidnapping.

Lauren retreated deeper into the folds of Alex's red and gray wool Doouglas tartan, trying to escape the chaos storming around her in this meeting. Her anger simmered just below the surface. She sat in the chair of the Co-Ruler on the Doouglas side of the giant tree-table. Her auburn hair hung in a lank braid draped over her shoulder. She listened, silently raging at the situation, not knowing if she would be allowed to exercise her right to rule. The cacophony of loud, angry voices filled the room as the Council of Terra argued. Shouts of "what do we do?" and "how do we proceed?" clashed with shouts of "do not delay." Pleas of "proceed with caution" and "we must plan" were lost in the mix.

"Who will lead us now?" Someone shouted. Lauren jerked in her chair and her heart sank, she couldn't tell who said it with all the noise. But Lauren had her answer; this Council would not follow her.

With this knowledge, Lauren's fear escalated as the interminable meeting continued, the shouts got louder and the arguments more heated. Finally, Lord McLaran, Chief of Clan McLaran, Leader of the Terran Black Guard, one of her most strident supporters, rose from his chair. His broad shoulders were hunched beneath his plaid of argyle-patterned green and navy, his black eyes lost beneath the folds of his drooping silvered brows. Deep furrows creased his normally smooth face. McLaran's emotions—anger, shame, sorrow, disbelief—beat at Lauren through her bond with his companion horse, Gríobhtha. The horse befriended Lauren when she was trying to escape back to Earth-reality. Gríobhtha was one of the first to recognize her as the Savior of Terra. McLaran's emotions warred for dominance within him, hammering Lauren deeper into her chair. She thought McLaran had aged more in the last two days than in all the prior two hundred and two rotations of his life.

"Councilors of Terra, please." He held up his hands for silence. "Let us not argue. Time is of the essence. We are in agreement. We must mount a rescue mission. We cannot delay further." As the council continued to argue, he shouted, "Quiet." His voice reflected off the gray granite walls and filled the circular chamber. The Councilors continued to argue. Their shouts only grew louder.

Lauren chuckled ruefully. *Right. Time. Something we don't have.*

Only eleven of the thirteen sides of the giant *Hyper-arborea sempervirens* tree-table were occupied. This species of fir tree was indigenous to Terra Prime, homeworld to the Terran people. It was reared from seeds, which survived the journey to Terra after the Comin bioweapon attack devastated the Terran Prime biosphere. Though its top was flattened into the council table, its core and roots still lived. The roots grew deep into the substructure of the Keep, fed and watered by the royal gardening technicians. The *sempervirens* possessed sentient properties and along with the sword of the Doouglas—the first Terran Foremother—the pair had intervened in several critical events in the last year.

Lauren laid her hands on the table, its energy warming her palms. *"Come on, I know you're listening. I need your guidance."* Despite her plea, the tree and the sword remained silent.

The two vacant sides of the table were where the traitors of Clans Cador and Stuart would sit. Somehow, they had escaped their imposed exile in the western islands and were now streaking away from Terra on the Clan Cador ship with Alex. Somehow, they had pulled Alex from within the quantum tubula as she crossed from Earth-reality back to Terran-reality, a feat only a psi-engineer of immense strength could accomplish. A feat, Gwenhwyfach—Chief of Clan Cador—did.

The backlash of psi-energy she released to kidnap Alex nearly destroyed the Keep. Giant cracks now split the boulevard into a patchwork of tilted yellow-granite blocks. The fifteen-meter-thick granite curtain wall which surrounded the Keep was so skewed, the postern and central gates would not close completely.

Several anorthosite monoliths of the sacred stone circle had rocked loose. Yet, only the traitors' clan stones had toppled over. Even now, the Keep continued to rock on its foundations as terra-tremors shook the area. These after-shocks were the planet releasing the last of Gwenhwyfach's massed psi-energy, trying to dissipate the strain accumulated in the crust from the attack. As Lauren thought of all the damage they sustained, the circular chamber rolled beneath them. Another terra-tremor. Dust drifted from the ceiling as the trembling slowly stopped. The Council room fell silent.

"We cannot delay. If we do not mobilize the fleet immediately, we will never catch the *Black Orchid*," Chief Graham demanded through his bristling red mustache. He wasn't listening to McLaran and seemed inured to the tremor. He continued to press his own opinions.

Lauren had had enough. "No." Her quiet disagreement sliced through the building anger within the room.

All heads turned to her. "What do you mean, no?" Hamish McLeod asked in disbelief, his face stained with grief. His brother, Chief of Clan McLeod, was missing and presumed dead. Admiral Iain McLeod had been in a construction flitter, and the sensor records showed images of the vessel caught in the weapons exchange as the *Black Orchid* escaped the Terran

Solar System. "If we do not launch the fleet immediately, we will never catch them."

Rising, Lauren gathered Alex's tartan closely around her shoulders and tried to suppress her shivering. She drew a deep breath and straightened. "There are only two things we must do immediately. First, determine how the traitor accomplished the kidnapping. And second, figure out how we can beat her to her destination."

"There is no destination. We do not know where the traitor is going. We have only two datapoints from the in-system sensors and that is not enough to triangulate a possible destination. They have a significant head-start and if we continue to delay, we will never intercept them." Hamish stood and leaned toward Lauren with a menacing air. "We cannot beat them to their destination when we do not know their course. We must give chase and catch them." He punctuated his point with a slap on the tree-table's smooth surface. The sound snapped through the silent room.

Lauren leaned in. "If we don't figure out how Gwenhwyfach snatched Alex from the quantum tubula and create a way to counteract another attack, any of us are vulnerable." Mention of the traitor by name caused several council members to hiss. Lauren ignored this reaction and swung around to Chief Psi-technician Newkirk in a silent plea for support. Lord Newkirk remained slumped in his chair, staring down at the growth rings in the table, his finger randomly tracing their concentric patterns. Lauren stood alone.

Hamish pointed at Lauren and turned to the others. "We cannot use a nexus to travel. We cannot transport enough troops and resources through a quantum tubula. We must utilize the fleet to transport our guard. Therefore, we do not need to know how she did it. We know she did. Now we have to go after her."

Lauren shook her head and stood even taller, looking at each clan chief in turn. Most looked away, others would not look up at all. *Well, there you have it, Lauren. Just what you expected, they're already defeated, and none believe you can do anything about it.* She sighed, frustration ripping through her.

"And what, leave Terra unprotected by dispatching the entire fleet to chase after them? What if this is a feint?" She paused to let her question be heard. "What if there are others, other traitors here on Terra, waiting for the fleet to depart. Ready to take over Terra in Cador's name?" Lauren's voice rose with her anger. Her cheeks warmed and she knew they matched the color of her hair. "What if the Comin are waiting? Ready to move in and conquer Terra. Then what?" She took a deep breath. "That can't happen. That won't happen. I will not allow us to leave Terra defenseless." She pulled Alex's tartan around her again. Her words and emotions demanded answers.

McLaran sank back into his chair. McLeod sat and looked away, dismissing her. Lord Graham stood. He took up the council's challenge, ignoring Lauren, as he turned to the others. "I demand this Council choose a ruler from among us, one to lead the rescue." His voice rose in volume with each word.

"I second that demand. We are leaderless and this needless debate is causing undue delay. We must act now." Lord MacBain stood and placed a hand of support on Graham's laurel green and black tartan.

"We aren't leaderless," Lauren countered. "You're ignoring Alex's last command." She turned to Alex's three companions where they sat along the outer walls. Angus, Robert, and Tavish sat behind each of their clan chiefs. "You all heard her." The young men she sought support from were raised with Alex and knew her better than anyone in this room, except Lauren. She knew they extended their loyalty to her as well, and she cherished their support.

Tavish MacDonald, Alex's strength and right arm, and Lauren's named Protector and Guardian sat behind his mother and chief of his clan, the Lady MacDonald. The tiny red-headed woman was the Terran Lady of the Ancients, historian and record-keeper of Terra. Tavish was a master blacksmith and had forged the rapier hanging at Lauren's left side. He nodded and stood.

Lauren turned to Robert McLaran, Alex's conscience and compass. He could be a prankster, but Lauren had grown to love the young man who never wavered in his support of Alex. He sat behind his father, Lord McLaran. He stood and gave a single nod, accompanied by a fist raised across his chest.

Lastly, she turned to Angus Newkirk, one of the foremost scientific technicians of Terra, and the companion she was closest to. He rose and placed his large hand on his father's shoulder. Lord Newkirk startled from his reverie of the table. "Yes, the companions all heard Her Majesty's final command." Angus repeated Alex's command verbatim, *"You will follow your Co-Ruler. She will lead Terra. You will honor and obey her. For Terra, for always."*

He pointed at Lauren. "I, Angus Newkirk, follow you. You are Her Royal Majesty, Lauren Beckwith Fraser Doouglas, Cáraid Rioghail Fuar Ćala, bondmate of Alexandra Aoeron Aonwyn nighean mic Fionnaghal, daughter of Clan Fraser, healing technician, nexus traveler, Captain of the

Ruadh làn-damh, Co-Ruler of Terra, Terra Prime, Luna Keep and all her realms beyond, and the Savior of All Terra." Lauren felt her cheeks heat again as he named her. He bowed and then turned to the clan chiefs. "I believe, with all that I am and on my bond to Alexandra, Co-Ruler Lauren Fraser Doouglas will again be the Savior of Terra and return our Ruler to us." He stepped around the table and knelt before Lauren, taking her left hand in his. She looked down into his solemn face. Then, he lowered his forehead to the back of her hand. "I apologize for this council's lack of trust in you, Majesty. You have proven your loyalty to Alexandra and to Terra. You are the one who saved our children. You are the one who will save our future. I reaffirm my oath and again swear fealty to you."

Tears traced down Lauren's cheeks, as Newkirk spoke. She squeezed his hand and then placed her hand on top of his bowed head. "I accept your oath and fealty. I swear to you, Angus Newkirk, I will do everything in my power to return our ruler to us." She looked up, sweeping her gaze around the table. "Know this Council of Terra. I will rescue Alexandra and I will protect Terra." She pulled Newkirk to his feet and dropped his hand as he stood at her left shoulder. His nearness gave her strength and formed a physical wall of protection around her. "If it is the last thing I do, I will do this with all that I am."

Lauren flipped the Doouglas tartan off her shoulders, folded it, and placed it reverently across the back of Alex's empty chair. She caressed the warm wool. Placing her hand on the hilt of her rapier, Lauren turned on her heel and strode from the room. As the great oaken doors closed behind her, she could hear the shouts rise again.

"We have a demand and second that must be voted on!"

"You will support your Co-Ruler as our Queen commanded!"

"We must leave now. The fleet is prepped . . ."

And then Lauren was too far away to hear any more. She moved rapidly away from the Great Hall and out onto the boulevard which led to her solar. She needed rest. She needed time to figure out what she was going to do. *And time is what I don't have.* She stopped. *Or do I?*

Lauren began to run.

Chapter Two
Aboard the Dubh Mogairle

Alex woke with a start. *Where am I?* The darkness so deep, she was unsure whether her eyes were open, and she ran a shaking hand over her face. She was huddled on a cold metal floor. *But I am alive.* Her heart pounded as she began to comprehend her situation. She had been unconscious for an unknown amount of time and did not know where she was. Panic rose in her throat, threatening to choke her. Alex rubbed her neck and felt her torque there. The torque was alive and her warm, metallic scales were rough against Alex's shaking fingers. She forced herself to breathe and to calm down. *Come on Alex, get it together. Take a deep breath.* She rolled her head to relieve some of her stiff muscles. *Think. You can figure this out.*

As she sorted through the cascade of memories streaming through her consciousness, Alex began to get her bearings. Earth, the nexus cave in the Zirkel wilderness, opening the quantum tubula, the companions traversing realities, Ffrwyn's young filly—Làireach's excitement at the adventure of going to Terra, Lauren's love and strength transmitted across the parallel universes, closing the nexus membrane on Earth, and stepping into the tubula. *Then, what?* This is where her memories stopped.

Another wave of panic rose and threatened to swamp her calm. Alex took another deep breath. In, out. And another. In, out. Just like Lauren taught her. A small smile formed on her lips. Lauren taught Alex this meditation technique to help manage stressful situations. She found it especially useful when dealing with her truculent Terran council and now it may prove the savior of her sanity.

When her breathing and heart rate returned to normal, Alex stood. Almost at once her head struck a ceiling, gasping at the sudden pain, she dropped to her knees. Once her head cleared, she reached out, slowly. Her fingertips just brushed a cold, metal ceiling. She stretched her arms to each side and touched walls, her arms still slightly bent at the elbow. Lying back down, she extended her legs, her feet pushed against another wall in front of her. She was in a box, a very small box.

Again, panic overwhelmed her, and she curled into a small ball. She closed her eyes to escape the darkness and tried to focus on her breathing, tried to make each breath deeper and longer than the last. In…out. In…out. As her breathing became regular, her panic receded once more.

Forcibly relaxing her muscles, Alex stretched out and extended her other senses outward. She felt the warmth of her torque around her neck and the minute flutter of her scales as the Old One also relaxed. She noticed a vibration which rose from the floor in rhythmic oscillations. Alex placed her palms flat on the walls of her box. She felt the same vibration, though less strong than through the floor. It was a familiar sensation—a gravitational wave drive. She was on a ship, and it was traveling at faster-than-light pulse speed. *Which ship? Going where?*

Alex continued to piece together information about her surroundings. She took another calming breath. *Wait, I am in a box, but I am able to breathe.* Fresh air was flowing around her. It had to be coming from somewhere, her box was not impenetrable. Her resolve to escape this box increased and her heart leapt.

As she felt each of the walls, a trickle of psi-energy tickled her bond. It was faint. Almost imperceptible. Alex reached out and pulled on the strand. *Yes!* A nanofilament of psi-energy so fine she almost missed it. *I am still connected to Lauren.* Even over the rapidly expanding distance, their bond held. Relaxing, Alex smiled in the dark. *She was not alone.*

On the Outer Hull of the Dubh Mogairle in a Terran Flitter

Lord Admiral Iain McLeod, Commander of the Terran intragalactic fleet and Head of Luna Keep, blinked sweat from his eyes and stared in disbelief at his pilot. Sarah Cameron's cheeks were a ghostly white. Her hair floated about her head in disarray, weightless in the zero-gravity environment within their flitter. It had escaped from its usual neat bun. She was slumped against the crash harness holding her in her flight couch. A deep crease marred her usually smooth forehead. He placed his hand on top of hers where it still held the throttle control in a white-knuckled grip.

"Easy, we made it." He looked out the forward transparency at the massive clan ship. Unbelievably, they were locked onto the hull of the *Black Orchid*.

"We did?" Small tremors shook her body and Sarah grimaced.

"Aye, we did, or should I say you did. We seem to be attached to the ventral side of the central cylinder, just aft of the thruster intakes." He turned back to his pilot. "A most impressive bit of piloting."

Sarah chuckled ruefully. "Luck. It was all luck." She opened her eyes. "If we had come in at a slightly steeper angle, we would have ended up in the thruster intakes, not behind them."

"Be that as it may, we are here and safely attached to the hull."

"What now? How long will the magnetic locks hold, given the shear of gravitational wave travel? We are creating an eddy as the wave travels along the hull. How long will our life-support systems last?" Sarah took a deep breath. "How can we gain access to the ship? How do we find Her Majesty?"

"Fair." Lord McLeod rubbed his chin. "All very good questions. Each of which will need to be addressed."

Sarah barked another laugh. "Addressed? How do we answer any of them? We are stuck here." She waved her hand toward the hull of the intragalatic ship filling the forward transparency.

Lord McLeod was nonplussed. "When Her Majesties visited Luna Keep, I had the privilege of many insightful discussions with the Consort." He smiled despite the gravity of the situation they found themselves in. *Gravity indeed.* "During our discussion of wave propulsion systems and faster-than-light-pulse travel, she struggled to grasp the mathematics needed for solving non-linear multidimensional field equations."

Sarah rubbed her forehead. "She is not alone in that. I can fly the ships but understanding how they fly has always been beyond me."

McLeod patted her hand. "Yes, well. You are a pilot, not a theoretical mathematician. And thank all the gods for that."

Sarah nodded, both in acknowledgement of the compliment and in agreement of the fortune of their being alive.

"I was defining linear state-space. I had hoped Consort Lauren would be able to understand the mathematics in two-dimensions before we moved on to multi-dimensional theory. The understanding came to her in a flash of insight." McLeod laughed at his memory, at how brightly Lauren had grinned when she began to understand the mathematics. They were touring engineering onboard the flagship of the Terran fleet—the *Iolar Mara*—Alexandra's *Sea Eagle*. He waved a hand as if to clear his wayward thoughts. "She said something I will never forget. Consort Lauren thanked me for my explanation and then said, 'I suppose anyone can eat an elephant if it is served one bite at a time.'"

"Elephant?" Sarah struggled to pronounce the alien term.

"Yes, in Earth-reality, there exists an immense herbivore, one which could not be easily devoured. When she showed me a picture of one on her analyzer, I understood." McLeod sketched a rough outline of the animal with his hands. "She went on to say, if you cut it into small chunks even this large beast could be eaten."

"How do we eat this elephant?" Sarah gestured out the forward transparency.

"We break it into small pieces, as the Consort suggested." Lord McLeod slapped the quick release on his chest harness and pushed off his acceleration couch, heading to the rear of their small flitter. "But first we must let Luna Keep know where we are."

McLeod dug into a little-used storage container beneath the rear-most seat, his feet floating to the ceiling as he muttered. "Where is it? I know we keep them on all construction-site flitters." He pulled various tools and safety packets from the container, releasing them over his shoulder, to float free within the cabin.

Sarah tried to peer over his shoulder into the container. "Where is what, M'Lord?"

"The . . . ah, here it is." McLeod flipped upright, a small silver cylinder in his hands. The cylinder was constructed of alumino-titanium, the smooth surface rippling with a muted rainbow hue in the flitter's dim light. Turning, he propelled himself back to the pilots' couches. Inserting the cylinder into a data port on the rear of the center control console, he spoke. He summarized their encounter with the *Dubh Mogairle* and the ensuing exchange of weapons' fire, and their successful attachment to the outer hull of the ship. Keying in a series of numerals on the console, he also attached their limited astro-navigation data. Once he finished, he pulled the cylinder from the port. "There, that should do."

"But, M'Lord?"

"One small piece at a time, Sarah." He held the small cylinder up knowing this was only their first bite of many. "We should be able to eject this safety beacon out the airlock."

Sarah shook her head and frowned. "That will not work. We're traveling at faster-than-light pulse speed. The beacon will not survive deceleration." Her frown deepened. "And the *Dubh Mogairle* will detect the beacon as it comes online."

"Remember your quad-dimensional physics?" Sarah cocked her head to one side in question as he continued, "Compressional stress of deceleration is proportional to the object's mass. And the tensional stress of gravitational wave travel is proportional to the object's shape."

McLeod pointed the beacon at Sarah to emphasize his point. "This beacon weighs less than two-hundred grams and is a smooth cylinder less than thirty centimeters long. Both of these attributes should allow it to weather the turbulence of deceleration down to normal speeds intact. And

I highly doubt anyone monitoring the sensors on the *Dubh Mogairle* will detect an anomaly made by such a small object."

Sarah arched an eyebrow. "They may not detect the beacon itself but I doubt anyone would miss the signal once it starts transmitting."

McLeod rubbed his chin. "Aye. What if we delay the transmission until it has reached normal speed?" He paused as he calculated the rate of deceleration in his head. "It should take approximately twenty-three point seven minutes for the beacon to reach normal space. And in that amount of time, the *Dubh Mogairle* will have traveled more than four-hundred and twenty-six million kilometers."

"And, if we limit the bandwidth to a microfilament directed away from our projected trajectory, they should not be able to detect it." Sarah pulled herself into the acceleration couch and punched numbers into her analyzer pad. "The microfilament transmission should also use an ultra-low frequency of less than three kiloHertz." Sarah looked up from her analyzer. "Does Luna Keep monitor frequencies in the microwave portion of the electromagnetic spectrum?"

Beneath Terran Keep, PSI-Laboratory
Sixth Subterranean Level

Lord Newkirk leaned over his junior technician's narrow tartan-covered shoulder, resting his hand on the high-backed brown leather chair for support. He was exhausted and the image on the technician's monitor wavered in and out of focus.

"There?" Newkirk pointed at the readout before them. "Is that the anomaly you saw?" The technician nodded and leaned forward, scrutinizing the readout. Newkirk leaned closer, too. "Could this be created by a gravitational-wave drive deforming spacetime?"

"I think so, sir." The technician split the screen with a wiggle of his fingers sunk in the analyzer's gel pad. He placed the current readings from the satellite-sensor array surrounding Terra on the left half and shrunk the readings recorded during the *Black Orchid's* escape from the Terran Solar System on the right. "See this?" Removing his hand from the analyzer gel pad, he pointed at a ripple on the right image. "It is in the same position in the real-time data; the only difference is the amplitude is diminished due to time decay."

"Can we see the trace from the sensors in the outer system as well?" Lord Newkirk squinted at the image, his tired eyes straining to see clearly.

The technician again split the screen, adding a third view. On this slice, he placed the current readout from the sensor array located beyond the Oort Cloud at the farthest reaches of the Terran Solar System. "There. The *Dubh Mogairle* crossed the Oort sensor array at that point. Using that point and the linear path data from the Terran near-planet array, we should be able to plot the ship's outbound course and obtain an approximate heading." The technician did not look up from his monitor, as he presented his hypothesis.

"Indeed." Lord Newkirk stood upright and stretched the knot out of his lower back. *Too much work, too much worry, too much uncertainty.* "Once you have a course and heading, please send it to me. I will be in the eastern solar with the Consort."

"Aye, sir." The technician never looked up as he was already deep into his five-dimensional spacetime field calculations. Newkirk turned and smiled. Hope lightened his steps as he made his way out of the lab.

Chapter Three
Terran Keep, Eastern Solar

Lauren sat in her chair, she was hiding, and she knew it. She needed to figure out what to do and how to do it. Jumping up, she went over to her aged-oak reading table where a large astro-navigation map of the Milky Way galaxy lay. Lauren traced a bright blue line with her index finger—the flight path traversed by the Terran fleet as it searched for a new home. She held a stylus between her teeth and when her braid flopped over her shoulder, she flipped it back with a huff. The sleeves of her white shirt were rolled above her elbows and her Fraser kilt hung askew. *I keep tugging at it.*

Lauren turned toward the analyzer embedded in the top of her large desk, over which a hologram of the galaxy floated, spinning slowly in a clockwise direction. The holographic galaxy sparkled in the late afternoon sun streaming through the solar's large octagonal window. Lauren had programmed the hologram to slowly rotate from a lateral-plane view, which looked parallel to the galactic plane, to a vertical-plane view looking down on the galaxy from above the galactic plane. This second view showed all the arms spiraling out from galactic center. The Milky Way was home to the Terran solar system and the solar system containing Terra Prime and the Comin Homeworld.

She highlighted both solar systems on the hologram—Terra's system was a pulsing blue dot in the Orion galactic arm. The Terra Prime system with its neighboring nebula and the outlying Comin Homeworld was a pulsing red dot located near the tip of the Sagittarius Arm. The arms were approximately sixty-thousand light years apart across the galactic center. Lauren struggled to comprehend this vast distance. She could convert the distance to kilometers, but five-hundred and sixty-seven quadrillion kilometers were difficult to comprehend. *It doesn't look that far on the hologram. It's all a matter of scale, I guess?* A headache began to pulse behind her eyes in time with the blinking dots. Time. *I'm running out of time.*

"Stick to the facts, Lauren. What do you know?" She heard her granddaddy's voice in her mind. *Okay, the facts.* The Milky Way is a barred-spiral galaxy with six arms: two major spirals, two minor arms, and two small spurs which shear off the major arms. The Terran solar system was in one of these minor spurs off the Orion arm. The galaxy is in constant motion, the arms spinning about the galactic center at more than eight-hundred and twenty-eight thousand kilometers an hour. It takes the Orion arm more than two-hundred and thirty million years to make one revolution about the galactic center. This immense time to complete one revolution gives one an idea of the size of the galaxy. The Milky Way galaxy was the second largest galaxy in its near neighborhood of galaxies within the universe. The size of the galaxy was overwhelming, and Lauren knew they had a great distance to travel to catch the *Dubh Mogairle.* She stood mesmerized by the spinning hologram.

Lauren knew the galaxy could be defined mathematically. The spiral arms could be represented by the Fibonacci sequence—1,2,3,5,8,13—a series of numbers often found in nature. The number of petals in a flower, the curved chambers of a nautilus shell, the arrangement of a pinecone bract. But none of that mattered now.

What else? Time—not enough. Distance—too far. Time—distance. Distance—time. *Wait, that's it.* Lauren's mind leapt as this new idea took hold and with this flash of inspiration, she dashed over to the large cedar storage chest beside the cold hearth. Pushing the heavy wooden lid up, she braced it against the stone wall. *Where is it?* She dug, leaning into the deep chest, throwing various items over her shoulder. Near the bottom, she found what she sought: a large drawing pad.

For her Investiture as Consort and Co-Ruler, Lauren was required to learn all fifty-four millennia of Terran history. She had organized the information into a number of matrices, each of which she diagramed on large, wall-size flash cards. She smiled. Alex and her companions had seen her flash cards the night before the ceremony. Robert McLaran stated, "Had I had your flash cards during my schooling I wouldn't have struggled so much with Terran history." Chuckling, Lauren recalled, Lady MacDonald's rebuke, "Having these would not have helped you, my boy. You were too focused on swordsmanship and sailing the stars to give a fig for our rich histories."

Lauren dropped the pad on her reading table and grabbed a marker. She wrote a large D on the first sheet. Tearing this off, she tossed the sheet to the side. On the second sheet, she wrote T. Removing this one, Lauren marked the third sheet with a V. She hung each sheet on one quadrant of her circular solar. Standing in the center of the room, she turned in a slow circle and let her mind relax. Lauren focused on the three letters and their combination $V=D/T$: velocity equals distance divided by time—like speed, miles per hour. Or with simple algebraic rearrangement $T=D/V$: time equals the distance they needed to travel divided by how fast they could go. Change any one variable and the equation's solution changes as well.

Questions cascaded through her mind. *How can I make the* Ruadh làn-damh—*the Fraser Clan's* Red Stag—*go faster? How can I shorten the distance the* Stag *had to travel to catch the* Black Orchid? *Can I decrease the time the* Stag *will need to travel the same distance?* Lauren looked back at the hologram and tried to see a way to modify the variables in this simple equation, to travel from the blue dot to the red dot and catch the *Dubh Mogairle* before she arrived at her destination—the Comin Nebula.

The arrival of Alex's companions interrupted her thoughts. She smiled at the three boys, who were fast becoming her stalwart companions, just as they were with Alex. Their loyalty and support warmed her heart and eased some of her fears.

"You're just in time. I need your help."

"Of course, Your Majesty, how may we help?" MacDonald responded quickly. The other two stood back, looking at the sheets covering the gray stone walls. Newkirk rubbed the side of his nose in contemplation.

Robert McLaran laughed, dropping into one of the large red leather-bound armchairs. "More flash cards? I thought your history lessons were over."

Lauren smiled. "This isn't history. This is how we're going to catch Cador's *Dubh Mogairle.*"

Robert sobered. "We cannot catch them. They have a significant head start. And they know where they are going; we have neither a course nor a heading to follow."

"They're going here." Lauren walked across the room to her desk and reached into the spinning hologram, pointing at the red dot pulsing in the galaxy's Sagittarius Arm. "The Comin Homeworld."

"We do not know that, Majesty. We cannot triangulate a course with the limited amount of data provided by the sensors within this solar system alone."

"I know that's where they're going. It fits with everything we do know." She stood and faced her companions. "We know Gwenhwyfach used a Comin weapon when she was exposed in the Council meeting, so she and Clan Cador have had recent contact with the Comin. The Comin patrol which ambushed Alex and I as we approached the Keep, after our trek from the nexus cave, knew exactly where we would go to open the shield, someone had to give them that information. Clan Cador were the ambassadors to the Comin Homeworld before Alex's great grandmother broke off diplomatic relations after her son was killed." Lauren pointed at the ceiling of her solar. "And they are headed in that direction."

"Where is that?" McLaran stared upward.

Lauren laughed. "That, my friends, is where my bond with Alex tells me she's headed."

"Bond? You can still feel Alex," MacDonald asked in awe. Newkirk stared at her slack jawed.

"Well, yeah. She's heading in that direction." Lauren pointed at the ceiling again. "She's alive. I can't talk to her but I'm getting sporadic emotion-thoughts." Lauren stroked her dragon torque. Though the torque hadn't spoken since Alex was taken, Lauren felt the dragon was somehow amplifying the strength of their bond across this vast distance.

Newkirk found his voice. "Emotion-thought? I have not heard of this before."

"I don't know what else to call it. It's how Gríobhtha described contacting Lord McLaran across realities—from Earth to Terra—to tell him about Làireach's birth." Lauren huffed as her frustrations built. *Why won't they believe me?*

"That is not possible." Newkirk scoffed. "A bond does not traverse intragalatic distances let alone cross realities. I never believed Gríobhtha when he told you that."

"It can. I know where Alex is. I know the speed she is traveling. I know the direction is she going." Lauren stamped her foot, much like Ffwryn, Alex's equine-companion, did when vexed. "Ask Gríobhtha, if you don't believe me. Let him describe how he did it. I don't understand it either, but I know, Angus, I know where Alex is."

Angus flopped onto the sofa and shook his head. "I must speak to my father about this. If anyone would understand how a bond can cross this distance, he would."

Waving a hand to dismiss his comment, Lauren paced around the room. "Everything points to the Comin." Lauren looked at her three companions. She saw their skepticism, felt their disbelief across the strengthening bond she felt developing with them. "Clan Cador was acting on an edict from their ancestors to remove the ruling Doouglas clan, each successive Cador clan leader knew of this edict and they've been preparing for a coup over the millennia. I'm also sure any of them would seek help from any quarter to accomplish their goal—to rule Terra." She paused and swallowed hard. "Even conspire with the Comin."

The room's occupants couldn't argue with Lauren's summary of the facts and MacDonald dropped onto the leather sofa next to Newkirk. He spoke into the silence. "But the Council is correct, the *Dubh Mogairle* has a lead and we cannot catch them. If they are going to the Comin Homeworld, we must send the fleet after them now. And remember Lauren, the Comin also have a formidable fleet. I am unsure if our meager fleet would be able to match them in combat."

Lauren stopped pacing and placed her hands on her hips. "We will not send the fleet." Her voice held an edge of steel and MacDonald shrank away from her anger, sinking into the soft cushions.

"But, ma'am, we must." McLaran leaned forward in his chair. "It is the only way we can stop that ship and save Alex."

She ignored McLaran. "I will not leave Terra without a means to escape."

All three boys started and looked at Lauren stunned by her statement. "A means to escape? From what, Lauren?" Newkirk asked.

A small smile curled the corner of Lauren's mouth, pleased that in this moment of high stress, he unconsciously dropped her title in favor of the more intimate use of her given name. Removing the barriers of rank would allow them to more easily brainstorm this problem together—Alex's companions —were now fully her companions. She knew this in her heart and she smiled.

Lauren circled the end of one of the other leather sofas, dropping into a corner. Her hands dangled between her knees. "As Co-Ruler of Terra, I can't leave this world and our people unprotected." The boys frowned. Perhaps, they didn't understand her reasoning. Lauren tried another tack. "As I stated in the Council meeting, what if the Comin are hiding nearby and ready to deploy another bioweapon, this time attacking Terra?" She paused allowing them time to consider her statement. "If we don't leave the fleet here, everyone will die, without a means of escape." She hoped they understood her reasoning, so she changed her tack. "How many ships would be needed to evacuate the population of Terra?"

"We have always had plans in place to evacuate the solar system in an emergency. Alex knew the Comin might find us." McLaran's eyes lost their focus as he organized his thoughts. "To evacuate the entire population would require the resources of a minimum of six of our clan ships."

"And Luna Keep?"

He shook his head, sadness clouding his fine features. "The population of Luna Keep was always designated to stay behind and fight the intruders. They were never included in the evacuation plans." McLaran swallowed hard. "The laser-weapon installations based there were to provide covering fire for the clans' escape."

Lauren jumped to her feet, unwilling to allow any Terran to die. "No, that isn't an option. How many ships would be needed for all Terrans?"

"Eight," MacDonald replied after some thought. "Eight would be able to manage, but it would be a tight fit."

"Can we automate the laser-weapon installations? Find a way for Luna's artificial intelligence systems to take control?"

Newkirk again rubbed his chin. "Perhaps, it would take some intricate reprogramming."

Nodding, Lauren sat back down. She pulled her legs up under her and leaned back against the sofa arm. "All right." She turned to McLaran. "Robert, would you please oversee the weapons reprogramming and get a plan together to include Luna Keep in the evacuation?" He pulled a small pad from his tunic. "Tavish, if Terra needs eight clans, then that leaves four to mount the chase." She looked at him. He nodded. "We can work with that. Our chase group will be four—the Fraser *Stag*, with the *Ruadh Leòmhann,* your *Red Lion*, MacD. McLaran's *Wild Boar*, the *Faol Muc-fhiadhaich*." Last, Lauren smiled at Newkirk. "And the *Ordha Speireag-ghlas*, your *Golden Kestrel*, Angus."

MacDonald extended his large hand. Lauren placed hers on top and the other two covered hers. They smiled at each other and tightened their grips, affirming their vow. "We have our fleet, but Lauren, we do not have the means to catch the fleeing ship." McLaran again highlighted their primary stumbling block.

"You're right. We don't." Lauren stood and moved to the first of the three sheets hanging on the walls. "But we will, if we can solve a simple equation and get physics to work for us. If my idea is correct, we can beat the *Black Orchid* to the Comin Homeworld and save Alex." Tears gathered in her eyes she said Alex's name. She reached out to pull her bond more closely around her soul. *Oh, Alex, I've gotta be right. This is our only chance.*

Newkirk looked at the sheets. "Are we using physics as we know it, or are we making it up as we go along?" The four companions laughed.

Terran Keep
Eastern Solar

The next morning, Lauren paced the perimeter of her solar studying the paper-covered walls. Robert and Angus were sprawled in the two armchairs before the cold hearth, while Tavish was draped across the length of the leather sofa, arm dangling to the floor, softly snoring. Lauren couldn't afford sleep. There wasn't time.

The four made great progress in the hours of darkness, filling two of the three sheets with scribbles and doodles and diagrams. The hologram now had seven traces crossing from the Terran system to the red dot of the Comin Homeworld. They were close to an optimal solution for her equation $T=D/V$.

Ideas were in place on how to shorten the distance by taking a different route. They had an idea about how to make the clans run faster, but time was still the sticking point. Lauren stood before the large blank sheet labeled T. She turned to her laptop and started another data-search when her other companions burst into the room.

Ice and Snow, Alex's white-wolf animal companions, arrived at the top of the stairs in a swirling ball of fur. Susan and Sharon, Lauren's closest friends from Earth, followed closely behind. Her friends had traveled across the nexus to Terra with Lauren and Alex. Dressed in blue jeans, a green wool shirt rolled to the elbows, and mud-covered riding boots, Susan's large muscular frame spoke of her profession—veterinarian. Susan had saved Ffrwyn's foal—Làireach, during a difficult birth. And then, much to everyone's surprise, Susan bonded with the filly. Sharon, her life partner, was small with a wicked teasing glint in her intelligent eyes.

Sharon respected her Scottish Highlands heritage immensely, and though she spelled her name differently, she was a Fraser and identified with Terran culture. Today she wore a bright red, green, and blue Terran-Fraser hunting tartan kilt. Her sash was held in place by a small silver pin in the shape of a sprig of yew, for her mother on Earth. Red garters held pristine, white knee socks in place.

By the time Susan and Sharon joined the group, Snow and Ice had already sprawled across the hearth, their large heads resting on crossed paws, eyes following Lauren. Last to make it to the top of the stairs and whiffling in protest was Boscoe who plopped down on his rounded bottom. The small black, tan, and white Pembroke Welsh Corgi heaved a large sigh, and then slid to rest flat on the ground.

"Looks like this is the place." Susan sat on the unoccupied leather sofa. "Seems you've worn the boys out." She nodded toward Lauren's three companions where they slept.

Sharon circled the room, obviously trying to decipher the scientific scribbles on the large paper sheets. "What's all this?" She pointed to the sheet marked D.

"Our hypotheses for ways to decrease the distance we've gotta travel to reach the *Orchid's* destination first." Various arced paths were drawn across the D-sheet, with the locations of known gravitational anomalies noted. The arcs represented proposed flight paths. They had also transposed them from the two-dimensional paper into the three-dimensional galactic hologram. Lauren continued to contemplate time.

"And this one?" Sharon ran her hand over a diagram of an undulating wave form on the V-sheet.

Lauren smiled; pleased Sharon was doing so well on Terra. Before they left Earth, Sharon was hesitant to make the trip. But now, she'd already spent a day with Lady MacDonald, discussing the parallels between the Scots of Earth and the Terrans. Lady MacDonald could not pass up an opportunity to learn about Earth and chronicle her learnings. Lauren and Sharon were convinced other Nexus-travelers had visited Earth in the distance past. There were just too many parallels between the two cultures for them to have developed independently. Shaking her head to clear these tangential thoughts, Lauren pulled herself back to the now, and their current crisis.

"Ways we can increase the overall velocity of the clan ships." Lauren waved her hand at the sheet.

"And this H_2-six-sided block?" Sharon tilted her head at a sketch.

Lauren walked over to Sharon. "A molecular representation of solid hydrogen."

This comment got Susan off the couch. She joined her partner and Lauren, looking close at the drawing. "Solid hydrogen? I thought that was only a theory. I remember NASA talking about using it as a high-energy rocket propellant, but they couldn't convert the gaseous form to a stable solid. As I recall, they didn't have a way to produce enough energy to compress it fully."

"You're right. On Earth it's only a theoretical construct. Here, we've got the means to produce it. The Terrans already use one variety of metallic hydrogen as a super-conductor in their quantum computer cores. This configuration—a three-dimensional construct of hydrogen—doesn't yet exist. But, Terrans possess the means to create the extremely high-pressures and temperatures needed to create this stable form of metallic hydrogen." Lauren could almost see the wheels turning in Susan's scientific brain.

"For what purpose?" Sharon may not have the scientific background the other two did, but she still possessed strong relational abilities. She often saw connections others didn't, whether between objects or humans.

"The Terran clan ships use a propulsion system which surfs gravitational waves." She pointed to the schematic of the wave on the V-sheet. "Terrans shunt the radiant energy carried within the gravitational wave into a fusion containment vessel and feed in gaseous hydrogen fuel."

"Holy-moly, they use fusion reactions to drive their ships." Susan's eyes flashed with excitement.

"You got it. They create a mini-sun within the containment vessel and use its power to drive their faster-than-light-pulse engines." Lauren turned back to the molecular diagram and pointed at the H_2 cube. "We're trying to figure out if concentrating the hydrogen fuel into a solid would increase the overall temperature of the reaction and thereby, increase the thrust output of our engines. We're thinking about using solid hydrogen in its metallic form as the primary fuel and adding a small amount of gaseous hydrogen as an accelerant to boost the explosive reaction."

Susan nodded, but Sharon frowned, looking lost, so Lauren tried to explain. "Solid hydrogen is a three-dimensional matrix of hydrogen nuclei which share each other's electrons. To produce this solid we would need to place a molecular condenser in front of the containment vessel to tightly pack the individual hydrogen atoms together to achieve a solid form. Then feed the solid hydrogen into the containment vessel as the primary fuel. What we're trying to do is add an accelerant to the fuel mixture—make it burn hotter and faster." When Sharon continued to frown, Lauren tried another analogue. "Think about this. You like auto racing, right?"

"Yeah." Sharon studied the diagram.

Lauren squeezed her shoulder. "Okay, consider a top-fuel funny car. They use a fuel mixture of nitromethane and methanol. The primary ingredient in the fuel is nitromethane, which burns more explosively than TNT. But add a little methanol and you increase the burn temperature of the explosive reaction even more and increase the rate of fuel consumption, producing more horsepower for the car to use in acceleration."

After a moment, Sharon smiled. "Like making ice cream?"

Ice raised her head from the hearth. *"Did someone say ice cream?"* The wolf's voice echoed in Lauren's mind.

"Not now, Ice." Lauren looked at the wolf, who growled at the slight. She turned back to Sharon. "I don't follow."

Angus lifted his head from the sofa, his voice thick with sleep. "That is an excellent example where an accelerant is used to change the rate of a chemical reaction, Lady Sharon."

"What do you mean?" Baffled, Lauren looked from Sharon to Angus where he reclined on the sofa.

"What Lady Sharon is referring to is the addition of salt to the ice used to freeze ice cream as it is being churned." Angus rose from the sofa and walked over to the diagram, waking the other two boys as he passed their chairs. They yawned and stretched. "As the ice melts, the salt is dissolved in the water. The resultant salty water has an increased capacity to absorb heat released as the rest of the ice melts. This ability to hold more heat allows the temperature of the salt-water solution to decrease below the freezing point of pure water, creating a super-cooled liquid. This super cold liquid then cools the vessel that holds the cream and other ingredients. Thus, ice cream."

Susan hugged Sharon around her shoulders. "Well done, love. See? You do understand physical chemistry." Sharon grinned and the group laughed. Even the wolves added their whiffles while Boscoe chortled.

"And that, Lady Sharon, is exactly what we are going to do on the four clan ships. Add a bit of salt to the mixture to accelerate the rate of reaction within the containment vessels." Angus' comment trailed off as he grabbed a marker and began drawing another sketch on the V- sheet.

Sharon moved back to the D-sheet. "What's with all the curved lines?"

"Those are sketches of proposed shortest-distance flight paths we could take from Terra to the Comin nebula." Lauren smiled, pleased to see Sharon trying to understand their ideas. "We're assuming the Clan Cador ship will follow the exact flight path the Terrans used to get to Terra from Terra Prime. We also assume they will forgo any side-trips and keep to the original course. Given these assumptions, we're able to calculate the total time for the *Dubh Mogairle* to travel back to the Comin nebula."

Susan placed a gentle hand on Lauren's arm. "That's a lot of assumptions, isn't it?"

"Perhaps, but it's all we've got to go on. With my bond-connection to Alex, we do have another point of reference. So far they're following the original course exactly."

Sharon arched an eyebrow. "Okay, how long is it going to take them? You've got to know if they choose another course, right?"

Lauren had to agree with Angus, working in a group did expand on her ideas and it helped slow her churning mind. She smiled at Sharon, "If we assume, they're following the original course, then we need to calculate a route across the galaxy for our clans. One which will get us to the nebula two weeks or more ahead of Cador."

"Well, that seems easy enough." Sharon walked over to the galactic hologram. She reached into the blue dot and stretched a line directly to the red dot. "There you go, the shortest course."

Lauren laughed. "True, that'd be the shortest-distance course if we were traveling on a two-dimensional surface. Like from New York City to Cleveland, Ohio."

When Sharon frowned, Susan draped her arm around her narrow shoulders. "Love, what Lauren is getting at is their course is through three-dimensional space. And they have to take into account the curvature of spacetime due to the existence of massive bodies."

Sharon sighed. "If you guys would just speak in small words, I'd maybe get it. You've lost me again."

Robert rose and pulled a blanket off the back of one of the sofas, gesturing to Tavis to help him. The boys drew the blanket tight between them. "Here is your flat plane, Lady Sharon. Lauren, would you place one of your balance balls on the rug?"

Lauren walked over to another cedar chest and pulled out one of the many balls she had used during her sword-training. She dropped the ball onto the stretched blanket. Its mass deformed the blanket and created a depression with the ball sitting in the center.

Robert tilted his head at the ball. "Lady Sharon, assume the ball is a planet or a star or a black hole, some massive object. Notice how it presses down on blanket?" Sharon nodded. "This depression is known as a gravity well. As the mass of an object increases the depth of the gravity well also increases. Therefore, it also increases the amount of deformation the object creates in the fabric of spacetime. Because of these deformations, we must plot a course which bends, following the gravity wells of the massive objects we will pass as we travel."

"Unbelievably, I get that." Sharon moved the ball across the blanket surface, watching the ball's gravity well move with it.

"It's why airliners flying from Europe to North America fly a great-circle route and not a direct line route across the globe. The great-circle is a shorter distance on a curved surface," Susan added.

Lauren felt her companion-bond grow as this small group came together to solve their problems, she needed them to get Alex back.

Newkirk joined in. "Therefore, we are trying to determine what objects are where, how massive those objects are, and how close we can fly to them as we calculate an alternate course. Plotting an exact course is difficult, as all the objects are in constant motion relative to one another. We will need to continuously refine the course as we travel towards the nebula."

The boys dropped the blanket and the group took up a discussion of the blank T-sheet. Lauren knew altering time would be their biggest challenge. Time was the one universal constant even Einstein couldn't bend.

Several hours later, a knock interrupted the group. "It's open," Lauren called down the stairs. The massive oak door swung inward and a gray-haired head peeked around the edge. "Lord Newkirk, come on in. We're just ready to order some lunch. Please join us."

"Thank you, Your Majesty, but I do not have time for lunch. I only came to give you some new information." He climbed the stairs and entered Lauren's private solar, looking around the room and acknowledging its occupants. "Well, it seems everyone I need is here."

"Please, M'Lord, grab a seat and tell us." Lauren's excitement built. Maybe things were moving in the right direction.

Lord Newkirk crossed the room and sank into the overstuffed leather chair young McLaran vacated. His haggard face was lined with exhaustion. Lauren felt the same; it had been a long few days for everyone.

"I will get right to it as I need to return to the psi-laboratory. I have come to tell you we have some additional data on the speed and heading of Cador's *Dubh Mogairle.*" He swallowed hard. "And, to share some difficult news."

"Difficult news? What are you talking about, M'Lord?" Worry creased young McLaran's forehead.

Lauren's heart rate increased. She knew this was going to be bad news. "What's happened?"

Lord Newkirk stood and clasped his hands behind his back as he began to pace the room. He nodded once and straightened his shoulders, turning back to the six. "We have lost him, Consort. Lord McLeod is gone."

Lauren gasped, and Newkirk spun toward his father, the marker forgotten in his hand. "What do you mean lost him? Where is the flitter? There would be wreckage. We did not see any on the replay of the *Orchid's* escape. The flitter could not have been caught in the cross-fire."

Lord Newkirk shook his head and he took Lauren's hands in his. "One partially-melted piece from the ventral fin was found, nothing more. If the flitter sustained a glancing strike from one of the lasers, we should have more wreckage. But if the flitter took a direct hit, which is what we assume, then the craft would be vaporized. In this case, we would find nothing. It is gone."

Lauren's sob caught in her throat as tears streamed down her cheeks. "No, that can't be. We just missed them in the confusion of the escape and ensuing firefight." Lauren's mind raced as her heart continued its galloping pace. A keening cry filled the solar and Boscoe added his howling compliant to the cacophony of the wolves' lament. "He can't be gone. We need him. I need him." She dropped Lord Newkirk's hands as if burned and spun toward the diagrams on her walls. "We can't do this without him."

On the Outer Hull of the Dubh Mogairle
In the Terran flitter

Sarah turned in her acceleration couch and peered into the rear of the construction flitter. *Feck, I hope this works. It could so easily backfire on us.*

Admiral McLeod stood in the hatchway and tossed the small silver communication beacon into the airlock. "Close the inner hatch, please."

Sarah turned to her control console and dipped her hand into the analyzer gel pad. The rear hatch slid closed with a snick.

"Depressurize the airlock and open the outer hatch."

She wiggled her fingers to follow McLeod's orders. The indicator lights above the interior hatch cycled from green to amber to red—indicating depressurization. A slight vibration ran through the flitter, as the exterior hatch opened, and the gravitation-wave turbulence increased. The turbulence grabbed the cylinder and sucked it out of the airlock.

Admiral McLeod nodded as he looked out the small viewport. "It is away, close the outer hatch."

The vibration died, as the indicator light cycled back to green.

"All right, what is next on our list?" Sarah asked.

"Next, we prepare to enter the *Dubh Mogairle*." Lord McLeod opened another storage locker, aft of the airlock hatch. He pulled out a white evacuation suit. The suit floated free, then he gave it a small push forward. He pulled a second suit from the depths of the locker.

Sarah pushed out of her pilot couch, catching the suit. "And how exactly are you planning we do that, sir? We are nowhere near a hatchway."

His muffled voice answered, his head was buried in the torso section of the second evac suit, "Through the thruster intakes, of course."

"The what?" Sarah's voice rose and she stopped struggling with the suit in her arms.

"The thruster intakes." Lord McLeod's voice held a bit of amusement as his head popped out of the neck ring.

"And just how do we gain access into the ship through a sealed thruster intake?" Her panic spiked again.

McLeod struggled to get into the leg-portion of his suit, his efforts causing him to revolve in a circle. "If they are called 'intakes' they are not completely sealed."

"Sir, respectfully, they open when in a planet's atmosphere, but we are in deep space. Now, they are sealed to increase the aerodynamic profile of the ship."

"True, but they do open." McLeod smiled. "But, there is another way in."

"Another way?" Sarah looked at the Admiral in disbelief. "Not that I know of."

"Remember your ship design?" He continued to revolve slowly about his center of gravity, his helmet and gauntlets floating near him. "How do the repair drones enter and exit the ship when the gravitational-wave drive is engaged?"

"Still not understanding, sir. Repair drones? What exactly are you planning?" She now had her suit locked together and was snapping her gauntlets in place.

Admiral McLeod stopped struggling with his suit and gave her his full attention. "What we are going to do is activate the beacon in twenty-six minutes, exit the flitter, and walk along the hull into the thruster intake. Once inside the intake, we are going to enter the *Dubh Mogairle* through the drone maintenance hatch."

Sarah's eyes widened. "Maintenance hatch? Sir, you do realize we will not fit through the drone hatch wearing evac-suits."

Terran Keep, Eastern Solar
Lauren's Personal Rooms

"You have other news, M'Lord?" Lauren pushed the news of Admiral McLeod's death down. She would grieve later, when she had time to process their horrendous loss. Now, she didn't have time or the energy for distractions.

Shaking himself, Lord Newkirk walked toward the hologram. "Well, it seems our new sensor array, deployed beyond the Oort Cloud on the outer edges of the Terran system, works well."

Lauren dropped her hand into the gel pad of her desktop analyzer and changed the hologram from the Milky Way galaxy to one of the Terran solar system. Once the hologram stabilized, she removed her hand but held it above the gel pad, ready to input Lord Newkirk's information. "Go ahead, M'Lord."

Lord Newkirk stared at the hologram. "The *Dubh Mogairle* crossed the boundary of the Oort Cloud here." He pushed his finger into the hologram and a dot formed at his fingertip. "With the velocity and directional data gathered at this spatial point, combined with the data points from the Lunar sensor array, we can calculate a course heading with some degree of accuracy. If you will allow me, Your Majesty?"

"Oh, of course. Sorry. Have at it." Lauren stepped back from her desk.

Lord Newkirk sank his hand into the gel pad and wiggled his fingers. Several datasets—small spreadsheets of x, y, and z coordinates—began to stream down the side of the hologram and he pulled data points from those. As each point within a spreadsheet was selected, a colored dot appeared within the hologram.

I didn't know it could do that. Lauren stared into the evolving hologram.

Soon, a multitude of points populated the three-dimensional representation of the Terran system. Lord Newkirk then pulled up more spreadsheets—velocity, heading, and time. A red line streaked through the hologram. Finally, he stopped and stretched. "Here is Luna Keep. The green dots represent the near-system sensor array around the orbital path of Luna. The blue dots are the new Oort Cloud sensors." He pointed at a cloud of azure dots outside the farthest edges of the solar system." A red line connecting all the highlighted data points crosscut the cloud of sensors and moved out of the solar system.

"The *Dubh Mogairle* was detected on five thousand, six hundred and thirteen sensors on her way out of the system." He sank his hand back into the gel pad and a cluster of sensor dots began to glow around the red line trace. "We are currently completing a five-dimensional spacetime calculation using the velocity and orientation information from these sensors. We should be able to then calculate a true course trajectory, including heading and acceleration."

"That's amazing. We'll have a starting course and speed. Were they at full speed when they passed the Oort sensors? Which course did they choose? How long do you think they will hold their course?" Lauren knew she was babbling but this confirmed Alex's position from her bond and hope sang in her heart. Lord Newkirk's data contained information they could use in their calculations.

Young Newkirk joined his father at Lauren's desk. He shrank the hologram while enlarging the datasets. He peered at the data and ran his finger down the columns of data marked—velocity and heading. "It appears the *Black Orchid* encountered their first gravitational wave here." He enlarged the hologram and pointed at a sensor cluster in outer lunar orbit. "It then dropped out of that wave here." He highlighted another sensor cluster in the inner Oort Cloud. "Picking up their second wave here. They maintained contact with that wave, through our last recording of their heading, as the ship exited the solar system."

"What's that tell you, Angus?"

Lord Newkirk answered for his son and gave Lauren a small smile. "It tells us they got lucky and found a wave moving in the direction they wished to travel while still in the Oort Cloud."

"How does that help us?"

"Well, we got lucky too. If that wave was oriented in the proper direction of their desired course, they will ride it as long as they can." Lord Newkirk moved around the desk and dropped back into the leather chair near the hearth. "You cannot jump from wave to wave without slowing to one light-pulse speed, reorienting the ship to the heading of the new wave, catching the wave and then accelerating using the new wave's gravitational energy. Hopefully, with these initial data, we will have a handle on their course and can give chase."

Angus joined his father, sitting down on the arm of the chair. He placed a hand on his father's shoulder. "M'Lord, her Majesty already knows where they are going, and I think she is correct. They are going to the Comin Homeworld."

Terran Keep, Roof of the Eastern Solar
Midnight of the Third Day

Lauren scanned the night sky, brilliant with stars made brighter due to the new moon. Her gaze finally locked onto one point, the *Black Orchid's* current position. Following the course her heart and soul had gone. *There you are.* A small smile crossed her face as her bond strengthened and thrummed. *I will always know where you are, Dearest.*

"That is true, Your Majesty." Lauren gasped as an aged voice echoed in her mind. This was the first time her dragon torque had spoken since Alex was ripped from the quantum tubula. Lauren had felt the Old One's utter exhaustion and was afraid she would not speak again.

"Now you speak! Where were you in the Council meeting?" Lauren's frustration spiked. "I could've used your support then; any acknowledgement of my right-to-rule would've help dissuade the nay-sayers. Or when the boys and I were trying to figure out how to beat the *Dubh Mogairle* to the Comin Homeworld, your intelligence and knowledge of our First Foremother's thoughts about gravitational wave travel might've narrowed our discussion."

A puff of stream and ruffle of scales told Lauren her torque was as frustrated as she. "We could not speak earlier because we are cleaved in two just as you are. It took this time for us to re-establish our connection and strengthen our bond. Even now, we are barely hanging on to the tenuous connection. It is very fragile."

Lauren sighed. "Tell me about it. I feel as though I'm merely a shadow, without substance or weight. Just a wraith existing in a torn slice of altered reality."

A scaly shiver tickled Lauren's neck. "Well said, Consort. That is exactly how we feel, as well. However, you must understand one thing, the longer you and Alexandra, and my mate and I are able to hold this connection, the stronger it will become." Another puff of steam warmed Lauren's neck and she shivered at the contrast with the cold night air. She pulled her red and black Fraser-tartan blanket around her shoulders and sat cross-legged on the granite flagstone roof tiles. "Your bond has not existed since the time of our First Foremothers. It is something we never thought to experience again. When we woke from our millennia-long deep sleep, we were shocked to feel that bond strength again." The torque ruffled her scales, hugging the contours of Lauren's throat. She wondered if her torque was seeking some comfort in a closer physical contact. "As you know from your readings, The Fraser and The Doouglas were able to find themselves across the vast *distances of deep-space. You can as well. You must seek your soulmate and soon. You cannot allow her to be taken to the Comin Homeworld."*

"I know. I'm trying." Lauren huffed in anger, her grief sharp. "We're trying. But we can't go harrying off on some mad dash. We've gotta determine our best course of action. We must plan and then execute the plan."

"And we will help you. My mate is fully awake now, which will strengthen our bonds further. Soon you should be able to communicate with Alexandra along your bond. Together the four of us will defeat the Cador bitch."

Shock spiked through Lauren at the venomous tone of her torque's thoughts. Her anger radiated through Lauren and stoked her own fury. She couldn't afford to give in to that anger. She knew she must control her emotions, something she struggled with continuously. To be successful, she and the boys would need their combined intellect, their boundless strength, and their cold courage. There was no room for the debilitating grip of emotions. Lauren stroked the metallic scales of her dragon. Drawing a deep breath, she tried to calm the beast. A beast which, if unleashed, could spell doom for her and Alex. If their torques were to act independently, attacking the traitor before the companions were ready, Alex could die.

"Easy now. I feel the same way, but we gotta solve this without emotion if we're to succeed."

Steam scalded the underside of Lauren's chin as her torque lashed out, emotions roiling. *"No, we must act now!"*

"Not without a plan, we won't. We can't afford to go off half-cocked." Arguing again. It seemed that's all she'd done in the last three days. Argue. And she was tired of it. "When we've got our plan, we'll act swiftly, whether the Council likes the plan or not. I, with the aid of our companions, will find Alex and bring her safely back to Terra."

Her torque huffed in frustration. *"Very well. We will help as we can."* Her torque seemed to accept Lauren's order. *"But I warn you, Consort, there is very little time left in which to act."*

Lauren's anger and frustration burst forth. "Bullshit!" She jumped to her feet and paced the waist-high granite rampart surrounding the rooftop of her solar. "Given the shortest time calculated using the clan's route on their hunt for Terra, it'll take the *Dubh Mogairle* more than four months to make the journey to the edge of the Comin nebula at faster-than-light pulse speeds. And then they need to slow to sublight speeds to traverse the nebula itself. So, add another four weeks to cross the nebula to the Comin Homeworld." She stomped her foot. Her torque remained quiet. "All we've gotta do is beat them to the edge of the nebula. That's where we'll face them and take back what they've stolen from us. There we'll get our bondmates back."

"You and the companions will determine the best course." Her torque's voice was resigned. Her voice softened further into a warm, almost motherly tone. *"But first, you will not succeed at anything if you do not rest."*

"You've gotta be kidding me. I haven't got time to rest. Too much to do." Lauren threw her arms up. "We've figured out a way to increase the speed of our clan ships using a new fuel. We've calculated a shorter-distance course across the galaxy." Lauren sat with a thud, dropping cross-legged onto the granite tiles. Her shoulders slumped. "And then." Her voice was a mere whisper on the night breeze. She swallowed hard, barely holding back her tears. "And then, we need to bend time to our will." She knew time was the one thing they couldn't bend. It was the one constant in reality, in any reality, in all realities. Maybe two and a half months, or three at the most to get to the nebula. "We've gotta get there first." Lauren punched her thigh. "We will get there first."

"Rest now, Your Majesty. Things will be clearer in the morning."

Lauren slumped over, exhaustion pulling her down into sleep. She curled into a tight ball, pulling the Fraser blanket around her. She yawned. Her jaw cracked. "Can't sleep, no time," she mumbled. Her mind continued to churn even as sleep crept closer. "Perhaps, we can combine time, velocity, and distance, to bend it. No, wait, not bend it but shape it." With a ruffle of scales, her torque's scaly smile tickled Lauren's chin. Lauren felt her dragon slide into slumber and she followed.

Floating. Lauren was surrounded by the vast blackness of space. Galaxies spun around her, but out of the multitude of stars, a single bright point of white light called to her, a shining beacon which eclipsed all others. Streaking across the celestial sphere above her head, the *Dubh Mogairle* was there. Lauren reached out to grab the speeding point of light. Missed. She turned to match the trace of the fleeing ship, trying again to reach her. To reach the *Dubh Mogairle*. And Alex.

"Alex, can you hear me?" Lauren's mental plea filled the space around her. *"Alex, please."*

"She is awaking, Majesty, we will help her hear you," her dragon replied.

"Alex, please wake up. We must talk. We need your help." A single tear broke free and floated before her, a frozen orb in the void. *"I need your help. I need you."* A sob tore through Lauren. She stretched toward the

trace of light. Lauren felt more than heard a gasp and a throat-deep groan. *"Alex? Can you hear me?"* Silence answered her. She asked her dragon, *"Why isn't she answering me?"*

"I do not know. I can hear my companion. She is trying to communicate with Alex."

A flood of emotion-thoughts hit Lauren all at once, overwhelming her. Anger, pain, loneliness, fear, and heartbreak were jumbled together. Each emotion fought to dominate the other. Yet, no words came.

Her torque said, *"She is awake, but her voice is blocked by an outside force. I will share your thoughts and my companion will pass them along to Her Majesty."*

Lauren's excitement rose but she wanted to speak with Alex directly, not have her thoughts translated. *"Okay, if that's the only way. Please ask her how she is. Where she is? Is she safe? Can she push through the block so we can talk directly?"* Lauren swallowed hard. *"Tell her . . . tell her I love her with all my heart and soul."*

"That she knows." Her torque fell silent and stiffened in concentration as platinum scales dug deep into Lauren's neck. *"Something is taking Alexandra's power, twisting it, throwing it back against her, using her power to create the block. She does not know how to fight herself."* Her dragon huffed, a puff of steam warming Lauren's neck.

"Then, we'll send her our strength. The bond is stronger than ever. I can sense all her emotions." Lauren shut her eyes and concentrated, feeling their bond hum as she poured energy into it. The hum increased as her dragon added her psychic energy. Time slowed to a stop, and the distance to Alex shrank as Lauren filled their bond with her psi-energy, feeding their connection. Lauren could almost see her bond as it stretched across intragalatic distances to the *Dubh Mogairle.* A fine thread of intense white traced across the blackness of space.

Lauren reoriented herself and began to physically follow the thread, pouring more of herself into her bond. She felt herself stretch and thin, as she left her body to follow her soul, reaching out to Alex. Suddenly she couldn't reach any farther. She was trapped, confined in a small box, unable to move. Fear ripped through her gut. *A box? Where have they got Alex?*

"No! Stop! Come back, Consort. You cannot follow physically, or you will be caught in the nothingness of your bond. Neither here, nor there." The torque spouted flame. Pain jerked Lauren's psyche back into herself.

Lauren shook her head to regain her equilibrium, her ears popped. She felt whiplashed, as she was snapped back into herself by her torque. *Whoa,*

I get it now, I feel like I'm nowhere. Like I don't exist. Traveling along the nano-fine thread of psi-energy, she had purpose and direction. Her bond filled with psi-energy made her soul sing. Lauren was going to be with Alex, but now she was back in herself, floating in the black void of space. Alone again. Carefully, she raised her hand to her chin and felt a large blister forming where her dragon had scalded her skin. She couldn't sense the confinement of the box anymore. She could still see the *Dubh Mogairle* streaking away. She could still feel her bond with Alex. It was stronger than before, strengthened by the addition of the dragon-torques' bond and their combined psi-energy.

Lauren pulled their bond to her—it now existed as a physical filament humming with energy. She sent a burst of emotion-thoughts to Alex. Need, worry, love. Alex responded in kind and their bond fully opened.

"There you are, dearest." Lauren smiled as their bond suddenly overflowed with energy. Her heart filled with love. Emotions rushed back to her. Alex's desire overwhelmed her, and Lauren's heart raced as her body responded. She sped toward physical climax, caught in the torrent of Alex's need.

Suddenly, the block between them shattered and words burst into Lauren's mind.

"Dearheart, I am sorry for overwhelming you. But I need your love. I need you." Alex's plea overwhelmed into her.

Lauren panted. *"I'm okay. Just give me a minute here."* Her heart rate began to slow, and she pushed down her physical responses. *"Phew, that was . . . well, I don't know what that was, but I'm going to have a heart attack if you do it again."*

A burst of concern filled their bond as Alex reached out again, but slower this time. Rather than a freight train bearing down on her, Lauren felt enfolded in gentle arms. Safe, protected, loved. *"Better?"* Alex's mind-voice was laced with concern.

"Much better." Drawing a deep breath, Lauren's worry came out in a rush of questions. *"Where are you? Are you okay? Can you escape?"*

"Easy. One question at a time, please. For now, I seem to be unharmed. But I am confined."

"I know, in a box."

"Yes, a very small box. I can turn over, but little else. It is not sealed, because I feel air moving around me." Alex swallowed and Lauren felt Alex's fear soar. *"I can feel her, Lauren. She is near."*

"Yes, we've determined Gwenhwyfach escaped to the Dubh Mogairle. *She then pulled you out of the quantum tubula as you crossed from one*

reality to the next. You never made it to Terra. We will get you back. The boys and I are working on a plan now. But Alex, we've lost McLeod. He isn't here to help." Lauren's sadness at their loss almost overwhelmed their bond.

A torrent of anguish slammed into Lauren, causing her to curl into a fetal position, trying to protect her soul. She knew how much Lord McLeod meant to Alex. How much she loved and revered him. How he was a mentor to Alex and the boys. She knew without his help and guidance, their exodus from Terra Prime would have failed. The loss of his knowledge and engineering skills, of his leadership, were nearly insurmountable for Lauren and the boys.

A strangled groan hit Lauren. "*How . . . oh gods, how?*"

"*Somehow in the weapons exchange as the* Black Orchid *made her escape, his flitter was destroyed. The salvage crews from Luna Keep haven't found anything. And Lord Newkirk's techs haven't found any engine power signatures either. It's as if he just disappeared.*"

Silence reigned, as Alex struggled to reconcile this terrible news.

"*Alex, this is a near crippling blow, but we've got the beginning of a plan. Lord Newkirk has new data which gives us the course and velocity of the* Orchid. *And I can refine her course through our bond. We know where you are.*" Alex's roiling emotions threatened to overwhelm their connection. "*But, Alex, the Council is against me, they're challenging my right-to-rule. I don't know if I'll be able to overcome their objections to take the clan ships and give chase.*"

"*You are Ruler of Terra. Gather your allies, complete your plan. Then execute the plan.*" Alex sent a burst of love and support with her encouraging statement. "*Use your power. Do not be afraid, Dearheart, I am with you.*"

"*The tree and the blade are silent. I know they're listening, watching, but not all of our allies agree with us or I should say with me.*" Lauren felt Alex's fear, a barely contained beast gnawing at the edges of Alex's consciousness. Alex was the one kidnapped, the one trapped on the *Orchid*. *I shouldn't be dumping all my worries and problems on her. I should be the strong one. But, god, I don't feel strong.* Lauren was scared, overwhelmed, and she needed Alex. But Alex needed her more. Lauren pushed down her fears. For her love and for Terra she would be strong. Lauren pulled herself together. Drawing strength from her torque, she wrapped herself in a cloak of psi-energy. This made her feel invincible. She became a bright white speck in the blackness. Her brilliance rivaled the stars as her energy coalesced.

"You have me, Dearheart. Together, we will triumph. I am—"

Alex's words were suddenly cut off. Lauren felt her bond begin to thin again. Her dragon roared as Lauren desperately grabbed hold of their connection. *"Majesty, do not let go."*

Lauren channeled her psi-energy into their bond again. She knew her supply of energy was not infinite, but she hadn't reached the end yet. The stretching stopped and the bond held, but just. She could feel Alex struggle as the block slammed back into place. Alex fought against it, using short bursts of energy, but her psi-energy just reflected back against her. *"Stop fighting it, Alex. Relax. Let our love push the block aside."*

Then Lauren felt her. Terror filled Lauren as a dark malevolent wraith slithered and coiled around her soul. Gwenhwyfach. The wraith reached out along their bond. Before Lauren could react, her torque unclasped from her neck and lashed out. Grasping the darkness in her maw, steam and flame erupted from her nostrils. Her dragon fought to consume the evil, to extinguish it. To kill Gwenhwyfach. But she couldn't do it herself.

Lauren felt her dragon's strength flag and she leapt into the fray. She threw psi-energy out in a sparkling bright web. Pure love recharged her energy, and she pulled the net closed, the evil caught within. The evil form lashed out and attacked the web again and again. Like a cobra, venomous evil was spewed in all directions. Where it hit the web, the golden-white strand would dim and darken. Lauren released more psi-energy. She was exhausted—emotionally and physically—but she would not allow Gwenhwyfach to win again. Their struggle became a nova in the blackness of space.

Then, her psi-energy web grew stronger as Alex poured her energy in, the strands thickened and brightened. Each venomous strike was now reflected back against Gwenhwyfach two-fold and then four-fold as both torques joined in, strengthening Lauren's web. The web began to constrict and the evil could no longer strike out. It coalesced, shrinking until only a speck of darkness remained within the golden-white web. With a final snap, it disappeared.

Lauren felt her dragon re-coil around her neck, settling with a ruffle of scales, and a final puff of steam. The torque sank into a deep sleep, exhaustion dragging her out of Lauren's consciousness.

"Rest, Oh Great One, you've earned it." She sent her message along their bond with a small burst of love and energy.

"Are you there, Dearheart?" Alex's voice was a soft caress in Lauren's mind.

"I'm here. Thank you. I don't know how much longer I could've held her."

Lauren felt more than heard Alex's chuckle. *"You had her, no doubt about it. I just added a little extra. She must be off licking her wounds. I can no longer sense her presence. She will think twice about going head-to-head with you again."*

"Be that as it may, we're still not out of the woods yet."

"Or the box, it would seem," Alex added, her voice strained, even as she made an attempt at humor.

"Funny, but not helping here. You must rest, too, Dearest."

"You are equally exhausted." Concern laced Alex's voice, now no more than a faint whisper carried on the galactic winds.

Lauren laughed as she spun in place in the darkness of space. *"I think I'm sleeping now. I'll probably wake up and find this all a dream."* She sobered and felt Alex's exhaustion. Alex's fear was a constant emotional drain along their bond. She knew they wouldn't be able to maintain this contact much longer. *"I need your help."*

"Yes?" Alex's faint voice tickled Lauren's consciousness.

"We're trying to change any or all the variables in the equation: V=D/T." Lauren sent a burst of images along their bond, equations and diagrams from her brainstorming sessions with the boys. *"That's V and D. Now, we're trying to figure out how to bend time."*

"Bend?" Confusion added to her exhaustion and diminished the strength of Alex's response further.

"Alex, stay with me here. I need something, anything you can think of that'll give us a place to start."

Silence echoed in her head, and Lauren was sure their connection was severed. She could still feel Alex, but she couldn't hear anything along their bond.

A faint jumble of words, then thoughts strangled and confused, came back to her. *"Field . . . q . . . use . . . use your Eins . . . like. . . Doogl. . . second . . . sh . . . p . . ."* Then nothing, only silence again.

"Alex? Alex!" Lauren screamed.

But Alex didn't respond, and their bond shrank back to the nano-thin filament, stretched taut, too small to carry their conscious thoughts across the intragalactic distance.

Sunlight pierced Lauren's eyelids, and she groaned, throwing an arm up to block the light. Lauren turned away from the light, right into a mass of damp fur as a wet tongue rasped across her cheek. Another swipe of a sandpaper tongue caught the edge of her jaw, Lauren's eyes snapped open.

"Stop that, I hate it," she gasped. Pushing against the mass of fur, Lauren struggled into a sitting position, shoving the wolf away. She felt light-headed, almost disembodied. She'd never been so tired in her life, or so cold. Even the fall through the ice and the following trek through the Colorado blizzard in wet clothes hadn't made her this cold. She felt like she'd been exposed to the absolute zero of deep space. That thought made fragments of her dream slip in. *Maybe I was exposed to deep space?*

"Lauren, Merilyn is looking for you." Snow pawed her in the shoulder, nearly knocking her onto her back.

"I'm up." Pushing the large white wolf away again, she swayed. "Give me a minute."

"Why are you up here? Why are the stones burned? Did you start a fire? It is not that cold out here." Ice paced around her, sniffing at the granite tiles.

Lauren rolled up onto her knees and hung her head, hair falling around her face in a curtain. "Ice, what are you talking about? There wasn't any fire. I fell asleep out here last night."

"But, Lauren, look at the tiles. They are charred." Snow began her own investigation of the area.

Lauren sat back on her heels and rubbed her sleep-filled eyes. Sure enough, she was kneeling in the center of an area of blackened tiles. The damage to the granite seemed extensive, flakes of minerals curled out of the stone and a thick layer of ash covered the area. Only exposure to extreme heat could cause something like this in solid rock.

"This wasn't like this last night." Lauren rose, careful to keep her balance. She swayed; her light-headedness exacerbated by the change in position. She rubbed her eyes, drawing her hand over her face and down her throat. White, hot pain flashed through her and she gasped. "What the—?" A large blister covered the underside of her chin and extended down her neck to where her torque lay sleeping. "Well, if this blister is any indication, we must've had a fire last night." More fragments of her dream rose into her consciousness. An image of a white web flashed through her mind, but before she could sort through the dream-images, Merilyn arrived.

"Oh, there you are. Hurry now, the Council has called another meeting and we are needed." Lauren turned her head toward Alex's Seneschal. The elderly, petite woman strode across the roof, her deep purple robes billowing around her ankles in the morning breeze. Merilyn stopped short of the charred tile circle and gazed around, indicating the tiles with a sweep of her arm. "Consort, what is this?" Her usually commanding voice now softened into the whispered question. Awe and concern laced her words.

"Don't know. I fell asleep out here and when I woke up this morning, the tiles were charred." Lauren looked down at the destroyed roof tiles.

Merilyn stepped closer, but she did not enter the circle. She peered up at Lauren, a frown marring her fine features. "And that burn on your chin, did that just appear this morning? Or did you have an accident before you came up here last night?"

"Errr . . . it was just here this morning?" Lauren's voice rose. She really didn't understand either. Again, she touched the large blister. Definitely a second-degree burn, she was sure her entire chin and neck were blistered, and the edges would be red and swollen. Her chin began to throb as the pain continued to build. "I'd better head downstairs and get something on it." Lauren took a step to exit the circle of charred tiles but Merilyn held up her hand.

"I need you to remain where you are, Your Majesty," Merilyn commanded. "I must call Lady MacDonald. I need her expertise to help explain this happening. You must not exit the circle until we know the cause." With a swirl of robes, Merilyn headed off the roof.

"Okay, but this burn needs attention." Lauren spoke to empty air. "Well, that's just great. Now I'm a prisoner too." Lauren crossed her arms over her chest and tapped her booted foot.

"*You are not a prisoner, Lauren, but Merilyn is correct. If this is what I think it is, you must not exit the circle until we can erect the necessary wards.*" Snow growled deep and sniffed at the edge of the circle. She sneezed and jumped back from a particularly dark tile.

Lauren faced her animal companion. "*Oh, come on. I need to get downstairs and continue working on our plan for Alex's rescue. I can't hang out up here all day.*" She easily slipped into mind-speech with her companions.

"*You are not hanging out; you are standing in the middle of a transitional bond portal.*" Ice continued to circumnavigate the circle of burnt tiles, while Lauren turned in a circle to follow her movement. "*We have only heard of them in stories from the days of the First Foremothers. This would be amazing, if you have created such a phenomenon.*"

"*Did you connect with Alex last night, Lauren?*" Snow asked. "*Did you speak with her?*"

"*I think so, or it could be I was just dreaming. I told her about McLeod's death. We talked about the Council. I explained our plans, and I asked for her help.*"

Ice and Snow sat down at the edge of the circle and looked at each other, having a private conversation. They turned their ice-blue eyes on her. *"Did you speak with anyone else?"* Snow curled her lip and growled at Lauren as she asked this question.

"No, I don't think so." Lauren tried to sort out the images of her dream. *"Well, just our torques. They strengthened our bond. Our connection kept failing. Alex's fear kept draining our energy, and then—"* Lauren's words caught in her throat and an icicle of pure terror dripped down her spine. Gwenhwyfach had attacked their bond.

"And then, what, Lauren?" Ice prompted.

Lauren went still, remembering the struggle they had with the traitor.

"I may have met Gwenhwyfach. She attacked Alex as we were talking. She had some kind of shield around Alex. It used Alex's own psi-energy to block our connection. We struggled against the block together. Gwenhwyfach attacked me, but I captured her within a net or web or something. I don't know really." Lauren sank to the tiles, her hands draped over her knees. She closed her eyes as she tried to sort out the memories. *"I thought it was all a dream. I threw a web around her as she was trying to sever our bond. I think Alex joined in and the torques and we suffocated her. I don't really understand what I did. I just did what I had to, to protect Alex."*

The wolves howled at this news and dropped to the tiles, growling as their hackles rose. Lauren was shocked by their reaction. "What?"

Before the wolves could respond, the boys arrived in a tumbled heap at the top of the stairs. Lord Newkirk followed them, breathing as if he ran a great distance to arrive on the rooftop with them. He grasped his knees, trying to catch his breath. Merilyn then arrived, with Lady MacDonald.

"Well?" Lauren swiveled and faced the group. She rubbed her forehead, as a headache began to pound behind her eyes. Ice and Snow sat to one side, their heads bent, listening, hackles still raised. "What's this about a portal something?"

Lady MacDonald knelt at the edge of the charred area. She reached out a hand, one slim finger touching the edge of the circle. A snap sounded and a tracer of golden white light arced from the tile to her fingertip. Lauren's eyes widened at the sight, and Lady MacDonald drew her hand back with a gasp. The air filled with the smell of ozone, as if rain was on the wind. Lady MacDonald turned to Merilyn. "You are correct. They have made the connection."

Merilyn took a deep breath. "I am in awe of their power. This is an ancient tale. Myth, really. Not something created on the rooftop of my tower."

"Come on, guys, what's going on?" Lauren struggled to her feet and raised her arms in a plea. "I need to get downstairs and finish our plans." She turned to the boys. "Angus, help me out here. Time is of the essence."

Young Newkirk stepped up to the edge of the circle and knelt to inspect the burned tiles. "I cannot help you, Majesty. I do not understand this phenomenon. I have only heard about it in my lessons about our Foremothers. Nothing has prepared me to actually see a portal." He looked up at Lady MacDonald. "M'Lady, how do we protect the Keep from an alien incursion across this open gateway? We will not be able to send the clans off to follow Cador if we must guard this access point. Clan Cador could send an invasion force here."

The other two boys and Lord Newkirk moved to the edge of the circle. Lady MacDonald held up a hand, halting any more questions from young Newkirk. She dropped her head, eyes closing in thought. After several minutes, she looked at Angus.

"We can ward this rooftop to prevent any travel through the portal." She pointed a finger at Lauren. "You must stay within the circle until we complete the necessary protections. You are blocking access, but if you exit the circle before we are ready, the portal will be open and remain so. You must not try and contact Alexandra again. This is all due to the power of your bond, and if you reconnect with Alexandra that power will strengthen the portal, opening it farther." The tiny woman placed a hand on Angus' arm. "Protect Her Majesty while she is trapped. We will return as quickly as possible with what we need to close this end." When Angus nodded, a grave expression on his face, Lady MacDonald glanced at Merilyn. "I need your expertise." And with a turn, she rushed off.

Merilyn looked at Lord Newkirk. "M'Lord, I need you to hold the Council at bay. I do not know how long this will take. Many are conspiring to remove Lauren and take over the Council. That cannot happen, or all will be lost. Please ask Lord McLaran to assist you." Her face fell and pronounced lines of worry creased her forehead. "Ask him to mobilize his Black Guard. Seal the Council in if need be."

"I understand." Lord Newkirk frowned.

Lauren focused her mind to open a connection to Lord McLaran's animal companion. After a moment, she spoke to the horse and then smiled. "I asked Gríobhtha to inform Lord McLaran." She tilted her head, listening. "They'll meet you at the Council chamber." Her voice took on a gravity the others rarely heard. "I do not want revolution, but I will not allow our plans to be derailed. Alex bestowed her authority on me, and I will fulfill my duties to the letter. I will do what I think is best for Terra. Even if that means we declare martial law." She knew what she said was an affront to everything Terra stood for and fought to preserve, but it had to be stated plainly. Everyone must know she would use all the means necessary to execute their plans and rescue Alex.

The wolves growled and the boys bowed. "We will obey, Majesty," Robert affirmed.

"Though martial law is an extreme measure, we will do our best to deal with this. The Black Guard will only be a last resort." Lord Newkirk left.

"Well, now what?" She addressed the boys.

"You will stay within the circle for as long as it takes, Majesty," Angus replied.

Lauren sank to the rooftop in a cross-legged position, her elbows on her knees, head in her hands. She fell into a semi-conscious sleep. The boys remained as guards until Merilyn and Lady MacDonald returned. Lauren yawned, rubbing her face to clear her grogginess.

Lady MacDonald carried a huge purple leather-bound book. It was closed with two platinum dragon hasps. She dropped to her knees and placed the book at the edge of the charred circle. When she opened the book, a golden light shown from within. The light was bright enough to compete with the morning sunlight streaming across the rooftop. Lauren felt a surge of energy fill her psyche. But this energy was different. This was an ancient energy, stored for millennia, waiting until it was needed. It drove her exhaustion away. *Whoa, how'd I know that?* Placing both hands on the tiles Lady MacDonald murmured in a language Lauren didn't immediately recognize. As the sounds continued, Lauren began to comprehend, words and then phrases became clear.

"This is the ancient language of the Terran ancestors from the isles of their birth," Ice explained, reverence evident in her quiet tones. *"This is what the original clans spoke before they were discovered by the people of the mainland on Terra Prime. It is a language lost to time and only known by a few now."*

"Alex, the Seneschal, and the Lady of the Ancients were taught this language. It was only to be used in secret communiqués. I have never heard it read aloud before," Snow added.

Merilyn walked around the charred tile circle, taking up a position opposite Lady MacDonald. She turned to the wolves. "If I may impose on the two of you, we will need your additional strength to close the portal and set the wards." The wolves scrambled into positions across from each other and at right angles to the Seneschal. "Thank you." Merilyn bowed her head. "Lauren, we need you to concentrate on closing the portal."

"All right, how do I do that?" Fear closed her throat and her breathing became labored.

Lady MacDonald rocked back on her heels and looked at Lauren, her gaze piercing. "Imagine closing a door, a heavy wooden door. Once you have this image in your mind, imagine throwing the bolts closed." Lady MacDonald rose and lifted her arms above her head, the sleeves of her robe falling above her elbows. Her lips moved in a silent incantation.

"Closing and bolting, okay, I can do that." Lauren closed her eyes and began drawing the mental image.

Suddenly, she could feel an oaken grain under her hands as she gripped the edge of the massive door. Pushing hard, she tried to move the massive door, but it wouldn't budge. The wolves joined her struggle. They stood on their hind legs and placed their forepaws on the door. Together, the three companions pushed. The door began to swing closed. Inch by inch, it moved toward the stone jamb.

Lauren heard a distant chanting. Monosyllabic notes rose to create a dissonant cacophony. The wolves added their howls. Slowly, these tones blended into a harmony which resonated within Lauren's soul. Her body began to vibrate. The door's resistance lessened, and she with the wolves swung the massive portal closed with a resounding boom. Reaching up, Lauren grasped the upper bolt and threw it home. She repeated this on the other five.

When the last bolt shot home, the harmony quieted into a low humming. The wolves dropped out of the chant and left Lauren standing alone before her closed mental door.

She spoke into the minds of the four. *"The portal is closed and bolted."*

"Do you see any light leaking around the jamb or from beneath? Or feel any air movement around the door?" Lady MacDonald asked. *"Do you feel any energy penetrating the door?"*

Lauren dropped to her knees and felt along the bottom of the door. She didn't feel any air movement. She placed her cheek against the cold stone floor and tried to peer under the door. No light. Standing, she ran her hand around the stone jamb. Nothing. Lauren reached out with her psi-energy, running it in a tight beam along the door edges. The golden-white beam didn't change, and the beam's harmonic tones remained constant.

"Nothing, no light or air is escaping through the portal. It seems to be a tight seal." Lauren heaved a sigh. Another task completed. So much still

left to do. Exhaustion reasserted itself, nearly driving her to her knees while cold crept into her limbs. *"Will I ever be warm again?"*

"Yes, you will. Your soul will be reunited with its other half and you will be whole again. We know you will be successful in your quest. This is only one small but necessary step." Her dragon was awake, and her words of reassurance carried a weight of belief so heavy Lauren could not ignore her declaration.

"All right, let's do this." Lauren shook away the mental image of the closed door and opened her eyes. She looked around the rooftop.

"You may step out of the circle now." Merilyn held out her hand. Her small hand was warm in Lauren's grasp and she felt a burst of love and support fill her heart. With a long stride, Lauren exited the circle. As she stepped onto the unburned tiles, a golden-white light erupted, blazing around her. Merilyn dropped her grasp and threw a hand over her eyes.

"Sorry about that. I didn't mean to let the sun in your eyes. Are you okay?" Lauren looked at Merilyn with concern. The light didn't hurt Lauren's eyes. It was only a flash of sunlight, after all.

Merilyn turned to Lady MacDonald. "Did you see that? Could it be an energy corona?"

Energy corona? It's just the angle of the morning sun. Lauren didn't understand.

"What are you talking about?" Lady MacDonald shook her head.

Lauren frowned and Merilyn patted her arm. "It could have been a trick of the sun, a reflection. I am sorry to startle you, Your Majesty." Merilyn waved her hand in dismissal.

Lauren noticed the look of suspicion on Lady MacDonald's face, but she turned away and smiled down at Merilyn. "All right, what's next? Is it safe to leave this here?" Lauren swung her arm around, encompassing the charred circle.

Merilyn grasped Lauren's hand again and brought her other hand up to cup Lauren's cheek. She returned Lauren's smile. "Yes, it is safe. I will post several of Lord Newkirk's psi-engineers up here as a precaution to guard against anyone or anything breaking through."

"Sounds like a plan. We need to get to the Council meeting. Don't want Lord Newkirk thinking we abandoned him to the wolves."

A growl rose from Snow. *"More weasels than wolves I think, Lauren."*

Laughing, Lauren sent an apology to her companion. *"I'm sorry, guys, I meant no disrespect."*

"And perhaps we should include several Black Guards as well. They could prevent anyone from here trying to reopen the portal," Lady MacDonald added.

"Please arrange for the guards, too." Lauren turned to Lady MacDonald. She still didn't understand the portal or the charred circle. Curious, she asked, "How did that thing form anyway?"

"Majesty, you created the portal." Lady MacDonald knelt down and closed the large book. Turning the dragon hasps to seal it shut, she hugged it to her chest.

"No way. I don't even know what a portal is, let alone how to create one." Lauren shook her head.

Merilyn put her small hand on Lauren's arm. "You and Alex have a bond of immense strength. So strong, in fact, it cannot be broken, even when you are separated by vast distances. You spoke with Alex last night?"

"I did." Lauren felt tears gathering in her eyes. "At least until that bitch blocked our connection."

"What are you saying, Lauren? Please explain." Merilyn's gaze hardened.

"Alex and I were talking." Lauren absently reached up and stroked her dragon's platinum scales, remembering the bits and pieces of her night. "Then Cador tried to intervene and I got really mad and then, I could see her. Well, I didn't see her per se, but I saw a blackness, a menace. I lashed out and threw a web around her. I pulled tighter, and then, Alex joined in." Lauren shrugged. "The darkness struggled against the web and then just disappeared. Kinda like it was snuffed out."

"That is not possible. No one has ever converted bond energy into a physical construct before." Lady MacDonald turned to Merilyn. "Have you read about such a thing?"

Merilyn shook her head and bowed to Lauren. "Your Majesty, what you have done has never been done before. You and Alexandra turned your bond into physical matter—the portal and your web are the resulting constructs. I do not know what else you are capable of, but I do not doubt you can achieve anything. Bond-energy is an almost limitless resource." She stopped and cocked her head to the side in thought. "Perhaps, you could even physically travel along your bond from one point to another?"

Lauren's lip trembled, remembering the box, Alex's fear. "I tried that, but my dragon stopped me."

"Stopped you?" Lady MacDonald asked.

"I tried to follow my bond to get to Alex. She was trapped in a small box and—"

Merilyn interrupted, "A small box? An energy sink?"

"Possibly." Lady MacDonald replied, tapping her chin with a slim finger. "Or perhaps, she has created a psi-powered dampening field and is using the box as a physical conduit?"

"I could sense Alex was trapped. I could feel everything she felt, as if I was in the box with her. Alex said she could breathe." Tears escaped Lauren's eyes, her heart aching. "I tried to reach her to get her out of the box. I began to physically travel along our bond, but my dragon stopped me. She said I couldn't do that. If I did, I would be caught between here and there, and be nowhere."

Lady MacDonald nodded. "Your dragon is correct. You would have been caught within your bond. You would exist as pure psi-energy without a physical state. You would have nowhere to return to, your body would die. I doubt anyone could survive in such condition for long, without losing their consciousness."

"I came back and then I lost my connection with Alex." Lauren frowned. "Well, what I mean is, our bond is still there, and I can feel where Alex is, and the direction she is going. But, I can't talk to her anymore. She tried to give me some suggestions about how to modify the clan ships, but I didn't understand what she was trying to say."

Merilyn clasped Lauren's hand again. "Try and relax, Majesty. Alexandra's words will become clear as your unconscious mind works out the puzzle. In the interim, we have a meeting to attend."

Thinking about the mystery surrounding them, Lauren asked Lady MacDonald, "Would you please investigate this phenomenon? Perhaps there is something you've both missed in the vast Terran archives."

When Lady MacDonald nodded, relief spread through Lauren. Now, she could focus on the rescue and not worry about this. She trusted Lady MacDonald and Merilyn to handle it.

Chapter Four
Terra, The Keep, Council Chamber
The Fourth Day

Lauren stood before the great council doors, her companions a phalanx of support around her. They were formally dressed in their clan tartans, a flock of bright woodland birds against the gray granite of the hall. Large jewels sparkled at their shoulders and flashed from the pommels of their broadswords, each armed for battle.

Lauren was dressed for work, not ceremony. She wore a muted Fraser kilt in an ancient hunting pattern of dull green, blue, and red. Her Doouglas plaid—silver, grey, and black—draped across her open-collared white shirt. Her place within the two most powerful Terran clans noted by her clan colors. A golden brooch in the shape of the giant *sempervirens* tree bisected by a blade—the blade, a symbol of power, and the tree, a symbol of her acceptance by the Terran ancestral grove—held her plaid in place. Her dragon torque rippled against her neck. The torque was symbolic of the bond she shared with Alex, and its direct tie back to the First Foremothers of Terra Prime.

With her sleeves rolled up above her elbows, her blue-scaled dragon tattoo was on display. The tattoo's piercing blue eyes were open and alert. Lauren had acquired the dragon tattoo when using Alex's blade to open the energy shield around the Keep. The energy surge she released from the shield transferred the dragon from Alex's blade to her arm. She was armed, with her rapier at her side and an antler-hilt dirk tucked into the top of her right boot.

Turning to the Seneschal, Lauren nodded. The elderly woman grasped the golden boar head knocker. Snow and Ice stood on either side of her, where the boys flanked her in a tight semi-circle, their hands rested on hilts of their broadswords. The five companions, ready to protect and serve.

Lord McLaran, in his formal Black Guard uniform, stood next to Merilyn. Lauren could see the lines of stress on his face had deepened over the last day. This meeting wasn't going to be easy or end well. But she had no choice. Terra came first and she would do everything in her power, exercise all her authority, and utilize all her strength to protect Terra and her clans.

She had a flashback to her Investiture and the oath she swore—*I, Lauren Beckwith Fraser, will guide, encourage, steward, govern, and protect*

Terra and her satellite Luna, Terra Prime and her satellites, and all our Realms beyond. I will stand as our Queen's Protector and Guardian. I will protect and defend her against all enemies that arise from within or without. I will rule in a just manner and facilitate her Majesty's rule in all things, from this day forward and forever more. Yes, forever more, I will not fail, Alex. Her dragon torque fluttered her scales in agreement, tickling Lauren's neck.

The throbbing resonance of the knocker striking home tore Lauren from her thoughts. As the sound of the third strike faded, the great doors swung open on silent hinges. Merilyn, staff in hand, strode forward. "Rise, all Councilors, and give honor to your rightful Ruler." She waited until all were on their feet. Lauren took notice of those who were slow to stand.

"I present Her Royal Majesty, Lauren Beckwith Fraser Doouglas, Savior of all Terra and her future." Merilyn turned to Lauren and bowed, swinging her staff along the floor in a graceful arc. She held the bow for ten heartbeats. Standing, she swung her staff up and struck the floor three times. "This meeting of the Terran Council is called to order. Be seated and hear your Ruler."

Lauren squared her shoulders willing herself to become Her Royal Majesty, the fifteenth ruler of Terra. She flipped her plaid away from the hilt of her sheathed rapier and strode into the circular room at the head of her group. A wave of animosity struck her full in the face.

"Do not cower, Lauren. You are our rightful ruler, as Merilyn said." Ice bumped her nose into Lauren's right hand.

"We are here with you. You will prevail in all things." Snow added her encouragement.

Then Lauren felt Alex's presence as if she was standing at her left shoulder. Her bond flared and a burst of love and reassurance flooded into her soul.

"Her Majesty is with us," her dragon torque whispered.

Lauren continued forward to stand between the two high-backed chairs on the Doouglas side of the table. This time she left the Doouglas tartan across the back of Alex's chair. *Let it stand for Alex, as I sit for her in the Co-Ruler's place.* Lauren took her seat at the table. She waited for the Councilors to follow suit.

Once seated, Lauren looked at each clan chief in turn. Three chiefs from clans—Graham, Campbell, and Buchan—would not meet her eye, looking away as her gaze swept around the table. There was the core of her opposition. She was worried those three might be an insurmountable challenge as some of the clans who provided the core of her support were absent.

Lady MacDonald was completing her research into transitional bond portals down in the Terran archives. Clan McLeod was represented by the clan second, as Hamish McLeod was preparing the funeral services for his brother. Clan Cameron's side of the table was vacant entirely. They too were preparing a funeral for the other missing crewman from the flitter accident, the chief's daughter, Sarah. Even with the three clans missing, the phalanx of Black Guards ringing the circular council chamber made a statement of controlled power and support for her position. Ice and Snow sat on each side of her chair, lips curled in a silent snarl, their white fangs glinting in the wall sconces' flickering light. Alex's three companions stood around her chair, covering her back.

"Well, you've called this meeting, what do you want?" Lauren placed both hands flat on the tabletop and leaned forward. She would not cower beneath Alex's Doouglas tartan as she had before. A feeling of warmth spread up her arms. *Perhaps, I won't need those three clans? The tree is with me.*

Lord Graham stood. "Clan Graham demands the fleet be sent out to chase down the *Dubh Mogairle* immediately. If you will not act, we will assume control of this Council and take over the rescue ourselves. You have neither the right-to-rule nor the capabilities to mount a rescue yourself." Clan Campbell's Chief nodded, obviously aligned with Graham, and Lauren bristled at this outright insult. She partially rose from her seat.

"Be easy, Lauren. Let us determine what support he has and then counter with your plans. You have not been idle these past few days." Ice's voice of reason rumbled through her and cooled her ire. She sank back into her chair. This continuous swing of emotions was draining energy she didn't have to give. She needed to get control soon or she wouldn't have anything left.

"I concur with Graham. This snippet of a girl, who is not Terran, has no right to be in charge during this crisis," Clan Chief Campbell shouted. "She is not one of us."

What? That does it. Lauren sprang from her seat as his insult lanced her heart, but Tavish MacDonald beat her to her feet. In a flash, he sprinted around the table and the tip of his broadsword came to rest on the throat of a spluttering Lord Campbell. Snow followed on his heels.

Lauren's resolved hardened. "Enough! Take your seats. I'll not have more blood spilled in this sacred room. This Council will obey your Queen's order, or you will be removed. We do not have time for this nonsense. If you will not recognize me and my rights, then martial law will be enacted." Lauren settled back into her chair. "I said, sit down!" Lauren raised her hand and the Black Guards lowered their pikes toward the councilors.

Tavish dropped his blade to his side.

"Furthermore, I neither need your approval nor require your input to proceed. Our plans to rescue Alexandra are nearly complete." Lauren's voice was cold as she skewered each of the combatants with an angry glare. No one moved. "Follow me or get out." Lauren swung her arm toward the oaken doors, which opened of their own accord. A small gasp rolled around the table at this show of power. Graham drew his sword but sat, placing his blade across the chair arms.

Snow sank down on all fours, her growl rumbled deep in her throat, her icy eyes boring into Lord Graham.

Chief Campbell scoffed, his face reddening. "We do not have to listen to you, you are nobody."

"Leave." Lauren's command sliced the room like a knife through soft cheese.

Clan Campbell's second and third stood and placed their hands under each elbow of their chief, pulling him to his feet. The clan chief's eyes never left Lauren's. The second leaned down and whispered something into his ear.

Then the red-faced chief nodded. "We will take our leave." Jerking his arms free, he faced the other councilors around the table. "But know this Council of Terra, if this bitch is unsuccessful in her rescue attempt or Alexandra is harmed in any way, we will charge her with high-treason." The others stiffened and gasped at this threat. "Clan Campbell will see her hanged, drawn, and quartered. Her remaining body parts burned, and her ashes cast out."

The three Campbells rounded the table and exited the room. The doors shut against their backs. Lauren remained still; her gaze focused on the remaining councilors. Graham sank deeper into his chair and hung his head. Snow let out a snort at his quiet surrender. She trotted around to sit at Lauren's right hand.

Lauren dropped her hand into the wolf's thick ruff. *"Thank you."*

"I will always protect you, Lauren." Snow blinked up at her, ice blue eyes brilliant with fury.

"As will I." Ice leaned against Lauren's left leg.

Strengthened by the surge of love and support from the wolves, Lauren straightened in her chair. "As I said, we've got a plan. While you've been arguing, we've been working." Lauren nodded to Angus and sat back into her seat, turning the floor over to her companion. "I ask Angus Newkirk to lay out our plan and list what is needed. If we're to successfully return Alexandra to Terra, each of our clans will need to participate." Angus moved around the table, handing out a sheaf of parchment and a data cube to each of the remaining clans.

"You do not know anything of combat, Majesty. How could you prepare a plan without the input of our military at Luna Keep?" The McLeod second spoke into the stunned silence.

"This is a rescue operation not a military action," Newkirk answered for Lauren.

The young McLeod shook his head. "That may be your hope, young Newkirk. But you must be prepared for all eventualities. And at this point, you do not even know where to follow."

Lord Newkirk turned toward Lauren, asking permission to speak. He rose from his seat after her subtle nod. "Council, we know the course and speed of the fleeing Cador vessel."

Lauren smirked as a gasp swept around the room at this news.

On the Outer Hull of the Dubh Mogairle
In a Terran Flitter

The tiny ship clung to the underside of the great clan ship as another wave of tremors vibrated through the flitter's hull, producing a harmonic hum. "They are getting worse, Admiral." Sarah's voice was muffled due to her position inside the center control panel of the tiny ship.

"Aye, but we are nearly done. Once we exit the ship, we do not care what happens to her."

"Do not care? What if this is our only means of escape?" Sarah pulled her head out of the control panel and turned an incredulous gaze on her commander. He did not turn nor did he answer. She presumed he thought her questions rhetorical and therefore did not warrant an answer. "But, M'Lord?"

"Do not 'but, M'Lord' me, Sarah Cameron. This flitter will not be able to maintain her magnetic lock with the hull much longer. It is a tremendous drain of power to maintain the magnets at full strength. If the turbulence from the gravitational wave shear does not shake her loose, then when the power fails, the magnets will release." He raised his hands in a gesture of finality for the tiny ship.

Sarah did not like to hear how the ship—*her ship*—would die such a traumatic death. To be torn apart as the *Black Orchid* raced across the galaxy was not right for the sturdy vessel who got them this far. Her voice grew cold. "If that is the case, how are we going to survive the wave-shear?"

Admiral McLeod chuckled. "Oh, ye of little faith. We will be fine. It is only a transit of one hundred meters to the thruster intakes. Our magnetic boots will hold."

"I am not sure that is such a good idea." Sarah felt her fear rise into her throat. "The turbulence was quite pronounced when we released the safety beacon out the airlock. And we are neither light in mass nor aerodynamic in shape."

"Sarah, think about this, we have a much smaller mass than this flitter. Yes?" She nodded. "And, the energy needed for us to maintain a magnetic lock to the clan ship's hull will therefore be less." He smiled when she nodded again. "We open the airlock, step out, and traverse to the intake ports. We are smaller so our profile will not extend up into the shear turbulence like the flitter does. Further, we should be protected by the intake manifold extending above our heads. You can see the shear wave arching over the manifold." They looked out at the purple-blue swirls of gravitational-wave energy as it moved past them. "Once inside, we break into the maintenance hatch and access the lower decks of engineering. From there, we find Her Majesty, disable the *Dubh Mogairle,* complete our rescue, and escape. One bite at a time."

A low rueful chuckle tickled the back of Sarah's throat. "Oh, is that all." She shook her head and returned to the task of pulling the communication module from the center console. "All right, we will proceed as you have outlined. But, if we get to a place where an escape vehicle is needed, do not be upset if I say 'I told you so.'"

He grinned. "At that point, I will simply remind you of the complement of support vessels aboard the *Orchid.*"

"As if we will have an opportunity to commandeer one of those." Sarah huffed and laughed at the absurdity of their situation. But then she paused. *Is our situation absurd?* They were alive, and for the moment safe within a ship. They had supplies and a plan to move into the *Orchid.* Maybe not a great plan, but a plan, nonetheless. She had all the faith in the world in her commander. Admiral McLeod had never let her or anyone else on Terra or Terra Prime or Luna Keep down.

After another few hours of preparation, the two Terrans stood within the airlock, facing the outer hatch, waiting as it cycled. Red lights morphed to amber and then settled into a steady yellowish-green. The airlock could be opened. They both carried large equipment packs on their backs and had numerous tools attached to their utility belts. Sarah looked at her admiral, and he smiled at her through his transparent face shield.

"Ready?" His voice sounded tinny on their small suit-to-suit transceivers. The tiny radio transmitters were not powerful enough to be detected by the communications technicians aboard the *Orchid*.

Sarah flashed him the universal sign of readiness—a circle made between the thumb and forefinger of her gauntlet-covered hand. She tried to ignore the trickle of sweat running between her shoulder blades. Fear clutched at her heart. This transit to the intakes was an impossible task. But, she reminded herself, one bite at a time. The airlock hatch rolled back into the outer hull and she looked out into the blackness of space, framed in the shell of swirling gravitational-wave energy surrounding the larger ship. A wall of purplish-blue energy rippled along the black hull, captured and shunted into the huge containment vessels.

Admiral McLeod drew a deep breath and she watched him take a tentative step out of the airlock to the hull several meters below. It was actually more of a fall than a step. They were in zero-G and he directed the force of his step away and down, as his boots touched down, he lurched forward. Sarah reached out, but then she realized as soon as his boots touched the *Orchid's* hull, he had activated his magnetic boot locks. His accumulated momentum caused him to sway in place before he was able to arrest the motion by moving his arms out and back in opposition to his upper body's motion, like swimming upstream against a current. Slowly his oscillations halted, and he came to rest in a standing position.

"All right, Sarah. Your turn. Watch the first step; it is more dynamic than I thought."

Just as she released her foot from the hatch threshold, a harmonic tremor rippled through the flitter's hull. The unexpected motion threw Sarah out of the airlock. She tumbled head-over-heels. Disorientation swamped her and her stomach rebelled. Sarah closed her eyes and swallowed hard against her rising nausea. The jerk of the tether she had connected to the hatch arrested her uncontrolled tumble. Sarah hung at the end of the fully-extended tether—a fish at the end of line, waiting to be reeled in. She opened her eyes. She was suspended at the edge of the swirling gravitational wave, parallel to the hull. A meter farther and she would have been torn apart in the shear turbulence, but another tremor could be enough to swing her into the shear. She grabbed for the tether and missed. Panic ripped through her and Sarah scrabbled to grab the coiling tether but could not turn her body around to reach it.

"Easy now. No sudden or erratic motions. Take it slow and easy. I am going to transfer the tether snap from the hatch to my suit." McLeod's voice came over her transceiver. She tried to rotate about her utility belt. "Stop that! You will get tangled in the tether. You could sever a limb if it pulled tight," McLeod ordered.

Sarah hung limp and unmoving, waiting, totally helpless. *Totally useless is more like it.* As her panic waned, her ire built. She hated relying on others. She was a woman of action, a decorated pilot, but here she was dangling at the end of a rope. Worst of all, her own actions got her into this mess. She regulated her breathing and took huge gulps of oxygen into her lungs. Sweat poured down her face and stung her eyes. Her face shield fogged, blurring her vision. Sarah felt the shear turbulence claw at her chest. Like a living thing it tried to grab her. Then, the tether began to move, and McLeod reeled her back to the airlock.

"Easy, I have you. Take slow deep breaths."

Sarah knew he could hear her staccato breaths through their open microphones. Once safe, she hung limp for a few minutes while her breathing calmed. She rotated her feet down to the hull of the clan ship. When her boots were within a few centimeters of the hull, the magnetic locks activated.

McLeod reached out and encircled her in his arms as best he could in their suits. "All is good?" He smiled at her, and she nodded.

Admiral McLeod transferred her tether to his belt. Now joined together, they would need to coordinate their movements. Each step at the same rate, by the same distance, and with the same force. Get out of rhythm and destructive interference could overwhelm their magnetic boot-locks and tear them from the hull. They moved in lockstep toward the intake manifold, only lifting their boots enough to lessen the magnetic lock but not break it. As they neared the edge of the manifold, the shear turbulence bent toward them. McLeod lowered his head below the shear turbulence stream. Then he stopped, raising his hand. "We will need to crawl under the shear stream. Can you move up behind me and retrieve the magnetic hand-holds from my pack?"

Sarah shuffled forward until she reached McLeod. She eased open his pack fasteners and reached a gauntleted hand in, removing the two sets of handholds from the pocket. Reaching over his shoulder, she handed him one pair. "Here you go." The other pair she slipped over her hands and crouched down, placing her hands on the hull.

They crawled forward on hands and toes. It was difficult, and they were both breathing hard. As they crossed into the intake, the shear turbulence lessened, and they were able to stand.

"Just a bit farther." Lord McLeod's voice sounded far away over the sound of Sarah's own ragged breathing. "We are in the clear."

Arriving at the hatch, Sarah looked at her suit's internal chronograph. It had taken them over an hour to traverse a hundred meters. She gripped her knees and tried to get her breath back. McLeod removed the pack from his back and after fastening it to a tether, dug through the contents. Pulling a long wrench out, he said, "This should do nicely. We can loosen the hatch containment bolts. You were correct. We are too large to enter through the drone hatchway. We will need to remove the central hatch disk itself."

Sarah eyed the hatch. It weighed over two metric tons and would normally open by rolling sideways into a recessed groove between the armored plates of the outer hull. "Opening the hatch will evacuate the maintenance bay atmosphere and a decompression alarm will sound on the bridge."

Laughing, McLeod pushed the huge wrench toward her and then returned to digging through his pack. "You are absolutely correct. An alarm would sound, but we are not going to let the atmosphere out."

"What?" Sarah caught the slowly spinning wrench. *How will we accomplish that?*

When Admiral McLeod stood, he was holding a small silver pack. *Did he bring the entire contents of the flitter with him? And, what is he going to do with a medical trauma bag?* The trauma bag was meant to be used by field medical technicians to treat massive soft tissue injuries caused by blaster bolts. An injured combatant would be wrapped in the bag and the bag then evacuated to vacuum, putting omni-directional pressure on the body—becoming a full-body tourniquet. He pulled the pack's woven red tab. A silver alumo-foil sheath unfurled. Once the large bag was fully open, McLeod grasped the bag with one hand and pulled a serrated survival knife out of his suit's leg pocket with the other.

"Grab on to the other side, I need to split the bag down the middle." Sarah hung the wrench from a utility hook on her belt and grasped the bag. McLeod ran the knife along the seam of the foil bag. Once split, they held a large piece of foil fabric between them. A small red box, marked "For Use by Trained Personnel Only" dangled from a corner of the fabric. "Hold on to this please, while I get the adhesive." Then, he flicked his side of the fabric at her.

Sarah held the gently undulating fabric. It roiled slowly in zero-G, affected by the most minute movements she imparted to it. The silver sheet had an odd pear shape. *I get it, he is going to create an airlock.*

"All right, I am going to glue the fabric's edge onto the jamb of the hatch. I will leave one edge free so we can enter the space. Once the adhesive dries, we will loosen all the bolts." He turned toward the hatch and began squeezing adhesive out of a tube he had pulled from another utility pocket. *He did bring the entire flitter with him.* Sarah chuckled.

Sarah and McLeod carefully aligned the cut edge at the bottom of the hatch. The admiral rolled the foil into the adhesive, smoothing as he went until the fabric stretched over half of the hatch. The quick dry adhesive worked by partially dissolving the foil and then fusing the melt to the metal jamb. The adhesive was unaffected by the cold of deep space.

McLeod turned to Sarah. "Let us rest a bit. Removing those bolts will not be an easy task, especially if normal maintenance has been neglected." Sarah knew what effort it took to keep a giant clan ship in working order. The *Dubh Mogairle* had been mothballed when Cador Clan Chief was exiled on Terra. She assumed this meant nothing had been done to the ship prior to her sudden exodus from the system. Even in the vacuum of space, corrosion accumulated as metals reacted with each other. This was especially true, when one end of a bolt was in the cold of space and the other was within the temperature-controlled environment of the ship's interior.

After a brief rest, they folded the foil sheet back and stepped inside their make-shift airlock. Sarah went to work on the first bolt using the wrench. She turned to McLeod. He nodded at her and she applied a counterclockwise pull on the wrench. The nut didn't budge but Sarah pulled hard enough to break her boot's magnetic lock. Her legs floated free of the deck before she could get her feet back down. Now, her feet were above her head.

"That is no good." McLeod put his hands on his hips and cocked his helmet to the side. "We will need to double the magnetic lock on our boots and do this together."

After several failed attempts, the first nut finally broke loose with their joint efforts. The rest came free more easily. Sarah was beyond exhausted, and McLeod was no better. She could see condensation accumulated along the edges of his face shield from the sweat pouring down his face. Sarah tapped a couple of commands into the control pad on the left sleeve of her suit to check its environmental statistics. The internal temperature of her suit was elevated—the cooling system could not keep up with her physical activities. She was critically dehydrated which added to her fatigue. With only four hours of oxygen left at her current rate of consumption, she did not know if they would have enough to gain entry into the ship. She slumped, trying to conserve her energy. The admiral swayed next to her, probably doing the same calculations. Time. They needed more time and more resources to finish.

After a bit of rest, Admiral McLeod clapped Sarah on the shoulder. She started. *Did I fall asleep?* "Let us complete our task, Sarah. You have done well and soon we will be breathing the air of the *Dubh Mogairle.*" He laughed, a hearty belly-deep sound which made Sarah smile. "And then, we can really create mayhem. Yes?"

"Yes, M'Lord."

They glued the remaining half-circle of foil to the hatch jamb and stood within the silver bubble. Their headlamps flashed as they removed the remaining nuts. Now the hatch was only held in place by its mass and the coefficient of friction along the jamb. "We will only need to roll it back far enough to allow us entrance. We must do this slowly." She nodded. "And I do not know if I have enough oxygen in my suit to bring our make-shift airlock into equilibrium with the atmospheric pressure inside the maintenance bay."

Sarah was dumbstruck. *Does the admiral mean to evacuate all the oxygen from his suit to fill the bubble?* "But, sir."

He held up a white gauntlet-covered hand. "I know, Sarah. But we must pressurize the bubble some way. Do you have any other ideas?"

Sarah looked back down at her environmental readouts and punched a couple of buttons. Data streamed on the inside of her face shield—partial pressure of oxygen, suit temperature, humidity, partial pressure of exhaled gases. *What if—?* Tapping another button, a red laser flashed from her helmet-lamp, making a tiny red dot on the hull between her feet. Looking up, she focused this dot on the edge of the jamb and then turned in a slow circle.

"Sarah?"

She held up her hand at the admiral, her focus concentrated on keeping the laser moving, a new plan forming as data scrolled across her face shield. "That should do it."

"Do what?"

Sarah laughed. This was the first time she was not the one asking the questions.

"The volume of our bubble is approximately forty-five cubic meters. And we need to fill it to one atmosphere of gas pressure, or our airlock will blow out as the pressure inside the bay rushes to equalize with our bubble. Creating a catastrophe we cannot manage." McLeod stared at her in rapt attention; this gave her courage to continue. "Our environmental suits store gas in the recycler at four-hundred bars of pressure. Therefore, if we release gas at that pressure into the zero-pressure environment of our bubble, we would need approximately one hundred and twelve point five liters of gas to fill the bubble."

McLeod clapped his hands. "Well done! Well done, indeed. You may not have a mastery of non-linear multi-dimensional wave equations, but you do understand the physics of expanding gases." He looked down at his own data pad and punched a few buttons. "I have approximately fifty-eight point nine liters of gas remaining in my recycler."

"I have almost seventy liters in mine. The total is more than enough." Sarah swept her arm around to encompass the silver fabric rippling gently around them.

"No, I will not allow you to endanger your life." He shook his head.

"Sir, my life is forfeit anyway if we do not successfully open that hatch." She pointed at the round door beside them. "You do not have enough gas left in your recycler to fill the bubble to the required pressure. I will need to add most of mine."

"I cannot allow that, Sarah."

"It is the only way. And standing here arguing is only using up more of our limited supply."

McLeod looked at Sarah with a pleading gaze. She could almost see the wheels of his mind spinning as he tried to figure out another way, but she did not give him the time to finish his thoughts. "I appreciate your concern, sir, but we are in this together, and together is the only way we will succeed in gaining entry into the *Orchid*." He shook his head again and dropped his gaze to the hull in resignation.

"We will proceed. But I do not think we need a full one bar of pressure. Eighty percent should be adequate, and the pressure differential between our bubble and the interior of the maintenance bay will provide an extra shove as we try to open the hatch."

They began entering commands into their data pads. Soon, gas was being released into their makeshift airlock. The gas—humidified for breathing comfort—contained water vapor, and when released into space's deep cold, it froze. They were now standing in a small snowstorm. Sparkling crystals swirled around their feet.

The foil bubble began to expand and became taut. "That is enough." Sarah watched the external pressure readings, closing the relief valve on her suit.

They moved to the hatch and the large handle of crossed metal bars. Grasping two of the bars they pushed the large hatch. It did not budge.

"Be easy. Let me pull for a moment and see if we can get the hatch to roll along its track."

Admiral McLeod stepped back a half-step and anchored his boots, then he grasped the bars and pulled. The hatch gave a fraction and began to roll away from the right edge of the jamb. Light poured from the bay and Sarah was pushed against her magnetic boot lock. Obviously, interior atmosphere was equalizing with their makeshift airlock. The hatch rolled open. Sarah stumbled as she tried to get out of the way.

Admiral McLeod grabbed the hatch edge and pushed. "Get inside now." He gritted his teeth, straining against the hatch. "I will try and hold it from opening all the way and tearing through the fabric."

Sarah released the magnetic locks of her boots and sprang toward the opening. She dove through the hatch, like a diver slicing into water. Her forward momentum propelled her into the maintenance bay. Once she cleared the hatchway, Sarah tucked into a tight ball and rolled. She popped up and reengaged her boots. Turning, she saw the fabric bubble was stretched to its limits and shivering against the pressure increase.

"Sir, hurry! The bubble is going to burst," she yelled. Sarah could hear air movement, a rushing-sound filled her helmet. Now that they had an atmosphere around them, sound waves had a medium in which to move. Images of all the space-action vids she watched rushed forward in her mind. In the vids, all the battle scenes had sound effects. *There isn't any sound in space, only hard vacuum.* "Come on, hurry!"

McLeod pulled himself around the edge of the hatch but did not let go. "Help me push it closed." Sarah rushed to grab the hatch edge and the two locked their boots to the deck and pushed. The hatch closed.

"Hold it." McLeod left her holding the hatch closed and moved across the maintenance bay toward the far wall. He tore open a large panel marked with a crosshatch pattern of orange and white stripes and pulled out a large white bundle. Turning toward Sarah, he shoved the bundle in her direction. It tumbled end-over-end in the zero-gravity of the bay. She grabbed it as it spun toward her. The bundle was an emergency hatch seal, used in decompression accidents or hull breaches during combat. Sarah turned back to the hatch and pulled the emergency seal out of the package. When she affixed the magnetic seams to the hull in one corner, the seal snapped around the hatch jamb. She activated the miniature force field generator in one corner. The generator whirred to life and a sparkling sheet of energy snapped into place between the magnetic seams.

Sarah stepped back and shook her head. They did it. They got out of the flitter and into the *Orchid*. She heaved a sigh of relief. "We made it."

McLeod smiled, and then leaned on his knees, trying to catch his breath. He straightened back up. "Aye, we did. Let us secure the seal in place and then have some real fun."

A great tearing rent the bay, and the deck bucked beneath their feet. Sarah crashed backwards into the emergency seal, as the hatch rolled open behind the energy field. She could see their tiny airlock through the simmering sheet of energy, but she knew the energy field was sealed and would hold the bay's pressured atmosphere. Sarah heard a pop, a snap, and then Admiral McLeod's scream echoed in the empty bay. She moved toward him. "No, the seal. You must . . . ensure . . . it is up." He wheezed. She continued to move towards him. "Now, pilot!" She did not care about the hatch; the seal was in place. *Must help my admiral.* She released the locking ring of her helmet and pulled it off her head, rushing to his aid.

The admiral had already released his remaining boot lock and now he struggled to control his motion as he floated about a meter above the deck.

"The flitter must have torn free of the hull." Sarah reached out to stabilize his erratic movements. Klaxons began to sound, and the steady white light of the bay changed to a deep strobing red. Sarah froze, looking back at the hatch. The energy shield was intact, but the crew of the *Dubh Mogairle* must have seen the flitter as it tore free from the hull.

The admiral's face was etched with pain, and he panted against it, his face shield fogging and then clearing with each breath. "Must get out of this bay . . . only have . . . few minutes before engineering techs . . . here."

"Sir, stop struggling. Let me get your helmet off." She grabbed the emergency release tab on the side of his helmet and pulled. Once the helmet was off, his rasping breath sounded loud in the bay. "Where are you hurt?"

"Not enough . . . time . . ." McLeod grunted. "Must get out." He pointed up and Sarah followed his gesture. A large ventilation shaft filled the central portion of the bay's ceiling. The shaft was covered by a welded-wire grid. McLeod swung his good leg down and screamed again as his torso rotated about his injured hip. "Go up."

Sarah released her hold on his arm and crouched. She swung her arms up and back, timing the release of her magnetic boot locks with the upward swing of her arms. Shooting upward faster than she thought she would, she crashed into the ceiling. Sarah got her fingers into the grid and slowed her wild movements. "Now, what?"

"Cut—" The admiral gasped. "Grid bolts."

Pulling a small utility laser cutter from the leg-pocket of her suit, Sarah cut the heads off six of the eight bolts holding the large silver grill in place. By the time she had the sixth one off, the admiral managed to propel himself up. *How did he do that in his injured state?* "Good job . . . pull . . . grid . . . free."

Sarah pulled one corner down and the admiral turned and flipped upward. Or tried to. His one leg dangled loose, unusable, and he hit his head as he swung upward into the shaft. He stifled another scream.

Sarah swung her legs around the corner of the grid and moved effortlessly into the space. She pulled the admiral the rest of the way into the ventilation shaft. The large shaft easily accommodated both of them. One squirt of adhesive from the tube McLeod handed her and the grid was back in place. Sarah squinted at the sparkling energy field. *I cannot do anything to conceal the emergency seal on the airlock hatch. Now, I must help the admiral.*

Sarah did not know how badly the admiral's hip was injured. She carefully moved upward, coming even with his body. "Where are you hurt?"

Unconscious, his head slumped forward. She continued moving up the shaft. When she was above his head, she hooked a safety line from her belt to the neck ring at the back of his suit. She needed to find a place where they could rest, and she could assess the admiral's injuries. Just as Sarah began moving along the shaft, away from the maintenance bay, she heard shouting. Someone found the emergency seal. She shook her head and continued to float along the shaft, away from the maintenance bay, trying not to bump the sides, while towing the unconscious admiral behind her. *Time for a game of cat and mouse.*

Chapter Five
Terra, The Keep, Council Chamber
Early Hours of Morning, The Fifth Day

After Lord Newkirk provided the Council with all the data on the *Black Orchid's* course and speed, Angus' presentation of their rescue plan took more than five hours. Lauren called a halt to the meeting around midnight and had a meal brought to the chamber. Once everyone had eaten and rested for an hour, the meeting morphed from a confrontation, to a debate, to a strategy session.

The Councilors now stood clustered around the holo-display of the Milky Way galaxy floating above the tree-table. Several flight paths cut through the display, each taking a different route from Terra to the Comin nebula on the opposite side of the galaxy. The course Lauren favored was highlighted in Fraser green. It arced out from Terra and passed nearest the galactic center. She knew what the center contained—a supermassive black hole. She planned to use this giant gravity anomaly in their flight.

Lauren had learned a lot about black holes in the last few days, including the difference between stellar black holes and supermassive black holes. Stellar black holes occur when a massive star collapses in on itself at the end of its life. They are randomly scattered about the solar systems of the galaxies. Stellar black holes were first proposed in 1784 by clergyman John Michell. In 1915, when Einstein developed his theory of general relativity, he postulated how the mass of an object affects the fabric of spacetime. Black holes warp spacetime, creating huge gravity wells. Their wells are so deep light from distant stars is bent around them. Einstein's theory was experimentally confirmed when the light from distant stars was measured during a solar eclipse. The light was warped by the calculated amount.

Supermassive black holes are different, and Lauren was going to use their differences to her advantage. These behemoths exist at the center of almost all galaxies. The characteristic she was going to exploit was its mass to density ratio. Density is equal to an object's mass divided by its volume. Even though a supermassive black hole has immense mass, it is spread across a tremendous volume of space. Using the formula for density: a very large mass divided by a very large volume equals one or less. Therefore, a supermassive black hole has a density less than water. And in turn, the gravitational effects at the event horizon—the hypothetical boundary between space and the black hole—would be similar to those experienced by a person standing on the surface of Terra. Hence, a ship skimming along the edge of the supermassive black hole event horizon would be safe from any damage caused by gravitational effects. Therefore, if she could safely navigate a curved path within the deep gravity well depressed in the fabric of spacetime, this great-circle route would shorten their flight distance across the galaxy. An additional benefit would be gained by using the black hole's gravity as a slingshot to propel her ships to greater speeds than their engines could produce.

She visualized the fabric of spacetime near the galactic center with its supermassive black hole and its deep gravity well, thinking about the blanket and exercise ball Tavish had shown to Sharon. Lauren had one more idea to explore, one she wasn't sure would work and didn't want to share just yet. She would discuss it with Angus when they were alone. *Maybe I can bend time using gravitational time dilation at the event horizon, too?*

The councilors accepted their plan after much debate, building on its best parts, pointing out weaknesses, and recommending possible alternate solutions. They even volunteered clan resources to the rescue effort. The most difficult hurdle was convincing the clans not every ship should rush off to give chase. Terra must be protected, and each citizen given a means of escape if needed.

As the first rays of sun colored the eastern clerestory windows, their plan was in place, but one argument remained. The Council wanted to send a ship after the *Dubh Mogairle,* following her exact flight path in case anything happened to her or she changed course. Lauren felt this was unnecessary as she could pinpoint exactly where Alex was at any time using her bond. Sending one of her four ships off as a vanguard would only weaken her remaining force. She realized she was clinching her fists in frustration—her dragon tattoo squirmed in discomfort. Lauren opened her hands, shaking out her arms.

"Councilors, if we divide our force, we weaken our ability to stop the *Orchid* from entering Comin space." Loud arguments meet her disagreement. Lauren held up her hand. "Please, hear me out. We don't know what forces the Comin have or if they'll send them in defense of Cador's ship. We don't know if the *Orchid* will detect the vanguard and attack it in transit. We don't know if the *Orchid* has been modified with Comin weaponry which could penetrate our shielding." She shook her head. "It is too great a risk to divide our forces and leave one ship isolated and alone against the *Black Orchid.*"

The McLeod second turned toward her. "Majesty, we must send the vanguard. If we do not and the traitors do change course, we will not know in time to react and they will be gone. Alexandra will be gone."

Pain lanced through Lauren's soul with this comment, but she forced down her fears yet again. She stood. "I will know the moment the *Orchid* changes course or speed. We'll be able to monitor her progress at all times." Lauren turned to the hologram floating above the giant tree-table. She pushed a finger into the three-dimensional construct and highlighted a single region of space. Angus tapped a command into his pad and a small purple dot appeared within the hologram at the end of Lauren's fingertip. Lauren withdrew her hand. "The *Orchid* is there."

"But, Majesty, you cannot know that," Graham argued. He had come around throughout the presentation and was now actively participating in the refinement of their plan. His clan resources would go a long way to protect Terra, if the clans needed to flee. "We do not have any more sensor data to confirm that position."

"I don't need sensor data to tell me exactly where my soul's other half is." Lauren drew a deep breath. *Should she tell them about the portal?* "I spoke with Alex night before last, and although she's confined, she is well."

Gasps sounded. Questions were voiced as their shouts swirled around Lauren. Before she could answer, Merilyn rose and rapped her staff on the table. "Lauren and Alex opened a transitional bond portal. They communicated and were able to defend against a psi-energy attack from the traitor. Lauren does know, and will always know, where her bondmate is, how she is, and what is happening where Alexandra is."

Now the councilors fell silent, stunned by Merilyn's declaration. "We do not know how this is possible or how the portal was created. Our Lady of the Ancients is in the archives trying to get answers to our myriad questions. For now, we must accept that Her Majesty does know." The silence deepened after Merilyn finished. Then as one, the council rose and bowed to Lauren.

Graham moved around the table and knelt before Lauren; his head bowed on his knee. "Majesty, forgive my ignorance and disbelief in you and Alexandra. What you have done is unprecedented. I swear my allegiance and the resources of Clan Graham to you in the successful completion of your plan, as well as in the defense of Terra." He stood and crossed his right arm over his chest. "I am yours to command."

"Clan Buchan is with you!" The chief clapped his arm across his chest, their earlier dissent overcome.

Chief MacBain, a tiny wizened man with long white hair and drooping mustaches, nodded from where he stood leaning heavily on his wooden cane. "We join. We will fly with Fraser."

"We will always support the Doouglas' clan, we are with you, Majesty." McLeod's second grinned at Lauren.

Alex's three companions—Angus Newkirk, Robert McLaran, and Tavish MacDonald—encircled Lauren. Each reached out and clapped a strong hand on her shoulders. "As we swore an oath to Alex, so we swear our oath to Lauren. We will follow you to the hells and back." Angus spoke in a deep, resonating voice for the three.

"Aye, Clan Newkirk stands with you!" Lord Newkirk nodded.

The sound of wood against stone began resonating within the chamber. Lauren looked around—each of the Black Guard was banging their wooden pike shaft on the stone floor. As her gaze swept over them, they raised their right arms across their chests in salute. Tears rolled down Lauren's cheeks, she was nearly bowled over by the rush of emotions filling her.

Lord McLaran stepped forward and dropped to one knee. "I have known you since you first came to Terra. I nearly shot you, mistaking you for a Comin invader. I am so glad I did not." He chuckled at his own joke. "For you are the one to rescue our Queen. My clan and I are with you in your efforts."

"Stand, Lord McLaran. You honor me with your support, but I will not see you kneel before me." Lauren pulled the Chief of the Black Guard to his feet. He smiled and moved to stand beside his son, Robert.

Merilyn stood before her. "I adopted you into my clan, based on the contributions you made to Terra and your selfless acts to foster and protect. Based on who you were. But the adoption was not without my own selfish desires." The tiny Seneschal grimaced. "For, in you, I saw a way to keep my clan alive. Now, you are no longer adopted." The councilors gasped, but as Lauren gazed into Merilyn's eyes she saw a twinkle in their depths and knew her admission was not a negative. "Now, you are the heart and soul of Terra. You carry her weight on your shoulders, much as Alexandra does. You will succeed. Terra will survive and flourish under your rule. I am with you, daughter."

A hush fell over the council with the gravity of Merilyn's words. This moment was one of historical proportion—a nexus in the long history of the Terrans. What happened next would determine if the clans survived to flourish or died at the hands of a traitor. No one knew their fate, but the remaining Terran clans were united.

A deep rumble filled each mind, the great tree-table spoke in its aged-voice. *"Today, the fate of Terra hangs in the balance. No matter the future, we stand with our Consort. She will traverse the stars, just as our ancestors traversed the seas of Terra Prime. The sword, our spokeswoman, will travel with her."* The sword of the Doouglas, Terra Prime's First Foremother, and the tree were partners in the protection of the Terran civilization. They agreed with the plan to take the clans across the Milky Way galaxy to the Comin Homeworld.

As one, the clans shouted their ascent, stomping and clapping. The wolves added their howls to the cacophony. Soon the granite walls began to resonate with the noise. Then another sound came from outside the chamber, and a hammering sounded against the chamber doors. Lauren raised her hands and the councilors fell silent. Yet, the hammering continued, and with another sweep of her hand, Lauren opened the great doors.

Stewart McGuiness, Swordmaster and the Champion of the People, stumbled into the room to land sprawled at Lauren's feet.

"What's going on, Champion?" Lauren asked.

Rising, Stewart stood before Lauren. Bowing deeply, he spoke in huffs as his breath caught, "Majesty, you must . . . must come . . . come now."

"We can't leave, Stewart. We're not done. We've gotta—"

The swordmaster interrupted. "Now, Majesty this cannot wait." He clasped Lauren's upper arm in a meaty fist.

Tavish jumped forward and drew his sword, pointing the blade at McGuiness. "Unhand her now," Lauren's guardian and champion growled.

Snow joined him, snarling. *"I do not care you are champion. You will not touch her if I am alive."*

Stewart dropped his hand as if burned, then knelt, bringing him eye-level with Lauren. "I apologize, Majesty. But this is a miracle and you must come and see what is occurring." The other councilors moved around the table at the champion's words.

Lauren gestured for Stewart to stand. Turning to the Council she said, "I apologize, it seems I'm needed elsewhere for a bit." She nodded at Tavish. "Please come with me." He sheathed his sword and stepped around the hulking champion.

"Angus, please finish this meeting. We need a decision about a vanguard. And if you decide to send one, who it should be." At that, Lauren rushed through the open oaken doors.

As Lauren exited into the great hall, a crush of people stopped her. The silent crowd parted, opening an aisle way toward the great hall's exit and the boulevard beyond. As Lauren passed through, the Terran people fell to their knees, heads bowed. Tavish strode at her left side. Snow trailed a pace behind while Ice led their pack, following on Stewart's heels.

Lauren glanced sideways. "What's going on Tavish? This is weird."

"I do not know, Majesty. Let us see what the Champion has discovered and then we may have an explanation." He smiled down at her as they continued to thread their way through the crowd.

Stewart led them out onto the damaged boulevard toward the circle of standing stones within the sacred grove. People lined the street all along their route, silent, bowing low as Lauren passed.

When their destination was certain, Lauren couldn't help but question their rush. "Champion, can't you just tell me what's going on, please?"

The Champion glanced back at her and paused. Ice plowed into the back of his legs and dropped to her knees, letting out an explosive breath, winded from the sudden collision.

"I cannot. You must see this."

Totally bewildered, Lauren looked up at Tavish, who shrugged.

Finally, they arrived at the foot of the sacred grove's Grand Approach, the path which bisected the *sempervirens* and continued on into the center of the circle of standing clan stones. Here the paving stones were undamaged. It seemed the terra-tremors which shook the Keep and the standing clan stones to their foundations did not disturb the path. The Champion marched up the approach but stopped at the entrance to the circle. He stepped to the side and turned to Lauren.

"Please, Majesty." He bowed and swept his arm before him, indicating Lauren should precede him into the circle.

She looked around at the standing stones, all of which stood tall, except the stones of Clan Cador and Steward. These had toppled and now were nothing but a jumble of broke pieces, littering the circle's floor. "Okay. We're here. Now what?"

"Please enter and see the miracle." The Champion's voice came as a whisper, which contrasted sharply with his size.

Lauren entered the sacred circle, where the power of the stones flooded her soul. It thrummed through her and strengthened her flagging energy. Striding toward the steps of the central altar, she couldn't see anything missing or out of place. The wolves kept pace at her side, their large white heads swinging back and forth, ice-blue eyes surveying the central circle. Tavish moved up behind her when she stopped at the base of the lower step. She looked back where the Champion stood in the center of the path, his hands clasped tight in front of him, knuckled white. He seemed to be vibrating in place, trying to contain his emotions.

"What—?" But before Lauren could finish her question, Ice howled.

"There," the wolf shouted in her mind. *"There! I do not believe it."* Ice leapt forward into the grassy verge around the central altar, with Tavish on her heels. Tavish suddenly fell to his knees. Lauren still didn't understand, but all this kneeling was getting old. They had work to do and distractions were eating up time.

"It truly is a miracle." Tavish's gaze never left the Fraser clan stone.

Snow nuzzled Lauren's hand. Lauren looked down into the wolf's icy-blue eyes, and she shivered. Swallowing hard against a flood of emotion, she asked again, "Well?"

The wolf stepped away. *"Follow me, please, Lauren. This is amazing."*

Lauren followed Snow to the edge of the grass. The wolf stopped and dropped to her haunches. *"There, Lauren."* She swung her muzzle toward the standing stone. *"Do you see them? The flowers, surrounding the base of the Fraser clan stone."*

Lauren saw a cluster of the most delicate white, pink, and violet flowers she had ever seen growing around the stone. Tiny orchids. They rose from the tall emerald grass on thin brilliant green stalks. They were magnificent.

Lauren smiled and walked to the nearest one. She bent low, reaching out a finger to stroke the white cap over the violet and pink bowl. "I don't know what to say. I've never seen anything like these before."

"Nor have we. They are steeped in legend and very rare. They have only been reported growing in the fens of the northern isles of Terra Prime. It is a crime against the crown to pick or remove any when they were found. None have been reported for over six hundred turns," Tavish explained. "I do not know how they could possibly be here. But here they are."

By now, Terrans from all over the Keep surrounded the sacred grove, trying to catch a glimpse of these beautiful flowers. A glimpse of this miracle. Lauren could feel the emotions rising around her—surprise, awe, excitement, humility. But one emotion rose above all the others—belief. Belief. Belief in Terra. Belief in the strength of their society. Belief they could and would overcome all adversity. Belief in her. Lauren was humbled by their collective support.

From the crowd beside the Fraser stone stepped the tiny figures of the Terran Seneschal and their Lady of the Ancients. "Well, it seems you have done it again. You have produced yet another miracle, Majesty." Merilyn stated, hands on hips, a small shake of her head. Lady MacDonald simply bowed her head to Lauren.

"I don't understand. Tavish said they're very rare and only found in a few places on Terra Prime. If that's the case, how're they here?" She dropped her voice to a whisper. "And what does their appearance mean?"

"These are *Cypripedium reginae* or the Queen's Lady-Slipper orchids." Lady MacDonald stooped low and traced a delicate finger across the top of one of the orchids. It shivered, though no wind disturbed the circle. "It is fabled their appearance occurs only when an event of great significance happened to the queens-line or was about to happen. The folks of the northern isles were told to maintain a lookout for them, as they were a harbinger of good fortune for the crown. They were to report any sightings." Lady MacDonald stood to her full but diminutive height, her sapphire eyes flashing. "Their appearance here today is most significant and signals we are on the proper path."

When Lauren shook her head, Merilyn admonished, "No, Lauren, you must not discount this happening. This is another validation of your position."

"*Our Lady is correct, Majesty. You must accept and acknowledge this miracle. This affirms your right to rule. The people of Terra will follow you, regardless how far you must travel across the stars.*" The deep rumbling of the tree spread through the minds of the Terrans surrounding the grove. Murmurs rose from the crowd.

"*The appearance of the Queen's orchids supports our Queen-consort's right-to-rule. Her decisions are final and will be followed as if Alexandra ordered them herself.*" The feminine voice of the First Foremother's sword added her agreement to the Tree's pronouncement. "*Terra is with you, M'Lady.*" Slowly, the crowd began to clap their hands and stomp their feet. The sound rose until the ground beneath Lauren's feet vibrated in sympathy. Loudest of all were Stewart's cheers, he stomped and yelled, "Consort, Consort, Consort!"

Lauren couldn't speak, her throat was closed by her tears. She bent and touched another orchid near her feet. "*Thank you.*" She projected her thoughts outward. "*I acknowledge your support. I accept the challenges before us. Before me.*" She smiled, the first real smile since Alex's kidnapping, her heart was warmed and strengthened by this miracle. "*I promise you. I will not fail to bring our Queen home.*" She touched the delicate blossom again. The flower warmed her fingertips.

Lauren stood and strode from the grove. The crowd stopped their noise-making and parted as she exited onto the boulevard, heading for her eastern solar. Stewart fell in behind her. The wolves rushed to catch up as she hurried away from the circle. Her heart raced and she could barely contain herself. She knew nothing would stop her now. But, her exhaustion claimed her again. She didn't know how long she could hold it together. Collapsing in front of everyone wouldn't be an encouraging sign.

"I am at your side, Majesty. Ask anything and I will make it happen," Stewart said in his deep rumbling voice.

"Thank you, Champion. I may need you soon." Lauren gave him a small smile as she raced along the boulevard. Another ally joined her ranks and he would pull his clan members with him.

"Lauren, slow down, you will fall on the stones," Snow pleaded.

"Can't." Lauren gritted her teeth and rushed on.

Ice tried to cut her off, to slow her down, by jumping in Lauren's path. *"I must get into my rooms. Ice, get Susan and Sharon. I need them."* When Ice didn't move out of her way, Lauren paused and knelt before the wolf, she stroked her muzzle and behind her ears. *"Please, Ice. I need them, and I need quiet. Just for a little while."*

Ice snorted and raced toward the stables. Lauren continued her dash toward the solar. Snow raced by her side. She looked down at the wolf and smiled again. *"I am so lucky to have you."*

"We are the lucky ones, Lauren. We are with you, now and forever."

Several hours later, the gloaming was settled over the Keep. Lauren climbed from the hot water of her bath and wrapped herself in a large fluffy towel. She felt more relaxed, somewhat rested, and ready for the next phase of this ordeal. Her discussions with Susan and Sharon always helped ground her. They supported her and didn't care what the Terrans thought. Now they waited for her to finish her bath.

The people were with her and Lauren knew the Council wouldn't balk any longer. Most had accepted her plans and pledged their support. Only one clan remained in dissent. Campbell. During her history lessons, Lauren hadn't read anything about this clan which would explain their behavior. They'd never sided with Cador or Steward that she knew of. She wished she could speak with Alex. Get her input into this particular clan. Determine what was driving their dissent. She shook her head, wet hair sending streams of water sprinkling onto her shoulders. *No, I can't always rely on Alex. I've gotta do this myself.*

The next parts of her plan were still a bit nebulous, although she had some ideas how to proceed. They had their course. They had the design modifications for the clans ready. But, if the vanguard gave chase along the flight plan of the *Black Orchid*, they would need a means of communication. *Can we devise a means to communicate across intragalactic distances? Maybe we could use the companions' bonds, animal and human? Or perhaps, utilize the bond between Ffrwyn—Alex's horse companion—and her foal, Làireach?* Susan would have to be involved and travel with them if they used the horses, and that was why Lauren asked Ice to bring them to her solar.

Dressed again in a hunting-tartan kilt and white shirt, Lauren descended to the second floor of her solar. Her wet hair was pulled back into a tight ponytail, which hung over her right shoulder and the ends mixing with the purple leather thong holding the tail in place. Susan and Sharon cuddled on one of the leather sofas, snuggled before a blazing fire set in the large stone fireplace. Alex's Doouglas tartan throw was draped across their legs. Lauren chuckled, pleased to see Sharon immersing herself in Terran culture. She was dressed in a Fraser tartan as well, her gray and red plaid wrapped about her shoulders.

"Hey, guys, thanks for coming."

"Well, refusing wasn't an option." Sharon snorted from their nest, wrapped protectively within Susan's embrace. "Ice would've freaked. Well, freaked more than she already was. But you owe us an explanation, Lauren, something big is going on around here."

"Yeah, things are happening." Lauren walked over to the fire and gazed into its depths.

"That's an understatement. Ice was upset. She kept saying something about flowers and the sacred circle and the council agreeing. Ffrwyn could barely understand her. Ice just kept spinning in circles, woofing at us to hurry." Susan smiled up at Lauren. "Làireach kept repeating how everything was going to be all right now."

"Well, it's been quite a day." Lauren smiled and dropped onto the other sofa, sprawling along its length as she stretched her legs out, head falling back on the broad armrest. Her six-foot frame filled the entire length.

"Seems it's more than an understatement, Lauren. Once we got back to the Keep's main boulevard, everyone was out, rushing about, and speaking in hushed tones. No one would stop long enough to tell us what was going on. We kept hearing something about orchids blooming. The Queen's orchids had appeared." Sharon looked at Lauren, waiting for her to explain.

"If you can hold on a little bit longer, we need to wait for the boys and the wolves. Then, we'll tell you everything." *Or as much as I understand.* Lauren didn't know what everything meant but she would try and explain it to her friends. *Maybe explaining will help me understand as well.*

"How'd the council meeting go? You seem in pretty high spirits, compared to how you were a few days ago." Sharon always drove straight to the heart of the matter. She didn't miss anything when it came to interpersonal dynamics, and Lauren never could hide her feelings from her.

Lauren regarded her friend. Sharon looked pensive but Lauren could see an encouraging twinkle in her bright green eyes. "Once we got past a difficult start, it went well. But then, I was pulled away, so I don't know how it ended. There were still a couple of loose ends which needed sorting. That's why the boys are held up. I asked Angus to finish the meeting for me. Robert stayed behind, too, in support of his father and the Black Guard."

The three friends settled farther down into the soft sofas and relaxed, waiting on the boys. No one seemed to want to disturb the comfortable silence. Lauren didn't know how the meeting finished up, so she didn't have much to add.

The warmth of the fire washed over her and her eyes drooped closed, sleep came quickly as she gave into her exhaustion. It seemed only seconds had passed before boisterous shouting disturbed her; the shouting interspersed with the woof-woofing of wolfy laughter. Lauren jerked back into consciousness from a very nice dream about Alex and hot tubs. She sat bolt upright. "What—?"

"Sleeping, really." Robert turned to his two companions. "We are doing all the hard work and she is up here sleeping. That is just rude." The bite of his words was softened by the huge smile on his face and the twinkle in his deep blue eyes. His black hair was tousled, an indicator not everything went as well, or was as easily as his smile implied. Susan and Sharon woke up and started to rise from their nest on the other couch. Robert waved them back down and took up his usual position, leaning against the mantle beside the fire.

Angus and Tavish laughed and then joined Lauren on the sofa as she swung her feet to the floor. "I take it the end of the meeting went well?"

"Yes, Majesty, we accomplished all our goals." Angus relaxed back into the soft cushions, grinning, but Robert's harrumphed guffaw seemed in opposition to Angus' positive take on things.

Lauren looked hard at the three. Each of her companions had a smile of varying size on their face. There were no visible injuries, so a sword fight hadn't been required to gain consensus. But something was slightly off. "I'll ask again, the meeting went well?"

Tavish dropped his clasped hands between his knees. "We have permission to take four of the clans after the *Orchid.*"

"Well, that's something at least. Did they agree to work up evacuation plans for the Terran and Lunar populations using the remaining clans?" Lauren sat forward.

Robert nodded. "Yes, they did. However, we will need to modify our plans to meet their other requirement."

"All right…" Lauren drew the word out, waiting for Robert to elaborate. When nothing was forthcoming, she bumped Tavish in the shoulder. "Spill, big guy. What's this other requirement?"

Tavish frowned. "We have to send a vanguard out along the exact course recorded by our sensors."

"But doesn't that weaken your plan?" Susan interjected.

Tavish nodded. "Considerably. If we are required to give chase with a vanguard, we reduce our own capabilities by almost half."

Half? Lauren titled her head, wondering about the reduction. "We'll still have three waiting at the nebula, if our planned shorter-distance course is correct."

"In absolute numbers, yes, we will have three lying in wait. But, fighting three ships limits some of our attack plans significantly." Tavish looked away and Lauren caught a blush bloom across his ruddy cheeks.

"And?" Lauren prompted as Tavish looked at his companions. He was nervous about something. "Just say it, Tavish, we've never kept secrets from each other."

"And, Majesty, you will be in command of one of the three."

Lauren frowned. "So, we will still have three against one and with the vanguard chasing, we would soon have four."

Tavish punched Angus in the shoulder. "I told you this was not a good idea. We should never have agreed. We must keep our forces consolidated. We cannot afford dividing our resources."

Angus glared at him. "If we had not agreed, we would still be sitting in that damned meeting, arguing over how to protect Terra. Agreeing to a vanguard was the only way to get them off the mark."

Lauren felt the companions' emotions swell along her bond, and sadness filled her heart. *I thought they were with me?* She was beginning to understand their hesitance, but Sharon beat her to the punch. "Oh, I get it." She pointed a finger at the boys. "You don't think Lauren can command the *Stag*."

Susan and Sharon had only seen videos and pictures of the great clan vessels in their docks in Luna orbit. Sharon thought they looked like a cross between an Imperial Battlecruiser and a Romulan Bird of Prey. Of course, this caused the group to have several late nights viewing the *Star Wars* movies and various *Star Trek* episodes. None of the companions were taken by Captain Kirk, but all of them, the wolves included, thought Spock and Darth Vader hung the moon.

Tavish hung his head. He wouldn't meet her eyes. "Lauren is not battle-tested, let alone battle-trained. The crew of the *Orchid* is made up of hardened veterans of prior conflicts and the *Orchid* is well armed. And, we do not know what the Comin will contribute once the *Orchid* is within communications range of the Comin Homeworld."

Lauren shrugged. "You're right. I'm not battle-trained. I'm hoping we won't get into a shooting match. As you said in Council, this is a rescue mission not a military—"

Tavish interrupted. "That is an unrealistic wish, Majesty. Clan Cador is obviously taking Alex to the Comin, to curry favor or receive some sort of reward." Tavish rubbed his chin. "Most likely, they want the Comin's agreement to help Cador take the Terran throne in exchange for her. We cannot assume we are up against only one adversary."

Robert joined in the conversation. "Our last intelligence information was gathered before we departed Terra Prime, so it is very out of date. But it told us the Comin has a deep space fleet of over one hundred ships. Twenty of which match the clans in size and capabilities. At the time of the bioweapon attack, we were starting the construction of additional attack vessels to blockade the nebula against an invasion fleet. But with the exodus, none were completed."

Lauren settled back, lost in thought. She couldn't disagree with anything said.

Susan took up the argument. "I agree with each of you."

Lauren's head snapped up at this, betrayed and hurt at her friend's immediate dismissal and Susan's ready agreement with the boys. Lauren sat rigidly on the edge of the sofa.

Susan held up a hand when she saw Lauren's reaction, giving her a soft smile. "Let me finish before you go off on me." When Lauren nodded, Susan looked at each of the boys. "You must understand the depth and breadth of Lauren's intelligence." Each of the boys agreed. "There isn't a problem I've ever seen her face she couldn't overcome with study and determination. This is simply one more challenge." Susan shrugged and gave the boys a crooked smile. "Perhaps it is out of her immediate area of expertise, but not an insurmountable obstacle."

Sharon continued for her partner. "There is an old Chinese paradox on Earth. 'What happens when an unstoppable force meets an immoveable object?'"

The room was silent as its occupants considered Sharon's question. After some time, Angus spoke, "I do not think it would be possible for two such things to co-exist."

"True, hence the definition of the Chinese word for contradiction—*máodùn*. Literally translated, this word means 'spear-shield.' In the third century, a story was written by a Chinese philosopher. In the story, a blacksmith created a spear and a shield. When he tried to sell them, he stated the spear could penetrate any shield and the shield could protect from any spear. When asked what would happen if he threw his spear against his shield, he couldn't answer the question. Thus, a paradox was created." Each of the companions gave Sharon their rapt attention as weapons were mentioned. Turning to Angus, Sharon acknowledged his conclusion. "Your hypothesis is correct, Angus. There aren't any unstoppable forces and therefore there can be no immovable objects." She relaxed back into Susan's broad shoulder. "At least that's what I always thought until I met Lauren."

Lauren's laughter rang out and joined with her companions, but Sharon continued in a serious tone. "Lauren is both the immovable object and the unstoppable force. You must all realize; she will never give up. She will never abandon her cause. She will never stop fighting. Do not underestimate her abilities, training or not." Sharon leaned forward to emphasize her point.

Lauren felt her face redden. She rarely had anyone believe in her before she came to Terra. Once here, it was Lauren who didn't believe in herself. *I wish Sharon had been in the council meeting, it wouldn't have been such a struggle.*

"As you say, Majesty, 'well alrighty then.' It seems we cannot argue with such an assessment of your character." Tavish conceded and clapped both hands on his knees. "But you will have much to learn as we travel across the galaxy. And time is not on our side. You will need to learn quickly."

Lauren frowned. Time was still the parameter controlling their success or failure.

Chapter Six
Aboard the Dubh Mogairle

Klaxons woke Alex from a deep sleep and she started, hitting her head on the box lid. During her captivity, she had become attuned to the ship and her daily cycles. The sounds she made while running at faster-than-light pulse speeds. The quiet of the night watch, as opposed to the flurry of activity during her daylight hours. But something had changed. The vibrations rising through the floor were slightly different, the harmonic vibrations of the gravitational-wave generators decreasing. The ship was slowing down.

Alex sat back up and carefully reached out along her bond, testing the connection to Lauren. The psi-energy sink, which suppressed her bond with Lauren, was nearly absent and she poured energy into her bond, reaching outward, stretching for Lauren. *"Dearheart, something is happening. Can you hear me?"*

"What . . . Alex?" Lauren's response came back dulled. Alex could see her, feel her. So close to her, Alex felt like she was in the room with Lauren. This was the strongest their bond had been since she was taken. Lauren struggled to throw back the down coverlet on her bed. *"What's going on?"*

"Something has happened, the Orchid *is slowing, the alarms of general quarters are blaring. The psi-sink around my box is absent. And, why are you not in our bed? You are in the eastern solar."*

"Bed?" Lauren shook her head.

"Yes, bed. You are in your solar. Not in our bed in the western solar. Why?"

"Wait a sec." Lauren looked around the dark room. *"You can see me? You know where I am? How's that possible?"*

"I do not know, but I can see you. Quite clearly, in fact."

"That's amazing. I wonder if I can see you?" Alex felt Lauren send energy out along their bond, their connection snapping fully into place. And then they were together. Or at least their wraith-forms were together. Alex opened her arms and Lauren fell into them. The warmth and strength of Lauren's hug nearly crushed Alex but she didn't let go. She simply hugged her back, tucking her face into the nape of Lauren's neck.

"Oh, Dearheart. You feel so good. I cannot believe you are here."

Lauren looked up into Alex's ice-blue eyes. *"Where's here? We're not in my solar, now."*

"I do not know." Alex looked around them. They floated in the darkness of deep space, the stars of the Milky Way spiraling around the celestial sphere. *"It seems we are somewhere in space."*

"Space? Again?" Lauren's mental-voice squeaked, as she gulped, her eyes widening. Alex remembered Lauren's reaction to her first EVA from the flitter to Construction Site Alpha. Alex hugged Lauren tighter. *I cannot let her fear overwhelm our psi-connection. It is so strong now.*

"It would seem so, but I have you. I would never let you fall." Alex again looked around them as they floated, serenely twirling in place. *"This is a miracle. The ability to hold you, feel you in my arms, this is the boost I needed."*

Lauren continued to look into Alex's eyes, obviously trying not to look around them. *"I know, Dearest. This is awesome."* Her smile rivaled the brilliance of the stars and it lit Alex's heart. Sobering, Alex did not know how much time they had until Gwenhwyfach discovered them, so she sorted her thoughts quickly.

Lauren must have noticed her frown. *"What's wrong? We're together and that rocks."*

"I agree, however, I do not know how long we will have. Let us make the most of our time, shall we?"

Lauren's smile diminished, quickly replaced with a serious expression. Nodding, she hugged Alex once more.

"What have you and the companions planned? When are you headed after the Orchid? *How will you catch her? We have a significant head-start."* Alex felt lost due to the lack of information. Her heart bled for Lauren. She was the one with the impossible tasks. *"And how is the Council behaving?"*

Lauren chuckled. *"You're sounding more like me by the minute. Calm down, Dearest, we got things under control. Our plan is almost complete, with only a couple of obstacles yet to top."* She paused. *"As for the Council, only one clan has withdrawn—"*

"Withdrawn? Who? This is an outrage! I sent my final command. They are choosing to ignore a direct order from their Queen. I will remove them from the Council permanently." Anger boiled in her veins, and Alex's vision tinged red.

"Easy, love. We've got it under control." Lauren seemed to be choosing her words with care. Alex raised a brow in question. Lauren placed a gentle finger on her forehead and smoothed the crease above her eye. *"No need to worry."*

"All right, if you say you have things in control, I will let it be. For now." Lauren laughed, so Alex switched gears. *"Tell me what your plan is? I need*

to know so when I have escaped from this damnable box, I can help, somehow." Alex's worry ratcheted up another notch. Something was off. Lauren was not telling her everything.

"*We've decided to send out a vanguard. Robert'll take Clan McLaran's* Wild Boar *with a full contingent of Black Guard and give chase along the exact flight path the* Orchid *is on. That leaves Tavish, Angus, and I. We'll take our three clans, but we won't follow the* Orchid's *course.*"

"Robert cannot stand alone. He and his Boar are no match for the firepower of the Orchid. You will need the firepower of all four to defeat her. Where are the Lion, Stag, and Kestrel going to be? Why are you not joining?"

Lauren gave her a small lopsided grin, the one she used when she knew something someone else didn't. Some of Alex's tension bled away. "*Our three will follow, but along a different course.*" Again, Alex felt her eyebrow creep upward. "*Our flight plan will take us to the Comin nebula using the shortest great-circle route across the galaxy. And using this course, we will sling-shot around the supermassive black hole at the center of the Milky Way, gaining a boost in overall speed. We're hoping to beat Gwenhwyfach to her destination and defeat her there.*"

"What? Are you out of your mind?" Alex's disbelief flared, and Lauren winced at her mental shout. "*That course is suicide. The clans will not be able to withstand the gravitational pull of the black hole. And if they do survive the gravity, how will you control the massive stresses which will build on their hulls from the strain of the excess speed you will generate?*"

"*One question at a time, Dearest.*" Lauren chuckled. "*We'll manage the excess stresses on the hulls the same way our flitters re-enter Terra's atmosphere.*" Slowly, things started to fall into place for Alex. "*We'll skim the outer edges of the supermassive black hole's gravity well, just outside the event horizon, maintaining a forty-degree angle of attack. Remember your astrophysics?*"

Alex shook her head in confusion and then it came to her. "*You are assuming the gravitational effects at the supermassive black hole's event horizon are lessened due to the inverse relationship between volume and mass within the black hole itself.*"

Lauren made a buzzer sound. "*Correct, the Terran Queen wins the bonus round.*" Alex appreciated Lauren's attempt at levity, but time was ticking, Gwenhwyfach could not be absent for long. Lauren continued. "*Our proposed course should reduce our travel time to the nebula by over fifty percent. I didn't want to send Robert off after you, but the Council insisted. I think they don't believe I always know exactly where you are. They're worried the* Orchid *will alter course and her destination is not the*

Comin Homeworld. They don't believe our proposed alterations to the clans' propulsions systems will increase our speed enough."

Alex was flabbergasted by the amount of work Lauren had accomplished in such a short time. *"Alterations? What have you done now?"*

A soft laugh was the only answer Alex got. Alex looked into Lauren's sparkling eyes and smiled. She truly was a marvel, and if Lauren thought she had it handled, then perhaps Alex should just go with it. This thought caused Alex to grin. Their emotions joined, Alex did not need to search her soul to know what Lauren was feeling, she just knew. Their souls continued to blend, even at this distance, they were continuing to meld.

"What?"

"Yet again you have taught me. I should never doubt you and your plans. You will not let me down." Alex held Lauren's gaze as she tightened her hug and smiled. *"So, tell me the rest. At least then, I will have something to think about while I am trapped in this damnable box."*

"Perhaps we can do something about that." Lauren looked around them at the swirling stars. She cocked her head as if listening. *"I don't feel the traitor anywhere near. Is that how you were able to make this connection? Do you have a feel for what's going on?"*

"I was woken by klaxons. Something has happened to the Orchid *and she is slowing. And when I realized the psi-sink was gone, I reached out to you."*

"Are you able to open the lid of your box? Can you do that while still maintaining our connection?"

Alex did not know what would happen to their connection if she tried to complete a physical task within the reality of the *Orchid*, while in psi-contact with Lauren. No, it was too risky, and Alex would not lose Lauren now she was in her arms.

"I will try, but after we complete our discussion. You were going to tell me about the modifications you are making to our propulsion systems."

Lauren detailed the changes they were making to the four clans. *"This modification should give us a twenty percent increase in overall thrust. With that and the shorter flight path distance, we'll beat them."*

"That is a lot of 'ifs', Lauren." Pride rippled through Alex. Lauren had done so much.

"That's all you can say?" Lauren snapped. *"I've gotta deal with the naysayers on the Council and now you don't believe in us either. Or, is it, you do not really believe in me?"*

Alex quickly realized how Lauren heard her comment. She obviously mistook it for criticism. *"No, you misunderstand, Dearheart. I am not being critical. I am amazed."* Alex saw the skepticism on Lauren's face. *"Amazed at the amount of work you have done. Amazed you understand the workings of the clans so well you can create such modifications."* Alex hung her head. *"Amazed and awed you would do so much for me."*

Lauren tilted Alex's chin up. Alex knew being trapped in this damnable box had destroyed her self-confidence. *"I couldn't do anything less. And I had help. A lot of help. Once Campbell left the council meeting, everyone saw what was needed and put aside their concerns to focus on the only thing of importance to any of us."*

"Picking a new leader?" Alex snorted in disgust.

"Alex, get real." Alex smiled sheepishly as Lauren continued. *"Everyone buckled down and committed resources, knowledge, and manpower to our plan. The clans are in their construction docks now being refitted with the new hydrogen condenser."*

"Well then, you have it in hand."

Lauren laughed and then heaved a great sigh. *"Not really. There's too much yet to do and too little time to do it."* She looked away.

"And?" Alex prompted.

"And, I'm exhausted. This is the first sleep I've had in I can't remember when. Robert is leaving in less than thirty-six hours and we still need to tell Terra what we are doing. We need to finish the refits and we don't have a way to communicate and I—" Lauren stopped her tirade of uncertainties and tightened her hold on Alex. Lauren sounded defeated. *"And you're still in a box and I've got no idea how to command a clan, especially if we get into a space battle."*

Alex cupped her cheek. *"Let us focus on the concrete. Why do you need to communicate? The clans have a perfectly adequate communication system. You will be able to talk to Angus and Tavish anytime you wish."*

"I understand that, but we need to talk to Robert in real-time, and he'll be across the galaxy chasing after the Orchid. *We'll need a constant update on the* Orchid's *course and velocity. How're we going to do that?"*

Alex realized how important this was as the combat situation became clear in her mind. She searched her memories, sorting through all the briefings she had had with Admiral McLeod over the years. A thought tickled her mind, she remembered something, but she could not pull it to the fore. *What had McLeod said was needed when they escaped from Terra Prime?* They were discussing splitting the clans up, sending them all off in different directions, but a lack of communications prevented that. At the time, Alex was too frightened of another attack to divide her forces. She relaxed and quit trying so hard to remember. She looked out at the immensity of the universe surrounding them where they floated. They were so small, so insignificant in this great vastness of space.

"Wait, that is it!"

"That's what?"

She beamed at Lauren, who looked at her in confusion. *"I know how you can communicate—"*

"That's impossible." Lauren interrupted. *"We've been killing ourselves trying to figure something out and you just say, 'you know how?'"*

"Admiral McLeod had a prototype communication device built while we were searching for a new home. Originally, he wanted to split the clans up, have each go in a different direction, but we could not stay in contact with our existing communications system. He worked on this project the entire time we were searching. Hoping to find a new communication method, so we could split the clans up, cover more space, search more solar systems."

"All right, you've got my attention. What happened?"

Alex stroked Lauren's soft cheek. *"We found Terra and our search was over. Therefore, the communication system was not needed. He mothballed his project in the archives on Luna."*

Lauren's smile lit the space around them. *"If we can find the system configuration and his project files, and it works, we could depart almost immediately after the refits are complete."* Lauren drew a deep breath. *"And get you back."* Lauren's belief in their success resonated in Alex's soul.

"Yes, back. Together."

Suddenly, Lauren reared out of their hug, a look of fear crossing her face. *"She's coming."*

Alex felt Gwenhwyfach's presence grow closer, tendrils of dark menace began to surround them. *"I must go back. I must get out of the box before she realizes what has happened. Find those files."* Alex pulled away and began returning to the *Orchid*, her soul shrinking back toward the ship.

"Files, right. I'm on it. I love you, Dearest. You're my heart and soul. I'll get you back." Alex heard Lauren's oath as she too faded away, back to Terra, back to the clans and all the work she needed to do. Alex couldn't let her go without her knowing all Alex felt. All she believed.

"Lauren, regardless of what happens, remember one thing, I love you and I trust you. You will never let me fall. You will never let Terra fall."

Terran Keep, Eastern Solar
The Sixth Day

The warmth of the fire washed over Lauren and she welcomed the heat. She struggled to sit up. "Did anyone get the number of the truck that just hit me?" She swiped her hand over her eyes, rubbing sleep away. Her head pounded and her mouth felt stuffed with cotton gauze. "What happened?" She pushed back the down coverlet, but it was missing.

"That is what we were going to ask you, Lauren. One moment we were discussing the outline for your battle command training and the next you were flat on the floor. We could not rouse you." Snow's concerned tone spoke volumes about how worried she was, especially as the wolf usually took things in stride. Nothing ruffled her fur.

"Battle training? I was sleeping in my bed." Lauren couldn't remember anything. Her mind was jumbled. The room spun around her. She dropped her head back to the floor with a thud.

Ice moved to looked down at Lauren, her eyes filled with worry. Her whiffled snort lifted Lauren's bangs off her forehead. *"Do you not remember? Did you have a stroke?"* Ice addressed the others in the solar. *"We should call the healing technicians, now!"*

"I don't think that's necessary, Ice. Just gimme a minute." Lauren pushed herself back up and closed her eyes, willing the room to stop spinning. Opening her eyes a crack, she looked around. The three boys knelt next to her and Ice was so close to her face she blocked more than half of Lauren's view. Lauren pushed the wolf away. "Help me up?"

Tavish lifted her up. The motion so fast the room again began to spin. "Whoa, hold on a minute." As she swayed in place, Tavish kept a strong grasp on her arms. "I'm okay, Tavish, thanks." He released her but stood near to catch her if she lost her balance again.

Slowly everything righted itself and the room stopped moving. Lauren looked at each of her companions and smiled. "I know how to communicate—"

The boys interrupted her, barraging her with questions. Their demand for information swirled around her as the room again began to move. She closed her eyes and gripped her head in both hands. "Stop, gimme a minute, will you?"

"Lauren, we do not have a minute. Everything is moving forward at faster-than-light pulse speed." A wolfy snort punctuated this remark.

"I know. But the room is moving at that speed as well."

Snow's quiet voice entered Lauren's mind. *"You must focus. We have much to do."*

"Really, Snow, stating the obvious? That's not like you." Lauren opened her right eye. It seemed with only one eye open the room remained steady and she could move without falling. She walked over to her desk and keyed the communicator in the analyzer.

After a few seconds, Hamish McLeod's voice snapped. "What? I do not have time for further interruptions." Before Lauren could answer, the voice went on. "Look, we have a service to prepare. I cannot take time for others."

"M'Lord, please give me a moment to explain the interruption." Lauren heard the stress in Hamish's voice and her heart went out to the new chief of Clan McLeod. *It must be agonizing to prepare a funeral in the midst of all that's happening.* Tears threatened as her memories of their lost friend rose in her mind. "It's Lauren. I appreciate how busy you are and how hard the tasks are. How much pain you're feeling, but I need your help." Lauren felt the companions' puzzlement. "We need to access Lord McLeod's archived files. Can you help us?"

Hamish's voice was softer when he responded this time, but he obviously didn't hear her earlier comments. "Your Majesty, my apologies, I did not check the ident on the call before answering." He cleared his throat. "How may I be of service?"

"No, I'm the one to apologize. I know the service is scheduled for tomorrow, but I haven't got time to wait. I'm so sorry. But to my point—"

Her thought was interrupted by Hamish. "Anything, Majesty."

"Thank you. Can you give me access to your brother's personal archives on Luna, please? It's of the utmost importance, M'Lord." Clan McLeod always backed Alexandra and were the first to offer their support and resources in the council meeting. Lauren hoped Hamish would allow her access.

"I cannot do that, Majesty."

"I only need access to one thing. Please, this is critically important. It's—" Ice nudged her hand, Lauren's words stuttered to a halt. She spun around to admonish the wolf.

Ice peered up at her, flicking an ear. *"Lauren, stop and listen. He is not saying he would not, he is saying he could not."* She thought about what Hamish said. Ice was correct.

Hamish continued, having no way to hear Ice. "I truly wish I could help, Majesty, but I do not have the codes needed to enter his personal archives." Lauren heard a gulp and sniffle, and then a deep breath. "He did not share those with anyone. I am afraid the data locked away in his archives are lost forever."

Lauren looked at each of her companions. "That's not possible. There's always a way into someone's systems." When Angus shook his head, she turned back to the analyzer. She pounded her fist onto the desktop. "There must be a way, damn it. There has to be."

"If there is, I do not know of one."

"Nor I, Lauren," Angus said from behind her.

Lauren hung her head, defeat rising up to swallow her. A heavy silence fell on the room and Lauren gathered her thoughts. *There has to be a way.*

Hamish was still on the line, his steady breathing echoing in the quiet room. *Think, Lauren. There has to be a way.* "May I ask why you need into his archive?"

"Oh, Hamish, I'm sorry. I'm so focused on our need to move quickly I'm not explaining things well." Lauren ran a shaking hand through her hair and leaned over the desktop. "I need to access the information on the communications system he was developing while the clans searched for a new home. Alex said he had a prototype ready, but you found Terra before he had a chance to test it."

Snow bumped her in the knees. Lauren's temper flared once again. They didn't have time for more interruptions. "What?" she snapped.

"Alex said? When did you speak with her?"

"Not now, Snow, we've got work to do here." Snow dropped to her haunches and gave Lauren a soulful look. Lauren frowned, knowing she'd hurt Snow's feelings.

Before she could apologize, Hamish replied, "Why did you not say so in the first place? You do not need to access his archives, Majesty. You simply need to access his personal storage vaults beneath Luna Keep. If he had a prototype ready, that is where he would have stored it."

Lauren turned back to the analyzer so quickly the room spun again. "Personal storage? How do we get into that? Where is this storage?" Her excitement rose. Maybe they could accomplish this.

"It is quite simple, go up to Luna and use your override codes to enter his storage vaults in the lowest level beneath the Keep."

"Override codes?" Lauren looked over her shoulder at the boys, each one shook his heads. "What override codes?"

Terra, Flitter Landing Field
Dawn of the Seventh Day

Lauren strode across the tarmac toward the *Y Ddraig Goch*—Alex's *Red Dragon*—her white helmet tucked under her left arm. Susan paced beside her, twisting with each step trying to settle her white evac suit. The speed things were moving didn't allow time to construct a custom suit for Susan, so she was using a cast-off from Robert, and it didn't fit quite right. The arms were too long, the legs too short.

"Are these things really necessary? I mean the flitter has a sealed system." She looked over at Lauren. "Doesn't it?"

Memories flooded back to the day Hamish fit her suit. "Well, funny you should ask. I asked the very same thing when I got my suit fitted."

"Yeah, but the key word in your statement is 'fitted.' This thing was pulled out the back of Robert's closet. I don't have a clue how old it is or even if it will do its job should that job be needed."

Spinning on her heel, Lauren faced Susan. *Can't everyone just get with the program?* Lauren's halt caused the vet to stumble as she tried not to run right over Lauren. "The trip is only going to take about thirty minutes. Really, Susan, can't you hold it together that long? You're the one who wanted to see Luna Keep. Now's your chance. If you don't want to go, just say so." Lauren's temper built. Her exhaustion, combined with all the stress of the last days, frayed her nerves to the breaking point. She knew it was unfair to take it out on Susan. So, she turned back toward the *Red Dragon* and continued across the tarmac.

"Whoa, easy there, kiddo. I didn't mean I didn't want to go, or I don't want to see Luna Keep." Susan gave the suit another tug to free the excess material from her crotch as she hop-skipped after Lauren. "But this thing is uncomfortable."

As they approached the large flitter, the boys stepped out from behind the dorsal wing and raised their hands in greeting. "Your Majesty. We have completed our preflight inspection and are ready to board." Tavish swept into a low bow.

As he stood, Lauren slapped him on the arm. "What's with the 'Your Majesty'? I thought we'd gotten past that?"

He smiled and gestured to the boarding ladder. "Oh, we have. But only in private," he whispered conspiratorially. "It would not do to have the ground crews hear me call you Lauren, Lauren." She gave him a smile as he helped her up the steep ladder. Tavish turned to Susan to offer her assistance.

Lauren leaned over the edge of the fuselage. "Watch the first step, it's bigger than you think."

Susan was perched on the second rung and promptly caught her toe on the next step. Cartwheeling her arms, she fell backward, straight into Tavish's arms. "I see what you mean." She wiggled out of his grasp. Laughing she added, "It's this damned suit."

"Right."

Angus' voice rose from the opposite side of the craft, "Seems I remember someone else saying exactly those words."

Lauren ducked back beneath the transparent canopy to settle in her seat, folding her crash harness back as Susan threw her leg over the fuselage edge to join her in the passenger area.

"Unbelievable. This is amazing, Lauren."

"It gets better from here." Lauren continued to adjust her harness. "And thanks for your patience, I'm sorry I sniped at you."

The boys got Ice and Snow settled and then took their places. Robert was in the last row, surrounded by numerous silver-gray storage containers. These would be transferred to the *Wild Boar* in preparation for her departure. Captain Bruce Cameron of the Black Guard was accompanying Robert on his vanguard mission and sat across from him. His black evac-suit contrasted sharply with Robert's stark white one. Captain Cameron's troops would arrive at Luna Keep via a troop-transport the following morning. Lauren noted the lines of stress and sadness on the captain's face. She knew he missed his cousin Sarah. Lauren shared his sadness. His departure on the *Boar* would cause him to miss Sarah's funeral. Tavish and Angus occupied the pilots' seats and were finalizing their pre-flight checklists.

Susan took in all the activity and Lauren was amazed how calm she seemed. Maybe it was her doctor's mask, always calm in the face of a stressful situation. But then Lauren noticed her glazed eyes. Susan was talking to Làireach, her young filly companion. Not wanting to be rude and "listen-in" to their conversation, Lauren waited patiently for her to finish. Susan gave a slight shiver and rubbed her forehead.

"Everything all right?"

"What? Oh, yeah. Everything's fine. Làireach was just anxious about me and my first space flight." Susan chuckled and shook her head. "If that horse was being totally honest with me, she would admit how jealous she was."

"Ffwryn is the same. She wants to travel to Luna Keep as well, but Hamish hasn't figured out how to construct a viable evac-suit for a horse." When Susan frowned, Lauren reached across the aisle and placed a hand on Susan's arm. "They'll come up on a transport when we are ready to depart, if we decide to take you and them with us as a means of communication. Once in the *Stag* though, they'll have free reign of the place." Both laughed at Lauren's unintentional pun.

Tavish turned in his seat. "We are cleared for departure."

Lauren nodded and noticed Susan grip the armrests of her crash couch. "Thank you, Tavish. Smooth ride, please."

"Well, that is what I needed to let you know." Tavish winced. "Your last trip was planned to minimize any inflight-stress, so we took a long flight path out over the western ocean. I am afraid this trip we will utilize a more direct route."

Susan gulped. "Direct?" Her voice came out in a thin, high squeak.

"Yes, Susan. We will be headed straight to Luna, without a tour of the upper atmosphere. So please tighten your harness and relax. The G-forces of acceleration will be absorbed by the crash couch." He turned back to his heads-up-display, his right hand dropping onto the gel-pad interface of the analyzer in the center console.

"I wish they wouldn't call it a crash couch." Susan whispered under her breath. Lauren grinned at her friend, but her heart rate began to accelerate.

Robert piped up from the back. "With Luna in perigee, our flight time will be limited. So, enjoy." He couldn't quite contain his small chuckle, as he nodded at Lauren.

"Hey." Susan looked at her. Lauren placed her gauntlet-covered hand on Susan's arm, feeling the muscles tremor through the thin material. "When we get to Luna Keep, remind me to tell you about my first EVA."

Snorts could be heard from the two wolves seated in front of Susan. "That's right, guys, yuck it up. But I was freaked."

"Freaked?" Susan squeaked again.

"*Not the best thing to bring up at this time, Lauren,*" Ice said. "*Perhaps, the story of McLaran chasing you through the northern woods would have been a better choice.*"

Lauren laughed with the wolf. "But that one has blasters and blizzards in it. And besides, she's already heard that one."

Susan wasn't really listening, her gaze frozen on the boys and their activities with the flight's controls. Lauren squeezed her arm again. "Really, it's going to be great. You're going to love it."

"That's what you always say right before we get into a mess." Doubt rang clear in Susan's voice.

"Please seal helmets and suits, tighten crash harnesses, departure in one minute," Angus commanded.

Lauren tested the helmet seals on the wolves and then helped Susan get her helmet over her head. She snapped the neck ring lock in place. Looking through the transparent face shield at Susan's face, Lauren winked. "Okay, can you hear me?" Susan swallowed hard and nodded.

"Let's get this show on the road." Lauren settled back and wrapped her harness across her torso, tightening the shoulder straps with a sharp snap.

"We are traversing space to Luna, Lauren. There is no road," Snow stated in a matter-of-fact tone.

"Funny, Snow, but not helping." The only response was a wolfy huff.

The vibration of the kinetic engines began to build as the ship rose off the tarmac. Tavish placed one hand onto the thrust control and grasped the joystick in his other. "Hovering at one hundred meters. Aye." Alex's *Red Dragon* rotated about her vertical axis and they now faced the sharp peaks of the Teton range to the west of the Keep. "Prepare for orbital insertion, in three, two, one—"

Tavish's next words were lost as the flitter leapt forward and Susan screamed. Lauren watched as they raced toward the jagged peaks. When it looked like they would strike the tallest one, they shot upward on a near-vertical trajectory. Lauren's crash couch rotated to align itself with the new attitudinal direction.

G-forces built and pushed Lauren deep into her couch. She could hear Susan huffing in tiny breaths. Through clinched teeth Lauren said, "Take a deep breath Susan, you're hyperventilating. Don't want you to pass out and miss space." The only response was a grunt.

Lauren chuckled. *"Alex was right, this is the best."*

"I know I am."

"Alex, is that you? Where are you?" But Lauren's question went unanswered. She tried to turn her head around the cabin, but she couldn't move against the force of acceleration.

"Orbital insertion in ten seconds, approaching thirty thousand kilometers per hour." Tavish's calm voice reported their progress.

"Tavish, we will need one orbit to reach Terra's gravity well exit point for translunar insertion," Angus stated.

"One orbit, aye." The *Dragon* rolled laterally. The planetary curvature of Terra filled half of Lauren's field of view, the other half was filled with the blackness of space.

"Forty thousand kilometers per hour, prepare for translation to grav-wave focus."

The *Dragon* shivered. A large hologram popped up in front of Tavish, drawing Lauren's attention away from her thoughts of Alex. He reached into the hologram and closed his fist around a purple streak crossing the three-dimensional construct. As he held the streak, numbers began to stream down the right side of the display. Lauren recognized the streaks crossing the hologram as gravitational waves. Tavish had chosen one aligned in the general direction of Luna, but outside Terra's gravity well.

"How do we catch that wave?" Lauren nodded at the purple wave within the hologram.

"We align our flight parallel to the wave direction and open the collectors leading to the containment vessel. Once gravitational radiant energy begins to flow into the collectors, the *Dragon* will be pulled into the wave. Since we are only traveling to Luna, the trick is only entering the wave a little bit. We will skim the wave and exit as soon as we contact Luna's gravity well," Tavish explained as the *Dragon* leapt forward, the gravitational wave streaming over the transparent canopy in a multi-hued rainbow of crackling radiant energy.

Lauren grinned, excitement coursing through her, and looked at Susan. Her friend's eyes were squeezed shut and she hadn't released her death grip on the armrests.

"Susan, open your eyes. You've gotta see this. We're riding inside one of Einstein's gravity waves. This is so cool!"

"No," Susan muttered. "Not going to open my eyes."

"Oh, come on. We're in space, on our way to the moon. Just think about that." Blackness surrounded the *Dragon*, as the ship left Terra's gravity well. Lauren felt swathed in a dark blanket. "Let go of the armrests, Susan. Look, we're in zero-gravity."

Susan cracked one eye open, a small slit of blue-gray showing. "Zero-what?"

"Gravity." Lauren let her arm float upward. "See?"

Susan's eyes snapped open and she turned her head. Lauren smiled as she watched Susan's expressions change from fright to awe. "Gotta love it." Speechless, Susan watched transfixed as the moon grew larger by the moment, its bulk filling the transparency.

Lauren laughed as the thrill of the flight tempered some of her worries. *"Alex, can you hear me?"* Lauren sent out a silent query. Silence answered her, but her bond was stronger than ever, psi-energy thrummed through her soul and she beamed as her heart rate settled.

She patted Susan's arm. "We're almost there. Luna Keep is on the dark side. Tavish will swing around and enter lunar orbit. Then the Keep will tractor us in."

Susan seemed lost in the view outside the transparency. "Right, tractor in."

The short time remaining passed quickly, broken only by the quiet instructions coming from the Keep's Orbital Command Center and Tavish's replies.

Chapter Seven
Luna Keep
The Seventh Day

The mood within Luna Keep was quite different from Lauren's first visit. Gone was the joy of something new and the security of their bright future, which the Terrans had held in their hearts. Now, the mood was somber. Their leader and chief was gone. Admiral McLeod's death hung over them all. No one spoke. No one smiled. Heads-down, they focused on the impossible jobs at hand. The various technicians rushed to finish their tasks preparing the clans for their departure. Lauren walked through the halls from Alex's suite to the empty observation dome. Once there, she willed herself to relax.

Robert's *Wild Boar*—the *Faol Muc-fhiadhaich*—hung in near-lunar orbit and filled most of the overhead view above the transparent dome. Lauren looked up in awe at the great ship. Her artwork of gold, brown, and red hair tinted with black edging was so realistic, she seemed poised on charging off on her giant yellow-tipped hoofs, tucked under her belly. Ready to extend and run, chasing her prey down. The tips of her white tusks just peeked around her snout. Small engineering flitters jigged and jagged around her in an intricate dance, while her massive holds stood open as huge transports moved in and out, ferrying goods and personnel.

"She is a sight, is she not, Majesty?"

Lauren turned and saw Robert standing at her shoulder. So lost in thought she hadn't heard his approach. "She is. Here, when she's so close, I feel like I can reach out and stroke the hairs on her flanks. Yet against the backdrop of deep space, she is but an atom-sized speck."

Robert placed a gentle hand on her shoulder and Lauren started. In all the time they spent together, he had only touched her once before. Warmth ran down her arm and she felt his emotions race through her soul. This had happened several times before with the companions, but it felt the strongest with Robert. His deep empathy fueled the contact. Now she understood what Alex was saying about him when they were first introduced. Robert truly was Alex's compass and conscience and now he extended those gifts to her. She knew how blessed she was to have this special friendship. Lauren placed her hand over his warm one and squeezed.

Robert chuckled. "When we were just sprouts, Alex always took charge, whether we were getting into mischief or out of it. She stepped up and led. I always thought there would not be another person like her in my life. One I admired so much. One I would follow anywhere."

Lauren looked up into his dark sapphire eyes, but they were not looking at her or at the *Boar*, they were looking at memories. Then his eyes cleared.

"Until now. You are doing the right thing, Lauren. Never doubt that. And no matter the destination of the course we are sailing, you have done what is best for Terra." He turned his hand over and grasped hers, kissing the back of her hand. "At the time of our greatest challenge the gods and goddess gave us Alex to lead us out of danger. And now, when we are challenged again, facing potential disaster, we are blessed with a second gift." A single tear tracked down his cheek. Lauren's heart clinched. He was saying goodbye. *Can he see the future?* "Be true to your heart, Majesty, for your heart is Terra's heart."

He released her hand, turned on his heel, and strode from the dome, away from her, away from Terra, but toward the future. Lauren couldn't see the future, but she knew they were on the right course. *Be safe, Robert. For you are as important to Terra as Alexandra or I.*

"Of all the times to be late, this is not one of them." Lauren, with Snow and Ice in tow, rushed through the raw rock tunnel and swept around a curved corner just as Angus finished his complaint. He stood before a circular metal slab which blocked the tunnel, its blue-silver surface flashing iridescent ripples of red and purple in the low light. The massive door appeared embedded in the surrounding rough-hewn rock walls. Tavish and Hamish stood beside him. Hamish had delayed his brother's funeral services to allow him to travel to Luna and aid in opening the Terran vault.

"We're here. Sorry." Lauren tried to get her breath back after running down the long tunnel. She bent over and grasped her knees. "But I had to see Robert and Captain Cameron before they boarded the *Boar*. They'll depart in a few hours, if we find the prototype. We've gotta get this open and find the communication device. We'll hardly have time to test any system as it is."

Angus placed his hands on hips. "Well, we cannot do any of that without you. As you can see, there is no handle, nor analyzer pad or any other obvious means of opening it. And we cannot cut through it because it is a unique alloy of noble metals—palladium, iridium, and titanium." He held up a small scanner for her to see the metallurgic-composition graph on its tiny screen.

"Majesty, when this vault was constructed, Luna Keep was already complete and we were working on the shipyards in lunar orbit to house the clans. My brother did this by himself. He knew nowhere on Terra would be safe from attack, so he built this." Hamish pointed at the door. Lauren began to examine the massive door. It appeared to be a solid slab of metal. "He wanted a vault to store the knowledge of Terra, as well as other precious artifacts. He wanted to create a place safe from attack or theft. The few who knew about it could return if needed, should we be chased from Terra." Hamish frowned. "If we lost the keeps and again needed to flee to the stars, he hoped it would be missed in any search. This archive is composed of the same noble metals as those found in natural abundance within the lunar crust, so it should not be detectable on distant scans. You probably did not notice, but the tunnel is mined with explosives. I fear if we try to open the door without the proper key, explosives will drop the tunnel on us."

"I am completely baffled. This is not a door. It is more a stopper in a bottle." Angus rubbed the side of his nose in frustration. The wolves approached the slab slowly, sniffing all around the lower edge. No one actually touched it, given Hamish's warning about explosives.

"I still think we should cut out the rock around it." Tavish pointed to the rock wall. "Then push the metal slab out of the way."

"Once a sword master, always a sword master, wanting to use brute force when something more subtle is needed." Lauren felt attacking the door would detonate the trap McLeod had set in place, and feelings were all she had to go on. Alex hadn't told her anything about this archive prior to her kidnapping. *I wonder why not?*

"I don't think that'll work, Tavish. Noble metals are non-reactive. They don't oxidize or corrode. This is a puzzle, wrapped in an enigma, thus leaving a conundrum for us to solve. Knowing Alex and Admiral McLeod this'll not be easy. We must find the key or suffer the consequences. If those two worked on this together, then it's a product of modern engineering genius and ancient psi-stealth. And, I haven't a clue where to start looking for the key. Alex never told me about this, nor did Lord McLeod during my visit to Luna."

Lauren was lost. She rubbed her chin in much the same frustrated manner Angus did his nose then turned to Hamish. "Did we ask Merilyn about this? Or Lord McLaran? Somebody's gotta have a clue." All three shook their heads. The wolves snorted negatively. *"Alex, what'd you do here? Give me a clue, Dearest."* She sent her plea out along their bond but heard nothing. Her bond was strangely quiescent, its normal hum of energy dampened, though the sense of Alex's presence was stronger than ever. It felt like she was in the tunnel with them. She wondered if the thickness of lunar mass above them was blocking bond. *Or did the slab dampen my psi-energy? Or was it absorbing it?*

Sometime later, Lauren sat cross-legged on the rough rock floor in front of the door, lost in thought. She was trying to relax enough to feel the energy in the slab. She had the strangest feeling she needed to touch the metal, but the possibility of setting off the explosives warned her away. The wolves snuggled close and she rested her arms around their necks. The others had stepped back to allow her room to think. Though she knew everyone was racking their brains, she could sense their overlying unease and bafflement.

The temperature in the tunnel was well below freezing and Lauren shivered, pulling her plaid more closely around her shoulders. She snuggled closer to Snow and Ice, sharing their warmth. Bored into the heart of Luna, this tunnel was far below the deepest level where the environment was temperature and humidity controlled for comfort. There was air to breathe, but it was stale, dry, and cold. Clouds of frozen condensation began to gather in the tunnel. Lauren stared at the door. Then, she inched closer. *That's not right.* Lauren leaned forward, her nose almost touching the metal and exhaled. Nothing.

"What the—" Lauren sat back, startled. Leaning forward again, she examined the metal to be sure she saw what she thought she did.

Angus knelt beside Ice, putting a hand on her furry shoulder for balance. "What is not right, Majesty?"

Lauren exhaled a strong puff of air on the iridescent surface. "That." She pointed at the spot.

"I do not see what you mean." Angus leaned forward as well, so close to the surface his breath brushed over the exact spot Lauren's had. "There is nothing there."

"Exactly. There is nothing there, and there should be." Snow leaned in and exhaled her wolfy breath on the door. Nothing again.

Tavish and Hamish joined them. "What should be there?" Hamish asked, his head tilted to the side.

"A fogged surface." Lauren stood and pointed at the spot she, Angus, and Snow had exhaled on. "As cold as it is down here, our warm breath should condense on the cold metal." Her words were punctuated by puffs of white fog in the cold air. "But it doesn't." She reached out a hand, fingers splayed, and nearly touched the slab.

"No!" Tavish grabbed her shoulders and pulled her away from the door. Lauren stumbled back into his arms. The wolves growled deep in their throats. "We do not know if it is some kind of trap. You must not touch it, Lauren."

She pulled away and straightened her plaid. "Yeah, I know with the booby-trap and all, but I've gotta touch it. The more I concentrate on the door, the more I feel I must touch it. I'm drawn to it. And it's warm." She looked at each of the others in turn. "Believe it or not, I feel like a part of Alex is in the door. I can sense her presence, though not enough to interact with her." She shrugged. "And what's really weird, is I can sense Alex nearby, though our bond is quiet."

"I agree, Lauren. Alex is here. Or has been here in the near past." Ice flicked her tail.

"No way," Tavish muttered.

Lauren laughed at Tavish's use of one of her idioms. *Maybe I'm melding with them as well as Alex?* Her bond with the companions seemed to be strengthening each day.

"Yeah, way." Lauren smiled up at him. "The metal should be in equilibrium with the temperature of the tunnel. If it was as cold as the air in the tunnel, our warm breath should condense on its surface." She leaned forward and exhaled on the metal surface. Nothing happened. "See, no fog. Therefore, it's warm." Again, she reached out a hand toward the surface.

"Majesty—" Tavish warned.

But before he could grab her, she placed her palm flat on the door. The warm surface undulated beneath her palm; concentric rings rippled outward from the spot she touched. "Whoa." She snatched her hand back in shock. The others jumped back as well.

"Indeed." Angus stepped up to the slab. He placed his palm on the door. Nothing happened. He pushed hard against the surface. It didn't move, didn't ripple. He turned to Lauren. "Do that again, and this time push against it."

She placed her palm on the door and pushed. Her hand sank beneath the surface, the metal flowing up around her wrist. Her hand disappeared within the solid surface. She yelped and pulled her hand out, jumping away from the door. Grasping her wrist, Lauren cringed as pain radiated across her palm. A deep burning sensation traveled up her arm.

Angus touched her shoulder. "Are you all right?"

Lauren's hand spasmed as minute muscle twitches rippled through it. Her skin was bright red. It tingled and burned, as if she touched something cold, colder than cold, yet it felt burned. It was like she'd sunk her hand into liquid nitrogen. Her nerves sang in sympathy with the metal. Her touch must have activated atomic vibrations in the metal's matrix which in turn stimulated her nerves. Lauren's sense of Alex being with them strengthened, it was as if she stood right beside Lauren. She shook out her hand trying to dispel the pins and needles racing up and down her arm. "That was weird. And it kinda hurts."

"Weird is all you say after sinking your hand into solid metal?" Tavish frowned. He took her right hand in his, turning the palm up. "Your hand is burning up." He placed his other hand on her forehead. "Cool. No fever."

She pulled her hand out of his grasp and turned to Angus. "Do you think what I think?"

"Majesty, thinking as you do is simply not possible." Everyone chuckled lightly. Snow and Ice whiffled in agreement. Lauren smiled down at the wolves. Angus cleared his throat. "However, do I think the metal is somehow attuned to you and your psi-energy? Then yes I do think that."

"Looks like I'm the one that's gotta do this then." Lauren squared her shoulders, staring at the slab.

"*You do not have to do anything, Lauren. We do not know enough about this to proceed safely.*" Snow's whiffle morphed into a growl. "*We cannot risk losing you, as well as Alex. We must take time to study this more closely.*"

Kneeling down, Lauren wrapped her arms around the wolf's neck and buried her face in her snowy-white fur. "*I love you for your concern, but you know I must do this. It's the only way. We don't have any time left, Snow.*"

"*Although I agree with Snow about the risk to you, we know Alex has been here, Lauren. Snow and I can feel her energy, too. Just as you can sense her presence.*" Ice tilted her large head. Lauren nodded, raising her head from Snow's warm neck. She did feel Alex all around her. "*While you were having your tours and lectures with Admiral McLeod, Alex went off alone for long periods. She would not allow us to accompany her. I believe she came here. And using your psi-energy pattern from your bond, she tuned the metal to include your signature as well as hers.*"

"*You're right, Ice. Alex is here. And I know what I gotta do.*"

Before anyone in the group could react, Lauren stood and stepped forward. She reached out her arm, piercing the slab with her outstretched hand and walked through the metal door, the slab flowed closed behind her.

Lauren heard Tavish shout, calling her name, but she didn't respond. She heard pounding on the metal. She turned and could still see the others beyond the slab. It was translucent from this side.

"Stop, Tavish!" Angus and Hamish shouted, grabbing his arms.

"But I must get to her. I swore to Alex, I would be her protector and guardian." He hung his head but stopped struggling against them. "I cannot protect her when I am out here, and she is—" He pointed at the door.

"I know, but you will detonate the explosives if you keep beating at the door," Angus replied.

Lauren spoke to Snow. *"Tell the boys it's okay. I'm okay. I'll be back soon."*

Lauren felt Snow open her mind to the other three companions. She felt their shock when the wolf's voice entered their heads. *"She will return. She is safe."*

Tavish swung on Snow. "You can tell this how?"

Snow sat quietly, staring at the blank metal slab. Lauren looked back through the slab. She watched Snow simply shrug her shoulders in a very human gesture. *"She spoke to me, I know."*

Lauren gave a quiet laugh before turning to face her next challenge.

A soft pink, diffuse light lit the room. It seemed to emanate from the rock walls themselves, casting no shadows. She leaned against the slab. *I just walked through solid metal.* A shiver streaked down her spine. Her nerves still sang with the vibration picked up from metallic matrix. She knew metals had a unique atomic structure. Metal atoms aligned themselves in uniform rows and columns creating a dense three-dimensional structure—cubes or hexagons. Each atom then shared their electrons with all the other atoms, releasing electrons from their outer shells, creating a cloud of free electrons which flowed throughout the matrix. These free-cloud electrons must have been tuned to the resonance of her psi-energy. The metal's cloud-electrons and hers reacted with one another electrostatically. She was able to "step into" the metallic matrix and pass through it without disturbing the structure.

"That's too weird for words," Lauren muttered.

She may understand the chemistry, but Lauren wasn't able to comprehend how Alex was able to impart her energy pattern on the metal. She shook herself and looked around. This space was more than a storage area—it was a workspace. Long laboratory benches extended down the roughly rectangular space, creating a central walkway. Several work-stations had been set up on them. Large analyzer gel pads broke up the smooth surfaces. Various pieces of equipment and partially constructed devices sat on the benches between the analyzers.

Lauren walked down the center aisle. Large cases had been stored beneath the benches, with more stacked around the edges of the room all the way to the ceiling. Reaching the end of the aisle, Lauren realized the entire back wall of the room was a huge monitor screen. She walked to the corner of the wall and looked along its surface. It seemed to be made up of a wafer-thin sheet of some sort of silica-based material. Curious, Lauren searched for the interface to activate the wall-sized monitor. She found it on the end of the workbench to her left.

"Let's see what we've got here." She dipped her hand into the analyzer gel and watched the monitor.

After several manipulations, the screen sprang to life. A blue symbol appeared on the monitor and began to rotate in the middle of a black background. "Oh my god!" Lauren staggered back against the bench behind her. She stared at the corporate logo for GeoDynamics:

"How's this possible?" Lauren whispered. The tetrahedron continued to spin. "Alex, what are you trying to tell me?"

As if Alex heard Lauren's questions, her voice filled the room, echoing off the rock walls. "If you are looking at this, you know what it is. Enter the name of the entity this icon represents into the pad on the bench." Lauren whipped her head around, looking for the pad. *There.* She grabbed it and entered, "GeoDynamics."

A quiet beep sounded, and the monitor blanked out. The screen rolled up into the ceiling. Another room extended behind what had seemed to be a solid wall. A room within a room. Lauren laughed. Of course, Alex would enfold objects within themselves. She loved puzzles. Lauren hoped she could keep up with Alex's complex mind. And as Alex had aided Admiral McLeod in the construction of this place, it would be a challenge.

Alex's voice echoed in the space again. "I do not know what happened to cause you to enter this vault without me, before I had a chance to show you this first. But you are here and must have an urgent need. Within this vault are the most-closely held technological secrets of Terra. You must not reveal the contents of this vault to anyone, Lauren. They must not fall into enemy hands."

Lauren stepped up to the entrance of the vault, carefully peering into the darkness beyond. Alex spoke once more, and Lauren shivered. Hearing Alex's voice made her keenly aware of her bondmate's absence. This voice was so cold and disembodied, it lacked the warmth of their love.

"Until our bonding and your adoption into Clan Fraser, only Admiral McLeod and I had the codes to open the bins within this vault. When we toured Terra, I tuned the entrance slab to our psi-energy and added codes only you will know to allow you access to each bin. If I am not with you or I have not shared this information, each bin will require a passcode. You will have only one chance to enter the correct passcode. If I have not shared the passcodes with you, it is still possible to access the vaults. You will however be required to answer challenge questions to do so. An incorrect answer will detonate concealed explosives and destroy the contents of this room. This is a necessary precaution should an enemy attempt to force you to open the bins for them. Doing so would destroy Terra's technological future and perhaps Terra herself. But graver than that, I will lose the greatest gift ever given me. You. Do not fail me, Lauren. Do not fail Terra."

"Oh god, Alex, what've you done?" The full weight of ruling Terra crashed down on Lauren's shoulders and she staggered. She grasped her head in her hands, the responsibility crushing her as all her insecurities rushed forward. Tears slid down her cheeks. "I can't do this. I can't, Alex. I'm sorry."

Alex's voice came again. "I know you are questioning your abilities. I believe you have the strength needed to protect and govern Terra. If you are here and I am not, you are queen. I believe in you. Our souls chose each other. We are two parts of one whole. My strength is your strength. If I am gone, I cannot imagine the pain your fractured soul is experiencing. Nor the toll this cleaving of our bond is taking on your psyche. But for Terra you must endure. I believe you can do this. Ruling is the giving of yourself, all of yourself, for the greater good of our people. You are not important. They are."

Lauren shook her head. *I can't do this.* But then she remembered the flowers, the Queen's orchids blooming within the sacred circle, and the Terran people's belief in her. She heard the council pledging their support to her, one by one affirming their belief in her. She remembered the love Alex had for her, the trust she bestowed on her. *I can do this.* Lauren felt strength envelop her, urging her forward. As if Alex's arms had surrounded her, Lauren gathered that strength and stood to her full height. The lights in the vault sprang on.

Lauren gasped as she took in what was before her. This room extended outward more than a hundred meters and where the outer room had walls and ceiling of rough-hewn rock, this one was encased in the same smooth iridescent metal as the door. She stepped forward and realized the room was a perfect sphere divided into four quadrants by gangways of metal lattice. Each quadrant held one large matte-black cylinder extending from the bottom to the top of the sphere. A data pad glowed green blue on the front of each cylinder. At the intersection of the two gangways, was a circular platform. A curved workbench of the same iridescent metal as the sphere sat on the platform, a single chair beside it.

Lauren crossed the gangway and stepped up onto the central platform. An analyzer was embedded in the workbench's surface. She tried to pull the chair out to sit, but it was fastened to the gangway. It swiveled on an upright pedestal, so Lauren turned the chair away from the workbench and sat. When seated, the chair rotated back and rose, adjusting its height to allow her full access to the analyzer.

"Well, here goes." She placed her hand on the gel pad. It was warm beneath her cold palm, and she sank her fingers into its surface. An analyzer monitor rose and tilted toward her. Again, the corporate logo of GeoDynamics filled the screen.

Admiral McLeod's voice spoke this time. "What may I do for you, Majesty?"

Lauren cleared her throat. "I need to find the prototype communication system you invented."

"Very good. That device is stored in bin three." The central platform rotated until she was facing what must be bin three.

"How do I—"

Before she could complete her question, the admiral interrupted. "I cannot help you open the bin, Majesty. You must do that yourself, using your passcode."

"I don't have a passcode."

"Then, I cannot help you."

Lauren swiveled out of her chair and walked up to the black bin. The bin looked almost organic, soft and pliable. The bin's dull, matte surface absorbed the vault's light. She couldn't see any imperfections, seams, or openings on the surface. Only the lit-gel pad marred its perfection.

What did Alex say? She would have only one chance to answer the challenge questions. Lauren extended her arm to the pad, letting her hand hover above the surface, fear trickled down her spine. *Alex also said I would know the answer.* Lauren rested her hand on the pad. "Let's see if she's right."

A machine-generated voice sounded. "Identified, Lauren Beckwith Fraser Doouglas, Consort-Queen of Terra." Nothing else happened, so Lauren kept her hand in place, waiting.

"Enter your passcode."

"Great," she muttered. "I don't have a passcode."

"Without a passcode, you must answer three security questions. Failure to answer any question correctly will result in immediate destruction of the contents of bin three and the detonation of the lunar tunnel. Do you understand?"

"I understand." Lauren's heart beat uncontrollably and her palm began to sweat against the gel pad.

"Are you ready to begin?" The mechanical voice lacked inflection of any kind, but Lauren thought she heard a hint of amusement in its voice. *Yeah right, Lauren, now you're anthropomorphizing an analyzer. You gotta get it together.*

"Question one. State the full name of the person most important to you."

She opened her mouth to answer but closed it with a snap. *That's too easy. Why would Alex ask me to recite her name?* Lauren stared at the black surface of the bin. *Come on, think, Lauren. Alex wouldn't set up a security question with an obvious answer.*

"You have one minute remaining to provide the correct answer."

No pressure. Thanks, Alex. Lauren bit her lower lip. *Most important?*

"Erle James Phillip Beckwith." Her heart clinched, as she stated the full name of her grandfather. She missed him so much.

"Correct. Question two. What term of endearment does a friend use for patients?"

Lauren tilted her head then smiled. "Furkids."

"Correct. Question three. What is your deepest fear?"

A shiver ran down Lauren's spine as this question struck a chord within her soul. *Damn it, Alex. How could you?* Her insecurities rose up once more, closing her throat. She swallowed hard against them. Alex knew she feared so many things, things beyond her ability to fix, or control, or overcome. *How can I pick just one?*

"You have one minute remaining to provide the correct answer."

Lauren wasn't able to pick only one. Too many things haunted her nights. And now her days.

"You have thirty seconds remaining to provide the correct answer."

Panic rose as she struggled to organize her thoughts. *Pick one, Lauren.* So many failings. Images filled her mind of patients lost, of village children with congenital birth defects caused by environmental poisoning, of fish floating belly up in jungle streams running red with mine-effluent, of the Terran children in stasis, of the Terran council challenging her. She couldn't help them. She couldn't save them. Of the Comin and the traitor. She wasn't good enough. So many insecurities.

"You have ten seconds remaining." A countdown began. "Ten...nine...eight...seven...six...five...four...three ..."

A discussion she had with Alex as they enjoyed a late-night soak in the hot springs at the Teton Cache suddenly eclipsed all the other memories.

"Self-doubt." Lauren blurted.

"Correct."

I did it. She staggered back on the gangway, physically spent.

A metallic snap sounded, and bin three opened along a central split, the two halves of the cylinder swinging open. Cold rushed out as a gas vaporized and engulfed Lauren in a freezing cloud. A gantry extended outward from the gangway into the center of bin three. "The prototype transmitters and receivers are in space three dash one-hundred and twelve dash twenty-seven alpha. Instructions for use exist in file three dash one-hundred and twelve dash twenty-seven beta in the central analyzer core of this vault," the mechanical voice said.

Lauren stepped onto the gantry, moving forward into bin three. Rows of shelves lined the bin, each holding numerous devices. A shelf extended outward into the center of the bin with the correct numbers. Three large alumino-titanium cases rested on the shelf. She grabbed the first case. Moving out of the bin, she placed it on the gangway. She pulled down the other two and placed them beside the first. When she stepped back out of the cylindrical bin with the last cases, the gantry retracted, and the bin closed. Lauren carried each case back into the workroom. Returning to the central platform, she dipped her hand into the analyzer pad and called up the file.

"Copy this file to a portable medium," she ordered.

Lauren watched as the communication prototype file opened and the analyzer began copying it contents. Diagrams, data tables, handwritten sketches streamed across the monitor. Once the data-stream halted, the mechanical voice stated, "Copy complete." A drawer beneath the work surface opened and Lauren withdrew a thin flexible sheet of nano-flimsie. She rolled this up and placed it in her sporran.

"Thank you," she whispered into the quiet of the vault.

"You are welcome, Queen-Consort," the mechanical voice replied.

Lauren stepped back through the metal slab and reentered the tunnel with the three cases. She put the cases down. "Here it is. Now all we've gotta do is figure out how it works, install it on the *Boar*, send Robert on his way as vanguard, and then prep the other three clans to head out."

"Is that all?" Hamish replied in an exasperated tone, hands on his hips. "What happened in there? What is in there?"

"I got what we need, and I can't tell you." Lauren picked up two of the cases and brushed past Hamish. She walked up the tunnel. When she realized no one was following her, she turned around. "Come on, guys. We don't have all day. Tavish, grab that other case." Lauren tilted her head to indicate the third case sitting by the door. "Let's go." She turned back around and marched up the tunnel. The wolves' claws clicked on the rock floor as they rushed to catch up. The sound of booted feet soon joined the wolves.

Good, now we can get this done. Lauren felt energized. Maybe it was Alex's belief in Lauren, or hearing Alex's voice, or having successfully answered the challenge questions which fueled her, but Lauren didn't really care what it was. All she cared about was they had taken another step closer to getting Alex back. Nothing else mattered.

Chapter Eight
Aboard the Dubh Mogairle

Alex sat up. Her head spun and she felt disembodied. She had snapped back into herself so quickly after her encounter with Lauren she did not know if she was all here or if she left some of herself behind, floating free in the black emptiness of space. Free was the operative word. *I have to get out of this box.* Alex carefully extended her psi-energy and used it to feel around the box edges. She was right. The dampening field holding the box closed was absent. Reaching her hands to the lid, Alex pushed. The lid moved a fraction. *It should not be this easy. Must be careful, this could be a trap.* She pushed harder. The lid opened and Alex slid it to the side, careful to leave it ajar. She did not want it to crash to the floor and alert the guards of her attempted escape.

Illumination shone down from a lightbar running around the room just above the floor. No one was in the room, so Alex stood up and stepped out of the box. It was so long since she had stood, she stumbled, tripping over the edge of the box. Falling forward, she landed hard on her hands and knees. *Watch that first step. It is a big one.* She laughed, thinking about Lauren's first ride on the *Dragon*. Standing again, her leg muscles quivered, weak due to her confinement, dehydration and lack of nourishment. Alex took a careful step, holding her arms out for balance. Slowly she regained her balance and could now fully take in her surroundings. She could not identify a door, just four smooth walls. *Great, another box.*

Alex relaxed and extended her psi-sense outward. The thrum of the faster-than-light-pulse engines was decreasing. The ship was slowing down. Either they had experienced a mechanical failure of some sort or had detected a threat from outside the ship. She heard the far-off sounds of alarm klaxons. Whatever the emergency, Alex really did not care. She was just happy it had created a distraction. And she planned to use this distraction to its fullest. Extending her senses outward, she could not detect guards near the room. Nor in the near vicinity on this deck.

Moving toward the wall she sensed abutted the corridor, Alex touched the smooth surface. Energy swept up her arm and tingled. She drew her hand away as a bolt of dark energy leapt from a force field. Alex grinned. If she could find the field-generator, which created the electro-magnetic energy, it would be no match for a psi-energy discharge. She could easily create such a discharge by drawing energy from her bond with Lauren. She closed her eyes and concentrated on the wall.

There. She felt an increase in energy flow in the lower left corner. That had to be it. Crouching, Alex focused her mind on the small area where she noticed the energy spike. Drawing a bit of psi-energy from her bond, she shaped the energy into a thin blade. She drove the blade into the wall, where it shattered the embedded generator. Sparks flew and acrid smoke rose from the hole she'd made in the wall. *Time to get out of here.* This time when she stepped up to the wall, it split in two. The halves slid silently apart.

Red light flooded the room and blaring klaxons nearly deafened her. She hugged one side of the door and peeked around the jamb, looking down the corridor. To the right, the narrow corridor ended in another door. To the left, the corridor teed into a much larger corridor. Just as she was ready to step into the narrow corridor, a cadre of armed Terrans ran down the large corridor. Alex shrank back into the room, her heart racing.

She waited a handful of minutes and then peeked around the jamb again. Not seeing anyone, she reached out mentally, searching her surrounding area. No one was near, the corridor empty, so she stepped out. Once clear of the door, it slid closed behind her. *Well, that leaves only one way to go.* She moved to the intersection with the large cross-corridor and peeked around the corner.

Alex knew each of the clans shared a common design, though each had unique interior designs. The *Black Orchid* was no different. She might not be able to locate a specific cabin or control room, but she would know where engineering and other support systems for the ship were located, on the lowest decks and to the aft. Living quarters and the flight decks occupied the middecks, centrally located where they were the most protected from hull-breaches. Command and control decks were always located forward, on the upper decks. Alex stepped to the main corridor and headed aft. *But what deck am I on?*

Alex moved down the large corridor, hugging the bulkhead. When she reached the next cross-corridor, she turned away from where her psi-senses told her others were located. She needed an analyzer to gain access to the ship's schematics. Ultimately, she would need to access engineering and find a way to sabotage the ship's propulsion systems. She knew Lauren's plan. Robert and the *Boar* were giving chase. If she could slow the *Orchid* down long enough, they might be able to catch up. As Alex crossed in front of a door, it slid open. She peered into the dark room. Stacks of alumino-titanium storage cases lined the walls, organized in neat rows, each container had a data pad glowing on the corner. *Perfect, a storage room. I should be able to access the analyzer core from here without raising any alarms. And maybe one of these cases will contain something I can use.*

Twelve decks above Alex, Sarah continued to move Admiral McLeod's inert body through the ventilation shaft. She could no longer hear voices, but the continuous blare of alarms masked any other noises. She needed to be careful and not stumble into something she could not handle. The enclosed space of the shaft was great for moving about the ship undetected—as long as she was quiet. She came to an intersection. *Where are we?*

To the left, a silver-blue force field sparkled, obviously in place to separate an area with no gravity from an area with normal gravity. Certain sections of the ship were maintained with little or no gravity to create areas of null gravity where massive objects or cargos could be easily moved, or if access to the exterior of the ship was needed for maintenance or evacuation. Sarah couldn't easily take down the force field without alerting the ship to their presence. The right shaft was clear, and she eased the still unconscious admiral around the corner.

At the next intersection, she stopped. This was a six-way intersection, four shafts branched out at ninety-degrees to one another on her level with one going above and another below the current deck. A ladder extended up and down this cross-shaft. This had to be one of fifty-two vertical maintenance shafts connecting the individual decks to one another. Through a force field above her, Sarah saw a large forty-three stenciled on a hatch. *That helps. We are on a sub-deck between decks forty-three and forty-four.* Built between decks, sub-decks ran the entire length of the hull from bow to stern. They carried conduits for all the systems needed throughout the ship—environmental, analyzer, filtration, and communications.

Sarah curled herself into a ball and relaxed as best she could, floating in the confined space, the admiral bobbed beside her. What she needed was a diversion so she could breach the force field above them and climb up to deck forty-two without setting off any alarms. The medical bays, ship stores, and flight decks with their weapons armory occupied deck forty-two. She needed access to one of the medical bays to help the admiral and get into the ship stores for supplies. She thought for a moment. *Is there any way to lower the field? Can I trick the ship's control systems into lowering the force field for me?*

Removing the admiral's tether, Sarah refastened it to one of the girders surrounding the sub-deck they rested in, ensuring the admiral would remain safely within the ventilation shaft. She grabbed a girder and flipped herself toward the ceiling. Examining the conduits running above her head, she pushed off the ceiling and examined the ones running beneath the floor grids. *What could I do to drop the force field? A diversion of some kind? Maybe? What would cause the field to fail?* A loss of power, an emergency requiring the crew to have access to all decks, a release of a fluid into a zero-gravity space, general gravity failure throughout the ship, a hull breach, a decompression event. *Wait, wait, wait. A fluid release.* Releasing fluids into a zero-gravity environment causes total chaos. The fluid separates into isolated blobs and if it is caustic, maintenance crews struggle to clean it up before it can damage anything vital.

Sarah reentered the shaft and traced their path to the last intersection. She remembered seeing a coolant conduit somewhere. When she did not find it, she continued back to the next. At the third intersection, she found the conduit where it entered the deck and turned aft. This conduit contained plasma coolant for the giant containment vessels which generated the fusion power for the faster-than-light pulse engines. During her flight training days, she learned the history of Terran intrastellar flight and the evolution of their giant clan ships. After the tragic containment accident and subsequent destruction of the First Foremothers' original ship, all subsequent ships were designed with tertiary cooling systems. Each coolant system originated from a different point within the giant ship. The engineers believed a triple-redundant system would protect against future catastrophic system failures.

The conduit above her head was painted yellow for the secondary system; the primary system conduits were painted red and the tertiary system green. If the primary coolant system failed and shut down, coolant would be shunted along this conduit to the containment vessels. Even though coolant was not flowing through this conduit now, it was still filled with plasma. Plasma existed naturally throughout the universe; the clans captured this plasma along with their hydrogen fuel. Within the closed system, it existed as a cold plasma where only the electrons of the plasma were thermally active. Sarah reached up and touched the conduit, it was cool. It was full of plasma.

When released into an open environment, the plasma became corrosive as it interacted with metal objects in the presence of various catalysts. *Like oxygen.* Sarah smiled and reached into the leg pocket of her evac-suit. She pulled out her laser torch. Positioning the torch nozzle against the conduit, she strapped it down to one of the neighboring pipes running parallel to the coolant conduit using a plastic tie-down. Once she turned the torch on, it would begin to cut through the conduit and eventually release the plasma into the ventilation shaft. This should cause the automatic emergency escape systems to activate. Once the emergency was detected, force fields between decks would be released to allow maintenance crew access to the damaged conduit and other crew to escape the danger zone. *I hope.* Sarah turned the tiny laser torch on and pulled herself rapidly along the sub-deck back to where she left the admiral.

Alex found a small analyzer pad located on the wall of the storage room next to the door. *This should do nicely.* Holding her hand against the gel, she activated the pad. A string of command code scrolled across the tiny screen next to the pad. "Identity unknown, please enter passcode." Alex held one of five command-level passcodes which allowed access to all the systems within any of the clans. This was a failsafe system Admiral McLeod instituted to allow Alex, her three companions, and himself direct access and ultimate command override should they need to commandeer a clan ship for emergency purposes. *As long as the crew left the original command codes in place, this should work.*

Alex entered her command passcode. Just as she entered the final character, emergency klaxons sounded. Alex recoiled from the pad. Frantically looking around the room, Alex tried to find a place to hide. She jumped behind the nearest stack of storage cases opposite the doors. She forced herself to calm down as she heard the warning.

"Emergency evacuation of decks forty through fifty. Plasma coolant leak detected. Move immediately to designated safe areas. This is not a drill." The warning repeated on an automated cycle.

Alex stayed put behind the wall of containers as she heard crew running through the corridors surrounding her tiny storage room. Time was not on her side. Soon, the bitch Gwenhwyfach would discover her missing and search the ship. Alex could hide physically, but she did not know if she could hide from a psi-search. She would have to find a way to move throughout the ship undetected and undetectable. From the sounds of the emergency klaxons, Gwenhwyfach had enough to handle without worrying about Alex. Moving back to the data-pad, she called up a ship's schematic, locating her storage room on deck fifty-seven. *Great, she would stash me in the bowels of the ship.*

This room was located near one of the emergency escape routes and should contain most of what she might need to remain hidden for as long as possible. Pulling down the first storage box, she accessed the data pad and reviewed the container manifest. *Clothing. Great, I do not need sixty pairs of socks.* Opening other containers, she began to accumulate a pile of survival gear: an evac-suit, lightsticks, a med-pack, emergency rations, water-sippers. What Alex really needed was a weapon of some sort, but she doubted weapons would be kept in an unsecured storage room. *I will have to find a way into the armory.* Her shoulders drooped. The armory was located on deck forty-two, aft of the flight decks.

Alex stuffed her gear into a carry-all. Looking around to make sure she had not missed any containers, then she caught sight of a large ventilation duct. *If I cannot use the elevator system, this may be the next best thing to access the upper decks.* Maybe she should abandon her plan of sabotage and try to make it up to the flight decks. Steal a flitter, head back along their flight path, and find Robert. She dropped her carry-all and began stacking containers into a large pyramid. She would climb to the ceiling and access the ventilation shaft above.

Sarah made it back to the admiral just as emergency klaxons sounded. She squirmed around the admiral's body and looked up the cross-shaft at the flickering force field above her. *Come on. Go down.* Something was happening. Gravity pulled her down to the floor grid. The admiral's body sank beside her. The force field snapped off just as her feet touched the floor-grid.

The newly equalized gravity was not her friend. Moving the unconscious admiral up an access ladder to the deck above would be difficult. Sarah moved to the edge of the vertical cross-shaft. The access ladder was located on the opposite side, and it was going to be a long jump. She pulled several large tie-downs from her pack. Wrapping them around the admiral's arms and legs, she created a sling to lash the admiral across her shoulders, leaving her arms free. Sarah squatted down, back to the admiral and grabbed the looped tie-downs. She stood, pulling the admiral onto her back and shoulders with an explosive grunt. The sound echoed down the shaft. Wincing, Sarah inched back to the edge and peeked out, hoping no one heard her. The shaft was empty in both directions. Backing up, Sarah took a deep breath and with five running steps, leapt into open space. She grabbed the ladder. Agony ripped through her as she slammed into the ladder upright. Then she shuddered again as she her weight settled. She hung from the ladder, panting. Her shoulder was white-hot fire. *Made it.* The jump trajectory arced downward. Now she was another half deck below deck forty-two.

Gathering her feet under her, Sarah stood, gasping for breath. Her right arm tingled, numbness spreading down the limb. *Great, dislocated.* With a rotation, she popped the joint back in place, trying to suppress her moan of pain. Once in place, the joint ached but her acute pain was gone. Luckily, the arm worked, but the joint lacked strength. Sarah shrugged to reposition the admiral more squarely across her back and climbed up to deck forty-two. She was several meters below the deck hatch when another hatch hissed open. Light spilled into the shaft about ten decks below her. Sarah swiveled to the left side of the ladder, putting the ladder between her and the open hatch. The admiral's weight threatened to pull her off the ladder. Her blaster pistol was in a holster under her left arm and she did not know if she had the strength to pull it free. Carefully, she reached for her blaster with numb fingers. She pulled the weapon loose, tightening her fingers as hard as she could. *Are my fingers even closed?*

Looking down, she saw a dark head extend out into the shaft. She aimed the weapon and tried to squeeze the trigger. Her forefinger failed. The blaster dropped from her hand, clattering against the ladder as it bounced down the shaft. The dark head looked up just as the blaster ricocheted off the opposite wall and struck the head between the eyes. Sarah cringed. *Sorry. That is going to leave a mark.*

Chapter Nine
Luna Keep
The Seventh Day

Back within the Keep proper, Lauren made her way to Admiral McLeod's workrooms, two cases in hand. Stepping up to the large bulkhead, Lauren stated her name and title and the doors swished open, allowing her access to the admiral's private space. The space definitely reflected the admiral's varied interests and hobbies. Workbenches ran along two walls, covered in the most modern technology available to the Terran engineer. Micro-analyzers gleamed golden in the harsh white light. Large monitors were interspersed between partially deconstructed piles of circuitry. The other two walls were a sharp contrast, covered in various examples of ancient Terran weaponry. Broadswords, maces, battle-axes, and early flint-fired projectile weapons hung in ordered rows, each labeled in the admiral's distinct tiny script.

Lauren walked over to the nearest workbench and placed her cases on the floor. Tavish joined her at the bench, placing the third case next to the first two.

"Let's get this done." Lauren turned to the nearest analyzer. "If I remember correctly, this analyzer is not networked with the Luna-wide system." She pulled the nano-flimsie from her sporran. Unrolling it, she fed the datasheet into the access slot embedded in the dark surface of the workbench. The analyzer sprang to life as it downloaded the information into its isolated storage bank.

Tavish pulled two stools over to the monitor just as the others joined them. "Close the door, Angus, and please call Robert. We'll all need to see this together. No need to waste time, sharing it with him later." Angus closed the workroom door and placed a security seal on it. Now, no one would be able to enter without their permission. He accessed the communication pad, as Hamish settled in next to Angus.

Several clicks and pops later, Robert's face appeared on the adjoining monitor. "Did you find it? Were you able to retrieve it from the vault? Does it work?"

Lauren held up her hands to stem the torrent of questions. "Whoa, slow down. We only just got up here with it. It took us a while to figure out how to access the vault."

"That is the understatement of the millennium." Tavish gave Lauren a glare.

Lauren shrugged. "There wasn't time to figure something else out, Tavish. When we were in the tunnel. I could feel Alex's presence. I just reacted to those feelings. I'm sorry."

Hands on hips, with a face matching his flaming hair, Tavish replied, "Fine, apology accepted. But your action of walking through a solid metal door prevented me from doing my sworn duty. I had no way to get to you if you encountered trouble. Do not do that again."

"Solid door?" Robert's voice squeaked. "What is going on down there?"

Lauren waved her hands. "It doesn't matter now. We got what we needed; now we'll see if we can get the prototype working."

"Knowing this is one of Admiral McLeod's inventions, I just hope we can figure out how the prototype works." Angus was already placing the first of the three cases on the workbench behind them. "Did you see this?" He pointed to the small character engraved in the latch of the case. Lauren, Tavish and Hamish looked at the small symbol etched on the latch. Angus started to open the case.

Lauren quickly looked at the other two cases on the floor. Each had a distinct character etched into its latch. The other two were: ¬ and ⌐. "Wait, Angus, we don't know what the symbols mean. They could be important. Let's look through the data files before we do anything." Lauren had a feeling the admiral had placed another safeguard on the cases.

Snow snorted, reclining on the brightly colored throw rug in front of the admiral's messy desk, tucked against Ice's side. *"You may be correct, Lauren. Alex and the admiral were cautious to the point of paranoia when it came to safeguarding our technologies."*

Lauren smiled over at the grinning wolf. "Thanks for the reassurance, Snow. I do understand their concerns. When the admiral and I were together, he was always reticent to speak about discoveries if others were within earshot."

Pulling one of the stools over, Lauren plopped down in front of the monitor. Data still streamed across the screen. She dropped her head onto her palm and waited. This would take as long as it took.

Some minutes later, the admiral's voice came out of the monitor. "You are attempting to access confidential files owned by the Crown of Terra. These data require passcodes to access." Hamish gasped as his brother's voice cut through the silence in the workspace.

"Terrific, I already played this game once. I'm not doing it again." Lauren began manipulating the files. Or tried to.

"Consort, you will not gain access that way. Forcible entry will result in the destruction of the data," Angus warned.

Lauren growled and brushed her bangs out of her eyes, glaring at the screen. "Well, what then? We need this communication system now."

"And you shall have it." The admiral's image appeared on the screen, smiling at her. "After you answer a passcode question."

"All right, I give. What's the question?" She sighed.

When the image chuckled, Lauren realized she was interacting with an artificial intelligence. An avatar in the admiral's image. She swallowed down the strange feeling she got in her gut talking to an analyzer-generated construct. "Funny you should mention 'biting.'"

"I don't get it. You've lost me, Admiral."

Angus cleared his throat. "Lauren, talking to the monitor is not going to aid in our data analysis."

She laughed and turned to look at him over her shoulder. Seeing his blank expression, she realized the others hadn't figured out this was an interactive avatar.

"That's where you're wrong, Angus. This is an avatar of the admiral. I'm sure we'll get all the information we need just by asking the correct questions." Turning back to the monitor, she continued, "Isn't that right, sir?"

"You are correct, Consort." The admiral's image turned to look past Lauren's shoulder at Angus. "Shall we continue, boy?" It asked Angus. Lauren chuckled at the tease in his voice.

"But how . . . this is not possible," Hamish exclaimed. He turned to the screen, hands on hips. "Iain was working on this type of interface, but he was unable to overcome the time-delay in processing speed."

Now it was the avatar's turn to laugh. "I do not have a problem with processing speed."

Lauren grinned. "Obviously. But we need to focus, guys. Time's ticking."

"I agree." Robert's voice cut in from the communications console beside them. "I am scheduled to launch within the hour. We do not have time to debate the admiral's technological genius. We have a challenge before us and need all the help we can get. If talking to the monitor helps, so be it."

"Well said, my boy. Shall we continue, then?" The avatar looked at Lauren.

Lauren nodded. Some of the tightness in her stomach eased as she realized some of the admiral may exist in this construct and be able to help them.

"Just go with it, Lauren, carry on as if the admiral was here with you, conducting another instruction session." Ice twitched her ears.

"Thanks, Ice," Lauren replied, marveling at this gift the admiral left for them. "Yes, if I remember, you were going to ask a question?"

The avatar took on a serious expression and cocked its head to the side. It appeared to be listening, listening to a speaker those in the room couldn't hear. "I have ascertained your true identities through our interaction. Therefore, I do not require a challenge question at this time." Lauren nodded. "You will need to open the cases in the proper sequence to access the technology within. Please place the three cases on the bench across from me, please."

Tavish and Angus each picked up a case and placed it beside the one already there. "Thank you. Now, each case is marked with an etched character. These characters come from a unicode language Her Majesty learned while visiting Earth-reality. Do you recognize them, Consort?"

Lauren looked at the symbols. "Not really." *I don't remember these.* "Wait a sec, did you say unicode?"

"That is correct."

Lauren tapped her chin, trying to remember. Unicode was constructed by assigning a unique number to every letter in any language so any operating system could read the message. Banking systems used unicode to supersede the differences between languages when completing international bank transfers. "But what language is this a characterization of?" *What had Alex been reading while we were on Earth?* She read so many things it was difficult for Lauren to narrow down the source for this code. *I know she read a book about computer programming.* Lauren snapped her fingers and moved over to the cases, pointing as she identified each case. "One." She pointed to the half-cross shape symbol, and then pointed at the case with the down L. "Two. And three." She pointed at the last case. "The cases must be opened in that order." Lauren reached out to case number one, ready to throw the latch.

"At the same time." The avatar interjected and Lauren jerked her hand back.

"Complete instructions would be appreciated next time," Lauren replied, her annoyance flashing to the surface. "If we open them at the same time, we aren't opening them in sequence."

"Yes, well. The admiral set it up that way. I did not," the avatar snapped back.

Angus, Tavish, and Lauren reached out and grasped the latch on the case in front of them.

"On three." Lauren counted down and they flipped the latches. As the cases opened, a cloud of super-cooled air escaped.

"Good, now, case one contains the primary transceivers. Case two, the secondary transceivers. And case three, the paired entangled-photon generator-laser," the avatar instructed.

When Lauren looked into case three, she was puzzled. "Entangled photon?"

"Yes, Consort. You will charge each transceiver with a stream of photons generated by the entanglement laser. Each transceiver will contain one half of a pair of entangled photons." The avatar seemed to lean closer to the screen. "Do you understand, Consort?" Lauren shook her head. The avatar turned. "Angus?"

Angus tapped the side of his nose with one long thin finger, his eyes lost focus as he tried to decipher what the avatar was saying. "Ah, I see." Angus grinned at Lauren. "I believe it concerns your cat." The wolves' heads snapped up. Snow and Ice growled.

"Eh, Angus, I don't have a cat."

"Angus is speaking of your Professor Schrödinger, and his 'cat in a box' thought experiment," the avatar explained.

"Admiral McLeod and I discussed Schrödinger and his cat when we were discussing thought-experiments."

The avatar nodded. "Indeed, that cat."

Lauren shook her head, trying to figure out how this all fit together. Her brain was getting whiplash. Snapped backward and forward through the complexities of quantum physics, entangled photon particles, and thought experiments. She rubbed her forehead. "Let me see if I get this. You mean the photons will exist in quantum superposition, occupying multiple states at the same time. This would be true, if you are using the thought experiment of Schrödinger's cat in an enclosed box as an example." Lauren outlined the experiment. "There is a cat in a box. When the box is closed, we don't know if the cat is dead or alive. Therefore before we open the box, the cat is both dead and alive at the same time. It exists in both states."

The avatar nodded. "Correct."

Lauren frowned, trying to put the pieces together. "But if we open the box, the act of opening the box predetermines the state the cat is in. It is then either dead or alive, not both. Our observation of the cat dictates its existence in only one state. It is the act of observation which is the determining factor."

"Exactly, well done, Consort. Photons are elementary particles—the primary quanta of electromagnetic radiation i.e. visible light. Photons have no mass but do have spin directions. For simplicity's sake, let us assume the spin is either up or down, similar to the cat being either dead or alive. Since we do not know which spin each photon has, it exists with both spins at once until we observe it."

Lauren smiled as the pieces started to fall into place and she visualized the photons—one spinning up and the other spinning down—a complementary pair. Since they hadn't observed the pair directly, they didn't know which of the pair was spinning in which direction.

"To create an entangled pair of photons, a laser beam will be sent through a refracting crystal, generating pairs of polarized photons, each sharing a complementary spin direction with its partner—up or down. The pairs will then be separated—one half of each pair stored in one of the transceivers." The avatar looked at Lauren and Angus.

Lauren leaned closer to the screen. "Go on—"

"Thus, until the spin is physically measured by an outside observer, the photons exist in all spin states at once."

"This duality of spin defines their quantum superposition," Lauren said, and then she stood so suddenly, her stool flew backwards striking the bench behind her. "Right. Right. Oh my god. You're going to use their quantum states to send messages in binary code."

Angus arched an eyebrow. "What are you getting at, Lauren? How are you going to send binary code across intragalactic distance using photons? The photon beam would degrade after a few thousand kilometers as it interacted with interstellar dust in deep space."

"Don't you see, Angus, we won't send a beam. We don't need to. We'll use the particles themselves, as they exist within each transceiver."

The avatar grinned. "The Consort is correct, my boy. Even though the photon pairs will be separated across vast distances, each half of the pair—isolated within its own transceiver—will know the state of its other half. Separation distance is irrelevant. Their quantum states—in this case, their spin direction—will remain linked. When you measure the properties of your photon, you will immediately know the spin direction of its mate on the other ship. Thus, entanglement."

Lauren vibrated in place, excitement thrumming through her. "It's Einstein's 'spooky action at a distance.' Each photon always knows what its partner is doing, no matter the distance they are separated from one another. Kinda like Alex and I. I know she's all right and I know where she is. Totally cool, right?"

"I do not know about cool. It's weird and most difficult to imagine." Angus smiled but Lauren could see the wheels turning in his scientific brain.

She spun around to face the communication monitor. "Did you get that, Robert?"

Looking sheepish, Robert shook his head. "Not exactly, Consort. Remember I am not the technician you and Angus are." He held up his hands in surrender. "I merely fly the clans. I do not need to know how the clan ability to fly was discovered. But, if you understand how this works and you feel it will allow us to communicate as we travel on separate flight paths, I say bring it on. My communication technician has constructed a secure alcove off the bridge for the device."

Lauren grabbed Angus by the shoulders. "What else do we need? Do we need to set up an encrypted code to safeguard the messages?"

The avatar interrupted. "The quantum device is ultra-secure, Consort. If anyone were to break into the message, or read the message, that act would alter the quantum state of the shared pair and garble the message. It would be the equivalent of opening the cat's box—you would know immediately if the cat was dead or alive, as it no longer existed in both states."

"All right, so we set up a simple alpha-numeric code in binary—zeros or ones. Each character corresponding to a photon spin state—up or down. Like the dots and dashes used in Morse code, here we'll use up and down." She paced in front of the workbench. "But we need a way to set the spin-direction we want onto one half of the entangled pair to send a specific pattern of up or down. Once we impart a spin direction on our photon, its mate's spin-direction, on the other clan, would be instantaneously set in the opposite direction and the message would be delivered. We just read up—down, zero—one. This is fricking brilliant. To impart the spin we want, we need to insert a third photon with known spin. How do we do that?" Lauren was off in her own world of discovery, her brain flashing ideas almost faster than she could comprehend them. She pulled her braid over her shoulder, twirling the end around her fingers as she tried to organize her ideas, her pace quickening. "When the third photon, with known spin, is paired with our half of the original pair in the transceiver onboard the *Stag*, it would set the paired photon spin in the direction we wanted to match the code. The mate onboard the *Boar* would immediately spin in a complementary direction which Robert could read."

Lauren looked at her companions. "What else?" No one spoke. They just gaped at her, looks of astonishment on their faces.

The avatar laughed. "The admiral told me about your flashes of brilliance. I just did not believe him. I realize I had to see it for myself. Well done, Consort. Well done, indeed."

That simple statement brought Lauren up short. Hearing this avatar use one of the admiral's standard catch phrases, spoken in his speech pattern, with his voice, was disconcerting and Lauren's soul bled.

"Yes, well, the admiral's the one who deserves the credit for this, not I." Her enthusiasm washed away as she realized what a great mind the Terrans had lost with his death. Grief ripped through her gut and she shuddered. *I swear to you, Admiral McLeod, I will not let you down.*

"The admiral was just completing the photon generator to create this third photon with known spin when Terra was discovered, and he put this experiment away. You will have to complete that before the communicator will function."

Lauren looked at Angus. "Well?"

Angus stared at her. "Consort, really? I have yet to catch up to you and the avatar. I am still in the box with the cat."

Tapping her foot in a rapid staccato, Lauren tried to hurry him along. "Time's ticking here, Angus. What do we need to create a single-photon source, where we can impart a specific, known quantum state on it? All we need is spin."

"Well, I suppose we could use some sort of nano-material, like a quantum dot, or a—"

"Great." Lauren didn't give him time to complete his thought. "Work that out and get it paired with transceivers. I'll work on setting up the entanglement generator and create the stream of entangled photon pairs. We'll test the devices and then install them on the clans." She turned to the avatar.

"Thank you. We couldn't have done this without you."

"You are most welcome, Consort. The admiral will be pleased to see his work used for such a noble cause."

Lauren's throat tightened. "I'm sure he would've been, if he were here to know." Her voice broke as the weight of her sorrow flooded over her soul.

"I do not understand." The avatar tipped his head to the side in a gesture so reminiscent of McLeod Lauren barely stifled her sob. "Why are you sad, Consort?"

Lauren wiped at the tears running down her cheeks. "He's gone."

The avatar frowned. "If the admiral is gone, I have one additional request."

"Of course, anything?"

"Take me with you." An earnest tone was evident in his synthesized voice. "I would be most grateful for the opportunity to contribute to Terra's defeat of the traitor. And to avenge the admiral's death."

"That's an idea." *Could this help us? Possibly.* "We'd appreciate your expertise. I've got one request for you in return." He nodded for her to continue. "What were you going to ask as the challenge question?"

The avatar winked at her. "What is your favorite herbivore?"

Lauren chuckled. "Only the admiral would ask that question." *First a cat, now an elephant.*

Chapter Ten
Terra, The Keep, Seneschal's Office
Eastern Solar—Evening of the Eighth Day

Robert departed lunar orbit four hours after their discussions with the avatar. Lauren and Angus developed the quantum dot nano-matrix, and the single-source photon generators were completed and paired with the transceiver to translate the coded messages. Lauren, with the remaining companions in tow, returned to Terra. There, they prepared to launch the other three clans: Clan Newkirk's *Golden Kestrel,* the *Red Lion* of Clan MacDonald, and Lauren's *Red Stag.*

As the *Wild Boar* exited the Terran solar system and accelerated to faster-than-light pulse speeds, Robert activated the quantum communication system and sent the first instantaneous quantum message to the paired transceiver on the *Stag.* It was acknowledged by the communication techs aboard the *Stag* and relayed to the Seneschal's office.

Merilyn's offices occupied the five floors below Lauren's residence in the eastern solar of the Keep. Tonight, her personal office was filled to overflowing, with Lauren, the wolves, Tavish and Angus, Lords McLaran and Newkirk, and Lady MacDonald gathered within the circular stone-walled space. The two elder men were settled comfortably in the ancient carved ironwood chairs before her desk, while the boys leaned against the walls nearest the door. The wolves stretched out on the flagstone hearth before a roaring fire. Lady MacDonald sat on one of the two red, leather-covered arm chairs facing the fire. The chair swallowed her tiny frame in its down-filled depths.

Merilyn looked up from the monitor embedded in her desktop. "We have a message from Robert." She read the message aloud to the group gathered in her office, "Departing Oort Cloud, gravitational wave acquired, course aligned with *Orchid* flightpath." She settled back in her chair; folding her hands deep in the sleeves of her gunmetal gray robe. Her gray braid draped over her shoulder. "Well, they are on their way and not a moment too soon."

Lauren paced, her impatience, frustration, and pent up energy evident. In constant motion, she pulled on her braid, moving first one way and then retracing her steps. She mumbled to herself. It seemed to be lists, but lists of what Merilyn did not know.

Merilyn shared Lauren's frustrations, there was so much more to accomplish before the other three clans could give chase. She might not understand any of what Lauren and Angus shared about this quantum communications system, nor about the alterations being made to the clans' propulsion systems, all she needed to do was keep them moving in a positive direction, using all tools she could provide them. Moving toward their goal of saving Alexandra. Which was why they were all present now. Merilyn had called this strategy meeting to gather her confidants and share information first hand.

Lauren stopped and faced Merilyn. "How will you know our progress? We can't communicate with you in realtime. Do we build another quantum transceiver pair?" Lauren did not give Merilyn time to answer before she paced up to Angus. "Well?"

"That is doable, Consort. If we have enough time, we could construct another entangled-pair system."

Lauren gripped her head. "Gods, time. Again!" She began pacing again.

"Sit down, please." Merilyn's quiet command halted Lauren in mid-step.

Lauren's eyes widened. "I don't have time to sit down, Seneschal."

Merilyn nodded. "Be that as it may, the *Boar* is off as vanguard. We must wait for their update as they draw within sensor range of the *Orchid*. The refits to your clans are not yet complete. You cannot depart until all is complete." Lauren spun on her heel and paced back. "Lauren, you must sit. We have much to discuss this evening. We must prepare a summary of your plans for presentation to the Council." Merilyn dropped her head. She knew her next statement would raise Lauren's anxiety level further. "And prepare your speech to Terra."

As she expected, that did it. Lauren stopped in front of the remaining vacant chair in front of Merilyn's desk and dropped into it. Merilyn winched in sympathy as the ancient wood groaned. "What are you talking about?" Disbelief dripped from Lauren's tone.

"The people must not be left with only rumors. They must have the truth, told to them by their Queen. And that is you." Merilyn pointed at Lauren. "They must know the plans and you must instill hope in them, as they wait for word of Alexandra's successful recovery."

"Rumors, what rumors?"

Merilyn chuckled. "You may think you maintained this secret. Keeping everyone in the dark." She saw a small smile tug at the corners of Lauren's mouth. "However, rumors are flying about the Keep, faster than your quantum communication devices can relay information."

"How's that possible? We've been so careful, only a few know what's going on." Lauren sounded incredulous.

"Do you really think refitting the *Boar* the way you did, by commandeering all the resources of Luna Keep to do so, is keeping it quiet?" Merilyn laughed. "Thousands were involved, Lauren. And all involved have family and clan members here on Terra. You did not institute a communications blackout. Thus, when the *Boar* was brought down into near-lunar orbit and the propulsion system refitted, all ability to contain information was lost. Messages flew between Luna and Terra."

Lauren rubbed her face. "Well, damn."

"You did nothing more than fully-mobilize Terra. What did you think would happen once the Council accepted your preliminary plans?"

"I guess I didn't think." Lauren shrugged.

Merilyn smiled at the amazing young woman seated before her. "Of course you did not think. How could you? I am amazed you could do anything at all, besides curl up into a ball and drift off into your bond with Alexandra." She sketched a wave in dismissal. "What we must do now, is prepare the summary for the Council and your presentation to Terra. Agreed?" Merilyn looked at each of her compatriots, they nodded. Lauren did not nod. She sat, staring down at her clinched hands. "Lauren, do you agree?"

The Queen-Consort of Terra looked up and shrugged again. Merilyn realized her mistake as she looked into Lauren's green-blue eyes and gasped. "You can no longer feel her." This was not a question. Looking more closely, Merilyn realized Lauren's aura was rift with dark streaks of fear, terror, and anguish. *Why did I not see this sooner? We are all overwhelmed and exhausted.*

"It's not I can't feel her. I can't communicate with her." Lauren shook her head. "It's like she's there, but not. I know she's fine physically, and I know exactly where she is." Lauren pointed toward the ceiling. "But I've tried to actually talk to her, reestablish our communication link along our bond, and I can't."

Merilyn made a snap decision. "Siobhán, please take the Consort up to her rooms and see she has a bath and some tea, and then is shown her bed. We will complete the summary and draft her presentation. Her need for rest is more important than our need for her contribution here."

As Lady MacDonald rose gracefully from her chair, Lauren protested. "But—"

"No, Lauren. You are exhausted to the point of doing yourself physical harm." Merilyn stood and leaned across her desk. "You will do as I say, daughter, or I will turn you over my knee. Do you understand?"

Lauren gave up and slumped in her chair. "I understand."

Merilyn watched as Lauren, head hanging, diminished before her eyes.

"Very well." Merilyn sat down with a flair of her robes as Siobhán stepped next to Lauren. She placed a gentle hand on the Consort's shoulder, and Lauren winched.

"I am sorry." Lady MacDonald removed her hand. "I did not mean to cause you pain."

Lauren dismissed her apology with a shake of her head. "You didn't know. Every time I get overly tired, my shoulder aches. It hasn't fully healed from my bout with the Challenger." She smiled crookedly. "I guess it never will after all this time." Lauren stood and walked around Merilyn's large desk. She gathered the tiny Seneschal in a gentle hug and whispered. "Thank you for taking such good care of me, Mom. I love you."

"Yes, yes, off with you now. The Lady MacDonald will treat you well." Merilyn turned her head and whispered back, "And I you, Lauren." She smiled up at the amazing young woman before her.

Blinking her eyes open, Lauren squinted against the glare of the setting sun refracted through the large octagonal lensed window of her solar. She had no ability to judge how much time had passed but she was blessedly rested. Her shoulder no longer ached and her head was clear for the first time since passing through the nexus when returning from Earth-reality. She sat up and pushed back the down comforter, she was warm, snuggled in her flannel pjs.

The tiny figure of Lady MacDonald was curled into a ball, almost hidden beneath a throw of Fraser green and black tartan, only a tuft of brilliant red hair in view. The Terran Lady of the Ancients slept in one of two leather chairs before the copper-hooded fireplace where a cheery fire burned. Someone had been here to tend it. It had been embers when Lauren fell into bed after her soak. She was hungry, and her stomach growled.

That is the sound which stirred Lady MacDonald. An arm and then a smiling face slipped from beneath the throw. "Ah, good, you are awake."

"So it seems." Lauren acknowledged the obvious and gave a light laugh.

"How do you feel?"

Lauren cocked her head. "Surprisingly well rested, and incredibly hungry."

"Well you should be hungry, considering you have slept almost thirty hours."

"That's not possible," Lauren swung her legs over the side of the huge bed. "Why'd you let me sleep so long?"

Lady MacDonald just looked at her with one of her inscrutable smirks. When she didn't respond, Lauren realized what they'd done. She crossed her arms and growled. "You drugged me."

"Yes, the tea. It has great restorative powers. Just what you needed." Lady MacDonald smiled blithely and folded back the Fraser tartan. Standing, she stretched her arms over her head and yawned until her jaw popped. She moved to the communicator on Lauren's bedside table. "She is awake." She intoned to whomever answered.

"And?" the disembodied voice questioned.

"And she is none too happy to have been drugged."

"Too bad, it was just what she needed." Lauren realized it was Merilyn on the other end of the call. She growled again. "Is that Ice? I thought those two had gone to the kitchen for a spot of dinner."

"No, it is not Ice, though the Consort is doing an admirable imitation of the wolf. And I imagine she is as hungry as the wolves at this point."

Lauren's stomach rumbled again in response.

"So I hear. I shall be up with the evening meal shortly. We will be able to review the council summary and her presentation then." The line closed with a snick.

Lady MacDonald turned to Lauren. "She is on her way. Best have another bath. I will lay out some clothing for you while you soak."

Lauren stood and stretched as the Lady had done. Once her shoulder popped, she dropped her arms. Then, made her way around the partition into the bathing chamber.

Merilyn, with two stewards in tow, arrived a short time later. Lauren could hear the Seneschal's voice drift up from her personal sitting room, giving orders as to the distribution of the dinner trays. "No, not there. The Consort will have your head on a spike if you disturb her work surface. Over here." The rest of the conversation was lost as Lauren stuck her wet head through the neck of a shirt and settled the sleeves and cuffs in place. She grabbed up the kilt and wrapped it around her waist.

She walked barefoot down the stairs into her personal rooms below. "Hey, guys, what's shaking?"

Merilyn and Lady MacDonald chuckled. "Nothing is shaking. No additional terra-tremors have been detected, Consort." Lady MacDonald seated herself in a chair, her feet dangling above the floor.

"However, your plans are progressing at a rapid pace." Merilyn stepped around the low table set before the hearth and gathered Lauren in a fierce hug. The top of the tiny woman's head fell just below Lauren's breasts. Lauren hugged her back with equal fervor. "We have scheduled your summary to the Council for the morning and your presentation to Terra for noon."

"Well, in that case, let's eat and discuss our next steps." But Lauren's tone didn't match her words. Her nerves showed, her voice was pitched higher than usual. Merilyn gave her one last squeeze before letting go.

Lady MacDonald interjected, "Shall we wait on the others?"

Lauren grinned. "I'm sure Ice and Snow will be along soon. Ice never misses a meal, and with all that's happened at Luna Keep and then our hasty return to Terra, meals were not high on our priority list."

The rest of Lauren's companions arrived shortly thereafter and they shared a quiet meal. Lauren approved of all the work they'd completed during her forced sleep. The summary presentation to the Council would be handled by Angus and Tavish, laying out the military strategy they'd prepared.

Although she was uncomfortable speaking before the people of Terra, Lauren knew they needed to hear from her directly. She needed to unite Terra, alleviate their concerns about potential dangers to Terra and Luna Keep, and prepare the populace for emergency evacuation if the need arose. More importantly, she needed to reassure them Alex was alive. To do this, Lauren would need to share more about her bond. *I don't know how much to share or how to share something so personal?*

Chapter Eleven
Aboard the Dubh Mogairle

The blaster ricocheted across the shaft, continuing its free fall below the level of the open hatch. A loud groan rose as the figure slumped into the shaft. Dark hair spilled around the figure's head, Sarah could just make out a glint from around their neck.

"Feck." Looking up, Sarah was glad no one seemed to hear the noise she just made. She needed to get up to deck forty-two. When the figure did not move, she readjusted the admiral's weight across her shoulders and continued climbing. Once at the hatch, Sarah peeked through the access-port into the corridor beyond. Empty. Sarah could see all the way down to the doors of the medical bay at the far end of the corridor.

She wrapped her other arm around the stay, opened the hatch control panel and pushed the entry button. The hatch slid open. Sarah stepped off the ladder and into the adjacent corridor. Just as her foot touched the carpeted deck, another set of klaxons blared. *Great. Now what?* She tilted her head, listening. She could not hear any sounds from the corridor, but she thought she heard groaning from the shaft behind her. She palmed the hatch closed and lowered the admiral to the deck. *Now, how do I bluff my way into the medical bay?* She crouched next to the admiral. Looking at his still form, a glint caught her attention and she saw his rank and clan insignias on his vac suit collar. This would definitely give them away, so she pulled his insignia off and yanked her own from her collar, too. She slipped them into a leg pocket.

Grasping the admiral's arms, she pulled him onto her back and moved down the corridor. Her muscles ached from carrying him, but adrenaline pumped through her body, giving her strength. As she reached the medical bay doors, voices floated down the cross-corridor. *I am out of time.* Hitting the large red square to the right of the bay doors, she stepped into the muted light of the medical bay.

A nurse in a black surgical suit looked up from her analyzer. "What's going on?"

"This crewman is injured. He fell down the emergency shaft when the gravity shifted." Without their rank and clan insignia on on their evac-suits, they were lowly crew, but if she allowed them to do a scan of the admiral, his DNA-print would identify him. Hopefully, the nurse wouldn't recognize them. If the nurse was from Terra, they would never have come into contact. If she was from Luna, all bets were off.

Stepping around the curved center console, the nurse waved them to the left. "Third bay down, number eleven. Place him on the med-table and I will contact the doctor. She is down on level fifty-two in engineering. I do not know how long it will take for her to return."

Without another word, Sarah made her way to number eleven. Sarah hoped the nurse would leave them alone as well.

The med-table was centrally located in the med-bay, surrounded by banks of analyzers. High-intensity overhead lights so bright Sarah winced were attached to a ceiling grid system, allowing them to be repositioned as needed. Glass-fronted cabinets covered the curved walls. After carefully placing the admiral down on the table, Sarah searched for the handheld diagnostic pad. The pad controlled all the analyzers in the room. She found it tucked in its charging dock on a small desk.

Grabbing the pad, Sarah ran it across the admiral's body. The surrounding analyzers came to life and began accepting information from the pad. A series of beeps and chirps rose in harmony as Sarah completed the scan.

A mechanical voice drifted from a speaker. "Scan complete. Dislocation left hip. Acetabulum intact. Iliofemoral ligament detached from greater trochanter. Blood supply and innervation compromised. Tear in medial circumflex femoral artery. Concussion. No internal cerebral hemorrhage. Unable to determine degree of brain trauma, additional neuropathological testing required." *Oh this is so not good. But he needs help and I am it.*

"How do I treat these injuries?"

"Dislocation of hip requires reduction under anesthesia. Muscles of the pelvis and thigh in tetany require muscle relaxants. Femoral head adducted. This dislocation requires abduction rotation during reduction. Nothing required in treatment of concussion."

"How do I abduct his hip?" Sweat began to run down Sarah's back. She had to get this done before the doctor returned.

"The leg must be held in full extension and moved away from body midline, inline with pelvis, as foot rotated. Procedure not recommended unless attending physician present."

Sarah frowned. "No time to wait on the doctor. Show me an illustration of the needed movements on the monitor."

A diagram of the human pelvis, hip joint, and leg appeared on the overhead screen. The leg was straightened as two hands gripped the foot and knee keeping full extension on the joint. Another two hands moved the leg outward and rotated the foot inward. Sarah only had two hands, and one was numb from her shoulder injury. *How can I do this without help? What can I do here?*

Sarah looked around the room. The track grids for the overhead lights caught her eye and an idea started to form. "Right, this is all about mechanics. I just need a set of fulcrums and levers, and we will get this done." She searched the cabinets for supplies. Sarah removed several rolls of gauze from one cabinet and found a knee immobilizer in another. She tightened the immobilizer around the admiral's left leg, the knee was now held in extension. Tearing off strips of gauze, Sarah braided them together to make a rope, throwing it over the the light grid above the med-table. She fastened the two ends of the gauze-rope around the admiral's ankle and tied a knot. His leg was now suspended a few centimeters above the med-table.

Thank the gods he is unconscious. Sarah wiped sweat from her forehead and rubbed her hands on the legs of her evac-suit. "Here goes."

She grasped his foot in her left hand and placed her right on the inside of his knee. Slowly she rotated his foot to the right as she moved his leg away from the midline of his body. The muscles of his hip resisted. *Come on, I can do this.* She gritted her teeth and pushed the leg harder. Just when she thought she would need to reposition her hands and try again, the ball of the femur slipped into the socket with a resounding pop. "Yes!"

"Hip relocated. Minimal additional injury noted. Minor bleeding continues from medial circumflex femoral artery. The joint should be stabilized with hip and upper thigh wrap." A diagram appeared on another monitor. "Bleeding should be monitored. No surgical intervention needed at this time. Antibiotics recommended. Pain medication without blood thinners recommended. Muscle relaxants recommended to minimize cramping."

Sarah found the hip wrap and asked the pharmacological cabinet to dispense the appropriate drugs.

"Antibiotics available. Pain medication requires attending physician authorization." The mechanical voice droned.

"Use this authorization." Sarah rattled off the code she heard the admiral place into their flitter's communications beacon. As Sarah wrapped his hips, the mechanical voice acknowledged the command-level authorization code and another pharmacological drawer slid open. "Thanks." She grabbed the drug packs.

"Okay, Admiral. Now all we have to do is find a safe place to rest. Then, I will need to find food and water, as well."

"Water and food rations available," the mechanical voice said. Another set of drawers slid open. "Please make your selection."

Part Two

The Chase

Imagination is Greater than Knowledge.
~*Albert Einstein*

Chapter One
Aboard the Ruadh làn-damh
Nearing the Milky Way Galactic Center

The semi-darkness of the night watch cloaked the bridge of Clan Fraser's *Red Stag*. A quiet hum of activity filled the vast space—stations were manned with crew and technicians efficiently attending to their duties. Lauren stood in the bridge's prow, isolated—alone, like a boulder in the middle of a rushing river.

The small spot of deck she claimed over the last weeks of their journey was at the apex of the starboard and port command and control stations. These two long ranks of softly glowing analyzers and monitor stations wrapped laterally around the bridge below the curved forward transparency. Lauren stood rigid, arms crossed across her chest, dressed in a full body suit of black energy armor. She should be wearing a pneumatic face shield with her energy armor, but she'd left it on her command chair, in blatant violation of safety protocol. She couldn't stand the claustrophobic feeling she got while wearing the face shield.

Braided and wound in a tight bun, Lauren's hair hugged the nape of her neck. Her platinum Investiture coronet held back her bangs. She touched the beak of the golden owl where it met the head of a golden wolf across her brow. Wisdom and cunning. At the moment, she didn't feel either wise or sly. Her hand drifted down to her two badges of rank pinned on her collar—two facing loons showing her place within Alex's royal lineage and her golden brooch in the shape of the sacred tree bisected by a platinum blade. This badge identified her as protector of the Terran Queen. In this she had failed. She had not protected her Queen. She knew the two badges flashed against the black background of her armor, much like the stars beyond the transparency sparkled against the black velvet of deep space.

No one approached her. No one dared interrupt her thoughts. Standing here, she was as close to the transparency as she could get. Lauren felt like she could touch the passing stars and grab the ball of light by simply reaching out. She placed her hand on the cool trans-alumino-polycarbonate surface.

The muted light of intragalactic space cast a long shadow across the golden spun sails deployed amidship. The giant sails were used to capture every bit of gravitational radiation from the wave they traveled in. If Lauren turned to her right, she could just see the edge of the shadow as it brushed the starboard corner of the bridge. The great clan ship and her two companions, Newkirk's *Golden Kestrel* and MacDonald's *Red Lion,* traveled at faster-than-light pulse speed across the empty space between two of the spiral arms of the Milky Way on their way to the galactic center. Having departed Terra's solar system in the Orion arm, their flight plan would take them around the galactic center to the Comin Nebula located in the galaxy's Sagittarius Arm.

Lauren willed the *Stag* faster. She found herself leaning forward, trying to add her physical strength to the great ship's massive engines. Her will alone didn't add anything to the ship's velocity, but she had to do something. The giant wedge-shaped clan ship rode the back of gigantic gravitational waves—rhythmic distortions in the fabric of spacetime, created by stellar collisions of massive proportions—merging black holes or colliding binary neutron stars. Lauren visualized the waves using a two-dimensional analogy. One of a pebble dropped into a pond which distorts the water surface in concentric ripples.

Once within the wave, giant spun-sails of gold-coated analyzer gel were deployed to gather the gravitational radiation. The gathered radiant energy was shunted to heat sinks where it would be used to prime large fusion reactors. Hydrogen would be injected into the reactors' containment vessels where the atoms were fused within the heart of a mini-sun, releasing the enormous amounts of energy needed to propel the clan ship to tremendous speeds. Lauren knew the physics, acknowledged all the leaps of imagination the Doouglas took to build the first Terran clan ships, and gloried in the genius of all the Terrans involved. *But is it enough? Will we get to the nebula before the* Black Orchid?

Time. We've used so much already. Have we wasted too much? Lauren's thoughts stalled. The memory of telling the Terran population of their plans swamped her and she sagged against the transparency, closing her eyes against the tide.

The sky was gun-metal gray and thick clouds scudded across the Keep, ripped from the black thunderheads building over the Teton Mountains to the west. Wind whipped Lauren's hair from her braid as she stood atop the eastern solar waiting for the herald to announce her to the Terrans massed along the boulevard below. The white-clad herald exited the door of the solar and removed his drooping hat. This day he did not carry his messenger bag, now he held only his hat in his hands.

"*Terra, I have no words for you this day,*" he said, and the crowd gasped. "*Today, I am here to ask you to hear our Queen-Consort's words. I ask you listen before judging. Think before reacting. For today, her words will set the course of our future.*" He bowed to the crowd and turned, pointing up to Lauren. The weight of governing Terra settled on her shoulders as the crowd swept their gazes upward.

Lauren gathered her courage and stood tall at the edge of the waist-high gray-granite parapet. She felt the flow of positive energy from those who stood with her on the rooftop: the Terran Seneschal, their Lady of the Ancients, and the chiefs of clans Newkirk, McLaran, and McLeod. All, her companions and friends. She began to speak, outlining their plans, sharing the presentation so painstakingly prepared.

Lauren had only begun her summary, her voice carrying out over the crowd, when she felt an unease grow from the crowd below. Discontent followed interlaced with an overwhelming sense of anxiety. Lauren's speech faltered and she fell silent.

Ice butted her from behind, and she stumbled forward into the granite. "*You must go on, Lauren. Ignore this. Finish. They must hear what you have to say.*"

"I can't make them listen, Ice." *Lauren was defeated. Just like the Council, the crowd didn't believe in her.*

"*But you must. Together we can overcome anything, divided we will not succeed. This is fear not disbelief.*" *A low growl built in Ice's throat, rumbling to match the thunder rolling in from the mountains.*

"*Lauren be strong, we are with you. All of us. Make them listen, your plan will give them strength.*" *Snow swept her massive white head from side-to-side indicating those standing beside Lauren on the rooftop.* "*This discontent is rising from small, isolated pockets within the crowd. Do not allow their fear to overtake the entire crowd. Take charge.*" *Snow moved up beside her and looked deep in her eyes.* "*Gather your bond around you and use it to make them listen. Because if you allow your fear to be heard by the crowd, it will be over. Do not have fear, we are together.*" *Lauren dropped her hands into the wolves' fur. She felt their energy surge into her bond. Tavish and Angus stepped up and placed their hands on her shoulders. Their power joined the wolves', filling her bond.*

Raising her arms above her head, fingers spread wide, Lauren pulled even more power from her bonded companions. She reached out to her bond with Alex, pulling energy from the love stored there. Then she gathered energy from the building storm, golden-white lightening crackled from her fingertips. The charred tiles within the transitional bond portal glowed with renewed energy as Lauren's power fed it too. Her voice—strengthened and amplified by her power—rang from the rooftop of the eastern solar.

"Hear me, citizens of Terra, I have spoken to Queen Alexandra. She is alive but held captive by the traitor Gwenhwyfach on the Dubh Mogairle.*" Boos and hisses rose from the massed crowd below. "We will free our queen. We will protect Terra and her clans from the Cador-Comin threat. We will prevent such heinous acts from occurring again. But I cannot do this alone. I need you. Alexandra needs you. Rise up, Terra. Join me in this quest. For, we will triumph over this evil. For Terra, for always!"*

A roar rose from the crowd and surrounded the solar tower in sound. Lauren dropped to her knees, her power draining out in a rush, leaving her spent.

"For Terra, for always," the cheer repeated, over and over.

Here on the command deck of the *Stag*, Lauren's ears still rang with the crowd's roar. If she opened her bond, she could feel the crowd's massed energy stored there, waiting to be released. Once she'd collapsed on the rooftop, Lord McLaran outlined the specifics of their plan. It was evident the crowd already knew most of the plan. Merilyn was correct; they weren't able to keep any secrets. But, that was weeks ago. Now, they were streaking across intragalactic space at unimaginable speeds, trying to beat time. Preparing to bring the hydrogen condensers online and increase their speed even more.

The sound of a quiet throat clearing startled Lauren from her memories. She turned. A small technician gripped a pad to her chest. "Yes?"

"Majesty, a message has been received from the *Boar*."

Lauren reached for the pad. "Thank you. Ailsa, is it?"

"Yes, Majesty." The young communication tech bobbed her head and blushed to the roots of her golden hair.

"I think I'd better take the pad, before you crush it." Still holding her hand out Lauren smiled, her voice soft with amusement.

"I . . . err . . . I am sorry, Majesty." The young tech nearly flung the pad at her. Lauren opened the message and read. The technician stood at rigid attention.

Looking up, Lauren eyed the young woman. "Easy there, we wouldn't want you to break anything." Ailsa's stance softened a fraction. "Is there something else?"

"No. Ah, yes?" She squeaked and blushed again. "A reply, perhaps? Or orders for the fleet?"

"Good thought." Lauren chuckled. Ailsa frowned. Lauren really wasn't cut out for this command business. The weeks she'd spent trying to learn just weren't enough. "Please send a message to the *Kestrel* and *Lion*. I'll need to speak to Angus and Tavish as soon as possible. This is good news which must be shared." Lauren's heart soared with excitement.

The tech bobbed her head again. "Aye, Majesty." She turned on her heel and nearly ran to her communication station.

Lauren's gaze went back to the stars. She aligned her body with Alex's current position. *"Oh Dearest, this is wonderful news. All may not be lost."* No response came from the empty space beyond the transparency. She placed her hand on the cool transparency, over the spot where Alex was. *"I love you."*

Within minutes, another tech called Lauren away from her spot, letting her know the messages were sent and acknowledged. She left the bridge and headed to her command cabin located off the port side of the upper bridge deck. The room was spartan. There hadn't been any time to make it her own. A couch sat beneath the long narrow transparency running the length of the room along the outer hull. The carpet was a Fraser hunting tartan—an ancient pattern of muted brown, navy, and green background crosscut by bright lines of red and white. Her sheathed rapier hung from a rack of elk antlers attached to the inner bulkhead. Two large sheep-wool throws occupied the floor in one corner, defining the wolves' place.

Settling behind a large curved desk, Lauren pulled her chair close. She placed her hand on the gel pad and two screens rose from the workstation's black surface. "Authentication, alpha-one-one-two-omega."

A synthesized voice acknowledged her voice input and the screens sprang to life. Angus glared from one screen, while the other showed a spinning GeoDynamics tetrahedron. "He is always late."

Lauren held up a hand and chuckled. "I know. We'd still be in lunar orbit if Tavish was in charge."

"I imagine he is trying out his new attack flitter in the simulator. He believes we will be able to transit between ships, while riding a gravitational wave." Angus shook his head. "I tell you now, I will not be the one to try that. Ship-to-ship communications is fine for me."

"With you there. You're not getting me on a flitter within the shear turbulence of a wave."

Angus began to respond when the other screen dissolved into the sweating face of Tavish. His red cheeks matched his flaming hair. "Sorry for the delay. I was sparring."

Both Angus and Lauren laughed. "We thought you'd be flying the new flitter. But sparring?"

"I cannot allow the leisure of long space flights to diminish my skills. This is something each of you must be cognizant of as well. Especially you, Lauren." He pointed a long finger at her, and Lauren reared back. The three-dimensional holo-transmission had such high-resolution, it looked like his finger came out of the screen to hit her in the nose.

Lauren cringed. "Be that as it may, we don't have time for sparring at the moment."

"Well, when I have my flitter ready, I will be over to the *Stag* and you will spar until you drop." Tavish smirked.

"Will you two stop," Angus demanded. "What news do you have, Lauren?"

Lauren took a deep breath, barely containing her glee. Her heart rate picked up and she couldn't keep a smile off her face. "Down to business then. We received a quantum message from the *Boar* a few minutes ago. They've recovered a communication beacon."

"They what?" The boys spoke in unison and looked at each other and then back at Lauren.

Angus was the first to recover his ability to speak. "That is not possible, who would leave a beacon that far from known space? Is it one of our old ones left during our search for Terra?"

She couldn't wait to let them in on the news, but she answered their question first. "It's a beacon from a construction flitter. Seems it was ejected into normal space from within a gravitation wave."

"Oh, this just gets better and better. I would ask you to have Robert check their environmental systems. The concentration of carbon dioxide in their atmosphere is too high and their mental capacity is diminished. Or they are not encrypting their messages correctly." Angus huffed. "Nothing could survive the gravitational turbulence of deceleration and remain intact."

"They recovered the beacon along the flight path of the *Orchid*." Lauren's smile nearly split her face now. This was the first positive news they'd had since Alex's kidnapping. "Admiral McLeod and his pilot," Lauren paused to catch her breath. "They're alive."

The boys spoke at the same time, their excitement spilling across the distance separating their ships. "By the gods, this is amazing. How is that possible? Their flitter was caught in the laser cross-fire."

Excitement pulsed through Lauren. "Indeed, but they were able to avoid weapons fire and escape undamaged. Remember, Lord Newkirk didn't find any debris. It seems they attached tractors to the *Orchid* and pulled themselves up to the ship, where they latched on to the hull."

Tavish frowned. Lauren could tell he was analyzing the flight parameters of such a maneuver in his head. "No, that is impossible. A flitter is not built to withstand the translational stress to gravitational wave flight. She would be torn apart."

"Tavish, you are forgetting who was piloting the flitter. If anyone could complete a maneuver like that, Sarah Cameron could," Angus interjected.

Lauren was bouncing in her chair. "There's more, guys. When they launched the beacon, they were preparing to exit the flitter and gain access to the *Orchid*. Their plans were to disable her somehow and find Alex. Then rendezvous with Robert in the *Boar*."

Angus' smile disappeared. "Lauren, I do not mean to be argumentative, but what you are telling us is a fairy tale. It is a false trail laid by the *Orchid* to send a vanguard off course."

Lauren sent the full data file over to the other ships, using a microburst transmission. "There, I just sent you the data from the beacon. It includes a voice report from Admiral McLeod, as well as astrogation position, flight data, and a video of their flight path. Look for yourselves. I don't think it's a hoax."

The boys turned away from their monitors as they reviewed the data stream. Lauren tipped her chair back, allowing the self-adjusting mechanism to remold to her new position. *Definitely heaven.* She made a mental note to have one delivered to her solar on Terra. It would relieve the strain on her shoulder when she was working on her analyzer. *If we make it back to Terra. Come on, Lauren, remember one step at a time.*

"I do not believe this, Lauren. This shows they survived a near-direct laser hit and lost most flight controls but were still able to avoid additional strikes. Then somehow, they were able to attach a tractor onto the *Orchid*, pull themselves up to the ship as it was translating to gravitational propulsion, and latch on magnetically. Really? To repeat your phrase, 'no way.'" Tavish looked angry with this information, not excited.

Some of Lauren's elation faded. Her doubts began to overshadow her belief they had survived. "Sarah is a master flight officer, and if anyone would be able to complete a maneuver such as this, she would."

"Well—"

Angus interrupted. "I agree with Tavish. This seems an impossible feat of piloting, as well as, pure fantasy." He rubbed the side of his nose. "And just how were they planning to enter the ship?"

"According to the report, they're going to enter the ship through some sort of maintenance hatch within the . . . hang on a second." Lauren pulled up the transcript. "Ah, yeah. The thruster intake."

Tavish shook his head. "That is not possible. The hatch is sealed from the inside and the interior maintenance bay would contain a positive atmosphere. If they opened the hatch, decompression alarms would sound, and the bay would automatically seal itself against the hull breach. They would be immediately captured."

Lauren looked at Angus. "Well, what do you think? You've gotten awfully quiet all of a sudden."

Angus didn't respond, but then he smiled at Lauren. "I would have to agree with Tavish this sounds impossible. However, if anyone could find a way around a clan's systems it would be the admiral." He looked from Lauren to Tavish. "Perhaps, we need another opinion? Someone who knows him better than we do."

For a moment, Lauren didn't have a clue what Angus was talking about. "Another opinion?"

"Well played, Angus. I think you are correct." Tavish's smile slowly creased his face. "Yes, Lauren, another opinion. You need to activate the avatar. Perhaps, he will have some insight into the veracity of this message."

Lauren turned to the shelf behind her desk. Reaching up, she pulled down a black crystalline cube. When she depressed all eight corners at once, a holographic head appeared; the admiral's visage floated a few centimeters above the top surface of the cube. "Good day, Majesty. How is the flight going?"

Lauren placed the cube on the work surface in front of the two communications screens, and she smiled at the hologram. "Well, so far. But we've received a message from the *Boar*. Seems they retrieved a communication beacon from deep space. It was within the flight path of the *Orchid*."

"Indeed. How intriguing." The avatar tilted his head. "Is it one of our beacons?"

"It appears to be a beacon from a construction flitter."

The avatar seemed to glow brighter. "And just how did a construction flitter's beacon come to be in such a place?"

"That's what we need your help figuring out, avatar." Lauren nodded at the two boys. "Neither of my companions believe the admiral's flitter could've survived to drop this beacon in deep space. This is what the information within the beacon implies."

"I see. Please allow me access to the entire datafile. I will review. The probability of the admiral surviving the exchange of laser-weapons fire within the Terran solar system is less than zero-point-zero-zero-one-five."

Lauren dropped her hand into the gel pad and data began streaming across a third screen in her desktop. The avatar didn't blink or react. "Are you getting this?"

"Yes, Majesty, the uptake is a bit slow as we are limited by the streaming speed in this particular monitor. I will work on that following my analysis of these data."

Several minutes after the data stream halted, Tavish cleared his throat. "Neither Angus nor I believe this report is true. We are concerned it is a false report placed within the *Boar's* flight path to lead us astray. The *Orchid* had to know we would give chase."

"I agree, my boy. That is a real possibility. This report outlines a feat of piloting unheard of in Terran flight history. A construction flitter is not designed to survive the shear stress of translation to gravitational wave propulsion. Add to that, their plan to transit the hull of a ship while she is traveling at faster-than-light pulse speeds is unprecedented." The avatar paused; both boys nodded. "However, did you look at the frequency of transmission?"

"What has that to do with this crock of lies?" Tavish's anger seemed to be rising again.

Lauren interrupted. "Let him finish. He knows the admiral better than we do. After all, in most ways, he is the admiral."

"Thank you, Majesty. In all ways but one, I would have to agree with you." The avatar turned back to the images of her two companions. "The beacon was set to transmit on an ultra-low frequency of less than three kilohertz. And the transmission utilized a microfilament burst."

The avatar paused in his analysis, Lauren prompted, "And—"

"Majesty, only the admiral would think to use such a low frequency. A ship would need to be literally on top of the beacon to locate it. Given the location in which it was found, a message transmitted with those frequencies would need an inordinate amount of time to arrive at Terra, which would render the information useless. The *Orchid* would know we had already departed to give chase. The message would miss our departure."

"And Terra does not regularly monitor the ultra-low frequency bands," Angus added.

"Very good, my boy. That is also true. I do not think if Clan Cador wanted to lead us astray, they would use this frequency. Most probably, they would broadcast using a broadband blast—shouting out the message for all to hear." The avatar shook its head. "Rather than whispering in the dark, as this one does."

Lauren's hopes were reinforced by this hypothesis. "But you seem convinced this truly is the admiral."

"Aye, it was sent by the admiral." The avatar seemed to smirk at Lauren. "He embedded his personal security code within the microfilament carrier wave."

All three laughed. Lauren grinned. "Of course, he did. And this means, the message is authenticated and the admiral's alive?"

"So, it would seem, Majesty. Our only remaining concerns would be their safe transit across the hull, their ability to enter the maintenance bay without detection, their success at finding Alexandra, and their ability to take the *Orchid* against a crew of four thousand."

"Right, only those." Lauren rocked back in her chair, fingers steepled under her chin. Her fears slipped silently away, replaced by hope. Her energies surged. "Given this, what do we do now?"

Chapter Two
Aboard the Dubh Mogairle

The anti-grav stretcher floated behind Sarah as she traversed deck forty-two back toward the maintenance shaft. She would need to move into one of the sub-decks since the stretcher would not fit through the ventilation shafts they used on the way to the med-bay. The sub-decks ran from the ship's bow to her stern and provided access to any system. Additionally, there were any number of maintenance nodes in which she could set up a safe haven for them to rest.

Back at the hatch, Sarah palmed it open and peered over the edge. Looking up, the shaft was empty, though another force field sparkled several decks above. That had not been in place when Sarah entered deck forty-two. It was probably erected when the coolant leak was detected to protect the upper decks. Sure enough, when she looked down, the shaft was clear all the way to the keel of the ship at deck sixty.

"Well, it looks like we are headed down." Sarah slid the stretcher into the empty shaft and let go. It floated within the center of the empty shaft. She grabbed the swing bar above her head and rotated out onto the ladder. Then she grasped the admiral's stretcher where it floated in the center of the shaft, turning it to gain access to the control panel at the head of the unit. She reduced the anti-grav level to eighty percent of normal and the stretcher began to slowly sink down the center of the shaft. Sarah gripped the vertical supports of the ladder and hopped off the ladder rung. Placing her boot soles on the vertical supports, she began a controlled slide down the ladder, following the stretcher.

By the time they made it to the keel of the ship, Sarah's shoulder was on fire. But they were safe and so far, undetected. *Just need to enter the sub-deck and move aft toward engineering.* When the admiral regains consciousness, he would know how to disable the *Orchid.* Stepping onto the keel brace, Sarah looked down the length of the sub-deck toward the bow. Clear. Then she turned aft and froze. A dark form blocked the hatchway.

"Hold there. Hands up. Turn around slowly," the figure demanded.

Sarah complied, facing the menacing form filling the hatchway. *Feck, the game is up.* Slowly, the tall lithe figure stepped out of the hatch. The black energy-armor evac-suit masked their gender and the pneumatic face shield distorted the voice. The person held a small laser torch in their left hand, finger on the trigger. Shoulder aching, Sarah lowered her hands.

"I said, hands up."

"I am sorry, but I injured my shoulder while escaping the coolant leak and I am trying to get my companion to medical help." Sarah inclined her head to the antigravity stretcher.

The figure looked at the inert body on the stretcher and gasped. Looking up, the figure growled, "That is Admiral McLeod. Who are you?" The person emphasized their demand by waving the laser torch at Sarah's face while flicking the trigger on.

"Sarah Cameron, personal pilot to Fleet Admiral Iain McLeod." She gathered her courage and took a step forward. "Who are you?"

The figure did not answer, and Sarah froze again as the laser torch continued to weave in front of her. Slowly the figure lowered the torch and flicked it off. A hand rose to the pneumatic face shield, pulling it away, revealing the face of her queen.

Sarah gasped and dropped to one knee. "Majesty." She lowered her head.

Alex chuckled. "None of that now. Stand up, Pilot Cameron." Alex touched Sarah on the shoulder. "Tell me, how is it you come to be here, in the bowels of the *Orchid*?"

Sarah stood and smiled. "That is a long tale, Majesty." She broke off and looked up the maintenance shaft stretching sixty decks above their heads. "And probably, one best told in a safer place than this."

Bending down, she readjusted the anti-grav setting on the stretcher and it rose to float a meter off the deck plating. Sarah sketched a small wave to indicate the sub-deck hatch Alex had exited. "Shall we? I was planning on setting up a defensible position in one of the nodes within this sub-deck. I was trying to find a place to rest and allow the admiral to recover. Then perhaps, figure out a way to disable the ship, rescue you, and escape."

"Very well. I will follow your lead in this." Alex stepped aside and Sarah pushed the stretcher through the sub-deck hatch.

The trio moved down the passageway. Alex and Sarah ducked beneath the myriad conduits and piping which crossed the headspace above them. After fifty meters, the sub-deck passage widened and a circular space opened around them. Storage lockers filled the exterior of this space. Sarah stopped the stretcher and turned left into the small space. It was like the sub-deck cut through the middle of a bubble. "This should do."

Sarah pulled one of the lockers open and removed the back panel, revealing a relatively large empty space between the locker and the curved bulkhead of the outer hull. Alex knelt down beside her, peering into the dimly lit space. "This is amazing. How did you know this was here?"

Sarah laughed. "This is the place I hid as a child when I needed to escape the torment of my brothers during our long voyage away from Terra Prime. It is quiet and clean." She swept her hand indicating the space before them. "And usually, empty. I furnished my space with light, heat, blankets, and readers. It was my hideaway from the world."

Alex gaped at her. "Amazing, I never knew these spaces existed."

"They were used as storage spaces for escape pods during the construction of the clan. Once the clan's keel was laid and her exterior hull in place they were no longer needed, and the escape pods were removed. Then, after the decks were laid inside her, these spaces were walled off and largely forgotten."

Together, they maneuvered the stretcher into their cozy space and began sorting out supplies. Once settled with a foil-wrapped ration bar, Alex said, "Now we are settled, please tell me what the admiral's condition is and how you came to be here."

Sarah plopped down on one of the rolled blanket kits she had taken from the medical bay supply closet. She told their tale in the succinct way of a pilot reviewing a flight plan. How the admiral was injured, and then their trip to the medical bay. Her cheeks flushed when she summarized her fixing his hip injury. *I am so grateful he was unconscious during that.*

"Then he will need additional medical care." Alex began to push off the deck.

Sarah waved Alex back down. "He got some. The doctor was detained elsewhere, and I could not let them scan him, not without giving away his identity. But the medical AI provided the information I needed to help him."

Alex looked away and the light caught a darkening bruise on Alex's temple in front of her left ear. Without thinking Sarah grasped Alex's chin, turning her head into the dim light of their storage space. "It seems you are in need of some medical care as well. That is quite the bruise you have growing there, Majesty. What happened to you?"

"I am not really sure. Just as I stuck my head out into one of the maintenance shafts to check if it was occupied, I got hit with some falling debris. Never saw what it was that hit me, I must have been knocked out for a bit. When I came to, I was hanging out into the vertical shaft. No one was in the area, so I climbed down here to begin my sabotage effort. I decided to put on the evac-suit to conceal as much of my identity as possible in case I encountered any of the crew. I did not know what all the emergency klaxons were for, nor did I know why the *Orchid* was slowing."

Sarah did not have the courage to tell Alex what the debris was. She turned her head to hide her grimace as she moved over to the med-kit and pulled out a regen-unit. "Hold still, this should not hurt." Sarah moved the unit's laser discharge across Alex's forehead. "There, that should do." Sarah turned Alex's head from side to side. The bruise was already shrinking. "I believe we caused both."

"Both?" Alex looked at her. "Both what?"

"Both the klaxons and the slowing. I mean we caused the slowing, and then I caused the klaxons. You see, once our construction flitter latched on to the hull—"

Alex's grunt of astonishment interrupted her. "Oh, I can tell this is going to be good. A construction flitter? Really?"

"Yes, Majesty, you see . . ." And Sarah continued the tale of their exploits from latching onto the hull to gaining access to the clan. Listening to herself tell it, she could hardly believe they were actually sitting here talking about such an extraordinary feat.

Chapter Three
Aboard the Ruadh làn-damh
Nearing the Milky Way Galactic Center

Sweat dripped from Lauren's chin and splashed onto the deck between her booted feet. She gripped her thighs, trying to regain her breath. Her white shirt was gray with damp and her kilt hung askew.

"Come on, Majesty. You can do better than that." Stewart taunted. "Pick up your blade. Defend yourself." Lauren's blade lay several meters away, where it landed after he disarmed her. They sparred with practice broadswords, weapons at the edge of Lauren's strength to wield.

Lauren held up one hand. "Enough," she gasped.

"No, it is not enough. Young MacDonald will have my hide and yours, too, if I do not maintain your fighting skills. Now pick up your blade and let us continue."

A wolfy snort came from the pile of tumbling mats stacked to the side of the hardwood fencing *piste*. *"You have gone soft, Lauren."* Ice growled.

"And lost your edge." The wolves snorted in amusement at Snow's pun.

"I said, enough." Lauren ignored the wolves. She raised her head and tried to stand, stretching her back to her full height, but stopped short as a stitch caught her side. Pain lanced through her and she stifled a groan. She hurt everywhere. "I can't continue when I'm exhausted to the point of injury. Leave off, Stewart."

She kneaded the knotted muscles in her side, growling at the grinning man. He had yet to break a sweat. His brow only gleamed slightly in the bright lights of the *Stag's* fencing arena. At this moment she hated him for it. The last weeks of stress, limited sleep, and even more limited food had definitely taken their toll on her physical strength.

Lauren sighed. "I've had it, and if we continue, I'll only hurt more. So, let's call it an evening and have some dinner."

Stewart shook his head and moved over to her blade. He picked her blade from the floor with the point of his. A flick of his wrist sent the blade spinning toward her. Lauren instinctively protected her face with her hand and caught the blade across the pommel. The blade bounced off and fell toward the deck, but Lauren's anger erupted at the callous move. She snatched the blade out of the air and swung around to meet Stewart's thrust with a glancing parry.

"I said," she gasped through gritted teeth. "Enough!" She swung her blade in a compound riposte, feinting first left and then right before she dropped low, spinning back left on the ball of her foot. This move swept her blade across Stewart's knees. She struck him in the left knee with the flat of her blade, his blade singing over her head. Overbalanced without her returning parry Stewart fell in a heap, thudding to the hardwood with an explosive grunt.

Lauren tried to stand but her knees gave out and she fell to the hardwood, landing on her butt. She relaxed back and ended up flat on her back, arms splayed out to her sides. Her blade dropped from her limp hand.

"I would call that a draw. What do you say, Ice?" Snow turned to her companion. Ice simply snorted in reply and shook her head.

Lauren glared at the wolves. "Are you two through? I don't see you straining yourselves to get any exercise."

"We are wolves, Lauren. We get exercise just by breathing." Snow whiffled at Ice's glib comment.

"Yeah, right. On Terra, you hunted your dinner. Here, they serve it to you on a platter. You're not getting any exercise."

"True, but we run the decks every night. All you do is sit in front of an analyzer."

"Run the decks?"

Stewart raised his head from the hardwood and grinned at Lauren. It looked more like a grimace. "They do in fact run the decks every night, Majesty. Perhaps, you should go with them one evening." He laughed at his own joke, his head dropping back to the hardwood with a thump.

Lauren had neither the time nor the energy to run the decks. She needed more time to develop her idea for further augmenting their propulsion systems. Hopefully, Tavish and Angus would soon be able to travel from their clans to hers. Meeting face-to-face would help her discuss a complex scientific theory. Tavish was confident his flitter would be able to make the transit—he was trying to build a shielding system to protect the craft from the turbulence of gravitational shear forces.

The doors to the gym swished open and the young communication tech, Ailsa, stepped into the bright white space, light flashing off her golden hair. She cleared her throat.

"Yes, Ailsa. What can I do for you?" Lauren was still flat on her back.

"I have a communique from the *Lion*, Majesty." The young tech walked across the gleaming hardwood and held out a data pad to Lauren.

Lauren sat up with a groan and took the pad. "Thanks, Ailsa."

Ailsa stood at parade rest, her hands clasped behind her back, her gaze locked on the white bulkhead over Lauren's head. Lauren looked up as Stewart stirred. "Is there something else?"

He pushed himself to his hands and knees. "I think this is enough for now, Majesty."

"Really, you think?" Lauren laughed and shook her head. "Why is it you're ready to quit only when you're the one lying on the ground?"

"You are exhausted and unable to continue. And I do not wish to tell Commander Tavish I damaged the Consort."

Lauren snorted. Ailsa's eyes moved rapidly from one to the other, trying to follow the conversation. Lauren couldn't imagine what she thought. If they'd been back in Earth's reality, she could have made a wisecrack about trying to follow a tennis match. But here, the joke would fall flat. She would need to explain tennis to both the tech and the Champion. It wasn't worth it. *I'm too tired and all I want is a hot bath.* Shaking herself from thoughts of warm water, Lauren focused on the pad in her hand. She thumbed the device on and saw a message from Tavish.

"Funny, you're worried about Tavish. This is from him." She waved the pad at Stewart and continued to read. Looking up at Ailsa, she said, "Please send a reply to Tavish and let him know I'll review this and send my comments back this evening."

"Very good, Majesty." Ailsa inclined her head and turned on her heel, walking smartly out of the gym.

Head throbbing, Lauren rubbed her temples as she tried to focus on the technical data swirling within the holograms floating above her desk. Terran maritime strategies from historical naval engagements were holo-projected there in three dimensions. The naval tactics used by the Terrans were annotated within the borders and streamed by as Lauren played the engagement from start to finish. She had to admit, Tavish was thorough in his lessons. More thorough than she felt she would need, or so she hoped.

They were two days from entering the gravity well of the supermassive black hole within the center of the galaxy and all Lauren had done during the weeks of travel was study naval battles. Once they began their planned slingshot maneuver around the black hole, no one knew what gravitational effects they would encounter within the gravity well. Nor, what those effects would do to their ability to communicate. So, Tavish had built this set of instructional holo-projections to give Lauren a crash course in naval command strategies. The boys needed her to be prepared in case the worst occurred, if they lost one or more of their clans in the well or had to battle their way through the *Orchid's* defenses to recover Alex.

Lauren's stomach roiled as she reviewed some of the battles. She couldn't imagine the staggering loss of life nor how the Terrans survived to victory when the odds were often so skewed against them. They hadn't always prevailed, but when they lost the fight, they always won the war.

Lauren scrolled to the next sequence and the holo-projector displayed yet another space battle. Sighing, she leaned back in her chair. *What created their success? Better technology, more experienced commanders, better trained crews, or more intelligence about the enemy?* No, when she distilled all she had viewed down to one through-going thread, it was the Terrans themselves. Their indomitable belief in themselves. Their unerring belief in their queen. Their ability to overcome and thrive. This realization caused Lauren's insecurities to bubble up again. *Would this crew believe in me and follow my orders? Can they? They have to; we must get Alex back!*

"*You must stop this self-doubt, Lauren. It is unproductive.*" Ice's cool mental voice caressed the edges of her mind like the whisper of a passing breeze. She looked over at the wolf where she appeared to be sleeping on her sheepskin rug.

"*I'm not a naval commander, Ice. And, I don't believe in solving problems using force. Most of all, I don't believe in war.*"

Ice rolled over and lay on her back, belly exposed with her four paws flapping above her body. "*We are not declaring war, Lauren. We are righting a wrong. I suggest you review the causes of the conflicts Tavish included in your holograms and ask who started the conflicts. They go back as far as the time of the Black Priests.*" Ice whiffled and rolled on to her side, a slit of ice blue appearing as she opened one eye.

Lauren smiled at the wolf. "*Who made you so smart?*"

"*I did.*" Snow replied from where she lay sprawled on the sofa below the large transparency in Lauren's command cabin. This declaration was followed by snorts of wolfy laughter.

"*I still don't know what I'm going to do. This is way out of my league. And we only have three ships.*" She pointed to the hologram floating above her desk. "*This battle was fought with four naval groups.*" Lauren leaned forward to read the list of ships engaged in the conflict. "*Sixteen ships of the line and more than one hundred supporting vessels. We've got three.*"

Ice stood and stretched, forepaws extended, back arched in a negative curve, butt in the air, a large yawn cracked her jaws. She stretched in the opposite direction with hind legs extended back. Trotting over to Lauren's desk, Ice put her paws on the edge of Lauren's desk. She studied the hologram and then pointed with her muzzle. *"That is the battle fought following the murder of the Terra Prime governmental representatives at an interstellar conference on the environmental hazards of deep space travel. Alex and the boys studied this in school."* Ice gazed into the hologram and then motioned again with her muzzle. *"Terra Prime had numerous ships engaged in this conflict but watch what happens when you remove all the clutter."*

"Clutter?"

Snow joined them moving around to sit beside Lauren, leaning her chin on the edge of the desk as she watched the hologram. *"Yes, take out all the support vessels and all the smaller consorts, leaving just the sixteen ships of the line."*

Lauren manipulated the dataset, the hologram fuzzed out and then re-coalesced with only the five Terran ships and eleven enemy vessels. *"Now, see how the Terran vessels are spread out in a shell around the enemy who are clustered together in the center?"* Ice looked at her and when Lauren nodded, the wolf continued. *"The Terran ships enter the area of engagement from various vectors, slashing past the enemy to the opposite side of the shell, then turn and recross."* Lauren watched the five tiny dots slice across the cluster of enemy over and over. The ships flew an arcing path through the enemy. As the Terran ships exited the center cluster of enemy ships, they emerged on the outer shell at a different point. As the number of passes built, more of the outer shell was covered by a flight path from one of the Terran ships.

Lauren laughed. "It's like a spirograph drawing."

Snow frowned, her furry eyebrows drooping. *"I have never heard of a scientific instrument called that."*

Lauren continued to watch the battle unfold. *"A spirograph is a child's geometric drawing toy. You insert a pencil into a cog fitted in a larger fixed toothed ring. Like sets of gears, one inside the other. When you move the inner cog around the inside of the outer ring, your pencil traces mathematical roulette curves. They draw paths like these."* She pointed at the elliptical flight paths enclosing the enemy in a solid shell of fire. *"Only here the flight paths are scribed in three dimensions instead of two. I had one as a kid. It was one of my favorite toys of all time."*

"Also, notice this Lauren." Ice whiffled at the filling hologram, drawing them back to the point of this lesson. *"With each pass, the Terrans focused their fire on only one vessel. This reduced the battle from five-on-eleven to five-on-one. They never stopped within the enemy cluster. Their constant*

movement made targeting difficult for the enemy." Lauren knew the Terran's were outgunned, outclassed, and outmanned in this engagement. But as the scenario progressed, the enemy vessels winked out one after another.

"*Interesting.*" Lauren watched the battle, mesmerized.

"*Another important point is the flight path trajectories.*" Snow interjected. "*Using arcing paths, the five Terran vessels cover the entire volume of the sphere with weapons fire in less than fifteen passes.*" Lauren reset the holographic scenario to replay at half speed, adding a different colored trace to each Terran ship's flight path. She allowed the scenario to begin again, stopping it after each pass of the five vessels. Lauren replayed it again, this time highlighting the weapon traces in a different color from the flight paths. After this replay was complete, she froze the hologram.

Snow touched Lauren's forearm with her nose. "*Now you can see how the entire volume of space was filled with weapon fire and the entire outer shell was defined by the arcing Terran flight paths. This maneuver conserves ammunition and allows for maximum maneuverability. When you add back the support vessels, you will see how the Terrans chose their flight paths to use these vessels as shields against the enemy's return fire. Eventually the enemy fired at random, chasing the Terran ships, not caring if they hit their own consorts or not.*"

"Unbelievable." She hugged Snow tightly. "*You two are the absolute best companions I could ever ask for.*"

"*We know.*" Came their dual response. Lauren didn't miss the smug looks on their faces.

Lauren chuckled softly. "*Of course, you do.*" She hugged Snow again. "*But how do you know all this?*"

The wolves looked at each other and cocked their heads, silently communicating. "*This is one of only a few historical engagement scenarios which Alex failed in school.*"

"*Repeatedly,*" Snow added with a huff.

Lauren sat back flabbergasted. "*Alex failed at something? That's just . . . kinda unbelievable.*"

Ice whiffled. "*She never got the geometry correct. Always too focused on disabling as many ships as she could, as quickly as she could. Blasting her way through the enemy with no regard to strategy.*"

Snow swept her tail across the deck in frustration. "*She always had a difficult time separating strategy from tactic. She got caught up in the minutiae of the situation and would lose track of the larger picture. A good commander must always keep the big picture in their mind.*"

Lauren shook her head. *"I've a hard time believing that. She is always so focused on Terra. You know, her needs are always outweighed by the needs of the populace."*

"That may be true now, but when she was in school, it was always about how big an explosion she could create. Be it in the lab or the simulators or her flight classes. It was not until Terra Prime was attacked, she realized how life hangs by a thread and the big picture is paramount to tactics."

Ice's growl rumbled in her chest. *"This trait of hers was why the Council struggled making her queen when her grand'mere and her mother were killed on Terra Prime. Councilors did not believe she was mature enough or patient enough to lead Terra. They worried she would want to blast her way through a situation without regard for the consequences."*

"Well, I don't think we need to worry about that now." Lauren bit her lip and looked at her pad. *"Now we need to worry about my ability to lead. And I need to complete reviewing these other thirty scenarios before we reach the galactic center."*

"Lion and *Kestrel* are peeling off, ma'am. They will take up station-keeping one million kilometers out from our entry point."

Lauren couldn't see the two ships veer away, but she could feel them do so. Her bond with Tavish and Angus diminished as the ships moved further away from the *Stag.* "Very well, let's do this. Just as we practiced, set a forty degree up angle and prepare to enter the gravity well." Lauren spun her command chair around and faced Ailsa at her communication console. "Please send a quantum message to Robert on the *Boar.* Let him know we're going in."

"Aye, ma'am." Ailsa turned to her analyzer. She tipped her head to the side, listening. "Receiving a message from *Lion.* Commander MacDonald says good luck and see you on the other side."

Lauren smiled. "Send a return, same to you, MacD. And a copy to Angus as well please."

The *Stag* leapt forward as she increased her speed. Lauren watched the inclination to the stars in front of the ship change as her bow angle increased. This was all so strange. They were entering the unknown but there was nothing to see outside the forward transparency, no indication where the gravity well began, or that the event horizon lay just in front of them. *How can something so massive be invisible?*

Then she saw it. Well, not the gravity well but the Doppler effect it caused. The distant white and blue stars suddenly turned red and seemed to skip across the transparency window into new positions. Lauren understood the effect—light from these far-off stars slowed down at the edge of the event horizon, causing their color to change as their light bent following the curvature of the gravity well. Just like the sound of a train whistle changes pitch as the train leaves the station and its distance increases from the listener on the platform. The same thing happened to the wavelengths of starlight. Even though she understood the physics, it didn't decrease her fears. Sweat trickled down her spine and she gripped the armrests of her crash couch.

A ripple ran through the *Stag's* hull and Lauren glanced around the bridge. "Everything, okay?"

"All systems nominal," the engineering tech stated. "All departments report stable."

Lauren tightened her grip on the armrests of her command chair, her gauntlet-covered fingertips sinking deeper into the soft brown leather. Snow and Ice rose from their position at the edge of the command dais and sat on either side of her, sharing their calm and strength. Everyone had dressed in their evac-suits with a skin layer of energy armor beneath, including the two wolves. Lauren placed a hand on each of their armored shoulders, wishing she could sink her fingers into their warm fur.

"We are accelerating, gravitational pull toward the black hole's event horizon increasing. We are bucking a large lateral drift," Byron, the *Stag's* pilot, said from his position forward of Lauren's command chair.

Her astrogator Ronan reported, "I am losing lock on course heading. Drift increasing to fifteen degrees below horizon."

"Correcting course. Increasing power to the starboard engines. Coming back on heading, ten degrees . . . five degrees . . . on course. Attitude at forty degrees up angle," Byron said.

Everything quieted, as the *Stag* continued on her course. Lauren exhaled sharply. She tried to relax but her muscles were stiff and sluggish. She rubbed her hands down her thighs and rolled her head from side to side to release her neck muscles. The wolves sat regally beside her, watching the bridge crew with intent gazes, as they took in all the activities swirling around them. They appeared non-plussed, but Lauren could feel their tension through her bond. *Wish I could be so calm.*

"It just takes practice. Why do you think Alex always sits sideways in her command chair? No one can see her clenched fist where she hides it behind her legs." Snow leaned into Lauren's chair and smiled up at her, all her teeth exposed in a wolfy grin.

"I should've thought of that."

"Engineering reports the internal temperature of the starboard containment vessel is increasing. Four hundred degrees to red-line." Ailsa's voice rose half an octave higher than her normal dulcet tone.

Lauren sucked in her bottom lip. "How much farther until our exit point?"

Ronan looked up from his holographic plot of their course. "Difficult to say. We entered the gravity well sixty-four minutes ago, but we are unable to plot our exact position due to the Doppler shift on the stars we use to triangulate our course."

"Our best transit time estimate before we entered the well was three and a half hours at current speed," Lauren replied.

"We experienced a significant acceleration as we entered the well due to gravitational slingshot. I estimate we are traveling at one point six times our previous speed," Byron stated, never looking up from his course plot, hands dancing over his gel pads.

"Engineering reports the sails are overcharging, radiant energy sinks are at capacity. Preparing to shunt excess energy into the hull," Ailsa interjected.

Byron said, his voice strained, "Lateral pull increasing. We are sliding below course angle again. Attempting to adjust."

Lauren sat bolt upright in her chair. *Damn, what do I do?*

"Take the problems one at a time. Prioritize them. Figure out what is needed, act, and then move on to the next one." Ice's calm voice settled her racing heart a fraction. She exhaled and tried to take in all the information being thrown at her. Her granddaddy's whispers joined Ice's. *'Calm down. You can't think if you are in a panic. This is just like sailing in a summer squall, Lauren.'* She settled back in her chair, mind racing through the possibilities.

"Furl the sails. Increase bow angle to fifty degrees. Maximum power to the gravitational generators. Cut thrusters. Drain all the radiant energy to the containment vessels, prepare to shunt the stored energy to the engines."

"Ma'am?" the engineering tech questioned. "The engines cannot take a sudden blast of energy like that." Lauren knew there were safety limits built into the engines.

"Now!" Lauren's voice cut through the bridge like a knife and her command presence as a trauma surgeon surged to the fore. A cool calm replaced her panic as she worked through the problems her *Stag* faced. She stood and stepped to the edge of the dais. Standing, she could feel the gravitational effects of the supermassive black hole. It pulled her in all directions at once. She felt squeezed and stretched, pulled and pushed, deformed every which way. Lauren was small compared to the large cross-sectional area of the *Stag*. *If I feel like this, what's my ship feeling? We could be torn apart.*

"Deploy shock harnesses. Prepare to engage gravitational engines on my mark." Their original plan was to use thrusters only and not utilize the gravitational engines. They were worried the release of gravitational energy from the engines would create destructive interference with the gravitational forces generated by the black hole. Lauren took a step off the dais and stumbled. She fell, but caught herself on the step, slamming her knees into the deck. Gravitational forces increased as the *Stag* fought her way up against the lateral forces trying to draw her deeper into the gravity well down toward the event horizon of the supermassive black hole.

"Sails are furled and reefed. Starboard sails jammed within the stay. Emergency lashes in place, aerodynamics of the hull nominal." Ailsa gave the sailing master's report, voice tense.

Lauren dragged herself to the astrogation table to look at the hologram. She grabbed the edge of the projection table and pulled herself up. Turning to the Byron, she said, "Let me know the second our inclination reaches fifty degrees."

"Fifty degrees, aye," the pilot acknowledged.

Out of the corner of her eye, she saw the wolves struggling to stay upright against the gravitational forces tearing through the bridge. "Ice, Snow! Get in the command chairs and deploy your harnesses."

"*But, Lauren,*" Snow protested. She knew two couldn't share a harness and if the wolves used them, she wouldn't have one.

"Do it. I'm good." The wolves dragged themselves into the two chairs and with their paws, hit the emergency deploy buttons on the armrest consoles. White webbing extended from the back of the chairs and snugged them down into the chairs. Ice yelped.

Someone grabbed Lauren around the waist, and she started. "Majesty, let me fasten this closure," Ronan said through gritted teeth as he fought to get a harness around her.

"You first. I need you to tell me when our heading is aligned with our exit point." Lauren and her astrogator were the only ones left standing.

"No," Ronan argued, struggling to get a harness around Lauren.

The *Stag* slewed sideways, and the deck heaved, knocking the astrogator off balance, slamming him into the astrogation table. Before he hit the floor, Lauren grabbed the young man by the neck ring of his evac-suit. She hauled him upright and smashed the emergency harness release in the edge of the table. The webbing deployed and encircled the astrogator, she let go of him. He slumped in the harness, unconscious. The deck pitched in the opposite direction, slamming Lauren into the table's edge. Pain blossomed in her side, tearing muscle already strained from sparring. Her body screamed in protest, but she grabbed the table edge and held tight, then her feet came out from underneath her.

"Gravity systems offline," the bridge artificial intelligence reported.

Her body flew out parallel to the deck, but she continued to watch the holo-projection. *"Come on, come on."* The numbers on the inclinometer crept towards fifty degrees. The *Stag* groaned.

"Gravitational shear increasing. We are at eighty-five per cent hull integrity and dropping," the engineering tech yelled over the sound of metal warping.

Lauren tapped a display function, an image of the *Stag* appeared beside the navigational hologram. Yellow and red strips ran along her length. The ship was being torqued about her longitudinal axis as the gravitational forces rolled along her hull. *She'll be a corkscrew if this continues much longer.*

Ailsa's soprano cut through the cacophony. "Hull breaches on decks forty-three to forty-seven. Force fields in place, no reported causalities." She put her hand over her earbud. "Deck forty-four is open to space between maintenance shaft four and fourteen. Internal structural integrity compromised. The environmental AI has shut down elevators. Repair crews are utilizing the sub-deck above deck forty-four to make repairs."

Lauren got her feet under her and deployed a crash harness around her torso. The webbing snugged and held her against the astrogation table. Looking at the command deck, she saw the wolves safely seated. "Can anyone make it to the command chairs and get helmets on Ice and Snow?"

The auxiliary control tech, seated nearest the dais on the port side of the bridge, released his harness. "I got it." He inched his way across the heaving deck to the wolves, placing first Snow's and then Ice's helmet in place. "All sealed, Majesty." He grabbed the armrest on the port side command chair as the deck rolled again. "You need yours, ma'am."

"Get back in your couch." She was focused on the bow angle as they continued to climb—forty-eight degrees up angle.

"But, ma'am—"

"I said sit down!"

Byron's voice cut in. "I am unable to hold this attitude. The lateral stabilizers are unresponsive. We have lost rudder control, yaw increasing.

We will enter a longitudinal flat spin if we continue." The clinometer read forty-nine point five degrees.

Lauren had to chance it. *Now or never.* "Now, Byron. Full power to the gravitational engines." The pilot shunted all the energy stored in the overcharged containment vessels to the gravitational generators.

Lauren could feel the *Stag* gather herself, just as Ffrwyn did before a fence. The great clan ship shot forward. G-forces increased on the bridge. Inertial dampeners failed with the sudden increase in forward velocity. The crew groaned, fighting against black out. Lauren did the same, struggling to turn her head. *I gotta see the stars out the forward transparency.* If they shifted back to blue, they had escaped the gravity well. Darkness overwhelmed her vision.

Chapter Four
Aboard the Dubh Mogairle, Deck Sixty

Alex jerked awake. "What?" Her bond was gone. She struggled out of her blankets and lashed out mentally, trying to locate it, but she could not find it. *Oh gods, what has happened?*

"Majesty, are you all right?" a groggy voice asked from within Sarah's tumble of blankets.

"I . . ." Alex stopped and shook her head to clear the cobwebs. "I do not know." Her shoulders slumped and she rubbed her temple. "I can no longer feel Lauren. It is like someone cut the filament connecting us." She sank back against the bulkhead.

Sarah rose from her nest of blankets and crouched in front of Alex, placing a hand on her knee. "What can I do?"

Alex looked up into concerned green eyes. Flecks of gold sparkled in the low light and Alex felt a sense of calm pass through her. *Kinda like Lauren's eyes, but not as rich an emerald and gold not blue flecks. Not Lauren at all.* "Nothing but thank you. I will continue to try and reconnect." Her command training kicked in, walling off her soul. "We will need to gather more supplies, ascertain the status of the ship, figure out a way to monitor crew movements, keep watch on the admiral, and gain access to the armory."

"Is that all?" Sarah chuckled. "Might as well throw communications onto that list, just to round it out."

In spite of herself, Alex laughed. "That would be good addition." She moved over to the stretcher. The admiral appeared to be resting comfortably, snoring softly in his nests of blankets. "Do we dare wake him?" She looked at Sarah, who was pulling a diagnostic pad out of the medical pouch.

"We will know in a moment." Sarah moved the pad over his body and sat back waiting for the data analysis to finish.

Shock rippled through Alex. "Where did you get that?" She pointed at the medical device in Sarah's hand.

"Lifted it from the medical bay. I am sure they will miss it eventually, though I am more concerned the nurse I spoke to will initiate a search for the two mystery crew men who disappeared from bay eleven."

"Patient in deep REM sleep. No further deterioration of cognitive state noted. Bleeding halted in medial circumflex femoral artery. Hip joint shows mild accumulation of fluids. Iliofemoral ligament remains detached from greater trochanter," the diagnostic pad droned.

Sarah brow furrowed. "Recommendations?"

"Nutrition, hydration, and rest recommended. Current levels of pain medications should be reduced or discontinued. A lower dose medica-tion substituted. Muscle relaxants continued."

"Alrighty, then." Sarah smiled at Alex. "We have an updated prognosis and a treatment plan. I suggest we continue."

Alex laughed. Sarah's head jerked up. "What is so funny, Majesty?"

"First off, it is Alex, not Majesty. If you call me that in front of a Comin crew member we would be found. And secondly, you sound like Lauren, 'alrighty, then' is one of her favorite phrases."

Blushing to the roots of her red hair, Sarah hung her head. "The admiral uses this phrase now as well. I seem to have absorbed it from him."

"Be that as it may, I think we should do as the med pad suggests and lessen his pain medications. This should allow him to wake naturally."

"Agreed, Majes—sorry, Alex."

Several days passed with the two doing limited reconnaissance forays. Alex knew eventually they would need to access more of the ship. The admiral remained unconscious despite the reduced pain medications and Alex was worried about the severity of his head injury.

Sarah left their tiny storage area over nine hours ago. Alex sent the young pilot out looking for supplies—food, water, supplements to the admiral's medical needs, and more importantly, information. They agreed Sarah had a better chance of not being recognized. So, wearing the purloined evac-suit with its *Black Orchid* insignia, Sarah had headed out.

Alex paced the small space, ten steps one way, turn, ten back. She still could not feel Lauren. Their bond remained painfully absent. Something had happened, something bad. Not knowing what was going on was driving Alex to distraction. Lauren could very well be dead, but Alex believed she would know if that happened. Her heart and soul ached with each breath, but she needed to ignore her pain and focus on getting them off the *Orchid*. Or, better yet, take over the ship.

Alex chuckled as she replayed the admiral and his pilot's adventure in her mind. *Good gods, how could they survive such a feat?* And then cross the hull of a clan while she was flying at faster-than-light pulse speeds was unimaginable. Yet they had, mostly whole, and ready to carry on the fight.

Once the admiral woke, they would formulate a plan for taking the ship or escaping.

A scraping noise sounded. Alex grabbed a laser torch and flicked it on. Its quiet hum sounded loud in their small storage bay. She stepped up to the right of the locker hatch and flattened herself against the bulkhead. If it was maintenance crew, she hoped they would continue past. Sarah had taken great care ensuring no light escaped from their tiny space, ensuring they would go undetected. Now her diligence would be tested. *Damn, the crew is not passing.* They stopped and Alex heard someone step into the bubble-space outside the locker. Seconds later, the locker latch released and the hatch swung outward.

Heart pounding, Alex tensed. She crouched, torch at the ready. Just as a head poked around the corner of the hatch, she chopped her arm down, flicking her torch to full power. A flash of red halted her attack and she dropped the torch to the deck plating.

"Whoa, sorry to scare you." Sarah's smile belied the fear written in her eyes.

"It is all right." Alex gasped for air, as her heart raced uncontrollably. "I was concerned when the noise I heard from the sub-deck stopped, worried a maintenance crew member was going to access one of these lockers." Alex panted out and gave the young pilot an apologetic grin. "Was your scavenger hunt successful?"

"Aye." Sarah pulled a large data pad from the leg pocket of her evac-suit and handed it to Alex. "This should provide the much-needed information on the ship's status, as well as other critical data about her crew."

While Alex thumbed on the pad, Sarah shrugged out of the large rucksack she had slung over her shoulders. "I was able to access the central analyzer cores."

Alex grunted and then glared at her. "And just how did you accomplish that without leaving an entry-trace?"

Sarah looked down at the deck, scrapping the toe of her boot across the decking. "The same way I overrode the medical protocols to procure the pain medications for the admiral without a doctor's authorization." She looked up sheepishly.

Alex stared at Sarah. The only way to countermand a ship's authorization protocols was to use a command authorization code override and to her knowledge there were only five in existence. This young pilot would not possess such a code. "And that would be?"

Sarah scraped the toe of her boot across the deck again as she seemed to make a decision. She snapped to attention and looked at a spot on the bulkhead above Alex's left shoulder. "By using the admiral's command code, ma'am. I realize this action is a court-martial offense and I will submit myself to the review board upon our return to Luna."

"I see." Alex rubbed her chin, though her gut clenched in warning. *Oh gods, is this woman a spy? Aligned with Cador? I must get to the bottom of this.* "Pilot, how did you come to know his command code?" If this young woman had stolen the code, Alex would put her in confinement now, regardless of how much she needed her skills going forward.

"I heard him embed his code within the communication beacon we released from the flitter." Sarah stiffened. "I used that code to get him medical care and again this hour to access the *Orchid's* analyzer cores. The admiral told me a command authorization code can be used to enter the cores, access information, download files, and exit without leaving a digital fingerprint."

Alex hummed in agreement, as she watched the pilot's face for any sign of deception. "So, you did not have the admiral's permission to use his code."

"No, ma'am. I did not."

"What else do you know about command codes?" Alex had to determine if this young woman was a Cador ally. A spy would know all about command codes and would attempt to mislead her about that knowledge.

"Other than the override capabilities, nothing. The admiral used it to authenticate his identity in the message he left within the beacon. He knew it was the only way to ensure whoever picked up the beacon would know he had left the message. He was concerned the beacon's message would be seen as a trap." Sarah cringed. "Especially, given the outlandish flight path we took to get onto the hull of the *Orchid*."

"Take a seat, pilot." Alex waved at one of the blanket rolls and stood over the young woman as she seated herself. She frowned and watched Sarah shrink away from her imposing figure. *Am I being set up here? Did she injure the admiral intentionally?* "I do not know what to do with you. Using a command code is bad enough but doing so without permission of your commanding officer could be considered treason."

"I understand and I am sure you think I am a spy, left to gather data for Cador and her treacherous allies."

Alex made a snap decision. "From now on, I do not want you out of my sight. I do not trust you, Sarah Cameron."

"Aye, ma'am." The young pilot hung her head.

A graveled voice cut through their confrontation. "And just how are you planning on doing that, Majesty? You must sleep sometime."

Alex spun on her heel and gawked at the now-conscious admiral. "You are awake."

He tried to push himself up but failed, gasping in pain he collapsed back into the stretcher.

"So, it would seem. And I awaken to find you harassing my pilot. I do not know what she did to earn your wrath, but I would appreciate her left in one piece when you are done." He coughed and sank deeper into his stretcher. "She is why we are alive, and whole. Or mostly whole."

Alex arched her eyebrow. *Seems McLeod thinks highly of her, has he been fooled, too?*

Sarah stood and pushed her way around Alex. "Admiral, how are you feeling? Do you need more pain medication, muscle relaxants, water?" Her concern trailed off in a whisper.

He placed a gentle hand on Sarah's forearm. "I am fine, but I do need a status report. Especially now. I do not know how you managed to find Alex and drag her along on our adventure, but I am sure it is a good tale." He tried to laugh but it morphed into coughing fit.

Sarah grabbed a water sipper and returned to the stretcher. "Here, try this." She held the drinking nozzle out to him. "It will ease your dry throat." While the admiral drank, Sarah fluffed blankets and pillows fussing over the man to get him comfortable as possible.

Alex stood in silence as the young pilot busied herself getting the admiral sorted. Her nervous tension eased a bit as she watched their interaction. Sarah rummaged through their food stores until she found a ration of soup. She pulled the tab and activated the internal heating mechanism. "This will be ready in a minute, sir. But really, how are you feeling?"

With a final slurp from the water nozzle, the admiral exhaled. "Better than before. I do not know what you did, but I am sure I dislocated my hip and I think I banged my head on the ventilation grid."

"Aye, you did." When he looked at her in confusion, Alex noticed the care and concern Sarah expressed for the older man. "Both, I mean."

"Both?"

Sarah blushed. "Dislocated your hip and hit your head." The admiral rubbed his head, but Sarah stopped him. "Easy, sir. You have a laceration there and I do not know how well the plastiseal will hold if you rub it."

The admiral looked up at Alex. "Has she told you how she got us onto the hull of the *Orchid*?"

"Quite a tale." The admiral smirked, and Alex mirrored his expression. "Had you not been along to corroborate, I am not sure I would have believed her. Here you are and thus, the tale must be true."

"It will be one for our Lady of the Ancients histories." The admiral settled back with a sigh as Sarah handed him the soup ration and a spoon. "I lived through it and I still find it hard to believe. It was quite a ride." He sipped the steaming soup and frowned. His next words were clipped. "But that does not explain why you are harassing my pilot, Majesty."

"Well—" Before Alex could continue Sarah interrupted her.

"Sir, I have committed a court-martial offense and at this time I turn myself over to my commanding officer." Sarah came to attention.

"Oh, sit down, Sarah." He waved the pilot back down. "I will get a crick in my neck if I have to continue to look up at you." He turned to Alex. "Just what have you done now?"

The admiral's voice held the whip-crack edge of command, and Alex felt like a flight cadet being called out for an error in the simulators. Her gut clinched and she straightened, looking forward. Then she realized what he was doing, a command maneuver to deflect her from the topic at hand. "She used your command code." Alex frowned over at the pilot. "Without your permission."

The admiral recoiled slightly at the gravity of Alex's words and looked over at his pilot, eyebrow arched. "Well?"

Sarah cleared her throat. "Her Majesty is correct. On two occasions, I used your command code."

He looked at Alex and raised the eyebrow higher, asking her to explain so she did. "Your code was used in the medical bay, and then just an hour or so ago to gain access to the *Orchid's* cores."

"And you feel these events are grounds for court-martial?"

His question stunned Alex. *Of course, it is. Why would it not be?* With his code she could have taken over the ship's analyzer cores, evacuated the breathable atmosphere from any deck or throughout the entire ship, zero'd gravity, overloaded the containment vessels. Alex's imagination ran wild from one scenario to another, all of which would end in disaster.

"How could it not be?" She gaped at him.

The admiral tried to pull himself into a sitting position, hissing against the pain but getting farther than his last attempt. Sarah moved to help, but he waved her away. "If I remember my code of military conduct, an officer in a position of command has license to utilize any and all means at her disposal to protect her comrades and thwart the enemy."

Sarah and Alex spoke at once. "Well—" "But, sir—"

"Enough." His voice cracked off the bulkheads of their small hiding place. "In my estimation, Sarah was in command." He looked at Alex. She nodded. "Second, she was attempting to gain access to medical care for an injured comrade." Alex nodded again. "And lastly, did you not order her to gather any and all information she could about the status of this ship?" Alex harrumphed. "Then in no instance did she commit a court-martial offense. The way I see it, she was doing what was needed to keep us alive and find a way forward." He frowned at Alex. "Agreed?"

"But, Lord McLeod." *How can he dismiss the possibility she could be a spy so out of hand?*

Admiral McLeod rolled his eyes. "Oh, now you pull out the titles. Put a sock in it, Alex. What do you think; she is a spy or something?" Alex did not answer. The admiral's cheeks flushed red and he glowered up at Alex. "You do. You think she is a spy."

Alex did not know what to say in response. She did think it was probable. *I do not know how deeply the Cador treason goes. And she is here, she knew how advantageous this would be for Cador. Does the admiral really believe he hurt himself?* Her gut tightened.

"Well, this is just great. If I were this young woman, I would call you out. Queen or no queen." He folded his arms across his chest and refused to look at Alex.

"Sir, I can understand Her Majesty's point. I did use your command code without permission. Knowing the code, if I were a spy, I could easily do tremendous damage to this ship or any other." Sarah swallowed hard. "And, I would not even need to be aboard."

"That is all well and good, but you are not a spy and Her Majesty is wrong in accusing you of such treason." He gripped his blankets with white knuckles. Pain evident in his drawn face. "However, she is not wrong in analyzing the possibility of you being a spy. She must be prepared for all contingencies. This being but one of many. However, this possibility is low on our list of priorities, given our current situation. This matter is closed." Both women nodded.

Well, not for me. I will keep an eye on her.

Over the course of the next half day, Sarah and Alex began executing the plan the three designed to sabotage and take over the *Orchid*. The information gathered from Sarah's foray into the ship's analyzer cores gave them a wealth of information—course, heading, velocity, flight plan, ship's status, damage reports, and surprisingly, the most interesting piece of information—ship's complement. The *Orchid* ran with only twenty-five percent of its normal ship's company. The odds for their group were now three to one thousand versus three to four thousand. This minimal crew number meant whole sections of the ship, those deemed non-vital to ship operations, were unmanned. Entire decks were vacant. The limited crew was concentrated near the bridge and within the engineering sections.

Alex had wondered how Sarah so easily penetrated the analyzer cores, the admiral's code notwithstanding. Now they knew; no one was on deck fifty-three. She had easily slipped into one of the geo-technical survey laboratories to access the analyzers there. Now it was Alex's turn to complete a scouting mission and determine if they could access the armory to recover weapons. Climbing up the access ladder within a maintenance shaft, she was headed to deck forty-two. Maybe while on that deck, she could also slip into the medical bay and gather some more supplies.

The admiral was healing well. The tissue generators embedded in the stretcher worked overtime on his hip, trying to repair the various ligaments. The diagnostic medical pad recommended he not try to stand or walk until this was completed; therefore, he was confined to the stretcher. He was not happy, but it allowed him time to catalogue supplies and develop plans of action for the trio.

Pausing to catch her breath just below deck forty-five, Alex looped one arm around the ladder stay and reached around her waist for her water sipper. She was just taking a drink when her bond sprang to life. Her connection with Lauren had been absent for more than three days and she had become inured to the silence.

Now the connection slammed into her psyche at full strength. Her vision fuzzed out, leaving her dizzy and gasping for breath. *Lauren's alive!* Overwhelmed, she lost hold of her water sipper and the ladder. She teetered backwards, desperately trying to grab the ladder, hands flailing. She missed. Her foot slipped off the rung. Alex fell back into the empty shaft. Then, her safety harness caught and arrested her fall. Once it pulled taut, she swung back toward the ladder and slammed into the shaft wall. Pain exploded through her body. Stunned, she dangled limp, swinging gently back and forth like a pendulum. Her water sipper disappeared down the shaft.

Thank the gods, the admiral demanded we use a safety tether. The tether was anchored to a makeshift harness Sarah and Alex had devised to aid Sarah climbing the long ladders with her injured shoulder. A fall for her was a real possibility. Alex had refused to take the harness and tether until the admiral ordered her to use all safety equipment. He argued there were only three of them and they could not afford another major injury or worse.

Slowly, Alex got her breath back. Panic gripped her heart as the possible outcome of her fall set in. *This could have been disastrous.* She hung several meters below deck forty-six. Her injuries seemed mild. She would be bruised where the harness pulled against her torso, but after several deep breaths she realized none of her ribs were broken. The harness cut into her groin and tingles ran up and down her legs. A simple swing and she grabbed the ladder stay and swung her feet onto the nearest rung. She hugged the ladder and tried to calm her racing heart.

Closing her eyes, Alex reached out along her bond to Lauren. She was there, but Alex could not establish an active communication link with her. Something still blocked them. Alex withdrew from their bond, leaving only the nanofilament connection. Joy filled her being. Lauren was alive and soon she hoped she would be able to converse with her.

Alex gasped. *What if I had poured more power into our bond? I would light up like a beacon on a dark night. Gwenhwyfach could easily find me.* This spurred another thought. *Why has she not found me? The bitch should have realized I am missing.* It had been almost four weeks since she escaped her box, and she had moved with relative freedom about the ship. She could sense Cador lurking at the edges of her psyche, yet she could not sense any active psi-search. *Why? What is going on? Has something happened to the woman?*

Alex hung from the ladder stays, lost in thought, trying to answer her own questions. Nothing recovered from the analyzer cores indicated anything about her captor. When she got back to their locker, she would try and determine the reason for Gwenhwyfach's silence. The hair on the back of her neck rose as she realized the danger she created for the other two. *I could lead her right to them.*

Shaking her head, Alex continued the long climb. Time was of the essence. They needed a plan and then Alex would need to figure out how to psychically hide. She would not endanger her companions if she could not effectively conceal herself from psi-search. She would isolate herself instead. *Nothing can stop their plan. We must capture the* Orchid.

An update on Lauren's activities would greatly improve their developing plans, but Alex would need to figure out how to fully activate their bond without alerting Gwenhwyfach. She had done it before and if she could figure out how, she would do it again. Then, she could get a message to Lauren. If her small band knew what was going on outside the ship, they could coordinate their actions.

Chapter Five
Aboard the Ruadh làn-damh
Nearing the Sagittarius Arm, Across the Galactic Center

Blaring sounds penetrated Lauren's consciousness. Her brain was sluggish; nothing made sense. *Where am I? God, my head.* Everything hurt. *I thought sparring hurt, but this takes the cake.* She groaned and forced her eyes open—the *Stag*. The bridge was dark. Warning lights flashed spasmodically on monitors all around her. She was slumped under a table, tangled in a mess of white webbing. Someone lay beside her. Blood streamed from a gash on his forehead.

Rising to her hands and knees, she pushed against the confining webbing. Shucking it off her shoulders, Lauren crawled over to the crewman next to her. Her astrogator, Ronan. She palpated his neck, feeling a strong carotid pulse. *Just hit his head. I'll check on his injuries when I get myself untangled.* Looking around, her crew was unconscious, slumped against their crash restraints. The wolves were sprawled in the two command chairs. "*Ice? Snow? You okay?*" She didn't get an answer.

Gotta get to the command chair, determine our position, get control of the Stag. The holo-tank within the astrogation table next to her was empty. Lauren tried hitting the harness release embedded in the edge of the table, but she couldn't quite reach. She pulled her legs under her and half stood, pushing away the restraining webbing tangled around her limbs, she slammed the release. The webbing fell away. Now she was able to stand, but her legs wobbled. The room spun around her and Lauren gripped the edge of the table. Closing her eyes, she tried to stop her visual disorientation. *Deep, slow breaths, Lauren.* That did seem to help so she slowly reopened her eyes. Stepping from the pile of tangled webbing, Lauren hit the second release and untangled Ronan.

Nausea rose in her throat, but she needed to get to her command chair. Gritting her teeth, she set one foot in front of the other and made it to the edge of the dais. As Lauren stepped up to the command chairs, the deck heaved, and she collapsed. More klaxons sounded, these with a strident tone.

A mechanical voice rose out of the cacophony. "Containment vessel failure imminent. Containment vessel failure imminent. Auto-ejection sequence initiated. Fifteen minutes to auto-ejection."

"What the?" Lauren crawled to her chair. Ice lay sprawled at an odd angle, her forepaw caught in the restraint harness. Lauren checked the wolf's pulse, strong and regular. *Can't worry about her now.* She entered her command codes into the small console on the armrest. Data streamed across the tiny monitor. Lauren squinted at the tiny numbers.

Punching another control stub, she said, "Engineering, this is the Consort. What's your status?" Silence. She tried the medical bay, the flight deck, the marine barracks, and navigational control, finally the sailing master. No response. A groan from her left startled her.

Ailsa struggled against her harness. A trembling hand reached out, the white gauntlet was torn and stained by a bright red slash of blood. The young communication tech released her harness and tumbled from her chair, landing in a heap. "Must watch the first step, it is a whooper." Lauren chuckled at the tinny voice amplified on the bridge speakers.

"Are you hurt?" Lauren asked.

The tech shook her head and looked up at Lauren through a fogged face shield. She twisted off her gauntlets and released her helmet. With a groan, Ailsa pulled it off her head.

"I do not think so, Majesty." She grabbed the back of her chair and struggled to pull herself upright. "No, I do not seem to be injured beyond a few bumps and scrapes."

"We gotta find out where we are. The holo-tank is down on the astrogation table. Must have lost external sensors."

Ailsa turned back to her communication console and dropped her hand into one of the gel pads. "If I can raise the *Lion* or the *Kestrel*, they should be able to triangulate on our position." She spoke softly into her mic for a few moments.

"Any luck?" The tech shook her head. "Keep trying. Do whatever you can. Have you tried the quantum communication system? I need to figure out where we are and I've gotta stop the containment vessels auto-ejection sequence." Lauren snuggled into her command chair, pushing Snow's inert body to the side. She activated the analyzer pad. A hologram of the ship appeared. Numerous areas flashed yellow or red. One entire section along the starboard side below the lateral plane was solid red. She flipped through displays until she came to the detailed view of engineering, groaning when she saw, several sections flashing red.

"Holy crap." Lauren grimaced at the massive damage to her *Stag*. The damage Lauren realized, though bad, was localized to just a few decks. "Okay, we can work with this."

"Ailsa, I need voice communications to engineering."

"Would the engineering AI be adequate?" The young communication tech glanced at her.

"Anything that gets me connected down there. We gotta shut down the auto-ejection sequence. I can't bypass the emergency shutdowns to reach the crew through the network. Manual data entry is too slow. We've only got a few minutes left."

More klaxons sounded. The bridge filled with a deep red light.

The young tech's fingers danced across two gel pads. She barked over the cacophony of these new alarms. "I have the AI, Majesty."

"Engineering, I need a status report and a way to stop the auto-ejection sequence."

Static crackled over the open link. "Containment vessels at maximum temperature. Coolant system failure. Hull breaches on decks forty-three through forty-seven. Deck forty-four is exposed to space and at hard vacuum. Gravitational generators are offline on decks forty through forty-eight. Fuel connection to the fusion reactors open. Hydrogen supply tanks one, five, and six are ruptured. External sensors are down. Navigational AI is offline. Life support systems compromised along the starboard beam. Internal communication down. Auto-ejection of containment vessels ten minutes."

During their weeks of travel, Tavish had drilled Lauren on ship systems and procedures. To facilitate her learning, Lauren viewed the *Stag* as a living entity. She had a circulatory system, a respiratory system, a skeletal system, an integumentary system, and a neural network. The artificial intelligence systems—associated with each of the major ship systems—were the brains of her neural network. The AIs were all linked in parallel, one able to overlap with the other and provide additional computational power and functionality when needed. In this instance, the *Stag* had lost her circulatory systems—disruption of coolant fluids and communication—and her integumentary system or skin was compromised. The ship had lost access to external sensors and navigational data—she was blind, and a number of her AIs had been damaged, compromising her nervous system. *Think, Lauren, what does she need?*

"Engineering, I need you to override the coolant system AI, reroute fluids through the secondary or tertiary conduit systems, and send it to the containment vessels."

Another burst of static crackled across the bridge. "Unable to comply, secondary and tertiary systems compromised. Auto-ejection in seven minutes, thirty seconds."

Lauren's panic rose. *Come on, Lauren, you can do this. Think, damn it.* "Conduits are damaged. They need fluids to cool the containment vessels." She mumbled.

"Coolant tanks six through twelve on the port side undamaged," the engineering AI replied in a cool, mechanical voice. *It must have overheard my mumbling.*

Her trauma training kicked in. "Or on the vessels? Cool the vessels from the outside. Subcutaneous fluid replacement, that's it." Lauren stood. "Engineering, where are the undamaged coolant tanks located?"

"Coolant tanks are through-going between decks fifty and fifty-four, fore and aft of the central spur."

Lauren gritted her teeth. She didn't know how to get what she needed. She heard Tavish's voice. *"Just ask for what you need. You are not alone. Let the AIs run the ship."*

"Engineering, can you flood the reactor rooms with coolant directly from those storage tanks?"

"Release of coolant into an open environment creates a catastrophic danger to equipment and personnel."

"Evacuate the reactor rooms and flood the compartments," Lauren ordered.

There was a pause. *Is the AI going to countermand my authority?* "Command-level authorization required to override safety systems and comply with request."

More klaxons sounded and the red lights on the bridge began to strobe. "This is an order, do it!"

"Command-level authorization—"

Lauren cut the AI off. "Authorization, geodynamic-alpha-one-susan-sharon," she shouted.

"Command code received and authenticated. Coolant release in thirty seconds."

Warning lights began flashing on the engineering consoles—morphing from green to yellow to red. A voice command was heard on the open comm-link to engineering. "Emergency evacuation of all engineering decks. This is not a drill. Containment reactor rooms will flood in thirty seconds."

"Auto-ejection in two minutes, audible countdown will commence at one minute to ejection." The contralto voice of the *Stag's* bridge AI warned.

Alisa yelled over the blaring alarms. "Majesty, I have a quantum message from the *Kestrel.*"

"Well?" Lauren shouted.

Ailsa turned in her chair. "They wish to know where we are. We have been off their screens for three days."

"Three days? What?" Lauren was stunned.

The engineering AI spoke. "Coolant release complete in reactor rooms one through four. Containment vessel internal temperature decreasing."

"Auto-ejection in one minute," the bridge AI said. A countdown began. "Fifty-nine, fifty-eight, fifty-seven . . ."

Lauren shouted, "Engineering, abort auto-ejection sequence."

"Internal temperatures remain outside safety limits. Auto ejection will occur to prevent loss of containment."

God, what's wrong? Why won't the temperature fall? And then Lauren realized her mistake. "Engineering, emergency shutdown of all fuel to the reactors."

"Forty-two, forty-one, forty . . ."

"All reactor fuel shutdown. Fusion reactions ceased. Temperatures falling at an exponential rate within the containment vessels."

"Thirty-three, thirty-two, thirty-one . . ."

"Engineering, abort auto-ejection!"

The alarms silenced all at once, but the noise continued to ring in Lauren's ears. Flashing indicator lights still pulsed on consoles all around the bridge, but the audible countdown stopped.

"Auto-ejection successfully aborted at T-minus seventeen seconds. Coolant drainage beginning in reactor rooms one though four. Clean-up may commence in one hour. Engineering repair crews report to decks fifty through sixty," the engineering AI stated.

Lauren slumped forward, head hanging between her knees. She gasped for breath, sweat poured off her face and dripped onto the deck. Her limbs trembled uncontrollably as unneeded adrenalin overloaded her muscles before it drained away. She ran her hands over the deck. "Well done, *Stag*. Well done, ind—"

"Majesty, I have *Kestrel* and *Lion*."

Lauren smiled at the young tech. "Please let the boys know we are alive and ask them to send our location. Tell them once we've cleaned things up, I'll contact them with a full report."

"Aye, Majesty." Ailsa cleared her throat. "Permission to speak freely?" Lauren nodded. When Ailsa spoke, her voice was laced with awe. "That was unbelievable. I know there are numerous naysayers below deck who did not believe in you or your abilities. But I do not believe even Admiral McLeod could have done what you just did. You saved us."

Lauren chuckled, still shaken from their near-death experience. "He would have found a way. I don't know enough to know what I don't know. I just did what any trauma surgeon would have done with a critically ill patient. Stop the bleeding, replace fluids, and protect vital systems." Lauren stood and ran a hand over her damp hair. "Now we've gotta repair the damage I caused and the damage the black hole caused. And I need to see to the wolves."

Lauren moved over to Snow. She seemed to have fared better than Ice and stirred within her web enclosure. *"Are you okay, Snow? Can you hear Ice? I think she's hurt."*

Snow's blue eyes were dazed and unfocused, as the wolf turned toward Lauren. *"I seem to be fine, but I have a headache and I cannot move."*

"Let me get you out of the restraints. Hang on a sec." Lauren raised the console on the other command chair and deactivated its crash harness. The webbing retracted. Lauren removed the wolf's helmet and Snow rubbed her snout with a gauntlet-covered forepaw, and then blinked her eyes rapidly, sneezing twice.

The wolf stood slowly and hopped out of the chair onto the deck. She took a step over to Ice and bumped the seemingly unconscious wolf with her nose. *"Come on, I know you are awake."*

Ice grumbled and opened one eye. She peered at her mate through the face shield of her helmet. *"What happened?"* Ice rolled over but yowled in pain as she pulled on her forepaw. *"My paw is damaged."*

"You must've gotten it caught in the harness when it deployed. Let's get you untangled, and I'll see if I can find something to splint it." Together, Lauren and Snow managed to get Ice out of the webbing without inflicting too much pain. Next Lauren removed the injured wolf's helmet. She pulled a piece of console cover off the side of her chair. Grabbing her survival knife out of a pouch on the leg of her evac-suit, she sliced some of the harness webbing into strips.

"I would appreciate my damage being repaired, Lauren." Ice's voice was cool.

"I'm on it, Ice, hold your furry knickers on."

Ice huffed. *"I cannot hold my knickers on with a damaged paw, now can I?"* Snow snorted in amusement.

"I suppose not." Lauren bent to wrap the wolf's paw in the makeshift splint.

Over the next hours, the crew of the *Stag* assessed her damage and began repairs. No one could quite believe they were alive. Spontaneous hugs and cheers erupted when crew came across survivors trapped within the middle decks. Unbelievably, only three crew members were killed. Four more were missing and presumed dead. All had been on deck forty-four when the hull breach occurred. Emergency force fields were in place to close off deck forty-four from open space, but Lauren's soul tore with each successive casualty report. Overwhelmed, the medical bay commandeered the halls of deck forty-two for triaged patients waiting their turn. All Lauren wanted to do was add her skills to those of the med techs, but she couldn't leave the bridge. Her focus had to be on healing the *Stag*.

Of the twenty-four techs on the bridge when they entered the black hole's gravity well, twenty had been seriously injured and transported to the medical bay by their fellow crewmen. The internal elevators were still inoperable and anti-grav stretchers were being used to move patients down to deck forty-two. Lauren treated the other four bridge crew for minor injuries. After a quick meal, those four were now manning the bridge.

Lauren sat in her command cabin, as the wolves ate their dinner. The *Kestrel, Lion,* and *Boar* were aware of her status and position, and were waiting to complete a plan of action. Lauren was grateful for the admiral's quantum communication system and her ability to remain in contact with the other three. The *Boar* sent a light-speed communication back to Terra to let Merilyn know their status. To maintain contact with Terra, Robert had dropped a series of light-speed relay buoys in his wake.

For Lauren, the task at hand was to make sense of the triangulated navigational data the other two ships had sent. At first glance, it appeared the *Stag* had followed their plotted course, entered the gravity well on the Orion side of the galaxy, skirted the event horizon, traversed thirty percent of the distance around the supermassive blackhole, and exited on the Sagittarius side. They had traveled approximately thirty thousand light years.

That was all well and good, but the puzzling thing was the discrepancy in total travel time. According to the internal chronometers on the *Stag*, the total time spent transiting the gravity well was approximately four hours. Whereas, the *Kestrel* and *Lion* reported them lost from communications for almost three days. It took Lauren a bit to figure out what had happened. Then she had it, time dilation.

Time dilation at or near the event horizon affected the *Stag* while it was within the gravity well. According to Einstein's theory of special relativity, time dilation was the difference in elapsed time as measured by two observers, each in a different relative location from the gravity anomaly. Lauren knew this was a proven fact on Earth: clocks on the International Space Station moved slower than clocks at sea level on Earth, due to their different positions within Earth's gravity well. The flight records of the first Foremother's second ship also proved it true.

In this case, the *Stag* was one observer and the boys' ships the other. Lauren accepted time dilation, but dilation could be caused by two factors: a difference in relative velocities between the two observers or a difference in the position of each observer relative to a gravitational field. The *Stag* it seems was affected by both causes. One, she accelerated away from the two stationary ships at tremendous speeds as she entered the gravity well. And two, as she neared the supermassive black hole, she was subjected to the gravitational field created by the black hole. While the boys were out in normal space, far from any gravitational anomalies. Thus, the boys experienced the progression of normal time, while time was accelerated on the *Stag*. Three days compressed into mere hours. Time created another conundrum for Lauren.

Now the three had new problems: repair the *Stag*, figure out how the boys' ships could safely traverse the gravity well and minimize their damage, and not lose any significant time in their overall journey to beat the *Orchid* to the Comin nebula. Lauren rubbed her temples. She needed to prepare another message with an update on their repair status, but she was concerned about the boys. Tavish was ready to follow, danger be damned. Angus demanded a more cautious approach, using a longer flight path—one that wouldn't dip as far into the black hole's gravity well.

The frustrating thing was they were limited to their quantum communication system and a three-way discussion in real-time was impossible. She decided to wait another hour before sending her update to the boys. This would give the engineering techs more time to refine their repair estimates.

Lauren finished her meal of roast and veggies and compiled the list of damages to the *Stag*. Her heart bled for her ship and those lost. Yet they had survived and traversed more than two-thirds of the way to the Comin nebula in less than three days. Lauren chuckled. Three days or four hours. *Who would've thought this possible?* Now, with the *Stag* back in normal space, she decided chronometers on her ship would be re-synchronized to the time on the other ships. Lauren smiled and rubbed her forehead. *Kinda like crossing the International Date Line, when I flew across the Pacific Ocean.* That always caused a sense of time displacement when she traveled. *What would it feel like this time?* They missed three entire days.

A quiet knock interrupted her thoughts of how she met Susan and Sharon in Australia. "Come in."

The door slid open and Ailsa stepped in. Snow raised her head from her sheepskin pad in the corner, but Ice didn't move, the analgesic Lauren had given the wolf having kicked in. Currently, Ice was draped across the sofa in a furry sprawl, injured paw cradled across her chest.

"I have a message from the *Boar*, Majesty." The tech held out a communication pad as she stepped up to Lauren's desk.

"Did you finish your meal?" Lauren took the pad.

The tech nodded, her blond hair now neatly tied back in a long tail. "Yes, ma'am. We have all eaten and are waiting on our relief."

Lauren began to read the message. "Good. Please get as much rest as you can. I know we're at station-keeping while repairs are underway, but you need your rest. You're the only one with real duties on the bridge and I need you at full strength."

"If I may speak freely, ma'am?" At Lauren's nod, Ailsa said, "You, too." Lauren looked up from the pad and quirked an eyebrow. Ailsa blanched. "What I mean is, you are as tired as everyone else, and you are injured. You need your rest as well."

Lauren shook her head. "Well, according to all the reports I've read about our First Foremother, she never rested when she was immersed in a situation. Crew and ship come first." Ailsa frowned and Lauren tried hard to hide her smile. "I will take your suggestion under advisement."

"Very good, ma'am." Ailsa bobbed her head.

Lauren continued reviewing the *Boar's* message and hummed at the news. "Have Tavish and Robert received this as well?"

"Yes, I forwarded it on as soon as I had a decryption."

Lauren stood and grimaced as the muscles in her lower back cramped. Sitting had not been a good idea. "In that case, let the boys know I agree with Angus' new course. As soon as the *Kestrel* is ready have her enter the gravity well. Once the *Kestrel* arrives here and we ascertain her status, we'll send a quantum message and the *Lion* will follow." She handed the pad back to Ailsa. "Also, please add 'may our Foremothers watch over you.'"

Lauren turned away so the young woman wouldn't see the fear in her eyes. Her stomach cramped. *If we lose one of those ships, what would I do then?*

Accepting the pad, Ailsa bowed her head. "Yes, Majesty."

"And, Ailsa, after you send the message, I expect you to get a full eight hours of rest."

"And you too, ma'am." The tech ducked out of the hatchway with a chortle of laughter.

Lauren knew neither of them would heed her order, but she moved over to the brown leather sofa beneath the large transparency. The stars were bright and steady even though they were within the maelstrom of the spinning galaxy. Lauren shook her head at the vastness of it all. *How can anyone expect to comprehend this universe?* This made her smile as she realized not only did they understand it, now they were bending it to their will. The arrogance of that threatened to swamp her fragile optimism. Yet they wouldn't be doing any of this without the need to recover Alex. She wouldn't be doing it without the need to heal her soul.

With one more look at the blanket of stars surrounding the *Stag*, Lauren gathered the Fraser tartan throw from the back of the sofa and curled up next to Ice, sharing body heat with the wolf. She wrapped her arms around Ice's furred chest. *Companions are the bomb* was her last conscious thought before she dropped into a dreamless sleep.

Chapter Six
Aboard the Dubh Mogairle, Deck Sixty

Alex arrived at their hideaway, her trip to the armory a success. She returned with a large cache of weapons—hand-held blaster pistols, laser rifles, and small charges with remote laser-charged detonators. Hopefully, none of this cache would be required, but if they were to protect themselves and perhaps take over the ship, all of them and more would be needed. She paused before entering the small storage room.

Her ongoing freedom still nagged at her. Gwenhwyfach should have discovered her absence by now. *Why am I still free? All anyone had to do was check the room with the box.* All it would take was a simple mental search and Alex would be found. *I wonder if I can dampen my bond energy enough to go undetected.* It was worth a try. Alex closed her eyes and imagined sitting in a small stone room. She visualized closing a massive stone door, and then shrinking the room until all it held was her psi-energy. With this image firmly in her mind, she opened her eyes and hoped isolating her psi-energy in this way would be enough.

Sighing, Alex shuddered. Cutting off her psi energy always made her feel hollow. Severing her bond-connection with Lauren felt like an axe to her heart. She shook her head to clear those negative thoughts. All these questions would need to be addressed, but now they had other things to worry about. As long as she was free, the trio would carry on with their plans. Shrugging out of her pack, Alex opened the top and looked through her cache. Perhaps, the admiral had found something in the analyzer core data to answer her questions. In the interim, if they got into a pickle, they could defend themselves.

A pickle? Thoughts of Lauren and a warm spring afternoon flooded Alex's mind. She closed her eyes and allowed the memories full rein.

Alex lounged on a blanket at the edge of the large lake near the Keep. Wildflowers were just emerging from the winter grasses and the afternoon air smelled of life and possibilities. The sun warmed her back as she leaned up on one elbow to watch her bondmate. Lauren knelt at the water's edge, a small stick in her hand stirring the silt-rich soil.

"Come on, Dearheart. We have a picnic lunch to enjoy and I am hungry."

Without turning, Lauren replied, "You're always hungry. You're as bad as Ice. Your stomach is never satisfied." She did not cease her stirring. "I'm looking for frog eggs. I want to gather their DNA and compare their genome to those in my database. I need to determine how parallel this parallel reality really is."

"Once a technician, always a technician." Alex chuckled. "Well fine, but do not complain when all the chicken is gone before you complete your search."

"Chicken? Fried chicken? Eloise's fried chicken?" Lauren's head snapped around to look at Alex.

"I do believe it is." Alex watched as Lauren dropped her stick and stood, wiping her hands on her trousers. She made it to Alex in three long strides, where she dropped cross-legged on a corner of their tartan blanket. Brown sticky mud covered her boots nearly to her knees and her hands were stained the same color. She reached for the basket. "No, absolutely not." Alex pointed to the lake. "Go wash your hands before you contaminate our wonderful lunch."

Lauren huffed but went back to the lake, rinsing her hands in the clear cold water. She walked back to Alex and raised her dripping hands for Alex's inspection. "Better?" The palms were clean, but her fingernails still held fragments of the sticky mud.

Alex handed her a small towel from their basket. "Much."

They removed their meal from the basket, and Lauren filled their plates. Bowls of fresh cut vegetables, tiny steamed potatoes dripping in butter, and crispy pieces of fried chicken released steam into the cool spring air. Condiments of mayonnaise, coarse stone ground mustard, and a tomato-based sauce Alex loved shared a divided container. Small pots of salt and a ground herb with a peppery taste came out next. A basket of hard-boiled eggs, neatly peeled, was placed between them to share.

Last, Alex removed two round cylinders—the silver-blue one contained iced tea, sweetened with honey from last year's hives, the green blue one contained a malted liquor similar to beer but with a finer carbonation. Alex knew Lauren had become fond of this beverage. She did not like the heavy-fermented wines the Terrans aged in wooden vats. Lauren said the wine tasted like old gym socks and she could not get past the green iridescent color. To each their own. Alex reached for the silver-blue one. With plates balanced in their laps, they shared their meal in companionable silence, enjoying the light breeze and the warm afternoon sun.

"This is amazing." Lauren held up a chicken leg and waved it at Alex. "Eloise has it exactly right. I don't think Grandmommy would argue with her results." Lauren had shared several of her favored recipes with the Seneschal's master cooking technician. Most were from recipes her grand'mere had made for Lauren when she was a child. Eloise had struggled to find substitutes for some of the Earth-ingredients. She still could not replicate the dumplings Lauren enjoyed on a holiday called Thanksgiving. Lauren thought it was the difference in the broth prepared from Earth's domestic turkeys versus Eloise's wild turkeys, or maybe it was the Terran flour.

"I miss pickles. We always had dill pickle spears with our fried chicken." A wistful look crossed Lauren's face. Alex knew how deeply Lauren missed her grandparents.

"I do not think I have ever heard of pickles."

Lauren smiled sadly. "I know, Eloise hasn't either and she doesn't know what a cucumber is."

"What does a pickle have to do with this cucumber?" Alex scooted closer to Lauren, placing a gentle arm around her shoulders, hugging her close.

Lauren settled back against her and Alex could feel her draw comfort from their bond. "Cucumbers are small gourds." Alex grimaced and Lauren laughed. "They're tasty as a salad vegetable and you can make pickles from cucumbers by soaking them in salt-based brine with various spices." Lauren set her plate aside and relaxed deeper into Alex's arms. "Grandmommy made the best pickles. We grew small cucumbers on the farm, and she canned pickles in the summer. I can almost smell the brine from the pickling crocks."

Alex laid back and pulled Lauren with her. She placed a small kiss on her forehead as Lauren looked up at her. "I know you miss them terribly, Dearheart." Tears ran down the side of Lauren's face, and Alex kissed them away.

"I do miss them. I was always safe with them. They never judged me or ridiculed me for anything. They were proud of me."

Alex chased more tears with her finger. "I understand, Dearheart. But you must know how proud I am of you. You have brought so much to us and shared so selflessly." Alex swallowed and voiced her concern. "And I hope we can fill some of the void created by their absence."

Lauren cupped Alex's face with a gentle hand. "I'm glad to help in any way I can. You know that. It's almost like I had to travel between realities to find my true home. Here, on Terra." Lauren smiled. "With you." Rising, she captured Alex's lips in a kiss of confirmation.

Alex returned the kiss and it deepened as their love lit their bond. Lauren pulled away and settled back down on the blanket. She reached up and Alex felt the buttons of her sweater slip open one after another. Not to be left behind, Alex dropped her hand to the drawstring on Lauren's shirt. When the shirt fell open, Alex captured a small warm breast. A moan rose on the *gentle breeze and joined the quiet buzzing of insects. Alex continued her exploration and captured Lauren's lips in another kiss. As Lauren's mouth opened to release a moan, Alex's tongue slid in and began to duel with Lauren's. Warm, wet, gentle strokes fueled the fire growing between them.*

Alex's sweater got tossed aside but they never broke their kiss. Her hand dropped to Lauren's belt buckle and soon found its way beneath. When Lauren pushed her away to pull Alex's shirt over her head, a cold breeze drifted across Alex's chest. Strong arms gathered her close again and as their warm bodies merged, she saw stars behind her closed eyes. The world dissolved away, and they were surrounded by their love. Alex explored Lauren's taut abdomen, tracing the ridges and valleys of her abs. She chased ripples in the muscles tickled into existence by her fingers. Her hand floated lower.

Alex gathered moisture on the tip of her finger and coated Lauren's bud before she began to caress it on either side with long languid strokes. She was careful not to touch the tip, wanting Lauren to enjoy this bliss as long as she could. Their bond swelled as did the bud beneath her fingers. Alex could feel Lauren gathering herself to fall into the ecstasy of them.

She pulled away and Lauren groaned. "Easy, Dearheart. Let us do this together. I know you are close. I will not tease you."

Then, while looking into Lauren's eyes, Alex stroked across the tip and slid two long fingers into her. Lauren gasped and arched off their blanket. Her fingernails drew a path down Alex's back as she tried to pull her closer. Alex held her gaze and pulled out to the tips of her fingers only to plunge back in, hard. Again, and again. Their fire became a raging inferno and emotions spiraled out of control. Alex's strokes became uncontrolled. She tried to slow her rhythm, but Lauren shook her head and her body opened farther to Alex. Another finger joined the first two, as Lauren pulled her in. Alex sank deep, deeper than ever before and then halted her motion, as her thumb came to rest on the engorged bud. Lauren screamed and pulled them both over the edge into a whirlpool of emotions. Their hearts sang. Their bond exploded. Alex collapsed across Lauren, lost. An echoing howl of wolves and whiny of horses echoed in the distance.

A murmur woke Alex. Raising her head from its soft nest between Lauren's breasts, she realized she was draped across her love amid the scattered remains of their picnic. She had never lost consciousness before, even in the throes of their most intense lovemaking. But Alex had. She relished in the amazing feeling of completeness. She moved to roll off Lauren.

"No."

"*Dearheart, I am crushing you.*"

"*No.*"

Alex began to withdraw her fingers from the warm, wet sheath.

"*I said no. Don't move.*" *A contraction rippled through Lauren.*

Finally, Lauren opened her eyes. "*Thank you.*"

Her gaze held Alex captured in its depths and she watched ice-blue streaks flash against the emerald background. Lauren's gaze pulled Alex deeper. Her soul was open, and Alex was stunned by what she saw reflected there. Herself. Lauren blinked and their connection vanished. But as Alex relaxed into their bond, she realized it was stronger, more attuned to them, more resilient. The contractions around her fingers lessened to the flutter of butterfly wings.

Alex slipped her fingers out and smiled into those emerald-blue eyes. "*You are simply amazing, Dearheart. I am so blessed you arrived here and found me.*"

"*The feeling is entirely mutual, dearest.*" *A frown crossed Lauren's face and she took Alex's chin in one hand. She moved Alex's head to the side allowing the afternoon sun to flash across Alex's eyes. Lauren smiled.* "*So, Merilyn was correct. Our souls are joined.*"

Squinting against the brightness, Alex asked, "*What was my Seneschal right about this time.*"

"*Ours is a true bond.*"

"*A true bond?*" *Alex tried to move her head to get her eyes out of the sun, but Lauren held fast.*

"*Yes, it's your eyes. They have more emerald now, and the green streaks flash in the sun.*"

Lauren dropped her hand and Alex placed a quick kiss on her love's lips before rolling to the side. Now they lay shoulder-to-shoulder. A flight of cranes soared overhead. "*Be that as it may, you share the same characteristic. I was trying to determine what was different about your eyes just now.*" *Alex grinned at Lauren.* "*Your eyes have more blue in them. So, we are melding, are we?*"

"*It would seem so.*" *Lauren smiled.* "*And I think it's great!*"

They both dissolved in giggles. "*How did we get here, when we were talking about your pickles?*"

"*Well, it could be we got here because of a pickle. I'll need to tell you about all the types of pickles one can experience.*"

Alex shook herself free of the memory and knocked on the locked hatch. Lauren had indeed told her all about pickles. From the kind you eat, to the kind you can get into, to the one that occurs within a sporting game called baseball. The one she was in now was a true pickle. *I only hope we can escape unharmed.* She needed to talk to Lauren. But Alex had to exercise caution, so she strengthened the walls of the stone room around her bond. Alex had to be the one to control when and how they reestablished contact.

Chapter Seven
Aboard the Ruadh làn-damh
Command Bridge, Deck One

Lauren leaned forward in her command chair. Tension rolled around the bridge as the crew waited for the quantum message from the *Lion*. Ice sat in the other chair; her injured paw braced on an armrest. The wolf was alert, watching, and waiting. Snow lay at Lauren's feet, her large white head resting on Lauren's left boot. She wasn't missing anything either. Lauren smiled at their support, her heart and soul warmed by their constant companionship. The *Lion* would let them know when the *Kestrel* entered the gravity well. It had taken Angus six days to recalculate a new route around the supermassive black hole at the center of the Milky Way. Six days her crew used to continue their repairs to her *Stag*.

The starboard portion of deck forty-four now had a temporary hull graft with a force field embedded inside it. The engineers agreed it would hold at faster-than-light pulse speeds. The coolant Lauren released into the containment room had been cleaned up and equipment damaged by the plasma replaced. All but one of the containment vessels were fully functional and already primed, waiting only on a charge of gravitational radiant energy from the spun sails to restart their fusion reactions. They would wait to initiate a fusion reaction until the three clans were together.

"Ma'am?" Ailsa's quiet voice sounded like a roar in the silence of the bridge. Lauren quirked an eyebrow in question.

"The *Lion* reports the *Kestrel* has entered the gravity well on course and headed for our position."

"Very well. Start the clock, please." Lauren spun her chair around to Ronan at the holo-tank. They calculated the time dilation for this new course would be approximately two days. They would not fly the *Kestrel* as deep into the gravitational well as the *Stag* had flown.

At the two-day mark, Lauren was back on the bridge. Minutes ticked by and became hours. As each hour passed, the crew's tension racketed up. "Do you have anything yet, Ronan?"

Her astrogator looked up from his holo-tank and shook his head. "Not yet, Majesty."

"Turn the external sensors toward the black hole at maximum magnification."

The hours continued to accumulate, Lauren leaned back in her chair and tried to relax. *Come on, Angus.* She knew her anxiety impacted those around her on the bridge. *What had Tavish said? A commander's calm is her crew's calm. Do not underestimate how attuned your crew is to you and your mood.* Well, in this instance she was hard-pressed to control her fear, but she tried for the crew's sake.

When fifty-one hours had passed with no indication of the *Kestrel*, Lauren reached out to Angus along her bond. All she felt was a void. Blankness filled the space her bond with him normally occupied. It wasn't as if the bond was broken. It simply wasn't there. Lauren needed to reassure herself her bond still existed, so she reached out toward Alex. She slammed headlong into a brick wall with a jarring force. "What the?"

"Ma'am?" Her pilot turned toward her from his console.

Lauren waved her hand to dismiss her slip. "Nothing." She tried again to reach Alex. Again, a solid wall blocked her path. Settling deeper into the soft leather command chair, she reached out to the wolves. Both turned their heads toward her in question. *"Sorry guys, just checking. I can't get through to Alex."*

Snow's gaze unfocused and Lauren felt their bond sing with a small surge of energy from the wolf. The wolf shook her head and sneezed. *"That is odd, neither can I? But this block is different. It is not the Cador traitor. It feels more like Alex has erected the block herself. It smells like her mind."*

"Smells?"

"Each bond has a unique smell and taste, which changes with emotions. We can always tell what Alex is feeling from the taste," Ice explained, tilting her head. *"This block tastes of caution and wariness. Perhaps Alex is trying to hide herself and does not want a poorly timed surge in your bond to be detected."*

Lauren considered this, and then smiled. *"This may actually be good news then?"*

"Precisely." Ice's tone was smug.

Lauren turned back to her astrogator. "Time, please."

Ronan looked at the chronometer within the holo-tank. "Fifty-three hours, thirty-three minutes."

This is taking too long. Her stomach tightened as her fear rose. She couldn't imagine what the boys felt waiting for her. Lauren felt the tension from the bridge crew ratchet higher.

Ronan looked up suddenly. "Ship detected." He dropped his gaze back into the holo-tank. "Two point five million kilometers off our port bow. It is the *Kestrel*. I am receiving an automated ident-beacon."

"Ailsa, please send a quantum message to the *Lion*. Let them know the *Kestrel* has arrived. And then open communications to the *Kestrel* please."

"Aye." Ailsa spoke softly into her headset transceiver.

"*Lion* acknowledges our message. Their reply: On our way."

"What? No." Lauren leapt down to Ailsa's chair, leaning over the back. "Tell them to hold position until we determine the status of the *Kestrel*. Without word from them, we've got no idea if the new course worked."

Ailsa did as instructed. "The *Lion* is not responding." She looked up at Lauren. "Nothing from the *Kestrel* yet, Majesty."

Lauren reached out along her bond to Tavish. She felt the same blankness she had with Angus. She reached toward Angus and felt warmth fill her bond as Angus smiled at her touch. *Damn it, Tavish. Why are you such a hothead? Why do you always go charging forward like that?*

"*Because he and Alex leap before looking.*" Snow stood and walked to the edge of the command dais. "*You have tempered Alex's impulsive nature. Perhaps your continued interaction with Tavish will have the same effect on him.*"

Lauren laid a hand on Snow's head. "*Let's hope we get that chance.*"

"I have a message from the *Kestrel*, ma'am."

Stepping up to her command chair, Lauren turned the monitor. "Send it over, please." Angus' drawn face appeared; deep lines etched his forehead. "Lauren, we have arrived and are mostly unharmed. We have lost external sensors and two communications arrays due to gravitational shear. We are floating blind. The crew is unharmed except for some minor disorientation. Once our stomachs catch up to our bodies, we will commence repairs." He grimaced, then looked away from the pickup and spoke to someone. "I have ordered us to rendezvous with the *Stag* at your current location. *Kestrel*, clear."

Lauren nodded to Ronan and sat down. "Please send the requested location data and let them know if they need us to go to them, we can. What was their total relative time of travel?"

The astrogator bent over his plot. "Total relative travel time was nine hours and fifty-six seconds. Total distance traveled is estimated at twenty-nine point six-eight light years." Ronan looked up at Lauren. "Plus, the two point five million kilometers, of course."

"Right. Of course." Lauren was still startled by the casual mention of such vast distances. *You're not in Kansas anymore, Lauren.* She chuckled softly.

"*Kestrel* is moving, Majesty. She estimates her arrival at our position in just over twenty-six hours. Her arrival is delayed by the need to use thrusters only and Commander Newkirk sends his apologies."

"Please reply, 'No worries, Angus. Travel safe.'" Lauren thought for a moment. "And let him know Tavish is on his way. If he arrives safely, we'll meet him halfway."

The *Lion* arrived in fifty-six hours. Her crew experienced some mild disorientation and nausea, but the ship sustained no damage. *Lion* took up station keeping beside the *Stag* and *Kestrel*. Lauren frowned. *Thank god they're okay. Tavish won't be when I get my hands on him. He's gotta learn to stop and consider. I can't lose anyone else.* Her heart stuttered as she thought about her lost crew.

"Ma'am, I have a request for communication from Commander MacDonald."

Lauren rotated her command chair toward the communication consoles. "Please send it over, Ailsa."

Tavish's smiling face appeared on her monitor. "How are the repairs coming, Consort?"

"Don't ever do that again." Her anger exploded and out of the corner of her eye, she saw Ronan flinch. "Your actions were reckless and could've resulted in the loss of your ship." Lauren's anger cascaded through her and the wolves growled. She was overreacting but her fear for Tavish and the *Lion* were foremost in her mind and her exhaustion was inhibiting her ability to hide her emotions.

Tavish's smile vanished. "Excuse me?"

"You shouldn't have jumped into the gravity well without a status report on the *Kestrel*. They could've been dead or damaged beyond repair."

"Lauren, I am—"

"But no! You had to charge ahead. Be the bold commander. Show everyone else how it's done. You are impulsive and reckless. Those traits will get you killed." Lauren felt the first tear slide down her cheek and her anger racketed up another notch. She dashed the tear away with a harsh stroke of her palm. She would not allow her crew to see her cry, but goddamn it, he could have been lost.

Tavish bent his head to the side. "I am sorry, Majesty. But time is not on our side and I did not believe waiting another six days for Angus to recalculate another course would have changed the outcome. You arrived, they arrived, and now we arrived." He flashed a small smile. "Now we can continue."

Lauren slumped back into her chair, crossed her arms, and huffed, as her anger faded. "Fine, but don't ever do that again. I mean it, Tavish, I will not survive losing another." A single nod was her answer. Tavish got her message. He knew the *Stag* had lost crew. No, she had lost crew, some still unaccounted for. Lost in the cold blackness of space. *A horrible death.* Lauren hoped he would think twice about doing something so rash again. She took a deep breath and decided to move on. "Repairs are progressing. By the time we're ready to continue, the *Stag* should be ready for faster-than-light pulse speed."

Tavish gave her a boyish grin. "Good. That is good. I will take a flitter over to the *Stag* within the hour and we can begin planning the second part of this adventure."

Gawd, he's just like Alex.

Chapter Eight
Aboard the Dubh Mogairle
Deck Sixty on the Clan Cador Ship

Over the last weeks, the trio continued to gather information and stockpile materials. The admiral began light physiotherapy the week prior and made steady progress. Sarah returned with a lower body exoskeletal system on her last trek to the medical bays, and now, the admiral could walk down the entire length of the subdeck. The partially mechanized brace also provided active stimulation to the muscles in his pelvis and hip through a series of electrodes, further aiding his healing.

The deeper they dug into the *Orchid's* analyzer cores, the more disturbing the information they found became. The admiral completed a full analysis of the ship's damage reports. When their construction flitter tore loose from the *Orchid's* hull, it took a large section of hull plating with it. A gash now ran from the intake manifolds to the edge of the ventral plane, which made fourteen decks uninhabitable. The bigger problem for the ship was the flitter also tore away the mast booms for one of the spun sails used to gather gravitational radiant energy. Without one of her sails, the *Orchid* would be limited to the lower range of faster-than-light pulse speeds, thus they were forced to slow the ship to accommodate this damage. Without all her sails, she could not gather enough radiant energy to fully charge the containment vessels. Currently, the ship was running on only two of the four huge vessels. All this information helped the trio prepare a plan to take over the clan, rather than sabotage her.

Alex had another problem. They found no information on Gwen-hwyfach. Other than a brief reference in the medical database to a patient recovering from a cerebral vascular accident, they were in the dark. Alex could "feel" the traitor at the edges of her psi-senses but nothing more. Alex maintained her block against her bond and Lauren but being cut off from her bondmate drained her energy. Alex could not sleep and eating made her nauseous. Of course, her command training would not let her skip eating entirely. But food was nothing more than fuel.

The trio was ready to attempt their takeover of the ship. Alex and Sarah prepared to execute the first part of their plan. Although the *Black Orchid* crew was one-fourth her usual complement, their trio would not stand a chance in an open confrontation and they could not run the giant clan ship by themselves. Also, the admiral was adamant—they would not utilize any of her crew. They had neither the time nor resources to determine who was part of the conspiracy versus who was conscripted into service when the clan bolted from the Terran solar system.

Currently, Alex lay wedged in a small ventilation shaft above the bridge, waiting. She was fighting her claustrophobia caused by this small space. *I cannot make noise.* The admiral had broken their plan into three parts. Part one: By using a series of staged accidents, they hoped to force the crew onto the central decks. Once they had the crew isolated, they would lock the decks down. Part two: Reset the ship's command codes and reprogram the ship AIs to respond only to their input and orders. Then, allow the AIs to run the critical ship systems. Alex and Sarah would control the bridge, with its navigation, communication, environmental, sailing, and weapons control systems. The admiral would take over engineering and maintain the containment vessels and fuel supplies. And part three: Attempt to communicate with the vanguard *Boar* and acquire additional crew from Robert. It all sounded simple enough, but now the time had come, and concern coursed through Alex, making her muscles twitch. So many things could go wrong. *And it is only the three of us.*

This morning, Admiral McLeod moved aft to prepare the accidents. From his vantage point within the subdeck beneath engineering, he could assess the engineering crew's exit. Once the crew vacated the space, he would move onto deck fifty-seven and takeover the master control space. This self-contained control room had its own environmental systems and could only be accessed through one door. A single crewman could run all the critical propulsion systems from this location. If a critical accident occurred within engineering, a crewman would be safe inside and able to interact with the various engineering AIs to fix any damage. Once the admiral barricaded himself inside, only an open attack by power-armored crew could breach this room.

Sarah headed to the analyzer cores. On Alex's signal, she would input the admiral's command codes and begin an auto-reset. This should shut the cores down and the reset would bring them back up under his codes, locking out everyone else onboard the ship. Alex had been wondering why no one within the *Orchid's* crew had done this already. If their command codes were removed from the system, their plans would fail. Alex knew their advantage lay in the fact Gwenhwyfach was not a trained commander. She was a priestess. Yes, she could kill with a psi-attack, but she could not command a clan. When the clans escaped Terra Prime, she was clan leader by right of birth. She left the running of her clan ship to her captain. Perhaps she did not know about command codes or how they worked.

Alex's muscles continued to dance with tiny twitches as she waited for the first of the emergency klaxons to sound. At this point she really did not care how much the bitch knew. The farther they were able to infiltrate the ship's systems the better the odds of successfully taking over the vessel.

Once the admiral started the cascade of emergencies, Alex would release a small amount of smoke into the bridge. Hopefully, this would cause the crew to vacate the area. The captain should reroute command and control to the auxiliary bridge located amidships. The captain would only discover their reroute was unsuccessful when they could not access the auxiliary bridge. *Then I can get out of this cramped space.*

With the crew isolated on the mid decks, Sarah would lock them in using a series of interlaced force fields. They would be safe and have all the necessary supplies to keep them comfortable, but they would not be able to access the maintenance shafts, elevator system, or subdecks. Sweat trickled down Alex's temple and dripped onto the ventilation shaft below her chin. *This is taking too long.* She reached out with her psi-sense. All the bridge crew was below her, manning their stations. She extended her psi-sense a bit farther, just sensing Sarah in the analyzer core. Sarah's calm told Alex she was waiting for the admiral. Alex could not extend far enough to reach the admiral's position in the engineering subdeck. That would take too much energy. So, she just had to wait. *I hate waiting.*

Time dragged on, and Alex got drowsy. Her lack of sleep had caught up with her. She closed her eyes and tried to relax in the tight space, but the walls of the ventilation shaft closed in as her claustrophobia ramped up. Alex woke with a start as klaxons blared on the bridge. She hit her head on the ductwork in the small shaft. Flashes of light danced in her vision. Stifling a groan, she crawled forward to the open grid and peeked down. The bridge was in chaos. Red warning lights flashed from almost every console within her field of view. The captain, in black body armor, bent over the dark navigational holo-tank. Alex could see a crewman's feet sticking out from beneath the astrogation table.

"I am sorry, sir. The controls are offline. I have lost power and access to external sensors. We are running blind." The crewman drew himself out from under the table.

"Containment vessels three and four are overcharging. Temperature and pressure increasing toward redline," a disembodied voice reported, probably the engineering tech.

Alex saw the captain spin around. "What is going on? We are only running on vessels one and two. How did those tanks get fuel?"

"Engineering reports fuel cut off to tanks one and two, sir. All fuel is now being rerouted to the other two tanks," the burley red haired engineering tech stated.

Alex could see the captain clench his fists and slam them into the holo-table. He strode up to his command chair and activated a monitor. "Tell engineering to get fuel into vessels one and two, and then initiate a cold restart."

Alex sucked in a quick breath. *Cold restart?* That could cause an immediate containment vessel failure. Pouring all that fuel into a cold vessel and then injecting radiant energy was a recipe for disaster.

"Sir?" This question came from several crew. The engineering tech's voice overrode the others. "Sir, a cold restart is not recommended. The fusion reaction is at zero in those vessels." *That is the correct analysis. Listen to your tech, you fool.*

"Just do it."

Alex had to prevent the crew from trying this idiotic maneuver. She removed a silvered canister from the small pouch strapped to her arm. Pulling her face shield down and sealing the edges, she eased open the valve and directed the gas flow down through the ventilation grid. A yellow-blue haze of nitrogen gas mixed with sulphur dioxide vapor began to settle toward the deck below. Heavier than air, the gas dropped quickly to the deck. The nitrogen gas acted as a carrier to dilute the sulphur dioxide. In high concentrations, sulphur dioxide was caustic due to its acidic properties, so Alex released a minimum amount. Just enough to cause a sharp burning smell. Both the color of the vapor and the smell should alert the crew to the existence of an open fire nearby. No one wanted to deal with a fire on a spaceship.

"Sir, engineering is not responding. I am unable to reach the master tech or the engineering AI."

The captain dropped into his command chair. "Alert the containment techs. Send a text-only message with my order. Open those vessels."

Alex could feel the great ship begin to struggle. Small tremors vibrated through her as the ship continued to slow and the gravitational turbulence within the wave took hold of her. If Alex was not able to get to the controls and maintain their speed and heading, they would be ejected out of the wave at faster-than-light pulse speed. If the ship slewed against the gravitational wave direction, shear forces could tear the giant clan ship apart. Like a rider thrown over the head of her mount as it refused a fence, the great ship would tumble stern over bow within the wave.

"Come on," Alex whispered through clinched teeth. "Open your eyes and noses."

The engineering tech spun around in his chair. "No response, no—"

"Fire!" Alex watched as his eyes grew huge.

"What, where?" The captain shot out of his chair and began to frantically look around the bridge. Standing brought him up into the settling cloud of vapor. "Clear the bridge, transfer all command and control to the auxiliary bridge. Activate fire suppression systems. Send out a ship-wide message to clear the upper decks. Fire has been detected on deck one."

Alex watched the crew initiate a complicated dance. Masks were pulled from beneath consoles and donned. The communication tech lifted a small transparency and dipped his hand into the gel interface below. The evacuation order was sent over the ship-wide communication net.

"Evacuate decks one through fourteen. Move to central decks. Emergency force fields will activate in four minutes. This is not a drill." The bridge AI continued to repeat the order and the crew filed out of the bridge. Only the captain remained. *Get your butt moving.* Alex chided the man.

"Fire suppression systems not responding," the bridge AI reported. Alex smiled. Sarah had control of the cores.

But the captain remained in his chair and continued to utilize the computer interfaces located there. She heard him mumbling but could only catch every other word or so. The vapor cloud continued to expand, and the captain had not donned his face shield. He coughed as the level of the gas now hovered around his knees.

With one final input, he swore and thumped the armrest with his fist. "This is not right. This should not be happening."

Finally, he stood and pulled his face shield down. He reached into the pocket on the side of his chair. He pulled something out, but Alex could not see what he held as he turned. With one look around the bridge, he stepped from the command dais and moved out of Alex's field of view. She heard the pneumatic bridge door swish open and then cycle closed. She could exit now. Just as she placed her laser torch over the first locking bolt to remove the fasteners from the ventilation grid, her psi-sense flared. *The captain is still on the bridge.*

Stuck, Alex went through her options. *Can I remove the fasteners without him hearing? Could I use a psi-energy burst to immobilize him?*

What did he remove from the command chair? She could barely see the command chair now, as the gas continued to rise. More klaxons blared, but they sounded far off. "Fires detected decks one, two, and five. Fire suppression systems down. Evacuate deck one through fourteen. Emergency force fields in place." The bridge AI's mechanical voice sounded harsh.

Dropping the laser torch over the first fastener, Alex thumbed on the tool. The metal began to deform as it melted and vaporized. She only had one way to go and that was onto the bridge. Attaching a small grappling hook to the grid, Alex moved the torch over the last fastener. Alex hoped she could drop down out of the shaft, using the falling grid as a distraction. *I can hide in the vapor and move behind the command dais.* The bolt head continued to melt. Klaxons continued to sound. The captain had not moved. *He is waiting.*

When the bolt failed and the grid dropped, Alex pulled herself out after it, diving out of the shaft. She flipped over in midair and landed crouched on the deck with a puff of vapor. A blaster discharged and struck the back of the pilot's chair over her left shoulder. She rolled to her left. Reaching up to her face shield, Alex activated the infrared mode on her visor. The sickly yellow-blue vapor disappeared, and shimmering images appeared. The pilot's chair glowed white-hot where the blaster struck, and the various warning lights blinked a muted yellow. Alex belly crawled toward the holo-table and the navigation console, hoping to outflank the captain. Alex pulled a small detonator from her leg pouch. If she could discharge the detonator close enough to the captain, she hoped the concussion would render the man unconscious.

Another blaster discharge singed across the bridge. This one struck the communication console, bathing Alex in a shower of sparks from a shattered monitor. Even through her face shield, Alex smelled something burning. *Melted analyzer components?* And then Alex realized their danger. *Feck, if he does not stop discharging his weapon, we will all be toast.* Another bolt streaked by her shoulder and hit the forward transparency. If the vapor Alex released into the bridge contained any sulphur monoxide—a complementary component to sulphur dioxide—the gas could ignite. When the admiral prepared the cannister he had no way to filter the sulphur dioxide, so he diluted the gas with nitrogen hoping to eliminate this danger. The captain's blaster discharges could create a firestorm. Alex could not risk that happening.

She stood and called out. "Over here, traitor."

The vapor behind the emergency control console swirled and the captain appeared as he too stood. He leveled his blaster at her, its red sighting-laser settling on the center of her chest. "I thought you would have died of dehydration by now. How do you continue to survive?" She could hear the sneer in his words.

"Just lucky, I guess." Alex gripped the tiny detonator in her left hand. "Where is the bitch, you call clan leader, traitor?" She inched toward him, hoping the swirling vapor would mask her movement.

"Gwenhwyfach is preparing for a meeting with our allies. Once we reach the nebula, we will join forces with them and return to incinerate Terra." The captain saw her movement and circled away.

"And then what? Destroy all the clans? The bitch would miss having everyone to order around." Alex chuckled and shuffled forward another meter. "And you would not have a homeworld. What then?"

"Then we return to Terra Prime and reclaim our true homeworld."

Alex gave a deep full-belly laugh. "As the Consort would say, fat chance, traitor. That planet lost its biosphere and hydrosphere. Without life and water, it is a dead rock in space." Another step. *Four more meters.* The detonator gave off a high-energy laser pulse, which would not ignite the swirling vapor.

"Not after we utilize the Comin terraforming technology to rebuild the planet's hydrosphere. The infrastructure remains. All we have to do is move in and repopulate our home." The captain continued to keep his blaster leveled on her chest as she moved toward him. "Hold there."

What is this guy thinking? Another step. *Three meters.* "You are as delusional as the bitch is, traitor. You will never be able to do that in this lifetime. Even if you do, you will be vassals to the Comin. They will come and strip Terra Prime of all her natural resources and leave you with nothing but a rock in space." One more step. *Two meters.*

"You do not know the Comin. They are our allies—" The rest of his words were cut off as Alex tossed the detonator. The bridge hatch hissed open.

The detonator exploded, releasing a blinding white light. Blaster discharges slashed across the bridge. Alex blinked the starburst of light from her eyes and saw the captain gaping at her. A red patch blossomed on his chest and he dropped to his knees, the swirling vapor swallowed his falling body.

Sarah looked around the edge of the hatchway before striding onto the deck, her blaster held in a two-handed grip, its muzzle pointed at the spot where the captain fell. "You did not answer your communicator and I was worried you were still trapped in the ventilation shaft and not able to take the bridge." Sarah looked around the bridge and nudged the captain's body with the toe of her boot. "Seems you were managing fine, though. Any more surprises for me?"

Alex shivered as unused adrenaline drained from her muscles. "No, I think we are good here."

"Alrighty, then." Sarah moved over to the environmental console and with the flick of a few fingers, activated the system. Fans sprang to life and sucked the vapor out of the bridge. "Let us continue. Secure the door next?" Alex dragged the captain's body out of the bridge as Sarah moved over to the pilot's console. The young pilot cried out. "What did you do to my chair? I cannot sit in this and fly the clan." A large smoldering hole pierced the back of the pilot's acceleration couch; the molten metal had solidified into a stalactite reaching toward the deck.

Alex shrugged in response and dropped into the captain's chair. She began entering her command codes into the bridge AI system. The bridge hatch hissed shut, the locks cycling closed. "I did not shoot your chair." Alex pointed over her shoulder. "He did."

Sarah sighed. "I will reroute ship propulsion and navigational controls to the sailing master's console. We will need to trim the sails as we fly her."

"She is decelerating. The captain was attempting a cold start on two of the containment vessels, when the admiral shut the other two down. We will need to maintain our heading with the wave, and then pick a place to drop out of it safely." Alex continued to manipulate a gel interface. "Come on, you know who I am."

"Alexandra Aoeron Aonwyn nighean mic Fionnaghal, Regain Rioghachd Fuar Ćala," a mechanical voice responded. "How may we serve?"

"That is better. I am now commander of this vessel. Transfer all command and control functions to me. Route all ship functions, except engineering, to the bridge. Ensure the auxiliary bridge cannot be accessed."

Static crackled through the channel, then the bridge AI responded. "Transfer complete. Auxiliary command bridge sealed. Gravity and life support suspended within that space."

"Status of the clan?"

The bridge AI paused. "Clan decelerating. One light pulse speed in approximately three minutes. Containment vessels three and four are fully fueled, no reaction established. Containment vessels one and two shut down. Auto-navigation systems engaged. Environmental systems failing decks one through fourteen. Internal gravity failing decks one through fourteen, emergency force fields in place. Bridge systems fully functional. Internal comm-links operational. Analyzer cores offline, reset underway. Time to completion thirty-one minutes. External sensors offline. External communications offline."

"Begin system function transfer. Lock down the analyzer cores. Deploy a beacon, with the following message." Alex transcribed a message. "And the crew?"

"All but five crew members are on the middecks."

"Five?" Alex looked over at Sarah and she shrugged. "Where are the five located?"

The bridge AI replied, "Four in engineering, attempting to access engineering control. One on bridge."

Alex jumped up. Sarah grabbed her blaster from the top of the sailing console. Sliding out of her chair, Sarah moved to the starboard bank of consoles in a crouch, looking along their length toward the forward transparency. Alex moved to the port side and did the same. "Where is the crew on the bridge?"

"Within console Alpha twenty-three."

Alex crept around the bank of monitors and moved to the holo-table. Console Alpha twenty-three was the main controls for the navigational systems and contained the holo-emitters for the projection system. Bending down beneath the table, Alex noted the access panel was ajar. She looked up and nodded to Sarah. Sarah aimed her blaster at the panel.

Alex brought her blaster to bear. "All right, come out. Hands where I can see them. You have ten seconds."

They heard a whimper. "No shoot, I come now." A tiny hand, covered in a golden gauntlet, curled around the edge of the panel and pushed it open. A small figure appeared, clothed in a golden suit of body armor. The suit glistened, flashing like the feathers of an eagle as the figure rose. A pneumatic shield of gold masked their face.

Sarah waved her blaster at the tiny figure. "Remove the face shield and drop your hood."

The figure reached up and pulled the face shield free, then pushed the hood back. A tan face, framed by plethora of tiny black braids—each tipped with a copper bead in the shape of a bird—appeared. Dark eyes, flecked with golden highlights, looked around her with disdain. No more than a meter tall, the young child puffed out her chest and placed her hands on her hips, eyeing Alex. "I, G'iad'a, first born Kall'ka, Supreme Ruler outer planets, heir to condor throne of mighty Comin." She turned to Sarah and sneered. "No point weapon at your goddess."

Sarah scoffed. "Sorry, but I will point my weapon at anything that threatens my queen. So, lose the attitude, imp."

"Imp? I have your head for impudence." She swung toward Sarah and made a slashing move. A tiny weapon flashed into her hand and she fired. The purple energy bolt struck Sarah in the shoulder, spinning her around. Sarah dropped her blaster.

Alex grabbed G'iad'a by her shoulders, turning her away from Sarah. "I am Alexandra, Queen of the thirteen clans of Terra. You will bow before your elder, child." The tiny girl tilted her head and stared up at Alex. "Sarah, are you all right?"

"Yes, Majesty. Just a nick." Alex glanced over at her. Blood seeped between Sarah's fingers and ran in slow rivulets down her arm. "I have my blaster."

"Get a quick-seal on your wound and take over piloting this ship. Then contact the admiral. See where he is and if he has control of engineering yet. Give him the information on the four crew members there."

"I bow to no one but my Empress." G'iad'a raised her weapon.

Alex frowned and lifted the child by the scruff of her neck. She grabbed the tiny weapon and jerked it free. Then she realized the child just gave away a key piece of intelligence. If the Comin were ruled by an Empress, what happened to Emperor T'iik'lac? This girl had all the attitude Alex always associated with the Comin.

"Well young heir, take a seat." She plunked her down in the navigator's couch and hit the crash harness release. The white webbing engulfed the tiny girl, binding her to the chair. "What were you doing in the navigational console? Why are you here?"

The girl huffed and shook her head, beads rattling. "I not talk. I not answer questions. Where witch? She gone long. She answer."

Another piece of intelligence revealed. "How old are you, heir?"

The tiny figure puffed out her chest as far as she could against the webbing. "I nine cycles of Homeworld."

Sarah guffawed from her seat at the sailing master's console. "Nine, then you are an imp."

"Not imp. Heir to throne."

Alex held her hand up for Sarah to be quiet and the tiny girl recoiled. Alex grimaced. Knowing physical punishment was the way of the Comin, she would need to watch her overt gestures. "I will not hit you, imp, but you will stay seated and quiet." Alex stared at the child, until she nodded and hung her head. "I will hold you to that, based on your honor." Honor was one of the tenets of Comin society. When the child nodded again, Alex stepped up on the command dais, dropping into the command chair. The chair was as hard as a flitter wing. It did not conform to her body as her chair aboard the *Iola Mara* did.

"What a dump." Alex shook her head.

"I have a comm link to engineering." Sarah's hands danced over the gel pads on her console.

Alex punched a stub on the chair's armrest. "Engineering, do you copy?"

Static screeched across the open connection and Alex winced at the sharp sound. "Engineering?"

"Here, Majesty." An explosion sounded in the background. "One moment please." Another explosion sounded, and then nothing but static came across the comm. "There, that is better. Now, Majesty, what may I do for you?" The admiral sounded calm, but Alex's gut was cramped with panic.

"What is going on down there?" Alex's voice rose half an octave.

"Nothing out of the norm. Several crew were attempting to gain access to the engineering command center. They were using cutting torches on the door. I am sorry to report their fuel tanks exploded."

"Exploded? How did that happen?"

Alex heard a soft chuckle. "Nothing you need to worry yourself about, Majesty. Let us focus on more important issues. Engineering is secure." Clacking could be heard—the admiral must be accessing systems manually. "I have control of the containment vessels, including the fuel tanks which are undamaged. I have rerouted plasma coolant from the tertiary system to an unused storage vessel here." Alex heard him grunt and the clacking continued. "Was someone on the bridge attempting to cold start fully-charged vessels?"

"It would seem so. The captain was trying to increase the *Orchid's* speed to be able to remain in the wave."

"What a fool." Admiral McLeod must have moved away from the comm mic, as his voice faded. "Well, you will need to drop out of the wave. We cannot restart the fusion reactions without draining the system, and that can only be done in normal space."

Sarah interrupted from her station at the sailing console, her hands in constant motion. "I have identified an eddy in this wave. I recommend we use it to exit. It will be a bumpy ride but safer than just dropping out of the mainstream flow. Our problem is the stuck sail."

"Did you hear that, Admiral?"

"I heard. That eddy is a viable option to exit the wave with some control. As to the sail, I would recommend we jettison it from the stays."

Alex sat up straight. If they jettisoned the sail entirely, they would permanently lose a percentage of their ability to gather radiant energy. She shook her head. "How much would this cut our overall speed once we acquire another wave?"

"Approximately fifty percent of our energy gathering capacity would be lost." Sarah turned to Alex. "Majesty, we have another set of sails in their lockers. It could be replaced."

Alex arched an eyebrow. "And just how are the three of us going to set the sail?"

"Well—"

The admiral interrupted. "Let's drop out of this gravitational wave using the eddy. We can then attempt to contact the vanguard and get some of their crew aboard to set the new sails. We cannot continue safely sailing this vessel for an extended length of time with just the three of us."

Alex tapped a long finger to her chin, deep in thought. "All right. Sarah, steer toward the eddy and prepare to exit this wave." She looked at the young child, who sat quietly in the crash couch. Her arms were crossed, and a scowl marred her smooth face. Alex shrugged. *I will deal with her later.* "Bridge AI."

"Yes, Majesty?"

"Did you send the message?"

"Yes, communication beacon dropped approximately four point three two minutes ago. Beacon will broadcast on all bandwidths once it achieves normal space."

"Very well. Once we enter the eddy, cut all fuel to containment vessels one and two and shut down radiant energy gathering. Send a message, text only, to the middecks and warn the crew to brace for a rough ride. AI?"

"Majesty?"

"Inform the other AIs of our plan and prepare the ship for an emergency wave exit." She looked down at the comm panel. "Admiral, anything else? I am a bit out of practice with this emergency scenario."

"You will need to reef the functional sails and jettison the one stuck in its stays. I will begin emergency shut down of all engineering systems. The fuel within the storage tanks must be dumped. The flow of plasma shutoff." She could hear him moving about, the servos in his leg exoskeleton humming. He chuckled. "Then hold on. This is going to be a rough ride."

Alex shook her head and smiled. The admiral was always energized by a challenging situation. "Let us do this." She nodded to Sarah and they both began entering commands into their consoles.

The exit from the gravitational wave could only be characterized as a jettison. Anyone not strapped into an acceleration couch would have been seriously injured, if not killed. Alex was glad the middecks had adequate safety couches for the crew. Once in normal space, Sarah fought to control the clan. Inertial dampeners failed, as did the internal gravity system. Loose pads and crew detritus began flying about the bridge in the zero-gravity environment. Movement outside the forward transparency caught Alex's eye.

"She has entered a flat spin." Sarah's report came as Alex watched the star field flash by, the ship's rate of rotation accelerating with each revolution. A flat spin occurred when a craft rotated uncontrollably about her central axis and fell out of the sky, like a Frisbee tossed on a breeze. In this instance, the *Black Orchid* spun about her central axis, but here in open space, she fell toward the largest gravity well in the area—a glowing white-hot star.

Alex gripped the armrests of her command chair. Panic rose, choking her. *Come on, Alex, think. How do you recover from a flat spin? What had the sailing master taught them? Use PARE.* "Sarah, forward power to zero, ailerons neutral, rudders full opposite the spin direction, elevators to neutral."

"PARE recovery, aye." Sarah's hands flashed over her interfaces. "I am unable to control the spin. I have no attitudinal controls. She is not responding to directional input." Sarah shouted as the *Orchid* groaned and their spin rate increased. Stars whipped by the transparency in a blur. G'iad'a groaned and heaved her last meal.

"Come on, you rust bucket." *What am I missing? Why is the ship not responding?* "Wait, this is a flat spin. The normal recovery method is to throw the ship farther into the spin and increase drag along one portion of the hull." Alex thought aloud, as she swallowed convulsively to force down her nausea. "All control systems full in the direction of the spin. Full power to the starboard thrusters."

The giant ship screamed as Sarah reversed the control surfaces. Finally, the spin slowed, and the nose of the giant clan tipped over, pointing the ship toward the heart of the star. White-hot solar flares filled the forward transparency. A thrill of joy pulsed through Alex, only to be replaced seconds later by panic as the ship began corkscrewing about her longitudinal axis. They had converted one spin into another.

"PARE again, Sarah." Again, the giant ship screamed as the pilot reversed the controls against the corkscrew direction. The metal bulkheads groaned, warped, and finally tore as the metal substructure began to fail around the bridge. Alex threw her arms over her head to protect herself from falling debris. "Face shields!" Sparks flew from damaged systems as electronic connections severed. An acrid smoke filled the bridge.

"I have control," Sarah shouted above the screech of tearing metal. The corkscrew slowed and soon the giant clan stabilized in a controlled flightpath toward the star. "We have been captured by the star's gravity field. I do not have sufficient power to exit."

"Reverse thrusters," Alex shouted. She watched in horror as Sarah increased their speed, accelerating toward the star. "Reverse thrusters!"

Suddenly, the great ship slewed to starboard. Thrown against her crash harness, the webbing cut deeply into Alex's shoulders and thighs. G-forces increased, and her vision narrowed to a tiny tunnel flooded with the blazing light from the F-type star. She nearly lapsed into unconsciousness as the starlight faded and the ship bucked once beneath her and then settled.

"Orbit achieved at seventy million kilometers from the star. External temperatures are rising, approaching four-hundred seventy absolute degrees. Damage reports are not available." Sarah panted, as she struggled to maintain their orbit.

Alex fell back into her chair. "How did you—"

Sarah shook her head. "I knew we did not have enough power to exit the solar gravity well, so I inserted us into a semi-stable orbit."

The admiral's panicked voice matched Alex's racing heart as it erupted over the comm link. "What is going on up there? We have lost all internal gravity on the central decks. Containment vessel three has broken free from its moorings. I have hull failures throughout the external skeleton. The keel may be deformed. Spun-sail stays have failed—"

Alex interrupted. "We are in orbit around a star. Route as much power as possible to the thrusters to maintain our orbital position. Send drones out to repair the sail stays and inspect the attitudinal controls." Alex turned toward Sarah. "Communications?"

"Negative, Majesty. We have sensors and are maintaining a lock on the beacon we deployed earlier. We will lose lock once we orbit behind the star," Sarah replied. Alex could see the tremors running along Sarah's arms from the battle she fought to control the ship.

"Admiral, are the analyzer cores responding yet?"

"Analyzer cores?" His voice rose with incredulity. "You exited the wave without analyzer assistance?"

Alex looked at Sarah and saw her nod, but she did not take her eyes off her consoles. "So, it seems."

Nothing came over the comm system. "Admiral?"

"Then, we have another story to add to the Lady of the Ancients records of flight prowess."

Alex watched as Sarah's ears pinked.

"Indeed. Our pilot was able to control a flat spin and then achieve orbit within a star's gravity well. Now, about the cores."

The mechanical voice of the bridge AI cut in. "Analyzer cores will complete reset in four minutes and three seconds. System AIs routing damage reports to engineering control. A full report of the flight recorded for future study. No clan has ever recovered from a flat spin."

Alex chuckled and wiped her sweaty palms down her thighs. "Well, pilot, it seems you have again achieved the impossible. Well played."

Sarah did not respond, she simply continued to fly the giant ship. "Majesty, we will need to roll the ship to distribute the stellar heat across the entire hull. We cannot differentially heat one side versus the other."

"As recommended, so ordered." The clan rotated and the star field shifted outside the forward transparency. Alex looked over at G'iad'a. "Are you all right, imp?"

The child nodded and wiped her mouth. "Some water would appreciate." It seems their exit from the wave cooled some of the young heir's attitude.

Alex released her harness and floated out of her chair. She pushed off the back of the chair, moving toward the supply bulkhead. Retrieving three water sippers and a self-cleaning towel, she gave one sipper and the towel to G'iad'a.

"Tank you," the child whispered. Alex smiled at her.

After giving the second sipper to Sarah, she retook her seat and took a long pull on hers. "Sarah, set up a schedule for ship rotation to mitigate the temperature differentials. Then, ping the beacon and ensure it is transmitting on all bands."

The bridge was silent for several long minutes. The bridge AI chirped. "Yes."

"All AIs report. Damage concentrated along longitudinal structural elements. Repair drones dispatched to critical areas. Keel warped. Hatchways unusable. Isolation fields in place. Force fields on central decks holding. No crew injuries reported middeck. Critical systems rerouted around damaged sections. Forward speed limited." *Thank the gods, we will not need to worry about the crew escaping the central decks now.*

"Very well, keep us posted on the drones' progress." The bridge AI chirped, and Alex turned her attention to the limitations of their navigation and flight controls. "Sarah, how is she handling?"

"We are maintaining a stable orbit about the star. Lateral controls are sluggish, and our only available power is thrusters." The pilot turned, pushing her red braid over her shoulder. Alex could see the worry etched across her brow. "At our current power levels, we will not be able to exit the gravity well."

"Understood." Alex rubbed her forehead. "Admiral, when will we have full power to the gravitational engines?" The open comm line crackled and Alex heard a muffled curse and a clunk. "Admiral?"

"One minute, Majesty. Things are a bit harried down here for an old man." The admiral cursed again. The environmental recyclers cut in on the bridge and the smoke from the damaged equipment began to dissipate.

"Environmental systems reset and functional." Alex heard the engineering AI report to the admiral.

"Very good." His voice strengthened as he got closer to the audio pickup. "Now, Majesty, what may I do for you? I needed to stabilize life support as I assumed breathing was more important than your question."

Alex laughed. "I would agree, breathing is important." Sarah snorted and Alex laughed again. "My question was—"

"Yes, power output. Until the drones repair the containment vessels, and fuel and plasma are rerouted around the damage amidship, we will only have thruster control." *At least we still have containment vessels.*

"Thank you. I have dispatched drones to assess and repair the structural damage."

The admiral sighed. "Then, we are where we are."

"So, it seems." The connection severed with a click and Alex stared at the armrest on the command chair. "He hung up on me."

"I would imagine he is busy rebuilding systems," Sarah replied.

"As are we." Alex stood. "But first things, first. Anyone hungry?"

Part Three

Recovery

What a sad era we live in,
when it is easier to smash
an atom than a prejudice.
                    ~Albert Einstein

Lauren was lost in a fugue state. Because she couldn't feel her bond with Alex, she was distracted. She was desperately alone. She couldn't sleep. Lauren was so tired she could barely keep her eyes open and she sat with her head propped up in one hand, toying with a stylus on her desk with the other, mesmerized by the twirling motion. The boys were aboard Lauren's clan to discuss tactics for their remaining journey into nebular space. She glanced up, bleary eyed, when the boys spoke.

"We are thirteen days from the Comin nebula." Tavish was sprawled across the leather couch beneath the transparency in Lauren's command cabin. His blue and gray plaid wrapped around his broad shoulders with his flaming hair a wild cloud about his head. The star field beyond the transparency streaked past, the great clan ship traveling at faster-than-light pulse speeds. "I recommend we drop out of this wave several days before then and approach the nebula at sub-light normal speed."

Angus didn't look up from the micro-analyzer in his hand. "That will add more than a week to our travels." His appearance was a stark contrast to Tavish. His red, gray, and yellow kilt impeccable even though he sat cross-legged on the deck, his white shirt was crisp, and not a black hair escaped his tight tail. He was the picture of command and control.

"We need the time to run sensor sweeps across the region, prior to entering nebular space. I am sure the Comin have a full patrol waiting on the *Orchid*," Tavish replied.

"You might as well send flares out. Active sensors will announce our presence to anyone lurking in the nebular cloud. Lauren, your thoughts?" Angus looked up at her.

Lauren gazed back, but sleep called to her. She could hear them, but comprehension just wasn't possible.

Tavish dropped his stocking-covered feet toward the floor, landing on Ice who lay along the length of the couch.

"Hey, watch yourself." Ice growled. She rolled away from the intrusion and yelped as her splinted forepaw caught beneath her.

Ice's yelp penetrated the fog in Lauren's brain, and she chuckled.

Ice lifted her head to Lauren. *"Do not laugh at me. It hurts."* Snow mewled in sympathy for her partner. *"It is crowded in here with all of us present, but it's nice to be together again."*

"*Well said, Snow.*" Lauren smiled sadly at the wolf. Snow could always temper a situation. "*I'm glad we're together, too. But we're missing the heart and soul of our cadre.*"

"*I know, Lauren, but we are closer to recovering her every day. Have faith. We will be successful in our quest.*"

Lauren nodded at the great wolf and received an encouraging fang-filled smile in return.

A single tear tracked coldly down her cheek. Lauren didn't know if she could continue with her soul shredded. *Each day is harder than the last. I was so sure I would know if something terrible happened to Alex. Now I'm uncertain of everything.* Lauren swiped the tear away before the others could see it, in case they took it as a sign she didn't believe in their plan. Her heart was a void of darkness. Her soul split asunder. The part she had left was rapidly dying without the connection to her love. Shaking her head, she cleared her maudlin feelings. "Is there any way we can scout the nebula before we arrive, but not announce our presence?"

Angus held up his micro-analyzer, a star chart displayed on the small screen. "If we deploy drones from a point approximately two light hours from the edge of the nebula, we should be able to receive their sensor information using passive sensors."

"No, no, no." Tavish stepped over the lounging Ice to peer at the display on the small screen. "Lauren, link to Angus' analyzer and display his chart on your holo-projector, please."

The two-dimensional analyzer chart popped up in a three-dimensional hologram floating above her desk. Their position and projected course highlighted. The Comin nebula appeared as a hazy, violet cloud.

"Thank you." Tavish smiled at Lauren and winked at her. *Damn, he saw my tear.* She sniffled. *I can't help how I feel.* He poked his finger into the hologram and highlighted a point in space. "If we deploy drones from here and send them forward, they will enter normal space within the nebula and fan out across the area." He highlighted the drones' recommended courses.

"That is all well and good, Tavish, but as soon as they begin transmitting their sensor data back to us, won't that give away their positions?" Lauren tipped her head to the side and tried to imagine the little drones moving across open space.

Angus tapped his chin. "Perhaps we should see if the admiral has any suggestions?" Reaching above Lauren's head, he got the avatar's cube down and placed it on the desk. He nodded at Lauren and she picked up the cube to depress all eight corners. The hologram of the admiral appeared.

"Good evening, Majesty." He bowed his head to Lauren. "How may I be of service?"

Lauren smiled at the image floating above the digital storage cube. His voice sounded less mechanical each time they activated him. "Avatar, we're nearing the nebula and need to know what we're flying into. Any suggestions?"

"I know where we are, Majesty. I have been monitoring all navigation data." He chastised her with a gentle tone.

Lauren snorted. "Of course, you have."

The admiral's visage smirked. "I would be remiss if I did not maintain an understanding of the operational status of the *Stag*."

"Thanks for that." Lauren smiled crookedly. *He's so like the admiral.* "But now we're considering sending drones out into the nebula. The boys are concerned about an ambush from within the cloud."

"Indeed." The avatar narrowed his eyes in thought. Lauren could imagine the calculations going on in his electronic brain. The avatar finally nodded. "Majesty, I recommend a single drone, equipped with a full suite of electromagnetic-spectra sensors to see through the interference created by the nebular gases."

"A single drone will not be adequate to survey the nebula." Tavish stepped up to her desk and took one of the two leather chairs. "We need to do a complete survey."

The avatar shook his head. "No, boy, you will not be able to complete an entire survey. One, it would require too much time, which we do not have. Two, sending out a full suite of drones increases the likelihood one would be picked up on a patrol ship's sensors and we need the element of surprise on our side. And three, we would not be able to mask the returning data transmissions from that many point sources."

Angus dropped into the other desk chair. "I worry even a single drone will be detected. Its gravitational drive emits a unique signature and once it begins transmitting, it will light up like a . . . what did you call it, Lauren?"

"A Christmas tree." Lauren knew the companions were not familiar with the concept of that holiday, but it was the best analogy she had for the sudden blaze of energy a drone transmission would emit.

"Yes, thank you."

"I see." The avatar narrowed its eyes, but then it smiled at the companions. His holographic image brightened. "You both raise good points, but all can be addressed. Allow me to demonstrate."

The hologram of the nebula changed color as the avatar fed data into it. The violet-colored cloud changed to a soft blue and the flight paths of Tavish's recommended drones were changed to a deeper blue. A new flight path appeared in deep maroon. This single path arced across the front of the gas cloud, skimming the outer edge. Regularly spaced fans of pink emanated from the arced path, piercing the leading edge of the nebula. These fans marked the volume of space covered by individual sensor sweeps as the drone passed. "There, that should do."

Lauren and the boys leaned forward to study the hologram. "Okay, you've maximized the nebular volume swept by a single drone. But we still have the problem of detection." Lauren rotated the hologram, so they looked down on the ecliptic plane of the nebula rather than across it. This view highlighted how far into the cloud the sensor sweeps would penetrate. The avatar's suggested sweeps would penetrate five light seconds into the cloud. *We'd see about three hundred thousand kilometers into the nebula.*

"To continue, Majesty?" Lauren nodded absently, not taking her eyes off the hologram as the avatar replayed the flight of his solo drone. "Once the drone slows from faster-than-light pulse speed and enters normal space, it will cut its engine and continue on a purely ballistic course. Unless it comes within a thousand kilometers of a ship, it will not be detectable on normal scans. We will use the same frequencies as the admiral's beacon to transmit the sensor data back. A Comin warship would not normally scan the ultra-low frequency communication bands.

Angus nodded. "That just might work. Can we fit all the needed sensors into a single drone? Tavish suggested we fit different sensor types into each drone, allowing us to scan across the entire spectrum."

"Another good question, boy."

Lauren saw Angus bristle at the avatar's continued use of the diminutive and she patted his arm where it rested on her desk, smiling at him.

"You are correct. It would be a tight fit to place all the sensor packages into one drone, but if we program the sensors to alternate frequencies in each sweep, we can cover the entire spectrum with fewer sensors."

The three sat back and contemplated the avatar's recommendations. After a few minutes, Lauren said, "If we can reengineer a drone to allow for alternating frequencies scans, I—" Her office chime rang. "Come." The admiral's avatar disappeared with a snick as the door slid open.

Ailsa stood in the hatchway; a data pad held in a white-knuckled grip. "Majesty, a message from the *Boar*." The young tech handed her the pad.

Lauren took the pad. "Is Robert okay?" *What's wrong now?*

Chapter Two
Bridge of the Dubh Mogairle
Orbiting an F-Class Star

"We are maintaining our orbit about the star, ma'am. Entering seventh orbit now," Sarah reported from her position at the sailing master's console. She had placed a compression patch over her blaster wound but her suit was still streaked with dried blood. "Energy consumption is nominal. Attitudinal controls remain sluggish."

Alex sighed. "Anything from the beacon?"

Sarah turned her chair around. "We are on the opposite side of the star." She looked back over her shoulder at one of her monitors. Alex and her pilot had divided the control functions between them, routing different systems to each of their monitors. All five of the command chair's monitors were deployed around Alex and actively reporting the status of various ship systems. "We will be back in range in approximately six point four hours."

Well, I cannot change the size of the star or our speed. At least we are safe for now. Alex looked over at G'iad'a. The young heir slumped against her crash harness webbing; sound asleep. Tapping one of the monitors, Alex asked, "Admiral?"

"Aye, Majesty." A slurp and a swallow came through the audio link. "Status of the repairs?"

One of her monitors flickered and the admiral's drawn face appeared. He looked as tired as Alex felt. She would need to relieve them soon for rest. "The repairs continue. Most of the hull breaches are sealed. However, I can do nothing for the warped keel. She will need to be dry docked if you wish to repair her or scuttled as soon as we have an alternate means of transportation."

Alex shook her head. Her heart stuttered at losing one of the clans, even this old rust bucket. "We will need a dry dock, then. I do not wish to waste a resource no matter how damaged she is."

"I understand." His voice dropped to a whisper. "Alex, she may not be salvageable. I only have the drone reports on the extent of the keel damage. Without a visual inspection, I cannot comment further, but I would not recommend any sudden change in speed or altitude. Tell your pilot, no funny moves." Alex heard Sarah chuckle at this comment. Alex joined in. Given her recent flights, all of Sarah's moves seemed to be funny ones.

"Very well. Until the *Boar* picks up our beacon, we are not going anywhere soon."

The admiral leaned toward his monitor his face filling the small screen, causing Alex to lean away. "And if I may be so bold, you need to sleep, as does our pilot."

"And what about you, sir?"

"I am headed for a nap now. I trust the engineering AI to maintain our power output and monitor the repairs, if anything was to arise, I will be warned."

They were all exhausted. "And our guests? How are they fairing?"

"Activities on the middecks have slowed down. We have had no further attempts to breach the containment fields in the last seven hours. After the last one was attempted through a subdeck, we stopped it by releasing sevoflurane in the ventilation shafts. No one else has tried again." Alex had not wanted to drug the crew, but they did not have the manpower to continuously monitor their activities. Releasing a fast-acting, minimally damaging anesthetic agent into the ventilation system seemed best.

"Any idea about Gwenhwyfach?" Alex shuttered when she spoke the traitor's name.

"Sensors indicate the flag officer's cabin has a round-the-clock guard and a med tech sleeping on a cot in the hall. The ship's sensors have been disabled within this cabin." The flag officer's cabin was a large suite of living quarters and office space, rarely used on any of the clans. The admiral, who was fleet commander and therefore a flag officer, could have used it but opted for the engineering master's quarters during their search for Terra. Alex could have used the flag officer's quarters on the *Iolar Mara* but elected to use the captain's quarters to be closer to the bridge.

"What does all that mean to you?"

The admiral shrugged. "I am speculating, but it seems the traitor is bunked there and needs medical care at a moment's notice. My guess, something has happened to her." He looked away from the video pickup and placed a data file on another of Alex's monitors. She read through the information as it scrolled down the screen. "Past sensor records indicate no one entering the cabin except the med tech over the last five or so weeks. Each time the tech entered, he carried several large cases of supplies, which were not brought out of the cabin when he exited."

Alex tapped her chin and hummed. She thought back to their encounter with Gwenhwyfach, when she and Lauren were linked across their bond. Lauren had stopped the bitch's attack with a psi-energy web. *No, that would not harm her.* She was too strong to be injured in such a way. But if the bitch was ill or injured, it would explain why no one had searched for Alex.

Alex blinked back to the present. "The only information I could find in the medical records was a crewman with a cerebral vascular accident, but his stats indicate a male many decades younger. Do you think they falsified the records to hide a medical accident?"

"Possible, but why? Did not the young heir speak about the witch?"

"She did. She said she had not seen her for some time." Alex rubbed her forehead and decided to drop this speculation. If the bitch showed up, Alex was the only one who could manage her, and she would need all her strength to do so, therefore Alex needed to get some rest. "At this point, I do not care. But the captain seemed surprised I was alive. He thought I would have died of dehydration by now. Seems tending to me was not in his orders."

The admiral's harsh laugh caused Sarah to turn around. She frowned at Alex in question, but Alex waved her concern away as the admiral continued. "Well, let us not take on more battles than those we have already volunteered for. Aye?"

"Aye. Get some rest. I am going to have Sarah sleep for a bit while we are on the back side of the star and then I will take a turn."

"Sooner, rather than later, Alex. The vanguard you spoke to the Consort about should not be far now."

"Agreed. Sleep well, sir."

"And you, Majesty."

Alex cut the link and looked at their pilot. Dark circles marred Sarah's fair complexion. Her braid had long since failed and now a mass of red hair hung lank over her shoulder, stray tendrils framing her face.

"You heard the admiral, Sarah. Pull out a sleep sac and get some rest. Transfer the beacon telemetry to my monitor. I will keep watch." Alex looked at the forward transparency as the giant clan began one of her scheduled longitudinal rotations. As the ship rolled, the light from the F-class star flared through the forward transparency. "Transparency to ninety percent opacity. Bridge lights to night watch." The glare from the star faded and with the bridge illumination dropped to twenty-five percent, shadows formed across the large, empty space. The young heir muttered in her sleep and struggled against her bindings. *I will need to do something about her soon.* "And unfasten the heir and get her in a sleep sac as well."

"Ma'am?"

"She will not bother us. She is as exhausted as we are."

"Aye, but it is when she wakes which concerns me," Sarah mumbled. Alex watched her pilot pull her blaster from the top of the sailing console and tuck it into a pouch in her suit.

Bridge of the Faol Muc-fhiadhaich
Clan McLaren's Wild Boar

Robert McLaran, his jet-black hair held back in a tight tail, paced around the command dais of his bridge. His navy and white tartan kilt swirling about the tops of his brown boots with each revolution. With sleeves rolled above his elbows, he looked more ready to spar than command a clan. Not wearing an evac-suit, he was in direct violation of ship policy, but he hated the confinement of the skin-tight body armor. Besides, this vanguard business was a complete bore. He knew they would not have any problems prior to reaching the nebula. It would have been a bit more challenging had he not been in constant contact with the other three clans, but their quantum communication system took care of that. Turning around again he strode to the starboard side of the dais. "Anything?"

His navigator flinched and looked up from the holo-tank. "Nothing, sir."

Robert knew his patience was worn thin and he must not take it out on his crew. "Sorry, Shamus." They had no contact with the *Orchid* and no new information since retrieving the admiral's beacon.

"No problem, sir. We are on course, following the Terra-search flight path. We have stretched our sensors to their resolution limits. At flank speed, we should be gaining on them. Just nothing yet."

Shamus was quite young to hold the position of chief navigator tech aboard a clan. He was Robert's first cousin, the eldest son of his father's youngest sister, and he had Robert's aunt's blonde hair and striking teal eyes. His expertise at hand-to-hand combat and marksmanship was legendary, but his small stature prohibited his effective use of a broadsword. Therefore, Shamus never rose through the ranks of the McLaran clan, but he was one of the best astrogators Terra had and if anyone could improve their sensors he could. He could distinguish a sensor ghost from a true return at more than five light minutes.

"Keep at it." Robert smiled at the black energy-armored man. "And be sure you get proper rest. You have trained your staff well. This will continue to be a challenging search and I cannot have my best astrogator limited by exhaustion."

"Aye." Shamus returned his smile and added a wink.

The hours passed on this watch and Robert retired to his command cabin to eat. His booted feet now rested on his ironwood desk and he had just dropped into a light sleep when klaxons blared. The night watch illumination flashed into strobing red. "Commander to the bridge. Contact at six light minutes. Commander to the bridge. All crew to battle positions," the mechanical voice of the bridge AI ordered.

Robert jumped up from his chair and removed his kilt with a single twist of the belt clasp. Grabbing his suit of body armor from the back of the sofa, he jumped on one foot while inserting his other foot into a leg, donning the armor. As he sealed the neck closure, he grabbed his pneumatic face shield and exited onto his bridge. The night watch was being replaced by day watch crew and the bridge was filled with rushing clan members.

Crossing to his command chair, he dropped into the soft burgundy leather and activated all the monitors. "Report."

The astrogator turned to him. "We have a sensor contact at just over six light minutes. Resolution and identification is inhibited by its location. However, it is a large contact."

"What is wrong with its location?"

Just then Shamus bolted onto the bridge, his black body armor suit open to the waist, his bare chest exposed, he struggled to get his arms into the sleeves as he ran. His silvered face shield was clasped in his teeth.

"Shamus, increase our resolution and identify that contact."

"Aye, sir," his response garbled by a full mouth. If the situation was not so dire, Robert would have laughed at his young cousin's struggles.

Successfully getting both arms into his suit, the young navigator dropped the face shield and bent over the holo-tank. "Ultra-violet filters please," he said to the night watch astrogator. The hologram changed to a dull red color as the ultra-violet frequencies of light were removed from the image. "Now, apply a temperature filter and remove hydrogen spectral lines at nine-seven-two, one-zero-two-six, and one-two-one-six ang-stroms." The hologram wavered again, the stars turning from a bright white to a deep violet color. "Very good, now magnify section two-twenty-three by one-ten thousand by twelve." The hologram winked out and when it reformed, a massive star filled the construct. Shamus turned to Robert and pointed within the holo-projection, highlighting a tiny smudge on the face of the star. "There. Something is in close orbit of this F-star. Our sensors detected a shadow, as it blocked a portion of the star's luminosity."

Robert moved to the holo-tank, peering at the roiling star. "I do not see anything."

"Here." Again, Shamus poked his finger into the hologram, highlighting a tiny speck moving in front of the star.

Robert frowned. "That is just an inner rocky planet, caught within the gravity well of the star. It appears to be in a death spiral with its sun."

"Too small to be a planet." Shamus manipulated another gel pad. "And it is giving off energy emissions." The tiny image blinked off and on. He looked up at Robert and grinned like a cat after a bowl of cream. "I think it is a ship."

Robert shook his head. "No ship could maintain an orbit so close to such a massive star. It would be bathed in lethal radiation from the coronal plasma discharge. And what about the temperatures? That is an F-class star."

Shamus pulled himself to his full height. "That is a ship or a satellite orbiting that star."

"I do not—"

"Transmission beacon detected." Robert and Shamus spun toward the communication console on the port side of the bridge. The tech placed his hand over his ear and leaned toward his monitor, listening. "We are receiving an incoming message. It is garbled. The voice message is degrading, sir. But it contains an encrypted data stream."

"Send it to my screen." Robert leapt to his command chair and activated one of the communication analyzers there. Data streamed across the screen in a jumble of characters. He sank his hand into a gel pad and manipulated several programs. The jumble resolved into a message. As the words scrolled across the screen, Robert dropped into his chair, his legs no longer able to hold him up.

"They have taken the ship," he whispered. "Feck, they have control of the *Orchid*." The remaining message was lost as the data stream degraded completely.

"Shamus, send that star's location to navigation." Robert leapt to his feet. "Pilot." The young woman at the *Boar's* helm looked back at him. "Take us to the star, at maximum speed." He laughed, joy piercing his soul. "It seems our illustrious leader, with the aid of the admiral and his pilot, has taken the *Orchid* and they are now in command." Astonished murmurs ran around the bridge. "Communication, send a quantum message to the *Stag*."

"Ready, sir."

"We found them and are moving to intercept the *Orchid*. The trio is in control of the ship. No further information is available at this time. Append our galactic position." He paused to take a breath and calm his racing heart. Gripping his tail in one hand, he twirled it around his fingers. "Ask for an immediate reply from Her Majesty." Excitement vibrated through him. *How could they have taken a clan against a crew of four thousand?* "Send out an acknowledgement of the beacon on all channels. Include an estimate of our arrival time. Ask how we can be of assistance."

"Sending our estimated arrival to communications now, sir," Shamus said.

"And add their beacon message was degraded," Robert replied.

Bridge of the Dubh Mogairle
Orbiting and F-Class Star

"Ma'am?" Sarah's voice cut through Alex's exhaustion and she flinched in the command chair. Gods, her back would never recover from the torture of sitting in this gods forsaken chair. *How could the captain stand it?* Alex swung around toward her pilot.

Sarah sat up and pulled the tabs to open the blue sleep sac she was swaddled in. "Your turn. You need some rest." The pilot stood and struggled into the torso section of her evac-suit.

"After we complete this orbit." Alex looked at the navigation plot on one of her command monitors. "We should exit the umbra of the star in approximately three hours."

"Then something to eat?" Sarah stretched, before turning to the food dispenser area in the aft section of the *Orchid's* bridge.

"Food would be good, thank you."

Alex looked at the small bundle huddled at the foot of the command dais. "I am sure the young heir is hungry, and we need her secured in her couch if she is going to be awake." Standing, Alex walked over to the green bundle and nudged it with her toe. The bundle rolled over and a small head popped out of the top.

"How dare. No kick heir to Empire." A frown marred the child's face.

Well, it seems her attitude woke as she did. "I did not kick you, imp. We simply need you awake so you can eat, and then we will talk." The small child crawled out of her sac and extended her arms out with a large yawn. She looked like a golden lion cub, stretching in the sun after a nap. Sarah handed Alex a food pouch and water sipper. "Thank you."

The young pilot looked down at the child. "And what will you have for breakfast, imp."

"No, imp." The child frowned. "But am hungry. Egg, sausage, allo-seed toast."

Sarah handed the child a small silver packet and a sipper. "Universal energy protein and water." A huff answered Sarah. Alex smiled at the tug of war between the two. The child's hunger must have won out as she shrugged and sat on the edge of the command dais to eat.

"G'iad'a, when did you last speak to Gwenhwyfach?" Alex sat in the command chair.

The child looked up from her meal. "Many day ago." She paused, tipping her head to the side as her braids fell across her shoulder, beads rattling. "Perhaps, four thirteen-cycle."

"How long is that," Sarah asked from her position at the sailing console, where she munched on an energy ration.

"Many day." G'iad'a slurped water.

Alex placed her meal pouch down and turned the command chair toward Sarah. "Please ping the beacon once we clear the umbra of the star." Smiling down at the child, Alex asked, "Why are you aboard the *Orchid*?" *I need answers so I can plan our next steps.*

The question seemed to catch G'iad'a by surprise and she flinched. "I no understand."

"Oh, I think you understand just fine." Alex leaned toward the child and G'iad'a leaned away, nearly falling off the edge of the dais. "Again, why are you aboard this ship?"

G'iad'a wiped her mouth on the back of her sleeve. "I taken by witch. As b'rac'rac."

"What is b'rac'rac?" Alex knew her pronunciation was poor, the harsh Comin consonances a difficult twist of tongue for a Terran.

Thinking for a moment, G'iad'a tried to find a translation. "Not know. Perhaps, insurance?"

"Insurance for what?" This could only mean one thing. The bitch was not sure of Comin support. Another tidbit of information. When the child did not answer, Alex turned the question. "How were you taken?"

Anger flared in the small dark eyes, making the golden flecks flash. "From the T'le'cac."

"The what?"

"T'le'cac. Gateway to planets." The child suddenly looked sheepish and hung her head.

No, the Comin have discovered the quantum nexi. They could go anywhere. Alex looked closely at the young girl and smirked. *I recognize that look.* She had it often as a child when she did something she was not supposed to. "And, you were not supposed to be near the gateway."

The child's head whipped up, her eyes meeting Alex's with a look of defiance. "I nine cycles. I heir to condor throne of Empire. I be where I want."

"But, not in the T'le'cac. Heir, did the witch come to your Homeworld through the gateway?"

Again, the child's head dropped, braids falling forward to hide her eyes. "Not in T'le'cac. She reach through, grab me from far."

Finally, the pieces were falling in place. Gwenhwyfach or one of her ancestors discovered a quantum nexus between Terra Prime and the Comin world. With this connection, they must have developed some sort of alliance with the Comin. *With the destruction of Terra Prime, they must have discovered another nexus on Terra as I did?* This would explain Gwenhwyfach having a Comin disruptor, the one she used on Lauren. *But to grab the young heir through a nexus? Did Gwenhwyfach have a nexus aboard the* Orchid? *Could she create one?* Alex extended her psi-senses outward, trying to sense a nexus aboard ship. She caught herself and stopped, aware of the dangers her search would create.

"Now here." The child interrupted her train of thought. She had tears in her eyes. "Now . . ." the heir sobbed out, ". . . now you have me. What will do me, now?"

Alex had no idea what she was going to do but having the heir here may be to their advantage. She watched fat crystalline tears slide down the child's dark cheeks. "We will not hurt you. I will do everything to return you home." The child's tears slowed. "When we are able. I cannot promise anything more than that." The child's shoulders sagged. Alex took a chance. "I will allow you freedom, if you promise on your honor not to interfere with our efforts. Do I have your promise?"

G'iad'a stood and bowed low, an arm crossed over her chest. "I promise." She looked back up at Alex. "Tank you."

"You are welcome. Finish your meal and if you are in need of something, let us know. We will try and provide it." Alex turned toward the sailing console. "Sarah, I will get some sleep. Please monitor the beacon. We should be in contact again soon."

"Aye." Sarah checked a monitor display. "Two hours, thirty-one seconds to exit the umbra."

Alex retrieved a sleep sac from the storage bin and unfurled it on the edge of the command dais. Snuggling down, Alex closed her eyes. *I will need to reach out to Lauren soon. I cannot maintain this block much longer. It is draining me.* Alex startled. *If this is causing this much pain for me, what am I doing to Lauren?* Her heart beat double time. Lauren must be near hysteria.

Bridge of the Faol Muc-fhiadhaich
Clan McLaren's Wild Boar

"Approaching orbital insertion." Shamus peered into the holo-tank. "The ship is on the opposite side of the star."

"Very well, establish solar-synchronous orbit above the beacon and wait for the *Orchid* to reappear from behind the star." Robert walked over to his command chair and sat on the edge of the seat, tucking his hair back. "Once, she is back around, hail her on all frequencies."

"All frequencies, aye," his communication tech replied.

Robert could hear the excitement in the young tech's voice. *Can we be this close to recovering Alex?* He did not know, but his hopes rose with every minute. "Have we heard from the *Stag* yet?"

"No reply on the quantum receiver, sir."

The minutes dragged waiting for the *Orchid* to come around to the front of the star. Robert stood and began pacing around the command dais. Tension ratcheted up on the bridge as the time for the *Orchid's* emergence approached.

"Re-emergence in one minute and counting," Shamus stated from the holo-tank.

"Send another ping to the beacon."

"No response, sir."

"Re-emergence, now." Shamus looked up at Robert. "We have a visual on the *Orchid*. She is maintaining the same orbit."

"Send the hail." Robert watched the communication tech send the message.

Turning back to Shamus, he stepped up to the holo-tank. "What do you think is happening over there?"

"I have no clue." Shamus sighed heavily. Robert knew, he worried about a trap, too. "I am still stuck on how those three could overpower four thousand and take the ship."

"Any ideas on how we would recognize a trap? The voice message was so garbled I could not recognize the speaker. The data stream carried the proper encryptions, but I am concerned we are walking into a nightmare."

"I agree. I would request visual communications, the next—"

The communication tech interrupted. "I have a message from *Orchid*, sir." He turned from his console. "Response, sir?" A hush fell over the bridge as the crew held their breath. Everyone knew how close they were to recovering Alex. *Can it be this easy?*

"Not until I hear the message." Robert sat in his command chair. "What is the transmission lag? Can we establish real-time communications?"

Turning back to his screens, the tech pulled the data up. "At this distance, approximately one minute and twenty-one seconds."

"Pilot. Maintain a safe distance but let us cut the transmission lag time as far as possible." Robert activated the comm console on his chair. "Send the message over, please."

As the great clan ship made headway toward the star, *Orchid's* problems were transmitted to the *Boar*. As Robert read the message, he realized the dangers they faced. While the *Orchid's* current orbit was stable, at some point her thruster fuel would be depleted and she would spiral into the star. Time was in short supply.

"Sir?"

"The ship is damaged and running low on fuel." Robert acknowledged Shamus with a nod. "I believe we can enter a synchronous orbit above the *Orchid* and using power from our radiant-heat sinks shunted to the external maintenance tractors, tow her out of orbit. Once clear of the star's gravity well, we should be able to maintain steerage way to a safe distance and rescue Alexandra, the admiral, and his pilot."

Standing, Robert rubbed his hands together. "Let us do it." He punched a comm link on the armrest. "Engineering, I will need all available power stored in the sinks to power the repair tractors. We are going to pull the *Orchid* out of the star's well." He stepped off the dais. "Set it up, people. I will prepare a quantum communication packet for the *Stag*." He walked off the bridge into his command cabin.

Aboard the Ruadh làn-damh

Lauren entered the bridge at a run. Her heartbeat uncontrollably. *My god, we've done it!* "All stop. Exit the wave and hold position. Send the same orders to the other two clans, please. Prepare to send the boys back to their respective ships." The boys followed her and moved to the rear of the bridge, stopping at the blast door.

"We will wait for word, Lauren. This is truly amazing news," Angus said. No one else on the bridge crew knew what was happening except Ailsa, and Lauren watched as she struggled to cover her glee. *I bet my smile is bigger than hers.* Lauren chuckled.

"All stop, aye," the pilot answered. The great ship shuddered as she made the translation, exiting the gravitational wave to normal space. Stars flared outside the forward transparency and then settled into stationary specks of brilliant light.

The navigator spoke from the holo-tank, "The clans have entered normal space and are coming along side our position."

"Communication, please send a message to the *Kestrel* and *Lion*, have them maintain station keeping above and below the *Stag* at one hundred klicks," Tavish ordered.

"One hundred klicks, aye, sir." Ailsa sent the communication off to the other ships.

Lauren walked back to the rear of the bridge, Snow and Ice in her wake. "Now comes the difficult part, Lauren." Tavish placed his large hand on her shoulder and Lauren looked at him in question. "Waiting. You must rest and eat. You must not forget yourself, while we wait for word. We must be strong. Taking care of ourselves is key. We do not know what will be asked of us, but we must be ready. A battle is ninety-nine percent boredom as one waits and one percent terror. Let us hope the one percent does not come."

Lauren swallowed hard at his pronouncement. "Yes, no terror, please." Tavish's comment tempered some of her excitement.

Angus broke in. "I recommend we send off the drone and gather what information we can. This will give us something to focus on while we wait." He smiled at Lauren; she nodded.

"Angus, why don't you prep the drone to the specs we discussed? We'll launch it after we receive the next message from the *Boar*." She reached out and the boys stepped into a group hug. In a voice low enough for only them to hear, she said, "I'm not very good at waiting. Patience isn't exactly my strong suit." *And I still don't know why Alex's blocking me.*

The wolves crowded into the circle. *"No worries, Lauren, we will keep you busy."* Ice cut in. The three laughed, foreheads touching.

"Indeed," Lauren replied.

The hours dragged as they waited for word from Robert. Lauren sat through two rotations of the bridge crew and now it was the middle of the night watch. She sagged in her chair and rested her heavy head in the palm of her hand. The dim bridge lights and quiet hum of conversation didn't help. Snow and Ice were curled in a large furry ball at the foot of her command chair, snoring. Commands chirped and beeped as they were sent and acknowledged from various stations around the bridge

Sometime later, Lauren was woken from a dreamless sleep by a throat being cleared near her. Startled, she leapt from her chair and crashed into a crewman. The tech fell backward and landed on top of the wolves, who yowled at the interruption of their sleep.

"What?" Lauren demanded her voice loud in the silent bridge.

Shakily, he held out a pad to Lauren. "A message, Majesty."

Finally awake, Lauren had to laugh. She pulled the tech to his feet. "Sorry, what've you got?" She took the pad and sat on the edge of her command chair, thumbing the device open at the same time. Although their quantum communication system provided real-time communication across vast distances between the clans, it didn't allow for complex messages or face-to-face communications. So, the four had developed a standardized communication format, simplified to use binary code language. Fourteen lines of message, divided into a header, text or message section, and an end.

BEGIN MESSAGE
CFRId CMcLFMf R 151412 ST
In orbit above the *Orchid*
Will attempt to pull ship from gravity well
Six hours to complete this task
Will transfer Her Majesty, the admiral and his pilot from
   Orchid to *Boar*
Then travel your location
Will send additional information in six standard hours.
END MESSAGE

Lauren sat in silence for a long minute, trying to decipher the message. Standing, she said to the tech, "Send a copy of this to the boys, I'll be in my cabin." She needed to figure out what Robert was trying to say. As she went into her cabin and sat at her desk, Lauren picked up the cube resting there and activated the avatar.

"How may I be of assistance, Majesty?" The visage of the admiral smiled at Lauren.

"We've received a communication from the *Boar* and I'm not sure I understand what Robert's trying to say." She let the pad fall to her desk, frustration rippling through her. Her earlier elation had disappeared. *Tavish is right, waiting is really hard.* "This quantum system is a marvel, but the messages leave a lot out."

The avatar looked at the pad and cocked its head as it pulled a data stream from the portable device.

"Interesting."

"Interesting?"

"Do you wish a literal translation?" She nodded and the avatar began to translate in a monotone voice.

"Message to Clan Fraser *Ruadh làn-damh,*

Message from Clan McLeod *Faol Muc-fhiadhaich,*

Message sent at the fifteenth hour, fourteenth minute, twelfth second ship time,

Message reads: in orbit above the *Orchid,* will attempt to pull ship from gravity well, six hours to complete this task, will transfer Her Majesty, the admiral, and his pilot from the *Orchid* to *Boar,* then travel to your location.

Will send additional information in six standard hours.

End message."

Lauren looked at the chronometer on her desk. It read 15:16:37. "Wow, only a three-minute lag. That's pretty good considering the distance between the ships." She thought of the admiral's genius and smiled. *What an advantage to be able to communicate and know what's going on half a galaxy away. Without the communicator, we'd only have my connection with Alex. Since that's missing, we'd all be in the dark.* Lauren swallowed hard against tears.

"Actually, there was no lag, Majesty. The difference in time was due to the time needed to decrypt the binary code string once the message was received." The avatar appeared to smirk.

"Don't act all smug, Admiral. Just because you speak binary, doesn't mean the rest of us do. And what's all this about pulling the *Orchid* from a gravity well."

The avatar smiled. "That data isn't held within the message. But if I were to postulate?" Lauren nodded. "The *Orchid* is stuck in a star's gravity well and must be tractored out."

Lauren sat bolt upright and nearly toppled from her chair. *Holy crap!* "Are they in danger? What's going on? How can we help? Oh, this isn't good. I can feel it." She stood and began pacing, the avatar's floating visage moving from side to side as it followed her motion.

"Calm yourself, Majesty. We do not have enough information to answer those questions. I believe something must have happened to the ship when the three took her, and the result is they became trapped within a star's gravity well. The *Boar* has more than enough power to pull the other ship free and rescue the trio."

"Fine." Lauren threw up her hands. She dropped onto the couch and let her head fall into her hands, her braid sliding over her shoulder. "I want her back. I want her back now. We're light years from their location and I can't talk to her and I can't . . ." Lauren's whispered plea ran out of energy and she collapsed onto her side.

The avatar gave her a gentle smile. "Once Robert has more information, he will send it. Perhaps then, we will be able to answer more of your questions. In the meantime, I recommend a nap for you. You will function more efficiently if you receive some rest."

Lauren sighed. "Although sleep sounds good, I don't have time."

"You must rest to be at your best when needed." The avatar snicked out of existence. Lauren let her body relax and sleep captured her immediately.

Chapter Three
Bridge of the Dubh Mogairle
Near-orbit F-Class Star

"Ma'am, I have an incoming message." When Sarah did not get a response from Alex, she looked over her shoulder. The lump in the sleep sac had not moved. "Ma'am," she spoke louder. No response. "Alex." Louder, but still nothing. "She is beyond exhausted. No wonder she does not respond," Sarah mumbled.

"No yell. Hurt ears," the Comin heir said from her seat at the navigation station, where she was munching on a protein bar.

"Imp, I need to wake the queen. Would you do that for me? I cannot leave this station while the message is streaming."

"Do this. Do that. I not servant. I heir." Braids flew as she tossed her head.

Sarah laughed. "Fine. Heir, please wake the queen. This is important."

The young girl hopped off her chair and walked to where Alex slept on the command dais. Leaning over, she shouted, "Up now! Message."

Alex recoiled and groaned. Sarah laughed as Alex rolled over. Though warm and somewhat comfortable, a sleep sac was not the easiest thing to get out of. "What? What now?" A head popped out of the jumbled sac.

"I have a message coming in, Majesty," Sarah replied.

"Right, give me a second here."

Sarah watched Alex struggle to get out of the sac. She failed, and then just ripped the closure open. Rising, Alex stretched. "Thank you, heir. But next time, no shouting."

"What I said. Hurt ears."

"Yes, it does hurt one's ears." Alex laughed and looked at Sarah. "Now, to business. What have we got?"

"I am receiving a message from the *Boar*. They have established synchronous orbit above us."

"Wonderful, now we can get out of here, and—"

Sarah interrupted. "It is not going to be that easy, ma'am. We have a problem with communications. The solar radiation from the star is playing havoc with our transmissions. Everything is garbled and they do not have a clear picture of what we need, therefore, they do not know what to do."

"That is a problem." Alex dropped into the command chair and traced her lower lip. "Have you tried a tight-beam transmission directly at the *Boar*?"

"They did. No luck, I am afraid. Their message is garbled by the time we receive it."

"And the admiral, what does he suggest?"

"He is still resting. I did not want to wake him until we had a go at this problem." Sarah turned back to her consoles, entering another string of commands into her gel pad. Her unease rose. *I thought we could figure this out.*

"Like witch." G'iad'a's small voice said around a mouthful of protein bar.

Alex moved to behind Sarah's chair and leaned over her shoulder, watching as the analyzers tried to make sense of the message's data stream. "Have you asked the bridge AI for its analysis?"

"Not yet. That was my next step."

"Said, like witch," the young heir repeated.

"I would try that, and if we cannot resolve the message, wake the admiral." Alex turned away and Sarah watched her drop into the command chair with another wince.

Alex turned to her screens and activated the bridge AI.

The mechanical voice snapped on. "How may I be of assistance, Majesty?"

"AI, we need to translate the incoming message and then establish clean communications with the *Boar*. We cannot communicate through the solar radiation."

Several minutes later, the AI replied, "I recommend pulsing transmissions in bursts. This star is a Cepheid variable. Luminosity is varying in a distinct pattern. If transmission was sent between periods of high luminosity, the radiation levels should be low enough to limit interference with the data stream."

"Sarah?" Alex glanced at her.

"What is the periodicity of the luminosity?" *I will need to determine the time between pulses to break up the message.*

"The rate of helium ionization within the outer photosphere is controlling the periodicity of luminosity. We will need another orbit to measure this accurately," the AI replied.

"We do not have time for another orbit. Make a guess." Alex huffed, her frustration evident.

The AI sounded indignant. "I do not guess."

Before Sarah could intervene in the growing argument between Alex and the AI, the young heir stood up and with hands on her hips, yelled, "I say, like witch."

"What?" Sarah turned in her chair and faced the child. "Like witch, what? Stop interrupting. We are trying to communicate with the *Boar*. Sit down and be quiet."

Alex frowned and knelt before the child. "What are you saying, imp?"

"Witch no need machine to talk." She looked hard at Alex and then Sarah, obviously, trying to make them understand. "Talk like her."

Alex looked at Sarah. "Really, can we do that?"

Talk like whom? Sarah was confused. "Do what? I am totally lost here."

"Communicate with Robert using our companion bond. Is that what you are saying?" Alex's words ran together, obviously excited. G'iad'a nodded, beads clacking as her braids swayed. "If we do this, I would be opening my bond up. The witch would hear me and come looking. I would be risking all we have accomplished. I would place all of you in danger."

"She no talk me many days. I no hear her. She sleep."

"If you can do that, it would be faster than us trying to punch through this radiation. And time is not in our favor." Sarah bit her lip as her heart rate accelerated. *Alex has not wanted to open her bond. Can we risk it now, when rescue is so near?*

"Very well." Alex sighed.

Sarah knew they could not hold their orbit much longer. Their fuel supply was running dangerously low.

Bridge of the Faol Muc-fhiadhaich Clan McLaren's Wild Boar

Robert paced from one end of his cabin to the other. Shamus had finally convinced him to leave the bridge. The *Orchid* was in sight, but they could not talk to her. It was driving him mad. All three senior communications techs were on the bridge trying to punch a message through the radiation. So far nothing. "AI, what is the comm status?"

"As before. We are unable to send or receive an intelligible message," the voice of his bridge AI replied.

"Not good enough." He sighed. Getting mad at his AI was as unproductive as trying to talk to his desk chair. *What else can we try?* His best people could not figure out a solution. He knew something was wrong with the *Orchid*, but without knowing what, he could not pull the ship out.

He could cause a catastrophic hull breech, if he did not know the clan's structural integrity.

Moving back onto the bridge, he ordered, "Send a quantum message to the *Stag*, ask her Majesty to ask the admiral what he suggests for punching through the radiation."

"Sir?" His chief communications tech questioned.

Dropping into his command chair, he waved his hand. "Send the message."

Shamus stepped up to his side. "Robert, you know the admiral is on the *Orchid* not on the *Stag*, correct?"

Realizing what he had said, he could not cover up his slip. Instead he whispered, "We found an avatar of the admiral on Luna Keep, when we discovered the quantum communications device. It contains a dump of the admiral's projects and analytical abilities."

"That . . . that is amazing."

Robert smiled at his cousin. "We could not believe it either, but Lauren brought the avatar with her. It might have some ideas."

Shamus looked at the communication tech. "You heard the commander, send the message."

"Aye, sir." The tech disappeared into the small niche where the quantum equipment was located.

Robert nodded. "Thank you." He felt a tug on his consciousness and then promptly collapsed.

Bridge of the Dubh Mogairle

We are so close to rescue. I will not risk everything we have accomplished. But Alex knew it was the only thing to do. It was the only thing to get them out of this pickle fast enough. She stiffened. If she opened her bond to communicate with Robert, Lauren would hear her also. *Gods, I do not have time to explain. What will she think of me? She is going to be furious. Unfortunately, it must be done.* Resolve filled her.

Standing, she raised her arms above her head and spread her fingers wide. Closing her eyes, she opened the door to the stone room and began to focus her psi-energy. Power coursed through her and she felt her psyche swell surrounding her in a curtain of invincibility. Alex continued to pull power from those around her. *Come on, I need more.* Once massed, she dropped the rest of her block and sent a burst of bond energy outward. From a distance, she heard G'iad'a cry out. The young girl dropped to the deck. Imagining her energy traveling outward, filling the universe, Alex focused her release in search of her companions. There. Robert was on his bridge.

Alex pulled him into their companion bond and poured more energy into link. The link faltered, then died. "What the?" Alex focused all her bond energy, targeting only Robert. "Come on, Robert. Hear me."

He is unconscious, but his mind is still open to our bond. Alex sent all the critical information to him, organized in a military communique format. Hopefully, once he regained consciousness he would remember and be able to act. A bolt of rebound energy pierced her heart. Lauren heard her.

Aboard the Ruadh làn-Damh

One minute Lauren was asleep, dreaming of wildflowers and picnics, the next she was wide awake. Her soul pierced as her bond sang to life. She bolted upright, throw falling from the sofa. *"Oh my god, Dearest, you're there. Here with me. Us. I can't believe it, after all this time."* Then her pain of separation rose and overwhelmed her excitement before she could control it. *"Why?"* Her question tore across the universe and ripped into Alex's soul. Silence rang through her cabin. Lauren couldn't hear anything over the thunder of her heart. *"Alex, answer me! Why?"*

"Lauren one moment, please. I must get Robert to understand," was Alex's whispered plea.

Lauren moved to her desk. The avatar cube sat there, quiet now, but Lauren felt as though it heard all, knew all, ready at the moment's notice. She hit the comm stub on her desk. "Ailsa."

"Yes, Majesty?"

"Send a quantum communique to the *Boar*. I've reconnected with Alex. She's trying to reach Robert."

"Ma'am?"

"That's all I know. I'm trying to get more information from Alex. Just send the message please."

"Aye, ma'am." Ailsa closed the channel.

Turning toward the transparency, Lauren walked up to the clear barrier, placing her hand over the section of the galaxy Alex was in. *"Alex, please. What's going on?"* Desperation mounted, she begged aloud. "Please, Alex."

"I am here, Dearheart. I apologize for my block on our bond, but I could not risk the bitch hearing us, or feeling our connection. The admiral, Sarah, and I had much to accomplish aboard the Orchid *and I was so concerned*

about being caught I could think of no other way to isolate my bond signature and protect us. Please understand."

Lauren shook her head. *The wolves were right. She did this to protect them.* Her soul was raw from lack of connection with Alex. Taking a deep breath, she tried to calm down and place herself in Alex's position. Of course, Alex was correct to be concerned. Gwenhwyfach could easily trace her using a psi-search if their bond was active. It would be a beacon on a stormy night. Lauren took another deep breath. *"Put your anger aside, Lauren. There will be time to talk later,"* her granddaddy's voice whispered in her ear. Lauren drew another deep breath and settled herself. *We're reconnected, rejoice in that.*

"I understand, Alex. Are you okay? Can you talk? What's going on? How can I help?"

A chuckle reverberated through her soul and she reflectively laughed along. *"One question at a time, please. For now, we are well and in control of the Orchid. And before you ask, that is a story for another time."* Lauren laughed again; Alex knew her too well. *"But we are stuck in the gravity well of a star and do not have the power reserves to escape. We will need the Boar to pull us free. Gently. The keel is warped, and the bulkheads compromised. I do not know how much the clan can take. I sent Robert the information along our bond, but I do not know if he heard or comprehended the message."*

"Send me what you need, and I'll transmit it to Robert using our quantum communication link."

"You found it and got it to work?"

Lauren dropped into her desk chair and rubbed her hands on her kilt. "Yeah, we did, and it works as you hypothesized."

"Indeed." Lauren felt Alex smile. *"Once we are pulled out of this gravity well, I want to transfer the four of us to the Boar. The Orchid will not be able to match her speed. I do not even know if she will be able to fly within a gravitational wave again."*

"She's damaged that badly?"

A feeling of worry crossed their bond. *"I do not know exactly how badly she is harmed. But we have had a bumpy ride so far. She was in poor condition to begin with. She is an old girl."*

Something Alex said hit Lauren. *"You said four. Who is the fourth? I thought we would transfer only you, the admiral, and his pilot."*

Worry—and is that embarrassment?—flashed across their bond when Alex replied. *"Well, we seem to have added another to our cadre. She was also taken by the witch against her will. I cannot leave her behind. I promised we would see her home, if possible."*

"Home? Who? Alex, what're you saying?" Lauren tried to tamp down her growing anxiety, but Alex's conflicting emotions filled their bond. *"Who else was taken from Terra?"*

"Not Terra, from the Comin Homeworld."

That threw Lauren for a loop. *Homeworld? What the hell?* Lauren frowned. *"Alex!"*

"It is the heir to the Comin Empire. G'iad'a is nine cycles old and next in line for the throne after her mother took control." Lauren struggled to silence her questions, but her curiosity would not be easily halted. *Just let her explain. "Seems Gwenhwyfach pulled her through a nexus from the Comin Homeworld to the* Orchid. *How, I do not know. For what purpose, I do not know. But she is as much a hostage as I was."*

Lauren thought about a young child torn from her home and taken hostage. How terrible and frightening that must be. However, they had more important things to worry about first. *"That's awful."* Lauren paused to gather her thoughts. *"One step at a time. Let's get you out of the gravity well and off the* Orchid. *Once you're onboard the* Boar, *we can speak in more depth."*

"Thank you. Please relay the information to Robert and ask him to pull us free. Once away from the star, we will be able to communicate directly and plan for our transfer." Lauren felt a burst of love swell in her heart. *"I love you with all that I am, Dearheart."*

"And I you."

Lauren entered a quick message into a pad and exited onto the *Stag's* bridge, walking over to the quantum communication niche. "Ailsa, I will need your help with a quantum message, please."

"Of course, Majesty."

She leaned down to whisper in Ailsa's ear, "I've spoken to Alex." Ailsa gasped. "Shhh." Lauren looked back over their shoulders to the bridge, hoping no one heard her. It seemed no one had. "No one can know we have made contact." The young tech bobbed her head, blonde hair moving in a shimmering cloud around her shoulders. "I've got specific information about their needs and the status of the *Orchid* which Robert will need to plan his rescue. Send this, please." She handed Ailsa a data pad. "The *Orchid* is badly damaged and could come apart if they aren't careful."

"Of course, ma'am." Ailsa thumbed the pad on and began to review the information. "To send all of this I will need time. It is a lot to convey within our sixteen-line message protocol."

"We can't wait. Don't worry about the protocol. Send it in one transmission."

"Very well." Ailsa entered the communication niche and began entering the header information using a keyboard. Lauren watched as Ailsa linked the data pad into the system and fed the information directly into the body of their message.

"Thank you." A rush of emotions rose goosebumps on Lauren's arms.

"You are welcome." Looking up at Lauren, Ailsa smiled. "You are looking better, Majesty. I am glad you got some rest."

Little did the young tech know it wasn't rest Lauren had needed but the reopening of her bond with Alex. Energy poured through her from their connection. She felt as though she could leap across the distance between their clans and pull the *Orchid* from the gravity well herself.

Stepping out onto the bridge, Lauren ordered the assistant communication tech. "Send a message to the boys. 'We've established contact with the *Orchid*. The *Boar* will begin rescue operations shortly. Please come aboard the *Stag* at your earliest convenience. End message.'"

"Message sent."

"All right, let's do this." Lauren rubbed her hands together and dropped into her command chair, waiting for the boys to arrive.

Chapter Four
Aboard the Dubh Mogairle
Bridge, Orbiting an F-class Star

"This is not going to be easy, Majesty," Sarah said from the sailing master console aboard the *Orchid*. "The stresses on the hull will exceed maximum tolerance where the tractors attach."

"Be that as it may, we do not have a choice. Our fuel supplies are at a critical level and we cannot deploy the sails to collect any radiant energy," Alex replied, gripping the command chair's armrests. "We have calculated the exact attachment points as well as we can."

Sarah turned from her monitors. "I would suggest we have the admiral transfer his engineering controls here."

Alex frowned. "Why?"

"If the ship were to come apart, the bridge module would survive the breakup. A tractor focused directly over the bridge would insure we would be pulled from the gravity well."

Alex understood, but she would not condemn a thousand Terrans to a fiery death within the corona of a star, regardless of their traitorous actions. She really did not know how many were involved in the witch's plot and how many were innocent clan members, unaware of the actions of their superiors. *No, I cannot abandon them.* "Your suggestion has merit. Have the admiral make his way here. I will not abandon the remainder of the ship." Reaching out along her bond, she called to Lauren. *"Dearheart?"*

Lauren's answering whisper was groggy, *"Dearest?"*

Alex did not have time for Lauren to wake up. *"You must save the entire vessel. If she starts to break apart, pull the bridge module and any crew quarters from amidship out. I will not abandon anyone."*

"But—"

"You will relay this message to the Boar. *It is everyone or no one. I will not allow the death of innocent Terrans because of the actions of a few traitors."*

For several long moments, Lauren was silent. Alex could feel Lauren's anger and fear—the two emotions warring for dominance. She knew Lauren understood. Alex would not sacrifice the innocent to save herself. *"Very well. Message sent."*

"Thank you, Dearheart. I love you."

"And I you." Alex's heart swelled as a burst of love and understanding blanketed her soul. She also felt the terror Lauren was struggling to control. Sitting in another part of the galaxy, so far away and unable to aid in this rescue must be hell for her. Lauren was a doer, a leader. Here, on the *Orchid*, they had actions to perform which tamped down the fear, as they focused on their rescue. All Lauren could do was wait.

"It will be all right, Dearheart."

"Just get your butt back here. Because if I've gotta come to you, I'll be pissed. Well, more pissed than I already am."

"We would not want that. A pissed Consort is not a happy Consort." They both shared a laugh across the galactic distance, their bond singing with love and concern for the other's safety.

Banging on the bridge blast doors signaled the arrival of the admiral. "Open the doors, Sarah."

"Aye." The giant doors slide partially open with a groan, then seized. It seemed the entire structure of the giant clan had been compromised.

The admiral stepped onto the bridge, his exoskeleton whirring as he stooped under the frozen door. "Seal the doors, Sarah. Without them closed, the bridge module is compromised." He moved over to the engineering console, eyeing the damaged pilot's couch on his way. "Seems things have been as interesting here as in engineering." He chuckled at his own joke then noticed the heir. "And who might this be?"

"Admiral, may I introduce, Her Royal Highness, heir to the outer worlds of the Comin, G'iad'a. G'iad'a, may I introduce, Lord Iain McLeod, Chief of Luna Keep and Clan McLeod, Admiral of the Terran Intragalactic Fleet."

The admiral extended his hand to the young girl. "I am most pleased to meet you, young one."

"Not young one. Heir." The child crossed her arms.

The admiral chuckled. "It seems we have an attitude, do we? I have just the thing to adjust that." The heir frowned at him, but still refused his hand. He turned to Alex. "Permission to enlist the young one in our mission, Majesty?"

Alex was confused but knew if anyone could adjust an attitude it was the admiral. "Very well. Proceed." Sarah turned, a smirk on her face and Alex grinned back. Obviously, she had been on the receiving end of one of the admiral's lessons. *Just like I have. Oh, this is going to be good.*

"Our plan is to be pulled from the gravity well of this star using focused tractors from the *Faol Muc-fhiadhaich*." He motioned the child forward. "You will be in command of the auxiliary controls. Have a seat and get strapped in." G'iad'a climbed into the acceleration couch in front of the auxiliary console, pulling the crash harness over her shoulders and buckling the webbing across her chest. "Very good, you have clan experience, I see."

"I not know clan. I fly attack eagle and battle dreadnought. I second in command." Her small chest puffed out against the harness with pride.

The admiral chuckled. "A battle dreadnought? How many tonnes is your ship? What is her crew complement? Her armaments? Her defenses?"

The heir swallowed. "I not know. I command, not need know that?"

Alex walked up to stand at G'iad'a's shoulder, leaning over. "Actually, you do, imp. Without a thorough knowledge of the ship you fly, you would not be able to fight her nor recover from an emergency situation."

G'iad'a was silent, though Alex could see she was thinking about the ramifications of her comment. "Listen to the admiral. He is the best instructor I ever had the honor to learn from." Alex peeked at him and noticed a slight blush staining the admiral's cheeks.

"So, young one, you will be responsible for monitoring the tractors at their points of contact." He manipulated a gel pad and a diagram of the *Orchid* came up on the monitor. Twelve red dots appeared; each marked an attachment point along the hull of the clan. "All of the contact points must maintain an equal pull on the hull, or the clan could be torn apart. These graphs measure the shear load at each contact point." He pointed to twelve small plots running down the right side of the monitor. Each showed a flat blue line. Then, he pointed to the left side of the monitor, where twelve images showed a small blue circle within a red square. "These icons monitor deformation of the hull at the point of contact." G'iad'a frowned and traced a small fingertip over one of the graphs. "If the tractor pulls too hard on the hull, these circles will warp into an oval and the square will skew into a parallelogram. Can you draw an oval and a parallelogram for me on this pad?" He handed her a stylus. The heir put the end of the stylus in her mouth as she thought before drawing the requested geometric figures. "Very good, young one. Very good, indeed. You will make an excellent auxiliary control tech."

"But what about graphs?" She tapped the stylus on one of the twelve blue graphs.

"Excellent question. If one or more of these starts to rise above the base line, the graph will turn from blue to yellow to red. That indicates—"

"The tractor is out of balance?" G'iad'a asked.

He is such a good teacher, let the student participate in her learning. Alex laughed. "Admiral, I think you have a new engineering student." Looking down at the child, she ruffled her hair, causing her bird-shaped beads to tinkle musically.

"So, it would seem. Young one, your job is to alert us if one or more of the graphs begins to change color or if one or more of the circle-squares begins to deform. Do you understand?"

"Yes, understand." She smiled up at the admiral. "Tank trust me."

"You are most welcome." He whirred over to the engineering console, where he took a seat and strapped into the acceleration couch.

Alex stepped up on the dais and dropped into the command chair, activating her crash harness. "Well crew, are we ready?" Nods all around answered her. "Pilot, prepare to release attitudinal control and cut thrusters on my mark." Sarah's hand hovered above one of the console's gel pads. "Engineering, are all safety measures in place?"

The admiral looked back at her. "Aye, crew has been warned and should be prepared for emergency acceleration."

"Auxiliary control, status of the hull."

"All correct. Blue, round." The young girl responded seriously.

"Very well, on my mark, tractors will engage."

Alex reached out along her bond. *"In one minute from my mark, Lauren. The* Orchid *is as ready as we can make her. Please have the* Boar *latch on to the agreed-upon points of contact and begin applying the tractor. Ask Robert to go easy. This is going to be dicey."*

"Awaiting your mark." Lauren paused. *"Robert acknowledges message and will apply tractor using gradually increasing load."*

Alex's heart overflowed with love. *"I cannot wait to be in your arms, Dearheart. We will be together soon."*

"I love you, with all that I am. Be safe, Alex."

Tears ran down Alex's cheeks. She poured all of her love into their bond. As her bond energy physically rippled across the bridge, the other three gasped. *"One minute from now."* Alex hit a timer on her armrest and the bridge AI began a countdown.

"The Boar *acknowledges and has started their clock."* Lauren did not say anything else; instead she sent a burst of pure love back to Alex. Alex opened her bond wide. In doing so, Lauren would know what was happening in real time on the *Orchid.*

Lauren's wraith shimmered into existence and Alex gasped. *"Dearheart? How?"*

"I don't know. This is new." Lauren reached out for Alex and Alex tried to take her hand. Her hand closed on empty air. *"But I needed to be with you, so here I am."*

Alex smiled at her soul's other half and sat back in the command chair. *"I am glad you are, but this is dangerous, Lauren."* Out of the corner of her eye, she saw the heir turn.

"It witch." G'iad'a gasped and covered her eyes, shivering.

"No, young one, it is the queen's consort, come to protect Her Majesty," the admiral answered in awe. "We are blessed to see such a thing."

Alex cautioned Lauren. *"If something happens, you must return to the* Stag. *I do not want you lost in the void of our bond."*

Lauren's wraith frowned. *"I'll remain by your side, as a consort should, Alex. Don't ask me to leave you."*

"No, Dearheart, promise me. If something happens, withdraw to the Stag. *You must live. Your duty will then be to Terra and no longer to me."* Alex hardened her tone. *"You will be required to lead Terra."*

Lauren nodded slowly, then smiled. *"I understand Alex, many need us. I know you'll be successful and soon we'll be together."*

"Very well." Alex returned the smile. *"I am glad you are here. My heart is full again."*

"Nine, eight, seven, six…" The bridge AI intoned the final seconds and Alex tensed against her crash webbing.

"All right everyone, ready?" Her crew nodded again.

"Three, two, one . . . mark." The great clan shuddered as the focused tractors from the *Boar* slammed into her hull. The ship writhed and groaned as the pull increased. Alex winced as she felt the *Orchid* strain against the tractors, caught as she was in a tug of war between the star's gravity and the *Boar's* tractor.

"Come on, you. Let go," she hissed through clinched teeth. Alex leaned forward in her chair as the star field outside the transparency seemed to shift. *Am I imaging the change?* And then the *Orchid* lurched to port. Klaxons suddenly blared and metal screamed. "Hard starboard, remain within the tractors."

"Starboard, aye."

Turning to the admiral, Alex said, "Pour all the fuel we have into the thruster pods, now."

"But, Majesty—"

"Do it," Alex shouted above the sound of rending metal.

"Hull breaches decks fifty through fifty-six. Hull plates failing across ventral plane. Engineering venting atmosphere," the bridge AI reported. "Internal thruster temperature rising. Fifty degrees to redline."

Alex turned back to the port side of the bridge. "Any changes, G'iad'a?"

"No. All same." G'iad'a replied, her voice a shrill squee.

"Thank you. Continue to keep a sharp eye." Alex gripped the armrests, lurching right as the ship slewed to port again. "Starboard correction."

"Attitudinal controls are at maximum. She is not responding to additional directional input." Sarah fought to maintain some command of the helm, her hands flying over navigational control gel pads.

More klaxons blared. These had a different frequency, urgent in their strident pulse. Alex's monitors flared red. *We are losing the ship. Structural integrity is failing.* The ship groaned so loud this time; Alex felt it in her bones.

"Queen, two circle-squares deformed. Too much pull," G'iad'a shouted.

"Which ones?"

The child leaned toward her monitor. "Three, nine."

Alex looked at the wraith shimmering at her right shoulder. *"Lauren, tell Robert to rebalance the tractors. Load is too high on attachments three and nine."*

The wraith phased out slightly. *"He acknowledges, requests you yaw the ship thirty degrees port about her longitudinal axis. He will attach additional tractors."*

"Sarah, yaw thirty degrees to port. Prepare for additional tractors." Alex dropped her hand into a gel pad. "Heir, I am adding more inputs to your monitor."

Once Sarah released the forced starboard control, the ship slewed to port. Sarah hit the lateral thrusters on the dorsal plane, adding additional acceleration to the move. The yaw halted suddenly, and Alex was nearly thrown through her crash webbing. A tremendous tearing sound exploded through the bridge, followed by a snap. Alex's ears popped and she swallowed convulsively. Hull plating failed around the leading edge of the *Orchid:* sheets of debris streaked past the forward transparency.

"Lauren, return to the *Stag* now! The keel has failed, she is coming apart."

Lauren's wraith shook her head.

"I order you to withdraw, Consort."

Tears slid down Lauren's cheeks. *"I love you, Dearest."*

Before Alex could respond, the bridge lights flickered and went out, giving way to blood red illumination as emergency power came on. The wraith had disappeared. Alex felt sharp relief. Lauren was safe and she sent her love out to the universe, as her soul opened farther, her psi-energy following Lauren across the galaxy.

"Prepare to jettison the bridge module." Closing her eyes, Alex grabbed onto Robert through their companion bond. *"Dìobradh!"*

Sarah looked over her shoulder, yelling over the klaxons. "Ma'am?"

"Jettison the bridge."

"But, the crew?" Sarah voice was laced with concern and disbelief.

"Will be fine. Trust me."

It happened in an instant. One second the sound of the ship dying surrounded them; the next, they floated in silence. The klaxons silent. A large blast shield slid closed over the forward transparency to protect it from impact hazards. The crimson glow of emergency lighting still permeated the bridge. Artificial gravity failed and loose objects spiraled around them.

"Face shields now." Alex knew life support would fail next, but she had no idea what other connections had severed when the bridge module jettisoned from the ship. "Sarah, do you have attitudinal control?"

"I cannot reach the emergency module controls from here."

Before Alex could stop her, Sarah hit her web release and spun around in her seat. She grabbed the edge of the monitor, floating upward. Pushing off, she shot across the bridge toward the pilot station. Alex watched in disbelief as the young pilot executed a perfect pirouette in front of the command dais and grabbed the back of the pilot's couch. She hung onto the couch as if she was standing on her hands and pulled herself down toward the control panels.

"Almost there." Sarah puffed out, struggling to reach the emergency controls. "The module controls must be released from under the console." Her hand searched under the console edge. "There."

A small plastic panel floated free. Sarah swung her feet down and under the console. Slamming her hand onto the web controls, the crash harness shot out, pulling her down into the couch. Sarah yelped in pain. She leaned forward, pushing against the harness, trying to sit up. "Must get off the damage."

The damaged seat. The pilot's couch had a blaster hole in the center of its back, the seat supports must be jagged. Alex felt the tiny thrusters located on the outside of the module flare to life in a synchronized pattern to gain control of the tumbling module.

"Very good, Sarah. Very good indeed. Another exploit to add to your growing list of amazing piloting skills." The admiral chuckled. He sobered when he turned to Alex. "It will begin to get very cold in here, Majesty. I suggest we deploy internal space heaters."

"I agree. Do we have external sensors?" The admiral released his harness and maneuvered toward the aft storage lockers, behind the command dais.

Sarah checked a readout on one of her monitors. "Not available currently."

Alex eyed the blast shield over the forward transparency. "Can we open the shield?"

"That we can do." Now they were free of the *Orchid*, the risk of hitting anything, or anything hitting them was significantly reduced. The view outside showed their slow tumble, as the star field rotated past. Sarah gained control, and the tumble stopped. The F-class star filled more than seventy percent of the view, with the remains of the *Orchid* taking up the remainder. Alex watched in jaw-dropping awe as the bulk of the *Orchid* began to come apart, large pieces fell away and became flaming strikes as they slid into the star's corona.

"May the goddess watch over the innocent," the admiral whispered into the silence.

The *Boar's* tractors continued to pull large chucks of the ship out of the gravity well and fling them into the surrounding space. Finally, Alex breathed a sigh of relief as a massive cylindrical shape was pulled free. *The middeck module.* "They will be fine. Robert has them."

"Indeed," the admiral replied. "That is quite a feat of engineering control."

The *Boar* flung the massive cylinder away from the star. It tumbled slowly end-over-end, coming to rest not far from their bridge module.

"Position, Sarah?" Alex tapped her command analyzer. "Do we have contact with the *Boar*?"

Sarah sent a position location map to one of Alex's monitors before making her way back to the sailing master console. "We are approximately two hundred and fifty thousand kilometers from the *Boar*. They are closing the distance. We are outside the stellar gravity well." Once she dropped back into the other couch, she answered Alex's first question. "I have telemetry to the *Boar*, but no voice communications."

"Very well. Send the following." Alex dictated a message containing their status and a request the middeck module be secured prior to picking them up. "Time delay for a response?"

"Communication lag, twenty point four minutes," the bridge AI reported.

"In that case, I recommend we relax and wait for pickup."

Sarah and the admiral laughed, but G'iad'a scowled at Alex and spat. "Not happy. No relax. You crazy. Want go home."

Alex smiled, relief and joy filling her. "As do I, young one. As do I."

Chapter Five
Captain's Cabin, aboard the Faol Muc-fhiadhaich
Clan McLaren's Wild Boar

Several days later, Alex sat with Robert and Shamus in the captain's cabin aboard the *Boar*. Three crystalline glasses, filled with Terran wine, reflected blue-green rainbows in the cabin's soft indirect lighting. Alex propped her white stocking-covered feet on the low table holding their glasses. She was sprawled on the soft brown leather couch, her Doouglas plaid swaddled around her shoulders. Lauren was ecstatic and Alex's bond overflowed with love and warmth.

"And, that is about the size of it." Her mouth was dry from the three hours it took to summarize her time aboard the *Orchid*. She picked up her glass and took a long drink. She owed the *Boar's* crew so much for their amazing rescue of her bridge module and the middeck module. *A dry throat is an insignificant price to pay.*

Shamus sighed and reached for his glass, condensation running down the stem over his slim fingers. "If I were not here to experience it all, I would call you a liar, Majesty. This is an adventure for the ages." He smiled warmly at her. "Not even the First Foremother could top it. Absolutely unbelievable."

"I agree." Robert looked away. "Fate was also on your side, Alex. Without the strong bond you share with Lauren and the companions, we could not have prevailed."

Alex felt her heart swell as Robert sent a burst of love toward her. "But prevail we did. And do not diminish the contributions you made. Finding and deploying the quantum communication devices was amazing in and of itself. The real achievement is the modification to your propulsion systems. You overtook the *Orchid* and were here to rescue us."

While the three enjoyed each other's company, recounting their adventures, Admiral McLeod was down in the depths of engineering. He could not believe what had been done to his precious engines. He was in his element and Alex doubted they would see him again anytime soon. Sarah on the other hand had the more difficult duty, she was assigned to supervise and maintain control of the heir. A task she stated emphatically was not in her job description as pilot to the admiral of the fleet. Alex chuckled as she remembered that conversation. She stopped to collect her thoughts as she swirled the green wine in her glass.

Looking up, she smiled at the other two. "Now we are on to the next part of this adventure."

Robert cleared his throat and looked at Shamus, a small flick of his hand signaled for his young cousin to answer. "As we see it, ma'am, we have several decisions to make while we transit to the other three."

The young astrogator did not immediately elaborate.

"And they are . . ." Alex asked into the silence.

"Well, you see." Shamus paused again and Alex sat forward trying to encourage him by opening her body language. She had not spent much time with the young man but was beginning to enjoy his intellect and earnest competence. This was someone she could easily take into their inner circle of companions. "The survivors. The heir. And the Comin."

Alex laughed, and Shamus blanched. "Do not mistake my amusement for disagreement, young astrogator. That was the most succinct summation of the tasks before us I have heard. You are correct on all three. I would add one more. The witch."

Robert coughed into his hand. "I believe we must deal with the witch, as you call her, first and foremost. She represents the largest danger we face."

"Suggestions?" Alex relaxed back into the soft cushions and drew her plaid more snuggly around her. Mention of Gwenhwyfach made her blood run cold.

"I am hesitant to say this, but I do not know another solution. You must confront her, Majesty." Alex stiffened and Shamus hurried on. "You are the only one with enough psi-strength to contain her and perhaps destroy her. She is too dangerous to be allowed to run amok within the middeck module while it is lashed to the underside of the *Boar*."

Currently, the *Boar* had the *Orchid* middeck module attached to her ventral plane. The clan's crew could access the module through an airlock via a flitter. The crew of the *Orchid* did not have direct physical access to their ship.

Alex nodded. "I agree, and the only way to do it is to ferret her out of the flag officer cabin."

"Hang on a minute. Lauren will have my hide for a rapier sheath if I allow you anywhere near the bitch." Robert frowned. Alex saw Shamus wince at such language spoken to his queen.

"Colorful imagery aside, Robert, you know as well as I, and Shamus has confirmed, I am the only one who can handle her if she unleashes any sort of psi-attack. Besides, I will have Lauren with me." *Yes, Lauren is with me.* Warmth filled her soul and Alex smiled.

After coordinating their plan to enter the module, Alex agreed to have a cadre of bodyguards in powered energy armor accompany her. Much like the plating on the hull of the clans, these miniaturized suits of armor were constructed of carbon nanofibers, perfectly formed cylinders of graphene woven into a sheet-like fabric then compressed together—alternating the warp and weft—to create an indestructible, yet flexible fabric. A fabric capable of withstanding plasma impact, disruptor blasts, decompression, submersion, and exposure to deep space. Bonded to a powered exoskeleton of alumino-titanium alloy, the armor was manufactured to the exact size and shape of the wearer. Although Alex never had a suit of powered armor made for herself, she had considered it for Lauren after Gwenhwyfach's disruptor blast nearly took her life. She laughed. No way would Lauren allow herself to be sealed into a metal suit. *What had she called it? Oh, yes, a tin can.*

Alex pulled on her black body armor and looked at the clothing laid out on the bed. A formal Doouglas tartan kilt would be held in place by a wide purple leather belt, the buckle two facing loons, for her mother. She had no idea how Robert accomplished this but wearing these clothes always made her feel invincible. *These are the symbol of my clan, my place within the lineage of my Foremothers.* A white long-sleeved shirt, a Fraser plaid of red, green, and blue with a fine cross-cutting white line, a red leather sling to hold a broadsword across her back, and a pair of knee-high purple leather boots completed the clothing arranged for her. As she pulled the sling over her head, she adjusted it so a sword scabbard would hang across her back. The door chime sounded.

"Come."

Robert entered carrying two walnut cases. A long slim rectangular case rested across his arms. On top was a smaller square box closed with a golden boar-head clasp.

"What is this? I believe I have enough." Alex indicated the clothing she had donned.

"Oh, I think you will wish to add these to your formal attire." Robert smirked, definitely up to something and quite proud of himself it would seem.

"Well?"

He placed the two boxes on the bed, looking her up and down, and then picked up the plaid. "Here, wrap up in this and then I have what you will need to fix it in place."

Robert took the smaller box from the bed and opened it, showing Alex the contents. She gasped. Inside on a bed of red velvet lay one of Lauren's badges of honor—a golden tree bisected by a thin platinum sword.

"This will do nicely." He took the badge and pinned it to the Fraser plaid draped over Alex's right shoulder. She pulled the sling free. "And I see your scabbard is empty, Majesty. If I may?"

He opened the long, slim case. Inside was the most magnificent *claidheamh-mór* she had ever seen. This great-sword had a cross-hilt with forward looping quillons, each tipped with a brilliant sapphire.

"No, Robert, I cannot." Even though she refused the magnificent sword verbally, her hand reached out to grasp the beautiful weapon. To feel its strength and balance, to hold such a weapon would be a wonderous thing.

"This belonged to my great grand'mere. She stood beside your grand'mere as they fought the Comin many rotations ago. It is my honor to share this with you." He lifted the claymore from its case and knelt before Alex, presenting the massive, two-edged sword hilt-first. "May it protect you, as it did her, from enemies without and traitors within."

Alex grasped the hilt and gasped. The blade felt alive, the hilt warm within her fingers. "Robert." Alex was truly at a loss for words. She swallowed and then raised the sword in salute. "I am honored to carry the weapon of your foremother and more honored still you believe me worthy to carry it." She placed a hand on his shoulder, and he smiled. "Thank you, for your fealty, trust, and love. You truly are my compass and conscience. You know me well, indeed."

Robert laughed and stood to his full height. "Well, let us not go overboard." He pointed to the hatch of the flag officer's cabin. "Shall we?"

Robert slid the claymore into its scabbard and slipped the scabbard into the sling across Alex's back. She twitched a few times to settle the great weapon's weight and then nodded. "Let's do this."

The trip to the flitter bay did not take long enough for Alex's nerves to overwhelm her, but she reached out to Lauren during the ride down to deck forty-two. *"It is time, Dearheart."*

"I'm here. Let's do this." Their bond swelled as Lauren's determination filled it. *"I'm tired of Gwenhwyfach spoiling our fun. It's time that ends."*

"Indeed."

Robert and Alex exited the lift onto the flight deck and turned toward the flitter which would take her to her confrontation with the witch. Her steps faltered. Before her stood a phalanx of Clan McLaran. Recovering herself, Alex walked between the rows of tartan-clad warriors. As she passed, each clan member knelt and bowed their head. Stopping before one young woman, Alex placed a hand on the girl's shoulder. *I cannot believe this. I am honored by their presence.*

Lauren chuckled. *"Believe, Dearest."*

Alex spoke to the group as a whole. "Do not bow before me. You are Clan McLaran. You are my rescuers. I thank you for your bravery and am honored to be in your presence." The clan rose, stomping their feet and clapping. The sound filled the vast flitter bay. Alex blushed. "Thank you for all you have done. Terra is forever in your debt." Then she walked up the ramp into the flitter, her heart racing.

"That's amazing, and so well deserved." Lauren's approval rippled through their connection. *"You're their queen, Alex. It's you they follow and honor."* Alex sniffled. *"Don't diminish their tribute."*

"I am not. But I am still in awe at what you accomplished to rescue me. What was sacrificed—"

Lauren interrupted, sounding a bit miffed. *"And what was gained. It's not a sacrifice to recover what was wrongfully taken. Terra wouldn't be the same without you, nor would she survive against our enemies. We did what we had to for you and for her."*

"Well said, Consort. Shall we be about this next task, then?" Alex took a seat among her guard.

"Yes." Lauren materialized beside Alex, her wraith shimmering in the low running lights of the flitter. Alex's guards, usually so calm and quiet, gasped.

"Lauren will be with us. One more guard against the witch," Alex said as the flitter exited the bay into space around the *Boar*.

A scant few minutes later, the pilot connected to the airlock on the *Orchid* middeck module and the group rose to exit the craft.

"I do not know what we will meet when we open the airlock. Allow the guard to exit first and then you follow," her guard master said, and Alex nodded. Weapons could be constructed from anything and a suit of power armor could withstand an attack far better than her body armor would. Lauren's wraith blinked out, but Alex felt her psi-energy ripple as Lauren moved to stand at Alex's right shoulder.

The hatch cycled open to reveal a scene identical to the one they left, a phalanx of Clan Cador lined up to greet their queen. Two senior crew members, the chief medical technician and the executive officer, waited at the bottom of the ramp.

"My Queen." The executive officer dropped to one knee. "We apologize for the actions of a few misguided and treasonous members of our clan. There is nothing we can do to erase the tarnish from our clan, but we surrender to you and your guard."

Alex stepped around her chief guard and stood before the man. "The deeds of the few will not taint the good of the many. I must deal with your clan leader first. What happens then I cannot say, but each of you will be fairly judged, and if you are innocent of these traitorous acts, you will be welcome to return to Terra."

"Majesty." A thin, aged woman bowed low. "I am Camella, chief medical technician for this crew. The clan leader is gravely ill. She has suffered a brain injury of unknown origin and is unresponsive. Currently she is in a vegetative state, maintained solely by external means."

"Ask what her diagnosis is," Lauren whispered.

"We wish to know your full diagnosis." Alex inclined her head, her low voice carrying a cutting edge.

Camella looked around the flitter bay, everywhere but at Alex. Her gaze finally settled on a spot beyond her right shoulder. *Can she see Lauren?* Alex felt Lauren begin to pull energy from their bond.

"Careful, Lauren, do not pull too much of yourself into our bond. I will not lose you now."

"I'll be careful, but we must ask questions to determine if this is a ruse, a trap of some kind." Lauren tempered and Alex felt her hand taken and squeezed. Alex could actually feel the wraith's hand. But Lauren's wraith had yet to materialize.

The chief medical tech tilted her head. "As I stated she is in a vegetative state and has been for some weeks. We do not know the nature of her injury or illness."

Alex did not like the response, and neither did Lauren. *"This doesn't feel right, Alex."*

"Take us to her, chief," Alex commanded and fell in behind a trio of her guards as the medical technician led them out of the flitter bay to the flag officer's cabin.

An armed guard and a medical technician waited outside the cabin, just as the data pulled from the *Orchid's* analyzer cores indicated. A pile of supplies had been stacked neatly to the right of the hatch. The slightly built, elderly medical technician rose and bowed to his chief when the group arrived.

Camella tilted her head. "Any change, Mangus?"

"No. She remains in a coma and is unresponsive."

"I thought you said she was vegetative," Lauren said out loud, as her wraith shimmered into existence. Alex gaped in awe at this expression of immense psi-power.

Mangus gasped and dropped to one knee.

The man peeked up at Lauren's wraith. "She would not qualify as vegetative, ma'am. She is non-responsive to pain, light, noise, or other stimuli. She is unable to move and must be rotated to preserve skin viability."

"I see. Your diagnosis for this state?"

The man stood with difficulty, his knees creaking. Alex winced in sympathy. "Unknown. We have tested for various endocrine syndromes, heart episodes, and toxins. There are no reported incidents of head injury or other trauma." He clasped his hands within the sleeves of his blue tunic. "We have found no reason for this state."

Lauren stepped around Alex. "May we see your patient, Mangus?"

"Lauren, be careful. We do not know what is happening here," Alex cautioned.

"Of course." He turned and placed his palm on the data plate beside the hatch. It swished open to reveal a darkened cabin with a single medical bed in the center.

They entered and Lauren moved to the side of the bed, checking the monitors and analyzers circling the bed. The room smelled of death and rotting flesh. Alex's nose wrinkled.

"We will need to work together to do an exam, Alex. Lift the eyelid on the right eye and move her head to the left." A chill ran down Alex's spine. *I really did not want to touch the witch.*

"Alex?" Lauren pressed.

Alex did as Lauren instructed. The witch's skin was cold and unnaturally clammy. The eye did not track in the opposite direction to the head movement. The stench of death was stronger as she touched the cold flesh.

"Now the other."

Alex reached across and repeated the test. Same result. Alex wiped her hands on her kilt.

"She's failed the oculocephalic reflex test. Her brain stem's involved in whatever this is. Alex, I need you to fill that syringe and shoot it in her ear." Lauren's wraith frowned. *"We must determine the degree of brainstem*

damage. If her eyes move toward the injected ear, then she is not totally brain dead."

Alex could not imagine how painful this would be. But she complied and shot a stream of cold solution into the witch's ear. No eye movement.

"Good job. Thank you, Alex. A chief medical technician would know the difference between vegetative and brain dead. Camella is hiding something, but I don't know what. What I do know is this patient is dead." Lauren shook her head and pointed at the chief technician. *"She is only trying to keep this body viable."*

Alex turned to the chief medical technician and frowned. "Guards."

Though she only spoke one word, she felt Lauren pull more power from their bond, anticipating a need to move. The trio of power-armored guards trained their weapons on the chief technician who stepped back toward the open hatch.

"Take her into custody," Alex ordered.

The chief technician began to raise her hands and Alex reacted. In one smooth movement Alex drew the claymore from over her shoulder and dropped low into a riposte, bringing the tip of the blade to Camella's throat. The woman shrank away from the blade, backing into the chest of an armored guard.

"Do. Not. Move. Or, I will remove your head." Alex held her blade in place. "Shackle her hands behind her back, do not allow her to raise her arms." The guards did so, and then one picked up the tiny woman and flopped her across his armored shoulder. *I cannot let her attack us using psi-energy. She is another of Gwenhwyfach's witches.*

Alex felt her bond stretch as Lauren drew more energy. *"I need to go back. Don't trust anyone here, Alex. Keep them isolated and off the* Boar. *Stay safe, Dearest."* The wraith flickered and then faded away.

"I love you, Dearheart."

"And I you."

"Bring her with us." Alex left the cabin, still holding the claymore and strode down the hall with the remainder of her guards pacing behind her. *I cannot get away from the smell of death fast enough.* Lauren was correct. *We can salvage nothing here.*

Once back in the flitter bay, Alex called the executive officer to her, as her guards loaded their prisoner on the flitter. "I cannot take the time to determine what is going on here. I will instruct the *Boar* to place the middeck module on the nearest habitable planet. We will leave a beacon in orbit." The executive officer hung his head, gray hair falling forward. Alex placed a hand on his broad shoulder. "I promise you, we will return when we are able to and sort this out. I will not abandon any Terran who is loyal and can be trusted. You will have all the supplies you need to survive and with the beacon, a link to some communications."

The officer nodded. "I understand, Majesty." Alex squeezed his shoulder and walked up the ramp into the flitter.

Dropping into a seat between her guards, Alex sighed. This was not how she had wanted this to go, or what she had wanted to do. She had no choice. *I must protect Terra and her clans.* The chief medical technician was strapped into a seat. Camella gave Alex an angry glare before looking away. Cold anger filled Alex. *Something is definitely going on here.*

Chapter Six
Bridge of the Faol Muc-fhiadhaich
Clan McLaren's Wild Boar

Alex stood behind the captain's chair, hands clasped behind her, as she watched the activity outside the forward transparency. Eight flitters latched tractors on to the *Orchid's* middeck module, which was then released from the underside of the *Boar*. They were in orbit around a small blue-green planet, the sixth one out from a young B-class star and well within the habitable zone of this solar system.

The planet had water and wildlife, but no other sentient life. Supplies and other survival needs had already been dropped to the planet surface. While Alex was not happy abandoning the *Orchid's* crew, there was no other choice. Robert sent a communique along the trail of beacons he left in their wake and by now, Terra would know the module's location and have a full summary of the rescue and their plans. The message also requested that Terra prepare a rescue mission for the *Orchid's* crew.

As the module swung away from the great clan ship, Robert turned in his chair. "I recommend best possible speed to join the others. We will not have the advantage of a great circle route around a black hole to cut our journey's distance, but the new propulsion system will decrease our travel time significantly. We have not had the opportunity to really open up the hydrogen condensers and test our maximum speeds, as we did not want to overtake the *Orchid* too quickly."

"Well then, let's do it." Alex stretched, anxious to continue their journey.

Robert smiled at her. "As you command, Majesty. Once the flitters are recovered, we will be on our way."

Alex entered the flag officer's cabin. Once inside with the hatch secured, she stripped off her kilt, throwing it and her shirt into the corner. She stepped into the well-appointed bathroom. A large tub sat within a marble surround. Swirls of McLaran clan navy blue and emerald green colored the marble. A few turns of the controls and the large tub filled with steaming water. She stepped in and sank to her neck, finally relaxing. Closing her eyes, she let herself float for a little while.

"We are on our way, Dearheart." She smiled. *"Robert is planning the fastest route possible. We should rendezvous with you in approximately three weeks."*

"Where are you? You sound awfully relaxed. Better than I've heard in a long time."

"Up to my chin in steaming water. The first bath I have enjoyed since Earth and Susan's hot tub."

Lauren's laughter rolled along their bond. *"I can feel you wiggling your eyebrows. And yes, I remember that hot tub, too."*

"I can feel you smirking."

When no answer came, Alex sat up, water sloshing onto the deck. *"Lauren?"* Nothing. *"Dearheart, are you all right?"*

Finally, Lauren did answer, but she sounded winded. *"Give me a sec . . . almost there."*

"What is going on over there?"

"Had to leave . . . was on the bridge . . . surrounded by crew. Couldn't let them see me like this."

Alex chuckled and stepped out of the tub, wrapping up in a large white fluffy towel. She could picture Lauren's face, flushed with arousal, as she bolted from the bridge. *"I tripped over Snow as I shot out of my command chair and almost face-planted on the deck. Not a very regal exit."*

"No worries, Dearheart. I am sorry I got you flustered."

"No, you're not," Lauren sassed.

Alex chose to diplomatically ignore that comment. *"Where are you now?"*

"In my cabin."

Alex heard a sigh, and somehow, she knew Lauren was shedding her clothing.

"I am amazed how open our bond is. I can feel you. And if I close my eyes, you are here, in the cabin with me."

"Then close your eyes, Dearest."

A smell of vanilla and wildflowers—Lauren's scent—surrounded her as she slipped between the sheets of the large bed. *"Don't open your eyes."* Lauren's whisper ghosted past her ear.

Fingertips trailed over her cheek and soft lips met hers in a tender kiss. Her eyelids fluttered. A palm traced over her abdomen, and another sigh escaped. *Was that mine or Lauren's? Does it matter?* Not one bit. Pleasure surged through her as the questing hand traced over her curls. The muscles in her thighs quivered.

"Relax."

Lauren took one of Alex's hands in hers and brought it to her lips. *How is this possible? Our bond must be so strong; we can both transcend the physical plane.* Alex stopped trying to understand when a tongue traced over her palm and she shivered again. Lips were back on hers and their tongues joined, fighting a tender battle, neither wishing to dominate the other. Hands slid up her sides and palmed her breasts. Thumbs tweaked her nipples. Their kiss ended. Alex leaned forward trying to recapture Lauren's mouth. A tongue stroked a warm wet line down her throat. She tilted her head allowing Lauren better access. Then the hands were gone, and her breasts felt cold. She gasped as wet lips enclosed a nipple, sucking hard. Those lips felt incredible on her skin, warm and soft.

Another groan escaped. *"Lauren?"*

The other nipple received the same treatment as the first. When hands descended again to the point of her hips, she squirmed. *"You're too thin."*

Alex laughed. *"Could . . . not . . . eat. Too . . . much . . ."*

"Shall I stop?"

"By the gods, no." Alex reached across their bond to capture more of Lauren, but her hands were caught in a tight hold. Her eyes snapped open and she was lost in the green-blue depths of her love's eyes. Shock ripped through her. *"How?"*

"It's my turn. No hands." Lauren's body slid against Alex's torso and lips captured hers again. Lauren began to move against her. She felt cherished by Lauren's soft ministrations.

Love and passion, worry and fear, anger and hatred, these emotions and a myriad of others exploded through Alex. She could not breathe. She could not think. She could only feel. Their bond grew, until it swallowed them whole. Alex gave in and released all her pent-up worry, fear, anger, and hatred to the universe. Love replaced all. Passion overtook her. Her climax was so strong, her breath caught, and her heart stuttered. *Will it start again?* Then joy surged through her, and she settled back into the warm bed. Panting, as her heart galloped.

Hands cupped her but went no further. *"I'll save this for later."* A final kiss to the wet curls and Lauren was no longer with her. Alex was not alone. She was surrounded by vanilla and wildflowers and another aroma, something uniquely Lauren.

Three long weeks followed as the *Boar* raced to join her fleet mates at the Comin nebula. Alex tried not to harass the crew nor demand more speed from the giant clan ship, but her constant pacing on the bridge drove everyone to distraction.

"Alex, you have got to settle down. We are nearing our destination. If you wear a hole in the deck plating my father will not be happy." Robert tried to temper her anxiety with humor.

She paced toward him. "I know and I am sorry." She retraced her steps away from the command dais.

"Shall we head down to the fencing arena for another round of sparring?" Robert suggested.

Shamus raised his head from the navigational holo-tank, an expectant look on his face. *I am driving the crew crazy.* "We are approximately two point one five hours from rendezvous. How about another tour of engineering? I am sure the admiral would love some company."

That she doubted.

The admiral was amazed by the changes to the clans' propulsion systems and had yet to leave his precious engineering space. Traveling at these speeds was dangerous and he needed to be there in case of an accident. But Alex knew better—he was there to play. She would not take pleasure away from him. When the medical technicians aboard the *Boar* had told her, the admiral may always need an exoskeleton for mobility, Alex was shattered. His hip had not healed properly and until they had access to the regeneration facilities on Luna Keep, they could not rebuild his joint. In the interim, she would allow him as much happiness as she could give him.

Alex sighed. "All right, I will leave you to it. I will head down to the crew quarters and see what Sarah and G'iad'a are up to."

"Excellent. If anything arises, I will call you." Robert sagged in his chair.

Walking past the dais, she placed a hand on his broad shoulder. "Thank you for tolerating me. I will be back in two hours."

He winked at her. "Anytime, Your Majesty."

Alex squeezed his shoulder and stepped from the bridge. Taking the captain's lift down to deck forty, she found G'iad'a and Sarah in the fencing arena. The large white room was divided into several areas with padded floors and several with planked hardwood *pistes*. Currently, the young heir had both hands wrapped tight around a half-length practice broadsword, while Sarah held a full-length broadsword. They circled each other on one of the padded sections, oblivious to their surroundings. Sarah wore the red of her Cameron clan, while the heir wore Alex's grey and black hunting tartan.

Alex smiled, remembering that dinner conversation. G'iad'a had decided Alex was her hero and followed her everywhere. One evening, she asked about kilt, and then asked to dress as Alex did. What followed was a lengthy discussion of clan traditions, including the wearing of a clan's colors. The heir stated she would gladly meet any clan requirement, if it meant she could dress as Alex did. With much ceremony, Robert, as captain of the *Boar*, officiated a small clan ceremony, much like an adoption. G'iad'a was now recognized as a member of the Doouglas clan. She wore Doouglas tartan all the time.

"I would call unfair, young one. Sarah has the reach advantage on you." Alex's voice startled the two, and the heir spun around to smile at her. Sarah slapped her on the butt with the flat of her blade.

"Foul," G'iad'a roared as she fell forward onto her hands and knees, her blade spinning away. Sarah and Alex laughed, which did not appease the young heir. "That foul. I no look."

"Your inattention to me does not stop me from taking advantage." Sarah reached out a hand to pull G'iad'a to her feet. "Never take your eyes off your opponent." G'iad'a picked up the small blade.

"Well said, Sarah." Alex went down on one knee to look the young girl in the eye. "And how is the heir today?"

"I fine. We learn sword today. Tomorrow, I show Big Imp how to fight muhaddab." G'iad'a was as enamored with Sarah as she was with Alex and began calling her Big Imp shortly after their rescue from the *Orchid*.

"Well, that I must see." Alex never fought with the long thin curved blade of the muhaddab the Comin favored. She had seen images of the deadly weapon in their databases. "I do not know how an imp your size could wield such a weapon."

"I not imp." But the smile on the girl's tan face belayed her disagreement. "And I use muhaddab often. It better than this." She waved the half-sized broadsword at Alex.

With a swift two-handed swipe, Alex disarmed the child, startling both combatants. Standing, Alex twirled the short blade between her hands. "Tomorrow, we will challenge each other. I with my blade and you with yours." She pointed the practice weapon at the heir. "Yes?"

"Yes!" The girl's cheer rang through the practice arena.

"Now, we are a few hours from rendezvous with the others. I suggest a bath and clean clothes if you wish to greet the Consort properly." The child disappeared out the hatch before Alex completed her sentence.

Sarah laughed and walked over to replace her broadsword in the storage racks. "That got her attention. Well played, Majesty."

"How many times must I tell you to call me Alex?"

"Not going to happen, ma'am. My clan would have my head if I slipped and others heard me call you Alex." Sarah's smile faded. "What are your plans for the heir?"

Alex knew the two had become close and Sarah's worry dripped from her question. "Not much of a plan really. Rendezvous with the others. Enter the edge of the nebula and return the heir. Retrieve the *Orchid* crew. Head back to Terra along the shortest, fastest route." Sarah frowned. "Live happily ever after?"

This brought a smile to the young pilot's face and she flipped her damp braid over her shoulder. "Indeed, Majesty." Looking down at her sweat-soaked shirt, Sarah chuckled. "I think I will follow the heir and have a bath." She left Alex alone in the large brightly lit space. Twirling the small blade once more, Alex returned it to the rack and headed to change her clothes as well.

Alex stood at the forward transparency, straining her eyes to get the first sight of the three clans. They had the ships on the holo-display, but Alex needed to see them.

"There." G'iad'a pointed a few degrees off their starboard bow. Alex followed her direction and saw the ships where they rested at station keeping.

"Aye, there they are. Good eyes, Heir." Alex laid a hand on the young girl's shoulder. Both wore the formal blue, green, and white Doouglas tartan with crisp white shirts. Where Alex had a plaid of Fraser red across her shoulders, G'iad'a wore a sash of blue green Doouglas cloth.

"Tank you."

"It will not be long now." Alex turned to Robert. "I am heading down to the flitter bay. We will head over to the *Stag* as soon as we are cleared for departure. Again Robert, I cannot thank you enough for all you did. Terra and I are in your debt."

"No thanks are necessary, but I am joining you." He rose from the command chair. "Shamus, you have the conn."

Shamus turned the navigation console over to a subordinate and stepped up on the dais. "I have the conn." He smiled at Alex and then looked down at the young girl at her left side. "You must take care of our queen, young one. That is your order for the day."

G'iad'a snapped a crisp cross-chest salute and bowed her head, making her braids sway and beads jingle. "Aye, me watch."

"Well, then. Let us be off." Robert led them from the bridge.

Their flitter traversed the distance to the other clans quickly. Alex gasped as they neared the *Stag*. "What the?" A gash tore along the starboard side of the great ship, and small flitters and fleets of repair drones swarmed over the large open wound.

"She is injured, aye, but the wound can be repaired. Seems they are making headway even now." The admiral looked out one of the many view ports and then he turned to look at Alex. "Though, I admit it is a grievous injury."

Alex felt her anger rise. Lauren had not said anything about her ship being damaged. The gash opened four or five decks to space and tore across more than a third of her length. *How could she leave such a detail out of all our interactions?* Then she felt something on her thigh. Looking down, she saw G'iad'a's small hand resting there. "It no worry. All good. No harm."

"Just how do you know that, Imp?"

"Because can feel. Ship fine. Consort fine. You fine. All good."

Alex laughed and her anger drained away. "How did you get so smart?"

"Learn you." The young girl turned away to look at the giant ship they approached. "She bigger than Robert."

Robert leaned over G'iad'a's shoulder and followed her gaze out the view port. "Aye, she is. She is the largest of all the clans. The *Red Stag* is the vessel of our Consort and her clan." The heir turned to look up at him. "And our Consort is adopted just as you are." He reached down and tweaked her nose. "You both have something in common."

Alex whispered, "Thank you."

Robert had picked up on G'iad'a's nervousness. The young girl realized she would not be Alex's center of attention once they boarded the *Stag*. His comment would hopefully stop any jealousy before it arose. The flitter continued to circumnavigate the *Stag*, swinging up and over the dorsal plane, where they looked down on the beautiful artwork portrayed there.

"She run fast." G'iad'a pointed at the image of the stag on her hull.

"Aye, she does run fast. That is how she was injured. Dancing with a singularity." Robert's comment filled in a few facts for Alex, but she was still annoyed Lauren did not warn her about the damage. The flitter had turned aft and was maneuvering toward the flitter bay. Off in the distance, they could see the *Kestrel* and the *Lion*. Their running lights winked in greeting as their queen arrived. "And there are our other two fleet mates."

The flitter entered the bay and settled gracefully onto the deck with hardly a bump to signal their arrival. Alex stood at the hatch, waiting for it to cycle. The heir stood at her left and the admiral at her right. Robert stood behind them. "Welcome home, Majesty. I am sorry we could not bring your *Sea Eagle*, but she was slated for evacuation duty if needed at Terra."

"I understand. No worries, Robert. The *Stag* will do nicely. She is Lauren's ship and a valiant substitute as I was not available to command mine." A shiver ran down Alex's spine as she thought about how close they had come to disaster, only just thwarting the witch's kidnapping. She stood feet away from her love and once united, all would be truly right again.

The hatch opened and Alex stepped down the ramp. A phalanx of Clan Fraser crew in formal red tartan stood on either side of a long purple carpet. As Alex's booted foot hit the ramp, a piper began the welcome anthem, his droning melody in direct counterpoint to the rapid beat of her heart. Because at the end of the carpet stood Lauren.

Lauren was dressed in formal attire, with brown knee-high boots. A purple belt hugged her narrow waist with her rapier sheathed there. Her auburn hair was tightly braided and the coronet circling her forehead glinted in the harsh white light of the bay. Ice and Snow sat on either side of her. Alex focused on her smile.

"Welcome aboard, dearest. Welcome home." Lauren reached out both hands to her queen and bondmate. Alex's heart settled into its normal rhythm for the first time since entering the quantum tubula.

Alex strode down the purple carpet and stopped in front of Lauren. Lauren started to kneel, and Alex caught both her hands and held her up. *"None of that. Here I am the subordinate."* She squeezed hard. "Permission to come aboard, Commander?"

"Permission granted." Lauren held on tight, her gaze penetrating Alex's soul. *"I'm so glad to see you."* She looked Alex up and down. "I was right. You're too thin." Alex laughed.

Ice growled as G'iad'a moved from behind Alex. She released Lauren's hand. "Consort, may I present—"

The young girl interrupted Alex and stepped around her. "I, G'iad'a, first born Kall'ka, Supreme Ruler outer planets, heir to condor throne of mighty Comin." She crossed her arm across her chest and extended her left leg as she bowed to Lauren. Ice's hackles rose, but Snow stepped up to the child and sniffed her. G'iad'a stiffened but allowed the giant wolf near. Snow lowered her massive white head to look into the child's eyes.

"Heir to the Comin." Lauren dropped to one knee and knelt next to Snow. "But you wear the tartan of Clan Doouglas. How'd this occur?"

"Like you. I 'dopt to clan. Now Doouglas and Comin," the child replied with a lift of her chin.

Lauren's laughter was music to Alex's ears and a balm to her soul. Another growl and Alex sank her hand into the soft fur around Ice's neck. *"Easy, Ice. She is a friend."*

"She is Comin."

Snow gave the young heir a wolfy grin. *"She may be Comin, but I believe she is a friend. Her aura smells right."*

Ice huffed. *"Be that as it may, she is Comin."*

"Let it go, Ice, she is our friend. You will see." Alex draped a long arm around Lauren, as she stood. "Shall we take this somewhere else and catch up?"

"Sounds good."

Alex motioned Sarah forward. "Please take the heir to the flag officer's quarters. We will see you at dinner."

"G'iad'a, please go with Sarah. We will all have dinner together and then you can tell the Consort of your adventures and your trip through the T'le'cac."

The heir hesitated before smiling at Lauren. "I see soon?"

"Yes, you will." Lauren gave G'iad'a a gentle hug.

Alex took Lauren's hand again. "Hopefully, that will be long enough for you to tell me why the *Stag* has a mortal wound in her side."

"Of course, Majesty. We had a bit of a bumpy ride." Alex felt Lauren's sorrow through their bond, though nothing showed on her face. She was learning to control a command mask and Alex was impressed again by her love.

Lauren held tight to Alex's hand. She was afraid if she released her, Alex would disappear again. However, irrational a thought that was, Lauren's wounded heart needed the physical connection to her soul mate. Stepping up to the captain's cabin, the hatch slid open and they entered the dimly lit space.

Alex stopped a few steps into the cabin. "Oh, Dearheart, I have missed you so." Alex pulled Lauren back and around. She followed easily, spinning into Alex's arms. She let her head fall forward and rest in the center of Alex's chest.

"God, you feel good." Lauren's arms came up and circled Alex's waist. She leaned away and looked into her love's eyes. Her anger, fear, despair, and guilt welled up at the sight of those ice blue orbs and her words came out harshly. "Don't ever do that again!"

"I hope to never repeat this. My soul would not recover another forced parting from you, Dearheart." Alex smiled and Lauren's heart swelled to bursting.

"See that you don't." Lauren tugged Alex toward the sofa. "Now, tell me how you are, really."

"Fine. Tired, well, exhausted really and hungry. I cannot seem to get enough to eat. And although Robert's galley offered the best food, nothing tasted right." Alex smiled sheepishly. "All I could think about was getting back to you. Everything else, eating included, was secondary."

Lauren settled onto the sofa, took Alex's hand, and pulled her down beside her. "I know what you mean. In my single-minded need to get you back, I'm afraid I ran over, through, and around our friends. I'm sure when we're back on Terra, I'll have to mend a lot of fences. But, right now, I really don't give a flying frick. You're here. You're safe. We're together." Lauren's voice trailed off to a whisper and she felt tears roll down her cheeks.

"Lauren, please do not cry." Alex hiccupped as her voice caught. "If you start, I am afraid I will follow and then I will not be able to stop."

Lauren encircled Alex in her arms, resting her head on Alex's chest. *We're together. That's all that matters.*

They relaxed, drawing comfort from each other's soul, as their hearts synchronized and settled into a gentle rhythm. Lauren smiled up into Alex's ice blue, green-flecked eyes. "Let's rest for a bit. We've got time before dinner." Alex nodded and Lauren drew a Fraser tartan off the back of the soft brown leather sofa. Its cool surface warmed to their skin temperature, creating a comfortable nest to cuddle in. Time ticked by as they held each other.

After a while, Lauren smiled and poked Alex in the chest. "Go ahead, ask. I know you want the details."

"Well . . ." Alex looked like a kid caught with her hand in the cookie jar.

Lauren laughed the sound ringing through the cabin. "Once a commander, always a commander."

"So true." Alex sat up. "I was shocked to see the mortal wound in her side when we approached." A frown marred Alex's brow and Lauren smoothed her forehead with a gentle finger.

"It's not a mortal wound or we wouldn't be here." Lauren's heart bled for the crew she lost and the damage to her ship. Somewhere in the last months, she had bonded with her ship. Ridiculous as it sounded, she was attuned to the *Stag*. Her sounds and vibrations told Lauren how the clan was doing and what she was doing. The smell and feel of the air circulating through her were indicators of her health. The faces and body language of the crew Lauren passed in the corridors and those she interacted with told her of their wellbeing.

"Be that as it may, I would still like to know how it occurred. You neglected to inform me of her injury." Hurt flashed across Alex's face.

"I didn't mean to keep anything from you, Dearest. With everything you were dealing with, I didn't want to pile on and add to your worry."

Alex frowned and Lauren knew she wouldn't get out of this conversation and proceeded to share all the events of their trip. How their route was chosen. Their trials as they followed it around the supermassive black hole. What engineering improvements they made and how the quantum communication system was invaluable. Alex listened, not interrupting unless she needed to ask a clarifying question.

"That explains it then." Alex bit her lip.

"Explains what?"

Alex took both of Lauren's hands in hers. "Why I lost my connection with you. Not long after I escaped and joined up with Sarah and the admiral, our bond was severed. Like someone cut the connection. I could not understand what happened. I knew you were not dead, just gone and our connection too. Sometime later it suddenly reappeared. I almost died falling down a maintenance shaft when that happened. But this explains it."

Lauren relaxed into Alex. "I know I'm exhausted but I'm still not getting this."

"The distortion of spacetime created by the black hole's gravity field severed our bond."

Curious about this explanation, Lauren started to rise but Alex pulled her back down, kissing the top of her head. "How could that influence our bond? We've traversed nexi, communicated across realities, even when one of us was unconscious we were still connected."

"I do not know. Our bond was severed when you were within the gravity well of the black hole. Perhaps, proximity to the event horizon extinguished our connection. We will figure it out. Or I should say, you will figure it out. But not now, now I just want to hold you."

Sighing, Lauren relaxed into Alex's arms. "That we can do."

Dinner was a raucous affair. Lauren relished having all her companions together once again. The addition of Robert, G'iad'a, Sarah, and the admiral only increased the feeling of family rejoined. Everyone got an opportunity to share some adventure or memory from their journey. Ice stuck to Lauren's side, but Snow stayed near the heir. The young girl frequently reached out and ran her small tanned hand through the soft fur on Snow's head. Lauren didn't miss her slipping morsels of roast to the wolf under the table and she smiled as Ice bumped her for the same.

The admiral sat next to her while Alex sat on her left. A multitude of Alex's favorite foods covered the large ironwood table: trays of roasted meat and vegetables, boats of thick gravy, and platters of fried chicken. Flasks of Terran wine and carafes of sweet tea were at hand to keep everyone's glasses full. Robert sat next to G'iad'a and whispered in her ear when she had a question. Angus sat next to the admiral, and the two would get lost in some technical discussion when the conversation didn't hold their interest. Tavish and Sarah went over the finer points of Sarah's flight. Yes, it was good to be back together.

"Majesty?"

Lauren started when the admiral placed a hand on her arm. "Sorry, I missed your question."

He smiled at her. "As you say, no worries. I asked when the *Stag* would be ready to run."

"The repair crews should be ready to seal the hull in the next few days. They're completing repairs to the structural beams now."

"And the infrastructure?"

Robert leaned forward. "I noticed the decks were sealed off and repairs were being completed only from the exterior of the ship."

Lauren hung her head as memories of crew lost came to the fore, her hair creating a curtain she hid behind. "Since we lost crew during the accident, it was decided to seal off those decks and leave them untouched until we return to Terra." All conversation stopped when she said those words. Sadness welled up and tears tracked down her face. Alex reached out a long finger and caught the drops before they fell. Lauren smiled at Alex and raised her head. "We felt we couldn't properly honor our lost comrades and therefore, should leave their quarters alone until their families could honor them with us."

"A noble decision, Consort," the admiral replied. The conversation lagged as everyone remembered crew lost. Then the admiral cleared his throat. "On another note, I would ask how you were able to get into our technology vaults within Luna Keep?"

Lauren laughed, glancing around the table. All eyes were on her. "Well now, that's a story." Lauren related their trials getting into the vaults deep beneath Luna Keep. How Tavish freaked out when she walked through a solid metal door and her encounter with the avatar.

"I had no idea the construct would still be viable, much less able to interact with you. Did you have trouble with the security questions?" The admiral gave himself away as he smirked, barely able to contain his chuckle.

"In all seriousness, it took a bit to figure out the answers but taking it one bite at a time, I was able to access the vaults." Lauren smirked back.

The admiral roared and had to grasp his sides. Out of the corner of her eye, Lauren saw Alex tip her head in question.

"Sir?" Sarah asked when his laughter began to die down.

He waved her off and grinned. "I am fine, Sarah. We are simply sharing a private joke."

Alex turned toward Lauren, quirking an eyebrow and Lauren gave her a small smile in answer. *"Later, Dearest."* She glanced at the admiral. "Should you wish to talk with the avatar, he's in my office."

"Indeed." The admiral nodded. "I believe I would like that."

Just as their dinner was winding down, the hatch to the captain's mess opened and Ailsa strode in. She hesitated, looking around the room. Then she squared her shoulders and approached Lauren. Leaning down, she whispered, "Majesty, the drone has completed its journey and the scan data are in." Lauren nodded and Ailsa moved back to the hatchway.

"Well, it seems we've got data to review. Tavish, Angus, Robert, you're with me." Lauren stood, placing her napkin beside her empty plate.

Alex looked up at her. *"What is it, Dearheart?"*

"We've got the data from our drone."

Aboard the Dubh Mogairle, Deck Sixty

Alex arrived at their hideaway, her trip to the armory a success. She returned with a large cache of weapons—hand-held blaster pistols, laser rifles, and small charges with remote laser-charged detonators. Hopefully, none of this cache would be required, but if they were to protect themselves and perhaps take over the ship, all of them and more would be needed. She paused before entering the small storage room.

Her ongoing freedom still nagged at her. Gwenhwyfach should have discovered her absence by now. *Why am I still free? All anyone had to do was check the room with the box.* All it would take was a simple mental search and Alex would be found. *I wonder if I can dampen my bond energy enough to go undetected.* It was worth a try. Alex closed her eyes and imagined sitting in a small stone room. She visualized closing a massive stone door, and then shrinking the room until all it held was her psi-energy. With this image firmly in her mind, she opened her eyes and hoped isolating her psi-energy in this way would be enough.

Sighing, Alex shuddered. Cutting off her psi energy always made her feel hollow. Severing her bond-connection with Lauren felt like an axe to her heart. She shook her head to clear those negative thoughts. All these questions would need to be addressed, but now they had other things to worry about. As long as she was free, the trio would carry on with their plans. Shrugging out of her pack, Alex opened the top and looked through her cache. Perhaps, the admiral had found something in the analyzer core data to answer her questions. In the interim, if they got into a pickle, they could defend themselves.

A pickle? Thoughts of Lauren and a warm spring afternoon flooded Alex's mind. She closed her eyes and allowed the memories full rein.

Alex lounged on a blanket at the edge of the large lake near the Keep. Wildflowers were just emerging from the winter grasses and the afternoon air smelled of life and possibilities. The sun warmed her back as she leaned up on one elbow to watch her bondmate. Lauren knelt at the water's edge, a small stick in her hand stirring the silt-rich soil.

"Come on, Dearheart. We have a picnic lunch to enjoy and I am hungry."

Without turning, Lauren replied, "You're always hungry. You're as bad as Ice. Your stomach is never satisfied." She did not cease her stirring. "I'm looking for frog eggs. I want to gather their DNA and compare their genome to those in my database. I need to determine how parallel this parallel reality really is."

"Once a technician, always a technician." Alex chuckled. "Well fine, but do not complain when all the chicken is gone before you complete your search."

"Chicken? Fried chicken? Eloise's fried chicken?" Lauren's head snapped around to look at Alex.

"I do believe it is." Alex watched as Lauren dropped her stick and stood, wiping her hands on her trousers. She made it to Alex in three long strides, where she dropped cross-legged on a corner of their tartan blanket. Brown sticky mud covered her boots nearly to her knees and her hands were stained the same color. She reached for the basket. "No, absolutely not." Alex pointed to the lake. "Go wash your hands before you contaminate our wonderful lunch."

Lauren huffed but went back to the lake, rinsing her hands in the clear cold water. She walked back to Alex and raised her dripping hands for Alex's inspection. "Better?" The palms were clean, but her fingernails still held fragments of the sticky mud.

Alex handed her a small towel from their basket. "Much."

They removed their meal from the basket, and Lauren filled their plates. Bowls of fresh cut vegetables, tiny steamed potatoes dripping in butter, and crispy pieces of fried chicken released steam into the cool spring air. Condiments of mayonnaise, coarse stone ground mustard, and a tomato-based sauce Alex loved shared a divided container. Small pots of salt and a ground herb with a peppery taste came out next. A basket of hard-boiled eggs, neatly peeled, was placed between them to share.

Last, Alex removed two round cylinders—the silver-blue one contained iced tea, sweetened with honey from last year's hives, the green blue one contained a malted liquor similar to beer but with a finer carbonation. Alex knew Lauren had become fond of this beverage. She did not like the heavy-fermented wines the Terrans aged in wooden vats. Lauren said the wine tasted like old gym socks and she could not get past the green iridescent color. To each their own. Alex reached for the silver-blue one. With plates balanced in their laps, they shared their meal in companionable silence, enjoying the light breeze and the warm afternoon sun.

"This is amazing." Lauren held up a chicken leg and waved it at Alex. "Eloise has it exactly right. I don't think Grandmommy would argue with her results." Lauren had shared several of her favored recipes with the Seneschal's master cooking technician. Most were from recipes her grand'mere had made for Lauren when she was a child. Eloise had struggled to find substitutes for some of the Earth-ingredients. She still could not replicate the dumplings Lauren enjoyed on a holiday called Thanksgiving. Lauren thought it was the difference in the broth prepared from Earth's domestic turkeys versus Eloise's wild turkeys, or maybe it was the Terran flour.

"I miss pickles. We always had dill pickle spears with our fried chicken." A wistful look crossed Lauren's face. Alex knew how deeply Lauren missed her grandparents.

"I do not think I have ever heard of pickles."

Lauren smiled sadly. "I know, Eloise hasn't either and she doesn't know what a cucumber is."

"What does a pickle have to do with this cucumber?" Alex scooted closer to Lauren, placing a gentle arm around her shoulders, hugging her close.

Lauren settled back against her and Alex could feel her draw comfort from their bond. "Cucumbers are small gourds." Alex grimaced and Lauren laughed. "They're tasty as a salad vegetable and you can make pickles from cucumbers by soaking them in salt-based brine with various spices." Lauren set her plate aside and relaxed deeper into Alex's arms. "Grandmommy made the best pickles. We grew small cucumbers on the farm, and she canned pickles in the summer. I can almost smell the brine from the pickling crocks."

Alex laid back and pulled Lauren with her. She placed a small kiss on her forehead as Lauren looked up at her. "I know you miss them terribly, Dearheart." Tears ran down the side of Lauren's face, and Alex kissed them away.

"I do miss them. I was always safe with them. They never judged me or ridiculed me for anything. They were proud of me."

Alex chased more tears with her finger. "I understand, Dearheart. But you must know how proud I am of you. You have brought so much to us and shared so selflessly." Alex swallowed and voiced her concern. "And I hope we can fill some of the void created by their absence."

Lauren cupped Alex's face with a gentle hand. "I'm glad to help in any way I can. You know that. It's almost like I had to travel between realities to find my true home. Here, on Terra." Lauren smiled. "With you." Rising, she captured Alex's lips in a kiss of confirmation.

Alex returned the kiss and it deepened as their love lit their bond. Lauren pulled away and settled back down on the blanket. She reached up and Alex felt the buttons of her sweater slip open one after another. Not to be left behind, Alex dropped her hand to the drawstring on Lauren's shirt. When the shirt fell open, Alex captured a small warm breast. A moan rose on the gentle breeze and joined the quiet buzzing of insects. Alex continued her exploration and captured Lauren's lips in another kiss. As Lauren's mouth opened to release a moan, Alex's tongue slid in and began to duel with Lauren's. Warm, wet, gentle strokes fueled the fire growing between them.

Alex's sweater got tossed aside but they never broke their kiss. Her hand dropped to Lauren's belt buckle and soon found its way beneath. When Lauren pushed her away to pull Alex's shirt over her head, a cold breeze drifted across Alex's chest. Strong arms gathered her close again and as their warm bodies merged, she saw stars behind her closed eyes. The world dissolved away, and they were surrounded by their love. Alex explored Lauren's taut abdomen, tracing the ridges and valleys of her abs. She chased ripples in the muscles tickled into existence by her fingers. Her hand floated lower.

Alex gathered moisture on the tip of her finger and coated Lauren's bud before she began to caress it on either side with long languid strokes. She was careful not to touch the tip, wanting Lauren to enjoy this bliss as long as she could. Their bond swelled as did the bud beneath her fingers. Alex could feel Lauren gathering herself to fall into the ecstasy of them.

She pulled away and Lauren groaned. "Easy, Dearheart. Let us do this together. I know you are close. I will not tease you."

Then, while looking into Lauren's eyes, Alex stroked across the tip and slid two long fingers into her. Lauren gasped and arched off their blanket. Her fingernails drew a path down Alex's back as she tried to pull her closer. Alex held her gaze and pulled out to the tips of her fingers only to plunge back in, hard. Again, and again. Their fire became a raging inferno and emotions spiraled out of control. Alex's strokes became uncontrolled. She tried to slow her rhythm, but Lauren shook her head and her body opened farther to Alex. Another finger joined the first two, as Lauren pulled her in. Alex sank deep, deeper than ever before and then halted her motion, as her thumb came to rest on the engorged bud. Lauren screamed and pulled them both over the edge into a whirlpool of emotions. Their hearts sang and their bond exploded. Alex collapsed across Lauren, lost. An echoing howl of wolves and whiny of horses echoed in the distance.

A murmur woke Alex. Raising her head from its soft nest between Lauren's breasts, she realized she was draped across her amid the scattered remains of their picnic. She had never lost consciousness before, even in the throes of their most intense lovemaking. But Alex had. She relished in the amazing feeling of completeness. Then, she moved to roll off Lauren.

"No."

"Dearheart, I am crushing you."

"No."

Alex began to withdraw her fingers from the warm, wet sheath.

"I said no. Don't move." A contraction rippled through Lauren.

Finally, Lauren opened her eyes. "Thank you."

Her gaze held Alex captured in its depths and she watched ice-blue streaks flash against the emerald background. Lauren's gaze pulled Alex deeper. Her soul was open, and Alex was stunned by what she saw reflected there. Herself. Lauren blinked and their connection vanished. But as Alex relaxed into their bond, she realized it was stronger, more attuned to them, more resilient. The contractions around her fingers lessened to the flutter of butterfly wings.

Alex slipped her fingers out and smiled into those emerald-blue eyes. "You are simply amazing, Dearheart. I am so blessed you arrived here and found me."

"The feeling is entirely mutual, dearest." A frown crossed Lauren's face and she took Alex's chin in one hand. She moved Alex's head to the side allowing the afternoon sun to flash across Alex's eyes. Lauren smiled. "So, Merilyn was correct. Our souls are joined."

Squinting against the brightness, Alex asked, "What was my Seneschal right about this time."

"Ours is a true bond."

"A true bond?" Alex tried to move her head to get her eyes out of the sun, but Lauren held fast.

"Yes, it's your eyes. They have more emerald now, and the green streaks flash in the sun."

Lauren dropped her hand and Alex placed a quick kiss on her love's lips before rolling to the side. Now they lay shoulder-to-shoulder. A flight of cranes soared overhead. "Be that as it may, you share the same characteristic. I was trying to determine what was different about your eyes just now." Alex grinned at Lauren. "Your eyes have more blue in them. So, we are melding, are we?"

"It would seem so." Lauren smiled. "And I think it's great!"

They both dissolved in giggles. "How did we get here, when we were talking about your pickles?"

"Well, it could be we got here because of a pickle. I'll need to tell you about all the types of pickles one can experience."

Alex shook herself free of the memory and knocked on the locked hatch. Lauren had indeed told her all about pickles. From the kind you eat, to the kind you can get into, to the one that occurs within a sporting game called baseball. The one she was in now was a true pickle. *I only hope we can escape unharmed.* She needed to talk to Lauren. But Alex had to exercise caution, so she strengthened the walls of the stone room around her bond. Alex had to be the one to control when and how they reestablished contact.

Chapter Seven
Bridge of the Ruadh lán-damh
Clan Fraser's Red Stag

The group clustered around the holo-tank at navigation control on the bridge of the *Stag*. Lauren motioned to the astrogator. "Ronan, your analysis, please."

Swiping his black hair out of his sapphire eyes, the young astrogator looked around the table at the esteemed group of commanders, the admiral, and his queen. He swallowed hard, as a small bead of sweat rolled down his temple. Pointing toward the holographic projection floating above his navigation table he started to give his report, but his voice squeaked on the first word.

Lauren laid a hand on his shoulder and whispered, "Be easy, Ronan. They're family." With a squeeze she nodded for him to continue.

"As the commanders know, with the avatar's help we modified a standard reconnaissance drone to carry a complete suite of electro-magnetic sensors to gather information on the position and size of any fleet hiding within the nebula." He pointed to a blue trace arcing just at front of the nebula. "The drone then directed its sensors into the leading edge of the nebular cloud, looking for Comin."

"How would the drone pass undetected?" The admiral leaned closer to the hologram.

"Once the drone approached within ten light seconds of the nebula, it cut its inertial engine and continued on a purely ballistic course." The admiral nodded and Ronan seemed to relax, leaning in next to the admiral as he thumbed another control on the edge of the holo-tank analyzer. A series of fans swept out from the flight path trace and highlighted the nebula. "We estimated the drone could approach within one thousand kilometers of a ship hiding within the cloud and pass undetected."

"Indeed."

Lauren smiled at the young navigator. *He's going to be a fine officer.*

"The drone has completed its pass and returned all the information to the *Stag* in a data burst transmission from the far side of the nebula."

"How did you keep the data dump from being detected?" The admiral frowned. "Your course plan was ideal, but you could easily have given it away when the drone returned its information."

Ronan turned to Angus. "Commander Newkirk?"

"We placed a miniaturized quantum transmitter in the drone. The drone used this to encrypt and transmit the data back to the *Stag*," Angus explained.

The admiral leaned over the holo-tank, his servos within his brace whirring. "No, that is simply not possible. A quantum transceiver would not fit within a drone, especially with the full suite of sensors tucked in."

"We gave up on 'not possible' a long time ago. Now, we're just making it up as we go." Angus, Tavish, and Robert laughed with Lauren, while the others looked puzzled. "Now to your point, a transceiver wouldn't fit, but just a transmitter pre-loaded with entangled photons would. And we've got the added security of knowing if the message had been intercepted."

Alex draped an arm around her shoulders. "That is amazing, Lauren. Another scientific feat."

Lauren grinned at her. "It was a seat-of-our-pants necessity, Dearest."

"I have no idea what pants have to do with it, but this is truly an amazing discovery," Sarah interjected. "To be able to speak to others within your fleet in real time will be a huge advantage in a space conflict."

"It's the admiral's discovery; we just utilized the device to meet our needs." Lauren looked back at Ronan. "What'd we learn, astrogator?"

"Well, we learned the Comin have three full squadrons of attack eagles interspersed along the cloud edge." He activated another series of analyzer commands and three clusters of red dots appeared at the nebular edge. Fifteen pulsing red icons flashed into existence deeper within the cloud. "In the rear fleet area, we found a vanguard of fifteen capital ships. They are condor-class, each approximately one point five times larger in tonnage than a clan." Lauren felt fear return with a vengeance and cold sweat collected along her spine.

Alex released Lauren and stepped to the tank, leaning over to study the naval formations in detail. "This is one of the largest concentrations of Comin naval ships I have ever seen. What would cause them to bring this many ships forward? The Homeworld must be unguarded."

"Wait witch. No trust. She took me." G'iad'a pointed at her own chest. Lauren gasped. She'd forgotten the heir was with them. *Damn, this isn't good. We're planning on attacking the Comin. What could she think?* Lauren's thoughts stuttered as she considered another angle. *Is she a spy?*

"*Be easy, Lauren. Her aura has not changed its smell. She is simply excited to be close to home.*" Snow flicked her ear to the side.

"*I would have to agree. The child is not hiding anything from us.*" Ice wagged her tail.

"Fine, I'll go with your feelings and Alex's belief in her. But keep an eye on her, please." Ice and Snow nodded to her.

Alex turned to G'iad'a. "This may be true, young one, but are they waiting as escort or as ambush?" *Alex may have some concerns as well.*

"Not know. Both maybe. Always ready strike if need." G'iad'a tossed her braids over her shoulder and stood on her tiptoes peering at the hologram over the edge of the tank. She turned to look at Robert. "Higher."

"What do we say when we ask a favor?" Robert asked with a small smile.

Her tan face darkened with a blush. "Higher, peeese."

"Of course, up you go." Robert grasped the child around the waist and hiked her up to his shoulder. She draped a slim arm around his neck. "And?"

"Tank you."

From her new vantage point, G'iad'a looked at the entire hologram. "This talon strike." She pointed a tiny finger at the leading group of ships nearest the cloud edge. "Talon first. Then beak." She then pointed to the six clusters of ships farther back from the edge.

Alex nodded, along with her companions as the heir pointed out the Comin attack elements. Lauren asked, *"Do you recognize this?"*

"The Comin used this same formation to attack the rear guard as our last diplomatic mission collapsed after the murder of the ambassadors."

"Two prong." The six clusters were arranged three groups above and three below the position of the talon. "If through talon, then close beak." The heir clapped her hands together. Robert winced with the sound so close to his ear. Last, G'iad'a pointed to the capital ships–the giant condors. "Then maw. Eat live."

It was a classic multi-layered attack formation. Lauren learned about the Terrans using similar formations from the engagements Tavish had her study.

Alex rubbed her chin. "We are four, they are over a hundred and their capital ships out number us three to one." Her frown deepened.

"Let's not give up before we begin," Lauren countered. "Remember another Comin engagement your great grand'mere fought?"

"Excuse me?"

Lauren pointed into the hologram. "If the eagles are considered support vessels and the only ships we concern ourselves with are the fifteen condors within the vanguard, then we do a spirograph maneuver." Everyone looked at Lauren like she was crazy. "Oh, come on guys, you studied this in school."

Snow and Ice chortled with wolfy laughs where they lay on the command dais. Lauren dropped her hand into a gel pad. The hologram split into two parts. On the left was the current Comin fleet. The right display filled with ships: five Terran clans orbiting a central cluster of eleven capital ships. Lauren initiated the action and the five clans ripped through the cluster of enemy ships over and over.

"I recommend we get them out of the nebula, so we can fight ship to ship." Lauren's voice dropped to a whisper. "But I would prefer we try diplomacy first."

Tavish snorted. "Are you kidding, the Comin cannot spell diplomacy." The heir sucked in a small breath where she sat on Robert's shoulder. "I am sorry, but it is true. Your people have proven over and over, they will turn on us when we are trying to negotiate."

"Know history. But you too." G'iad'a tapped Robert on the head. "Down peese." Robert lowered her to the deck. The young heir walked up to Lauren. "I, G'iad'a, first born Kall'ka, Supreme Ruler outer planets, heir condor throne mighty Comin. On honor, we talk. I talk commander. No shoot." She held out a small hand.

Lauren grasped her hand and sank to one knee, bringing her eye-level with G'iad'a. *"I don't know if I trust her, Alex."*

"We have no choice. We are severely outgunned. She is our advantage in negotiating. If they massed this many ships within the nebula, they are motivated by something. What that is, I do not know. So, let us talk with them."

"I accept negotiations on your honor. We'll talk first." Lauren heard Tavish suck in a breath. "But our guns will be primed and aimed at the heart of your fleet. Do you still accept?"

"On honor, accept." G'iad'a pumped Lauren's hand. Then she stepped back and crossed her arm across her chest, bowing to Lauren. "You honor me, teach me, 'dopt me, trust me. I trust you." She stood to her full height, which reached just above Alex's waist. "What do I for you?"

"I ask that you represent us truthfully. We come as friends. Our only wish is to return the Comin heir safely."

G'iad'a smiled up at Lauren and nodded once.

Lauren looked at Alex and raised an eyebrow in question. *"What do you think, Dearest?"*

"I really do not know," Alex answered after a moment's thought.

"Do you trust her?"

Another minute passed. *"She is Comin, but I believe I do. She was taken much as I was, and we have a certain connection."* Alex looked deeply into Lauren's eyes, the blue flashing ice cold. *"Do you sense any deceit?"*

Lauren studied G'iad'a. *"No, not really, but I don't have the same connection. At least not yet, I need more time with her. I think—no I feel—this feud must end somewhere. Now's as good a time and place as any."*

Alex cleared her throat. "Robert, if you had not augmented your propulsion systems, when would you have arrived at the nebula?"

Lauren shook her head to clear her thoughts, Alex's question seemed tangential. *Where did that question come from? What's Alex getting at?*

Robert tipped his head in thought. "Ronan, if I may?"

"Of course, Commander." The young astrogator stepped back from the holo-tank.

"We increased our overall speed and took a more direct route to this rendezvous." He manipulated the hologram, decreasing the scale to include the F-class star where the *Orchid* was trapped. He drew their course between the two points. "Had we followed the original flight path all the way to the nebula, we would have ended here." A pulsing purple dot appeared approximately three million kilometers from their current location.

"Interesting, the tip of the Comin talon formation is pointed directly at that point," the admiral said. Lauren stared into the holo-tank and tried to see what the admiral was pointing out.

"If we recalculate the original route and lower our speed to the clan's original flank speed." Robert paused as his input parameters were recalculated. Another trace popped into the hologram, the projected original flight path. "We would not arrive for approximately another ten days."

"Thank you, Robert."

"What do you think, Lauren?" Alex asked when Lauren did not respond to Robert's analysis.

Lauren continued to study the data displayed within the holo-tank. "I know we've rushed to get to this point as fast as possible. I've pushed us hard, but finally time is working for us. If the Comin think the *Orchid* won't arrive for ten or so days, let's use the time to complete the *Stag's* repairs, rest, gather more information on the Comin fleet, and prepare as best we can, given our resources. Then in ten days, we talk to the Comin." Heads nodded around the table. Alex clapped Lauren on the shoulder and squeezed.

"Ailsa." The young communication tech popped up at Lauren's elbow, her blonde braids swirling around her head. "Orders to the others, please. 'Communications limited to quantum messages only. I do not want any stray transmissions leaking out. Commanders will stay aboard *Stag* for another day, and then return to their clans to prepare to move. We will be sending out another drone shortly.'" Ailsa nodded and turned toward her communication alcove containing the quantum transceiver.

To those gathered around her, Lauren said, "Let's complete a battle plan, should talking go poorly."

Chapter Eight
Bridge of the Ruadh lán-damh
Clan Fraser's Red Stag

Alex sat in one of the two command chairs on the bridge of the *Stag*. Lauren sat beside her, relaxed, legs crossed, one brown-booted foot idly swinging. Alex could feel her tension through their bond. After an argument about experience and capabilities, Alex had finally agreed to take temporary command of the *Stag* for this portion of their battle plan.

"Fifteen minutes until we engage gravitational engines," Sarah said from the pilot's console. G'iad'a stood at Alex's left shoulder, a tiny hand on the armrest of her command chair. Snow and Ice lay draped across the foot of the dais behind the pilot's acceleration couch. They hid their tension as well but were ready to spring into action in protection of their companions if needed. Their helmets were between the command chairs.

"*Boar, Kestrel,* and *Lion* are taking up flanking positions at the three cardinal points," Ronan said from astrogation as three icons began to flash on one of Alex's screens. "Course plotted and transferred to the pilot." The three escorts would form a triangle behind the *Stag*, with the *Kestrel* above her and the other two below and off her starboard and port flanks.

"Course received. Gravitational wave identified," Sarah acknowledged. Alex's anxiety ratcheted up. This was not her *Sea Eagle*; this was Lauren's *Stag. I must be cautious. No more injuries.*

"Sails deployed, radiant energy flowing to the sinks," the sailing master reported. Alex knew the overall profile of the clan ship increased three hundred and fifty percent with the sails unfurled. The sails opened in large arcs off each side of the ship. It made the clan look immense. Alex's palms began to sweat against the chair's armrests.

Ailsa turned from the communication console. "The clan mates are in position and prepared to engage gravitational engines. They have captured the same wave."

"Very well, charge the containment vessels, initiate fusion reactions, prepare to engage gravitational engines and intercept the wave. Prepare flyby of the nebular edge." Alex turned to the starboard sections. "Status of our particle beams and antigravity missiles."

The young Fraser tactical officer looked over his shoulder from his displays. "Batteries are manned and weapons are armed. Safeties remain in place."

The four giant clan ships leapt forward, catching the passing gravitational wave. Once they were within ten million kilometers of the nebula, they would be in sensor range of the Comin fleet hidden within the cloud. The fleet had not moved in the ten days since the *Boar* arrived to join her sisters. The eagles remained within their talon strike positions, while the condors maintained position in the rear fleet area.

"Bring active sensors online at ten million kilometers."

"Aye, ten million klicks." Ronan replied.

Alex settled back and felt the chair readjust to her change in position. She sighed in relief, thankful for the comfort surrounding her. Lauren took her hand. *"Back bothering you?"*

"No."

Lauren looked at her. *"Alex, don't lie to me. I can feel how you feel as easily as you can feel me. Your back's in knots."*

"Sitting in that fecking captain's chair on the Orchid and sleeping on the deck for days in a row may have permanently damaged something." Alex wiggled again.

Lauren dropped her hand into one of the gel pads on Alex's chair. *"This should help."*

"What?" Then Alex felt warmth build in the chair and her muscles began to relax. *"Oh my, heated command chairs."*

Lauren giggled, causing Ailsa to turn from her console. *"Pretty decadent, right?"*

"Absolutely, but wonderful."

"Gotta love heated seats. Living in Colorado, it was one option I always included in my cars." Lauren looked at Alex and smiled sheepishly. *"Even used' em in the summer. Helps with aching backs on long road trips."*

"Thank you, Dearheart."

"Anytime." Lauren winked. *"But don't tell the admiral of this modification. It might just be the straw."*

"Straw?"

Ronan turned to them. "Active sensors coming online. Data filling the hologram now." Alex watched as icons began to fill the three-dimensional construct.

Alex arched an eyebrow. "Time delay?"

"Zero. This is real-time information." Ronan gave them a smug smile.

Alex looked at Lauren for an explanation, which Lauren willingly gave. "Tachyon scanners. A suggestion from the avatar as we were traveling to the galactic center. We were trying to improve the clans anyway we could." Alex knew what tachyons were but had no idea how Lauren and Angus were able to control these exotic sub-atomic particles, which traveled at faster-than-light speeds.

"Seems like a good modification."

Lauren chuckled. "When we were building duplicate quantum transceivers, we discovered this as a side effect of the quantum field generator. The generator creates a number of exotic particle byproducts when producing the paired photons used in the communication device. We simply filtered for tachyons and saved them for the sensors. I think it's awesomely cool."

"Yes, very cool," Ronan muttered from the holo-tank. Having real-time sensor information would provide an invaluable advantage in a space battle fought at fractional light hour or light day distances.

The two relaxed and waited, watching the swirling purple-blue nebular cloud fill more and more of the forward transparency as the clans sped toward the hidden Comin fleet.

The blare of klaxons overwhelmed the quiet beeps and chirps of the active bridge consoles. "Missile launch. Missile Launch. Incoming missiles. This is not a drill," the bridge AI reported.

Red streaks filled the hologram, plotting the trace of numerous Comin missiles. All headed toward the projected approach vector of their original flight path. Their missiles headed toward empty space. Perhaps, the radiation within the nebula caused problems for the Comin sensors.

"The fleet is moving. Sensors indicate emergence from the cloud in three minutes. Their first barrage was deployed blind," Robert stated.

"Maintain our course. Prepare to drop out of the gravitational wave and deploy defensive—"

Lauren interrupted Alex's string of orders. "Ailsa, send the prepared message, please."

"Aye, message sent on all frequencies."

Heat bloomed across Alex's cheeks. "*Thank you, Dearheart, I forgot our message.*"

"*No worries, I'd forget things, too, with a swarm of missiles headed my way.*" Lauren gave Alex's hand a quick squeeze. She leaned forward in her seat to look at the young heir. "G'iad'a, any thoughts on how your kinsmen will react?"

G'iad'a shrugged. "Only watch simulations. But if Commander L'illa'ka, any possible."

Alex stood and moved over to the holo-tank. She studied the floating hologram. "Hold position at five million kilometers. Let them come to us, once they see us."

"Condors moving to lead position. Eagles falling back to the flank," the tactical officer reported. "They could be preparing a strafing run from the rear as we are distracted by the condors. The eagles are capable of a sprint speed of zero point nine five of light without a gravitational wave boost."

"Projected course of the Comin fleet?" Without comment, Ronan added a red trace into the hologram, and Alex continued, "Add a ten, seven and a half, and five-million-kilometer shell around the enemy fleet." Translucent spheres appeared around the advancing fleet. "When they crossed the seven-point-five sphere, fire a warning shot across their bows."

"Any response to our message?" Lauren asked Ailsa and Alex glanced over her shoulder at the young tech.

"No, ma'am." Ailsa shook her head, not looking up from her analyzer screens.

"Please resend it." Lauren then stood and joined Alex at the holo-tank. *"Dearest, is there anything we can do without firing our missiles?"*

Aghast at Lauren's question, Alex's tone came out tinged with anger. *"They fired first."*

"I know they fired first, but can't we do anything to de-escalate the confrontation?"

Alex felt Lauren's plea through their bond. *She does not want to lose any more lives.* Alex understood the feeling. Alex clasped her hands behind her back. Images of the destruction of Terra Prime flashed through her mind. She was still staggered at the massive loss of life. Her mother's death pierced her heart. *The Comin did that.* But Alex took a moment to consider Lauren's question.

"Ailsa, message to the clans, all stop on my mark. Pilot, prepare to bring the *Stag* to station keeping." Alex turned to the tactical officer. "Bring all weapons down to standby. Have the battery crews remain at their posts."

"Ma'am?" The young officer turned to look at Alex. She raised an eyebrow. "Aye, weapons to standby." He flipped a number of transparent covers down over his firing controls. "Crews report at post and standing down to readiness status."

"Very good. G'iad'a?" Alex smiled at the young girl, amazed at how much she looked like a young eaglet in her golden evac-suit. The suit shimmered in the bright-white light of the bridge. "I want you to send a real-time message to your fleet. Please let them know you are aboard and include a brief summary of the events of your rescue from the witch. Ailsa, please send the heir's message as a holo-projection."

Ailsa rose from her acceleration couch and motioned for G'iad'a to join her at the communication consoles. She pointed to a spot on the deck. "I will need you to stand here, please. The holo-cameras will capture your image in three dimensions, while we record your message."

G'iad'a nodded and stood on the indicated spot. When Ailsa nodded, she began, "JIH cho'wI' g'iad. ghu'vam witch wej yo', HIboQII' yo' vo' ghaH. yIn owe jIH Alex. ghaH ta'be' Terra. jIHvaD Qam tlham. wej bach yIjatlh, maH." Alex cringed at the harsh consonants.

When a small beep sounded from one of Lauren's screens, Alex joined her. *"Seems Ailsa is translating in real-time."* Lauren's mind voice betrayed her excitement, one which Alex mirrored. A stream of text appeared on the small screen:

[I heir G'iad'a. Witch take me T'le'cac. This not witch's fleet. This fleet save me her. I owe life Alex. She Queen Terra. Stand down. Order me. We talk, not shoot.]

Alex placed a hand on Lauren's shoulder. *"We may get out of this without firing, Consort."*

Ailsa turned to them. "There is a transmission lag of four minutes, seventeen seconds."

"Well then, we have about ten minutes to see what they say." Alex settled back down in her warm command chair.

G'iad'a came back onto the command dais. "All right me?"

Before Alex could answer, Lauren knelt in front of the young heir and took both her hands. "You did great. I'm proud of you. Thanks for helping us." The heir blushed to the roots of her dark braids.

Ice stood, yawned and stretched, then stepped up to G'iad'a. The large wolf lowered her head and looked in the child's eyes. *"I will add my thanks as well. I may have misjudged you when we first met."*

"You did right. Protect pack. We friends?" G'iad'a's mind voice was a soft tinkling in Alex's mind, as she reached out and placed her small hand on the wolf's large head.

"Yes, friends." G'iad'a squealed in delight and hugged Ice close to her.

Alex looked back and forth between the two. "Can you hear Ice, G'iad'a?"

"Yes, speak well." G'iad'a continued to hug the great wolf. She dropped her head into the soft ruff and sighed.

"*Alex, she can hear Ice. How's that possible?*" Lauren's shock rippled through their bond.

Turning to Lauren, Alex shrugged. "*I thought she could hear some of the conversations we had when I was aboard the* Orchid. *When we were preparing to tractor out of the gravity well, she was monitoring strain on the hull. She acknowledged my questions and orders faster than I thought possible, almost reading my mind. Now, I know she was able to. Her psi-abilities are quite strong. This may explain how the witch was able to recognize her and pull her through the T'le'cac.*"

Lauren turned to G'iad'a where she now sat cross-legged between the reclining wolves. She had an arm draped over each of their ruffs and leaned into Ice's warm body. "*Heir, can you hear me?*" Alex heard Lauren project her thoughts. The child started slightly but did not respond. "*I know you can hear me, quit playing opossum.*" A soft chuckle underlay Lauren rebuff.

"*No laugh me. I not pussum.*"

Lauren grinned. "You are, if you don't respond to my question. And it's an opossum. An opossum is a large marsupial, indigenous to my country on Earth. It protects itself by playing dead when in a dangerous or threatening situation. Just like you, playing dumb about being able to hear us and speak with the companions."

"Incoming message." Ailsa interrupted Lauren's impromptu biology lesson. Several of the crew had turned, curious, listening to Lauren's explanation.

G'iad'a jumped up and ran over to the communication tech. "Who call?"

"I do not know." She smiled at the child. "Transferring message to the holo-projectors."

An image of a woman in golden energy armor appeared. She stood in the center of a darkened bridge. Consoles around her provided a soft green illumination. Her black hair was braided in a manner similar to G'iad'a's, with golden orb beads containing flecks of reddish translucent stone. As the woman began to speak, Ailsa overlaid a real-time translation. "I L'illa'ka, commander Comin nebular fleet. You invade our territory. This not allow. Withdraw immediately or risk destruction. Your use image dead heir make crimes more heinous. You ten micro-cycles to reverse course. Leave space."

G'iad'a huffed. "She not believe my message. How dare her." She punched through the frozen holographic image of the Comin commander, her golden gauntlet piercing the woman's chest.

"That will not aid us in convincing them of your presence here." Alex knelt beside the child and gathered her in her arms. G'iad'a pushed against Alex's chest, anger sparking in her dark eyes.

"Easy, we must think this through. You cannot allow anger to cloud your ability to reason." Alex felt out of her depth and looked beseechingly over the child's shoulder at Lauren.

"G'iad'a, why would L'illa'ka not believe you were here?" Lauren asked.

G'iad'a looked at Lauren. "I not know. Think dead. Hate witch." She struggled to get out of Alex's arms and Alex released her.

"Can you think of a way to help?" G'iad'a hesitated, Lauren pushed a bit harder. "You're the only one who can convince the commander you're here. Convince her we aren't trying to trick her."

"I not know. Must think." She turned back to the frozen image of L'illa'ka. G'iad'a began pulling on her braids, the beads rattling against each other. She froze, looking down at the braids in her hand. "Have idea. Need knife."

Alex watched in fascination; Lauren was so good with the child. She got her to calm down and focus on the problem. Alex pulled her dirk from a pocket in her evac-suit and handed the blade to G'iad'a hilt first. As G'iad'a raised the blade to her throat, Alex lunged forward. "No!"

The child dropped the blade and staggered away from Alex. She seemed to realize what Alex thought was happening and smiled. "I not harm me. I need bead." She bent down picking the dirk up and grasped a handful of braids, sawing at the hair. Once they were free, she sat on the edge of the command dais, sorting through the hank of braids and beads. After choosing one braid, G'iad'a used the dirk's tip to pry one of the beads open. A tiny scroll fell out and bounced on the deck.

"What the?" Alex exclaimed. *I wonder what else she has hidden in those beads?*

"This work." She picked up the scroll and walked over to Ailsa, thrusting the tiny piece of flimsie toward the communication tech. "Here, send."

Ailsa unrolled the tiny scroll then looked at Alex. "I do not know what this is, therefore, I do not know what to send, Majesty."

G'iad'a put her hands on her hips. "Code, send."

"All right, but I cannot send something I do not know what it is," Ailsa explained. Alex moved toward the communication console, as Lauren stepped off the dais and exited the bridge into her office.

Alex raised an eyebrow. "Lauren?" All she got in response was a raised finger indicating Alex needed to wait a minute as Lauren disappeared through the hatch into her command cabin.

Lauren came back carrying a small black cube. "This should help." She walked over to Ailsa and pushed all eight corners on the cube before placing the cube on the tech's work surface.

A holographic image of the admiral's head appeared. "How may I be of assistance, Majesty?" Alex gasped as the hologram spoke with the admiral's distinctive brogue.

"We need to translate this." Lauren held the tiny scroll up. "And transmit it to the Comin commander in its exact form."

"Please place it in the data slot." A small slit opened in the side of the avatar's cube. Lauren fed the flimsie into the cube. When it disappeared, G'iad'a gasped.

"It'll be fine." Lauren smiled at the child.

The avatar closed its eyes and hummed. Alex quirked an eyebrow and G'iad'a leaned close to the holographic image. "He make noise."

"He's thinking." G'iad'a frowned at her and Lauren chuckled. She placed a hand on the heir's small shoulder. "Working through our request to translate your scroll into something Ailsa can send to your commander."

Alex leaned down. "That is the admiral, you recognize him?"

"If admiral, he smart."

Lauren laughed. "Yes, he's very smart."

A stream of text scrolled across one of Ailsa's communication monitors. "Please send this."

Ailsa nodded and the message was off.

The Comin fleet continued to advance on their position. A warning bleep sounded at the astrogation holo-tank. "The fleet has crossed the seven point five-million-kilometer mark," Ronan said, and the tactical tech looked over his shoulder at Alex.

"Continue to hold position," Alex ordered. "Bring defensive counter-measures online and prepare to deploy the defensive drones."

The seconds stretched to minutes as tension on the bridge rose. After more than nine minutes had passed, Alex stepped up to the holo-tank and said, "Deploy countermeasures. Have the clan mates prepare defensive maneuver alpha-beta-three-one."

Alex turned to the sailing master. "Charge on the sinks?"

"Fully charged, excess radiant energy is being shunted to the hull."

"Gravitational waves in the area?"

Several undulations appeared within the hologram as Sarah transferred information to astrogation. "We have several possible waves to use with that defensive maneuver," Ronan replied.

"Identify the optimal wave and prepare to engage."

When five more minutes had passed, Alex went to the pilot's position. She leaned down and whispered in Sarah's ear, "I do not want to engage the Comin, if we can avoid it. Prepare to enter the appropriate gravitational wave to place us on this course at maximum speed. On my command only." Alex entered the course using a gel pad on the pilot's console. Sarah nodded as information filled her screen.

"Aye, Majesty."

Alex spoke in a normal voice. "Ailsa, open a channel to the clan mates."

"Channel open."

"Let us assume the Comin are hesitating as they decrypt G'iad'a's message. If they do not respond in the next ninety minutes, engage gravitational engines and depart the nebula on the agreed course. We will meet at the designated coordinates."

"All respond in the affirmative. They will depart in ninety minutes," Ailsa confirmed.

Alex sat. She hated waiting, but in this instance, waiting allowed them time to plan and execute. The Comin fleet continued to advance on the Terran position.

"Incoming message." Sixty-three minutes had elapsed. Everyone on the bridge heaved a sigh of relief. "Uploading to the holographic projector."

Again, the image of L'illa'ka appeared before them. She looked angry, a frown pulling the corners of her mouth, but Alex sensed relief in her stance. *She is trying to maintain the Comin image of dominance.* "Your received message translated. How you code, knew translation, we not know. It old code, out of date. If message true, we require proof heir wellbeing. Put her on shuttle to these coordinates." The image flicked her left hand and a stream of astrogation coordinates scrolled across the base of the projection.

"Sending to astrogation, now," Ailsa replied, hands dancing over her gel pads.

"We require meet in quarter revolution. No weapons, guards allowed." The image froze with her last word.

"Well, G'iad'a, what do you suggest?" Alex turned to the young girl.

She stood from her place between the wolves and huffed. "Why no believe? I heir, have code."

Lauren laughed. "Not everything goes as planned, young one. Sometimes, patience is required. Tell us about your Commander L'illa'ka. Does she play fair? Is she one to lie or dissemble? Is she speaking the truth about this meeting or is it a trap?"

G'iad'a stood in front of Lauren. Alex was amazed at the rapport the two had established so quickly. *Lauren is thinking strategically.* Obviously, she learned much during their journey from Terra. *We make a great team.*

Lauren glanced at her. *"Always together, Dearest."*

"Ah, listening in. Should I be concerned?" Alex smiled in question.

"Not at all. But there aren't any barriers anymore."

Alex sank into their bond. *Lauren is correct.* All the physical limitations of their bond were gone. They stood as one within a pulsing tower of power. Lauren reached across the armrests and gripped her forearm, squeezing it once. She then turned to the heir. "G'iad'a, what do you think? Can we trust your commander?"

"I trust." G'iad'a thought for a moment. "But cautious."

"Well said." Alex laughed. "We will trust, but only to a certain point. I say we meet your L'illa'ka."

After much debate, it was decided each of the ships would send a flitter out to meet the Comin. Lauren would accompany G'iad'a with a cadre of bodyguards. Alex would remain on the *Stag*, much to her consternation. Everyone agreed, both of them could not be at risk. *Now, I am the one to wait and worry.*

Chapter Nine
Captain's Quarters of the Ruadh lán-damh
Clan Fraser's Red Stag

Lauren lay on the sofa beneath the large transparency in her cabin, reviewing historical recordings of past Terran-Comin interactions. She wanted to be as familiar with Comin culture and customs as possible. Their current truce was constructed of gossamer threads, easily broken if anyone were to slight the other party.

The meeting with Commander L'illa'ka went as well as could be expected, considering the Comin's suspicion about G'iad'a and how the Terrans had her with them. It turned out no diplomacy was necessary in this meeting, as it all came down to science. Once the heir's DNA was verified and it was determined she was not a clone, she then answered questions only she would know the answer to, the rest of the meeting went well.

The only sticking point was G'iad'a's refusal to travel to the Homeworld aboard the commander's *Golden Condor*. G'iad'a insisted she would finish this journey aboard the *Stag*, adamant this was her right as an adopted member of Clan Doouglas. L'illa'ka nearly had a heart attack at this news. It took Lauren more than an hour to explain what clan adoption meant. No, G'iad'a had not given up her position as the Comin heir, explaining her status as heir was enhanced and enriched since she was now also recognized as a member of Clan Doouglas.

Currently, the four clans were on their way to the Comin Homeworld, to received thanks from the Empress for rescuing her daughter and to open diplomatic talks between their people. Seven condor-class dreadnoughts flanked the Terran clans, with L'illa'ka's giant *Golden Condor* in the lead. The rest of the Comin fleet remained at the edge of the nebula on patrol against invaders. Tavish was not convinced of their truce and had the clans running weapons drills throughout their journey. Several plans were programed into the clans' automated defensive systems, should a surprise attack come from any of the surrounding Comin condors. A simple command would activate a coordinated escape from within the heart of the Comin's fleet.

Alex was off sparring with G'iad'a. Even though the child barely came up to Alex's waist, her skills with her muhaddab impressed everyone. Her speed and agility with the wicked curved sword made up for her lack of physical stature. Lauren had witnessed how easily the heir got under Alex's guard. The weight of the Terran broadsword limited Alex's ability to parry G'iad'a's flashing attacks and limited her ability to counter with an offensive thrust. Alex was convinced with enough practice; she could defeat the heir's muhaddab. Fewer bruises and cuts after each match were the only indication Alex was making progress with her goal.

The cabin's hatch swished open and Alex came in, perspiration beaded across her face and her once white shirt soaked gray with sweat. Several streaks of red marred the sleeves.

"Success?" Lauren rose from the sofa to retrieve her medical kit.

"Do not make fun of me. That child is a menace. She is fast as lightning and strikes like a bird of prey, talons first." Alex dropped into one of the three leather armchairs before the sofa.

"Perhaps you should make her fight with one of your broadswords to even the odds."

Alex laughed and their bond swelled with Alex's humor. "No, she cannot lift a broadsword, but tomorrow I will fight with the muhaddab. Then we will see how she fares."

Lauren pushed up Alex's sleeve and looked at the rows of long thin, parallel cuts which ran from her elbow to her wrist. "I'd say you did get in a fight with a bird of prey. These look like talon scratches." She pulled out an antiseptic pad, swabbing Alex's arm.

"Ouch! That hurts." Alex jerked her arm back.

"Don't be a baby. I need to clean these and apply a dermasheet. They'll be gone by morning." Lauren held Alex's arm in a firm grip and continued swabbing the wounds. "Will I need to treat the heir tomorrow?" *I think Snow is wrong. Alex and Tavish are just as aggressive as ever.*

Alex chuckled. "No, I am sure she will once again get the better of me. It seems to be more a matter of size than of weapon or ability. She is within my guard before I can react. I am just getting old."

"Not old, Dearest. Simply a different style of combat. You should have a look at some of the videos from early Terran meetings with the Comin. There are even videos from Comin athletic and military competitions. Perhaps, you can learn something for tomorrow."

"You are becoming quite the strategist." Alex placed her other hand on Lauren shoulder.

After she applied the gelled dermasheet, Lauren released Alex's forearm. "Perhaps, but I'm as concerned about this meeting as Tavish is. Something isn't right. Things were too easily agreed to with the commander. In everything I've read, the Comin are cautious to the point of isolationism. They scheme, plot, and attack against everyone, especially among themselves. Their court's a real hornet's nest of intrigue and treachery. They advance their society through the theft of technologies from others."

"I cannot disagree with you, Dearheart. I was shocked when G'iad'a told us her mother was Empress. What could have happened to Emperor T'iil'lac? When I entered the Comin Homeworld through the nexus to recover the bioweapon data files, he was emperor. Still young, with many heirs. For her to become Empress, many would need to be dispatched, if not outright killed. Theirs is a violent and tragic existence."

Lauren sighed as she finished dressing the wounds on Alex's other arm and left leg. She dropped into a cross-legged position the floor; her kilt draped across her knees. "And at the same time, they're combating global environmental disaster. The amount of energy needed to maintain their domes must be extraordinary. I can't find any reference to the use of renewable resources or alternate energy sources."

She pulled a jet injector from her medical kit. Alex shrank back in her chair. "To that end, I prepared an immuno-booster for all of us who'll travel to the surface of the Homeworld. I've got no idea what infectious bacteria, viruses, or fungi we'll be exposed to, or what inorganic contaminants may exist in their environment. I want to boost all our immune systems as much as possible." Alex squirmed again. "You're such a baby. This won't hurt at all. If you think this is bad, you should've seen the needles used to give me vaccinations back on Earth. Those hurt." She placed the injector on Alex's thigh and pulled the trigger. A tiny psst was the only sound. "There, that should do." Lauren placed her hand over the injection site and sent a burst of caring along their bond. Her hand warmed the spot she'd injected.

"Thank you for always taking the best care of me," Alex said.

Lauren was startled by Alex's comment. *I haven't always taken good care of Alex.* A cascade of memories ran through her mind of all the times Alex was hurt.

"Stop that. You are not to blame for the actions of others. You do take the best care of me. I would never have survived my injuries if we had not met when we did."

Lauren smiled at her soulmate. "Well, if we're going to give credit where credit is due, then we've gotta thank Ice. She was the one who pulled me through the nexus after all."

"Be that as it may, had our bond not begun to resonate she would never have felt you through the nexus membrane."

"And then where would I be?" Lauren finished in a whisper as she slid her hands beneath Alex's kilt and up her thighs. She relaxed and simply enjoyed the moment, the closeness, and the intimacy of being with her love. "Not here, which is the only place I ever want to be."

Alex kissed the top of Lauren's head. "Shall we take this somewhere we can get comfortable? If I sit here much longer, I will stiffen up and not be able to stand."

Lauren stood, grasping Alex's hands and pulling her up. "Yes, let's."

The distance to the large bed wasn't far but it could have been lightyears, as the two traversed the space lost in their bond. Lauren pulled Alex's shirt from her kilt and ran her hands over her ribs, thumbs sliding down to rest above her navel. Then, she traced a path up and over her breasts. She breathed in Alex's warm scent and drank in her nearness. This is what she was missing while Alex was on the *Orchid*. Now her soul was whole again and she relished this feeling of completeness. Her world spun as Alex gathered her in her arms and cradled her close, taking the last few steps to the bed. Alex placed her on the bed and Lauren looked up into ice blue eyes, green flecks sparkling in the low light. Her heart rate accelerated as Alex settled next to her and with a stuttered double beat synchronized with Alex's.

Lauren rolled onto her side and slid her hand across Alex's shoulder and down, to pull the shirt over her head. She tossed it aside. Her own shirt soon followed, and then her kilt. Alex raised her head and their lips joined. Sparks flashed behind Lauren's eyelids, and their bond sang as they sealed their physical connection. Alex's fingertips traced a random pattern across her spine then around her sides. Lauren slid down Alex's long lean body, smoothing fingers over curves of muscle and bone, the softness of her breast in sharp contrast to the steel-hard muscles of her abdomen.

"I can't get enough of you," Lauren whispered.

Alex smiled. "You have me." Her eyes filled with tears.

"Don't cry, Dearest. I'll never let you fall. This is a joyous moment."

"Too much, too fast."

Lauren kissed her nose. "Then, we'll take it slow and see where this exploration takes us." *I can't believe I can turn this powerful, confident woman into a tearful mess.* She kissed Alex again, pouring all her love into their bond. Without warning, they were swept into a maelstrom of emotion, sucked deeper into each other, before an explosion of supernova proportion tore through them. Crashing over them, in a blast of sensation so powerful, they both went rigid. Lauren couldn't breathe in enough air to speak. Alex lay shaking beside her, tears running down her cheeks, tiny shudders racing through her. Lauren wrapped her arms around her love, as the storm slowly abated. She lowered her head to Alex's shoulder and held Alex in her strong arms, listening to Alex's heartbeat thunder in her ear.

"Thank you," Alex whispered.

Lauren chuckled. "No thanks necessary, Dearest. Rest now. Tomorrow we're going to be busy, what with your sparring session and our arrival on the Homeworld."

Chapter Ten
The Comin Homeworld

G'iad'a vibrated with excitement as the Terran flitter descended from the *Stag* toward the planet's surface. The heir stood between the pilot couches and gawked at her red-brown, rocky planet through the forward transparency. Lauren could see streaks of lighter reddish brown where massive sandstorms tore over the planet surface, while thick pea-green clouds covered other areas obscuring the surface. Lightening arced between clouds and disappeared in the miasma of thick atmosphere. Lauren couldn't see any visible signs of water.

The heir had shared the history of her planet and the Comin people with them as they traveled from the nebula to the Homeworld. She talked about the grand palace and the condor throne, on which her mother now sat. She schooled them in Comin etiquette and what would be expected upon their arrival. Lauren worried one of their party would misstep and create a diplomatic incident. G'iad'a told them the size of various objects within the governmental center. It seemed the Comin were obsessed with the number thirteen or its mirror-image the number thirty-one. This was the number of gods and goddesses in their history—thirteen each. The number of ruling families, through their history—thirty-one. Even their mathematical systems were base-13, not base-10 as used by Terra and Earth. Lauren puzzled over this mathematical anomaly and had even asked the admiral's avatar and Angus about using this archaic system. Neither could figure out how the Comin ever figured out space flight using such a difficult mathematical system.

The companions would each take a flitter from their clan down to the surface in formation with the Comin commander's shuttle. Their party would be limited to Alex, Lauren, Angus, Tavish, Robert, the admiral, and their six bodyguards. Ice and Snow would accompany Alex and Lauren.

Their flitters were on course for landing at the Imperial space port, on the edge of the grand palace complex. They would meet with the Empress, return the heir, and hopefully lay the groundwork for a new alliance between their two people. Lauren knew this was a great opportunity to put an end to this destructive feud. *If everything goes well that is, but so much can go wrong.* Lauren caught her bottom lip in her teeth.

Sarah turned from her place in the pilot's seat. "Are you excited about being home, Imp?"

G'iad'a smiled. "I no imp. I heir."

"We got that." Sarah laughed and turned back to her flight controls.

Lauren smiled at the young girl. Although she had moments of insecurity—*and who wouldn't, given what she'd been though*—she was strong. In spite of her status as the heir, G'iad'a always respected Alex. Listening and learning all Alex shared with her. Perhaps being only children burdened with huge expectations created this bond. Lauren was an only child as well, with expectations piled on her by her parents, but it wasn't the same as the pressures placed on the future and current rulers of their people. *I'm glad they have each other.*

Alex and Lauren had dressed in formal tartan and wore their badges of honor and right-to-rule on their plaids. Lauren had her rapier at her side and Alex carried Robert's great grandmere's claymore across her back. G'iad'a had said no one could come armed into the presence of the Empress, but they hoped the weapons would be seen as ceremonial. After all, it was one ruler meeting another.

G'iad'a also wore the formal tartan of the Doouglas clan, to represent and respect those who saved her from Gwenhwyfach. She wished to let her mother know how important Alex and the Terrans were to her. Lauren knew this could go two ways—be seen as a sign of inclusion or an act of defiance. G'iad'a wore her muhaddab across her back in a shoulder harness.

Well, it was too late to change things now. Their flitter dropped through the thick polluted atmosphere and made a sweeping turn toward the glittering surface of the environmental dome covering the Comin governmental city.

Sarah's soft murmurs could be heard as she requested entrance through the barrier. An oculus opened in front of the descending flitter and she slipped the dart-like craft through with the ease and elegance of a skilled pilot. The flitter flared to bleed off forward velocity and touched down. Lauren saw G'iad'a lean down and whisper in her ear.

Sarah nodded. "I promised and we will. Let's see to what is needed before we add something else to your plate."

"Well, let us be about it, shall we?" Alex indicated G'iad'a should stand before her at the hatch. Lauren stepped up to Alex's right shoulder and smiled at her love. Initially, she had questioned Alex's desire to return the heir in person. *Now I see the benefit.* Alex once again placed her needs second to the needs of the Terran people. This was an ideal opportunity to remove the potential threat from the Comin, allowing the Terrans to live peacefully, focusing on advancing their society rather than advancing their military. She mentally crossed her fingers, hoping this was the right thing to do. Ice and Snow nuzzled her hands as they stood at her sides.

The other three clan flitters settled down around theirs and once the dust cleared, the hatch opened with a gentle hiss of releasing atmospheric pressure. Heat rolled over them in waves, as they stepped out and descended to the tarmac. The light had an odd greenish hue and the air smelled stale, loaded with manufacturing byproducts which left an odd chemical taste in the back of Lauren's throat.

Alex and Lauren followed G'iad'a toward an honor guard, a phalanx of Comin in full battle dress of golden energy armor, each holding a wicked looking scimitar before them. Their arms were outstretched parallel to the ground, the points of the weapons aimed to the sky. Commander L'illa'ka led the guard. A large, golden raptor sat on her left shoulder, its intelligent eyes taking in everything around it. It turned its head toward the commander and opened its maw in a silent appeal. *Or is it communicating in some way?* The commander tipped her head toward the large beak, as if listening.

Lauren was puzzling this out, when Ice bumped her hand. *"It speaks, though we cannot understand its words. I think it is a female."* Lauren placed her hand on Ice's neck in thanks and nodded.

The commander sketched a brief salute of right arm across her chest to Alex. "Welcome, Queen." Then she turned to G'iad'a and bowed her head. "And to you, young one, we pleased you return safe."

G'iad'a rattled off a string of Comin and Lauren knew it was a formal greeting of return. "We speak later, now see Mother."

"As you wish, so I obey, young one." G'iad'a tensed at the diminutive, clearly rankled.

G'iad'a had shared all she knew about a formal audience with the Empress. Where it would occur and what was expected. Lauren was shocked by the grandeur of their surroundings. The child's description of the Imperial grounds was inadequate to say the least.

The governmental center was a huge complex set within a tridecagon over fifty kilometers across, each corner was marked by a three-sided pyramid. The pyramids were constructed of a pinkish red limestone. The two nearest pyramids flanked the grand approach, each guarding the edge of the flitter tarmac. Lauren could just make out the fossilized remains of giant aquatic creatures trapped within the limestone blocks of the pyramid.

As the Commander L'illa'ka stepped aside, a great road stretched from the tarmac off into the distance. "This way."

As they followed the commander, the Comin guards fell in on either side of them. Lauren looked behind them and realized the Comin had their group surrounded.

Alex glanced at her. *"Easy, Dearheart. We are safe for now."*

"But for how long? I don't like this feeling of claustrophobia." Lauren took a half-step closer to Alex, resting her hand on the hilt of her rapier.

"As long as it takes, I suppose." Alex smiled. *"Let us see what the Empress has to say."* Ice and Snow trotted at Lauren and Alex's sides, forming another layer of protection between them and the Comin guards.

"Very well, but I reserve the right to say when we leave." Sweat slid between Lauren's shoulders. The heat was oppressive. The red sunlight was glaring. It seemed to multiply in intensity as it refracted through the glittering dome.

After a ten-minute walk, their party passed under a grand archway. G'iad'a had explained this was the Arch of Heroes, constructed to memorialize those who died in battle defending the Comin Homeworld. The great archway stood over fifty meters high, arcing over the hundred-meter-wide road. Friezes of battle scenes covered the white granite surfaces. Lauren could see scenes from land and space. A secondary arch intersected the great arch at a right angle and allowed exit from within the structure. This was the Arch of Cowards, an exit for those deemed unfit to cross through the Arch of Heroes onto the path of the immortals.

Once through the arch, the road narrowed. Thirteen rune-covered pylons flanked them here, carved from blocks of reddish marble, each pylon was separated by a statue of an eagle with spread wings. *Amazing.* The artists had used the swirls of white and pink imperfections within the stone to highlight eyes and talons, feathers and beaks.

Their approach ended at a massive dais; thirteen high steps rose above them. Each step held two massive guards in golden energy armor, patterned after feathers. Anyone approaching the throne would need to pass between the guards. Sweat now ran freely down Lauren's back. *Is the heat getting to me or is this show of dominance?*

On the dais sat the gigantic golden condor throne, the bird's wings were spread wide and curved forward as if it would enfold the throne's occupant. The head was also bent forward; the bird's large beak open in scream. It appeared ready to snatch the ruler's head from her shoulders if displeased. The eyes fascinated Lauren. Two huge green diamonds sparkled in the fetid red light of the Comin sun as it filtered through the polluted atmosphere. The eyes seemed to move and follow her, never leaving her, judging her as she came before the throne. Behind the throne rose a pure-white obelisk, tinted pink in the fading light. Its shadow cast a line straight down the road.

"Lauren?" Alex whispered in her mind.

She started. *"Sorry, just lost in thought."*

"I understand this is an amazing site, but we must focus."

Lauren straightened and followed at her love's shoulder. Alex ascended the thirteen high steps to stand before the condor throne.

The Empress sat on the throne; a tiny figure almost lost within the bird's enclosing wingspan. She stood and Lauren could feel command-presence radiate off her. This was something Alex also had in abundance. Dressed in a simple sheath of white silk, gathered at the waist by a golden rope, the garment stopped below her knees at mid-calf. Sandal-straps wove artfully around her lower legs. *Her nails are painted purple, interesting use of the royal color.* A single gold coronet encircled her head, holding her braids in place, her hair was so black, it reflected deep-blue highlights in the reddish light. Where G'iad'a wore braids tipped with beads carved in the shape of eaglets, the Empress's braids were tipped in golden talons. She stepped down one step and met Alex on the wide ledge surrounding the throne.

The Empress held out both hands, palms up. "Wec'ome, Queen Terra. I, Kall'ka. I owe you heart Comin people for return my child and heir."

Alex took the Empress' hands in hers, towering over the diminutive woman. "Greetings from Terra and her clans. I am pleased to be able to aid the Comin and her Empress in returning her heir."

"We sure heir lost all time, when disappear through T'le'cac." She frowned at G'iad'a. "Seem heir very good at evasive maneuver. Slip guard, step through gateway."

Lauren could see G'iad'a stiffen and open her mouth, probably to respond in anger at her mother, but Alex beat her to it. "I do not believe the heir stepped through the nexus of her own accord."

Kall'ka started and looked up at Alex, her onyx black eyes seeming to penetrate Alex's soul. Lauren could feel Alex pull energy from their bond to construct a mental barrier as the Empress tried to search her mind.

When Kall'ka didn't respond, Alex motioned to Lauren. "May I introduce my Consort, Lauren Beckwith Fraser Doouglas." Lauren stepped even with Alex and inclined her head, her left hand never leaving the hilt of her rapier. Kall'ka smirked, but she nodded greetings to Lauren.

"And my companions." Alex introduced each of the Terrans in turn.

Kall'ka pointed to the wolves. "And beasts?"

Alex motioned to the wolves. "May I present Ice." The wolf dropped her massive head. "And Snow. My companions since birth." Snow extended one paw forward and bowed.

"They behave well, better manners than heir." G'iad'a audibly huffed and Kall'ka smiled indulgently.

"As to the misdeeds of your heir, I believe she was taken," Alex said. "Kidnapped by the traitor Gwenhwyfach, through no fault of her own. The witch sensed the heir through the nexus membrane and pulled her across the quantum tubula to her ship. I believe she was going to use your heir as insurance against your potential treachery. However, the only treachery in this affair is that of the traitor. Your heir behaved with honor and valor, helping us overcome many near-fatal mishaps along the way. In fact, I would be hard pressed to say who rescued whom in our escape from the traitor's ship."

Kall'ka scrutinized Alex, weighing the veracity of her words. "We wait many rotations for Gwen'fack arrive. No word since left your planet. We know not what happen 'til you arrive nebula." Kall'ka seemed to make a decision. She stepped back from Alex and dropped her hands, nodding to an attendant. "Bring chair, drink. We talk. Much discuss."

A semi-circle of chairs was arranged around the front of the throne, one for each of the Terrans and L'illa'ka. G'iad'a sat cross-legged at her mother's feet, her colorful tartan kilt a sharp contrast to her mother's white sheath. Small redwood tables held drinks and light snacks. The Comin food was pleasant, and Lauren enjoyed the sweet fruity snacks and iced fizzy drinks. As the discussion continued into the late evening, torches were lit around the dais. The flickering light made the wings of the condor throne appear to be moving, ready to take flight.

Alex was masterful in the discussion, never giving anything, which wasn't met with an equal gift in return. Compromise and compassion were forefront in the discussion on both women's part. "War not answer, now. We too many battles here to fight." Kall'ka waved her hand around indicating the sparkling environmental dome overhead. "No waste resources elsewhere."

Lauren glanced sideways at Alex. *"Now?"*

"Now."

"I understand your dilemma, Highness." This was the first time Lauren had spoken all evening. "Your planet is struggling to survive, and your people are suffering." Both G'iad'a and her mother stiffened. "I mean no disrespect. But as we traveled here, G'iad'a shared stories of your history, your great past, your current state, and your uncertain future." She leaned forward and opened her hands. "I'm a physician by training and spent my career studying environmental hazards across my planet and what environmental contaminants could do to the physical health of the populace. Harm done by poor decisions or a need for resources elsewhere."

Lauren took a deep breath. Alex gave her a mental nudge forward. "And greed. Individuals who place a planet and her people second to personal desires. Perhaps Angus and I could be of assistance?" She pointed at the young Newkirk.

A dark scowl marred the Empress' fine features. Alex and Lauren had discussed how to offer assistance to a civilization which saw asking for help as a weakness. They decided to just put it out there, in as unthreatening a way as possible. That's why Lauren led this portion of the discussion.

"No, not need help." Kall'ka slapped her hand onto the arm of the condor throne. Silence reined. *Did I overstep, say too much too soon?* Kall'ka's face continued to darken and the guards took a menacing step forward. The atmosphere around their small group changed. Ice and Snow growled low and Lauren dropped her hands onto their ruffs.

"Stop!" G'iad'a jumped to her feet and thrust her hands toward the guards. "I say stop." The guards hesitated in their advance.

"You impertinent child, no command my guard." Kall'ka raised her hand to strike her heir. The young girl turned to her mother, dropped to one knee and placed her small hands on her mother's sandal covered foot. No one spoke but Lauren knew the two were communicating. After several minutes, tears escaped Kall'ka's eyes and slid down her tan cheeks. She nodded at her heir and stood. "We stop now, rest, eat, meet on morn." She placed a hand on G'iad'a's shoulder. "Come, explain more." The two disappeared around the throne and walked off into the dark toward the towering obelisk.

Lauren sighed. "I'm sorry, Alex. I think I blew it."

Alex remained seated, lost in thought, and then she shook her head. "I do not agree, Dearheart. I believe we touched on a highly sensitive issue, but one which needed to be broached. Now, we wait and see what happens." She stood and gathered Lauren close. Lauren sank into her arms and relished the feel of her love.

A servant came from behind the throne and motioned at the small group. "Come."

The Terrans were led away to a beautiful set of apartments within the Imperial Palace, their suites overlooking the parks and gardens on the periphery of the environmental dome. Lauren's anxiety increased as they made their way to their rooms. "Relax. Tomorrow is another day, Dear-heart."

"I hope you're right, Alex. I'm afraid I may have created another diplomatic incident."

Chapter Eleven
The Comin Homeworld, Imperial Court

Lauren stood on the balcony looking down on the splendor of the tended gardens beneath their suite of rooms. Even this early in the morning, the heat was nearly unbearable. The twin suns had barely slipped over the horizon and the temperature skyrocketed. Obviously, the dome didn't protect from the accumulated greenhouse heating outside.

Lauren speculated it would take too much energy to cool the inside of the dome, so the Comin allowed the temperatures to equilibrate across the shimmering boundary, while using the dome to block pollutants and other toxins. At one time, the Comin had cooled their domes, but their use of non-renewable energy resources created more pollution. Lauren looked up and saw the billowing pea-green clouds swirling around the dome boundary. From their chaotic flow, the winds would be hurricane-force and with sand embedded in the winds, a person would be flayed to the bone if exposed outside the dome.

Alex came to stand behind her and encircled her in long arms, resting a chin on her the top of her head. "My heart bleeds for the Comin. They have destroyed their planet. I understand why they so desperately need another home."

Lauren turned in her love's arms. "Regardless of what the Empress says today, I think we should release the nanites from orbit and then go home."

"Perhaps you are right." Alex frowned. "But, what if the nanites fail? Are we are sentencing this world to death? I do not know if I can allow that. At least now they are holding everything in check."

"But for how long and at what cost, Alex? My gawd, don't you see?" She swept her hand at the clouds streaming past the dome. "This isn't sustainable. They're burning through their resources faster than they can produce them. And if what G'iad'a said is true, their conversion to nuclear energy isn't going well. They've already had four near meltdown accidents. They're headed for a China Syndrome accident."

Alex cocked her head. "What does dishware have to do with the use of nuclear energy?"

Despite the gravity of the situation, Lauren chuckled. "Not dishware. China Syndrome is an analogy for what happens during an uncontrolled nuclear reactor meltdown. The lava-like material created within the melted core of an uncooled nuclear fission reactor melts through the floor of its containment building. This corium-melt continues melting downward into the underlying ground. If and when it encounters groundwater, it superheats the groundwater into steam creating an explosion. This ejects the hyper-radioactive material upward into the atmosphere. The radioactive plume would contaminate the entire planet. On Earth, a movie hypothesized the corium would melt all the way through the planet, coming out the other side."

Alex tipped her head in thought. Lauren felt her struggle through the elements of this scenario. "I do not think that would happen. If the mass made it to the planet's core, gravity would prevent it coming out the other side."

"Exactly, but it made for a scary movie, nonetheless. Here, their fission reactors are open to the sky and even worse they are built over a pool of water. They run pipes through the pool to route coolant around the reactor core." Lauren glanced at the swirling green clouds, before settling her gaze on Alex. "Surface pollution wouldn't be a problem for them if they had a meltdown. Their environmental domes would not protect them from nuclear radiation and the associated fallout. And, Alex, they've got over a hundred open-core fission reactors now. It's just a matter of time."

"All right, then we press ahead. Offer them the nanites to clean up their environment and our fusion reactor technology to replace their fission ones. What else?" She looked at Lauren.

Lauren tugged her braid over her shoulder, thinking. "If they can build the fusion plants and decommission the fission plants, that's a start. The nanites'll take care of their global environmental pollution, as we hope to do on Earth. What about the outlying tribes? They're exposed to the pollution all the time, what environmentally-produced medical issues do they have? And if their domes fail, that part of the population would be infected with the plague the bioweapon released upon Terra. The nanites won't address that."

Alex stepped away and stood at the balcony's edge, grasping the balustrade. She looked out over the gardens, but Lauren knew she wasn't seeing them. Alex turned to look at Lauren over her shoulder, her face etched with grief. "Would the treatment you gave our children work here?"

"Perhaps." Lauren furrowed her brow. "The treatment protocol would work but we would need to find the Comin 'Neanderthal'—a person uninfected by the desert retrovirus—and sequence their un-infected DNA, build a new retrovirus based off that clean Comin genome. Decide on a dispersal system." She slipped her arms around Alex and rested her head against Alex's strong back. "That's a lot of work. Should we just offer to relocate them?"

"I do not know."

Lauren felt like they were giving up before they even tried, and it made her angry. *I won't give up.*

Alex and Lauren shared a leisurely bath. As they were dressing, G'iad'a burst into their room. "Come, breakfast, talk."

"And how are you this fine morning, young heir?" Alex ruffled the girl's shining braids.

"Good. Mother understand. Come now." She tugged on Alex's sleeve, dragging her from their room into the hall. The other Terrans waited there. Lauren followed the pair.

"Ah, I see, no one else had the nerve to bang on our door." Lauren grinned. Everyone laughed and followed G'iad'a down the wide hall of the palace.

After a full breakfast of fruits, juices, and various roasted meats and vegetables, the Terran party was led to another room, a large audience chamber strewn with pillows of varying sizes and colors. One wall was open to the outside and a breeze billowed sheer white curtains into the room.

G'iad'a walked up to the pile of pillows. "Sit. Mother come." Everyone but the admiral dropped to the floor. G'iad'a seemed to realize what was wrong. She turned to one of the guards standing at the side of the entrance door. "Bring chair, now." She turned to the admiral. "I sorry, no think good."

"You think fine, young one. I am sorry to cause a problem for you, but I do not think I could get to the floor or get off it if I did." He patted her shoulder.

"You elder, me no think." The guard returned with a chair. G'iad'a gathered several pillows from the large pile on the floor and placed them on the chair, fluffing them. "There, better. Sit."

"Thank you, young one." The admiral settled into his soft nest with a sigh and a whir of servos.

Not long after, Kall'ka arrived in a swirl of brightly colored robes, entering through a hidden door across from the open wall. Everyone began to stand, but she waved them back down. Walking over to the pillows, she dropped to the floor in a graceful move. *She moves like a swan. I feel like an elephant.* Alex chuckled at Lauren's self-deprecating remark.

"G'iad'a talk long. I listen. Need more information." She pointed at Lauren. "You explain."

Lauren blushed. Rubbing a hand across her hot cheeks, she drew a deep breath and outlined what technical aid the companions had decided to offer. Lauren only stopped when Kall'ka asked a question or requested an explanation of a technical term which didn't translate into Comin. Lauren reviewed everything about the nanites—what they were, how they worked, how they would be produced and distributed across the planet. She used Earth as an example for the various types of pollution they would resolve.

Then she turned the floor over to Angus so he could explain Terran fusion technology and how it could replace the Comin fission reactors. He highlighted the unlimited power the plants would produce, without producing nuclear waste. The one waste product fusion reactions did produce—hydrogen—could be combined with atmospheric oxygen and produce water, a resource the Comin needed. Neither Lauren nor Angus said anything about the plague. Lauren felt Alex's worry. They worried a discussion of this topic would stray too far into classified weapon technology. Alex didn't want to offend the Comin nor give away the Terran cure which was an advantage against this bioweapon.

Kall'ka was silent for long moments, her tan fingers steepled beneath her chin, eyes half-lidded in thought. "I not know how talk next thing. Ask speak only Queen and I. Rest go." She waved her hands in a shooing motion at the Terrans. The companions rose and exited the room.

Alex stood from her nest of pillows. "I ask if you wish to speak together, Empress," Alex inclined her head. "Lauren stays as well."

"Fine, fine. G'iad'a said you say. G'iad'a stay. Bear witness." Lauren had no idea what that meant.

Their private discussion began once everyone had cleared the room. Lauren knew Alex had many questions and now was the time to get some answers. Alex needed to determine what the deal with Gwenhwyfach was. *Are we being played by the Comin to gain a strategic advantage? What did Kall'ka want from the witch? What does the witch want from the Comin?*

Alex asked, "What is your business with Clan Cador? And why was Gwenhwyfach coming here?"

"Not my business. T'iik'lac start long time. Continue on from past." Kall'ka waved her hand in dismissal.

But Alex didn't let it go. "If it was T'iik'lac's doing, why maintain communication with the witch?"

"I no talk witch. I look G'iad'a. Witch talk here. I no answer."

Alex bristled. "Then why was Gwenhwyfach coming here if T'iik'lac was no longer on the throne?"

Kall'ka frowned. "I need information. She could give. Must find heir. Never thought her dead."

Lauren felt Alex's anger rising, their bond sizzled. She placed a gentle hand on Alex's arm. "What information? What could be so important you would consort with a traitor?" Emotions flashed across Kall'ka's face before she could hide them. "Why do you think someone who betrayed their own people wouldn't betray you as well?" Lauren pressed.

"Information more important than actions. We crush Cador if betray us." She closed her hand in a tight fist and thumped her thigh.

"What information is that important?"

Suddenly G'iad'a stood and wrapped her mother in her slim arms. "Tell, they friends."

Lauren watched tears fill Kall'ka's eyes and she reached out and took the slender hand in hers. Compassion flowed outward from her bond with Alex and Kall'ka gasped.

"You feel?"

"I feel. We'll help however we can." *In for a penny, in for a pound.*

Kall'ka broke down in sobs as G'iad'a held her mother close. Soon the storm passed and the woman and mother Kall'ka was took a back seat to the Empress she must be. Her expression hardened into a mask Lauren had seen on Alex's face.

"Planet dying. People dying. Family lost to sickness. You know." She pointed a slim finger at Alex. "I child when weapon released. Know need new home long time. Those before me try, take not theirs. Even child know wrong. But others send weapon anyway. Weapon dissipate in time. We take Terra Prime, new world for us. As older, know very wrong. Then hear about you come. Take weapon data. I think why need data? Not on planet Terra Prime any more. Then I understood, I school, study biogenic warfare."

Lauren gasped. *How could this gentle soul study that?*

Kall'ka glanced at Lauren. "Father make. Not choice. See how develop. Now know weapon from here, natural. Planet sick. People sick. Need help. I understand how make weapon, no understand how stop. Know, if chance, I take condor throne and make cure. Take throne, with weapon. But, still no understand how cure." Then she turned and spoke to the guards in the room. "Leave now. Close door."

The guards clapped a clinched fist over their chests and bowed, leaving through the main entrance. The doors banged shut.

Kall'ka motioned to G'iad'a. The child went to one of the carved wooden chests on the inner wall. She pulled a drawer open, removing a silver cylinder from its depths. Returning to her mother, she handed her the device. Kall'ka twisted the top of the cylinder and a faint blue glow grew from one end. When a blue bubble engulfed the four, where they sat on their pillows, Kall'ka explained, "Cloaking needed."

The Empress stood and approached Alex, kneeling before her. "Queen Terra, I need help for people." She looked up at Alex and Lauren felt their bond sing as Kall'ka pushed into it. *"I know heart good."* She looked at Lauren. *"Consort heart good."*

The Terrans should have realized the Comin Empress would be fully briefed on Alex's clandestine travel to retrieve the bioweapon data from their Homeworld. Or at least, have the means to retrieve that information. It meant Kall'ka knew of the existence of a nexus between the planets. One of the questions they always had—was how Kall'ka felt about it? Lauren and Alex now knew how she felt. She wanted to help her people not use the nexi as a weapon of war. She only wanted information from Cador.

Lauren reached out along their bond. *"We'll help however we can. We've got a cure for the bioweapon, but we can't reproduce it without information from you."*

Kall'ka looked puzzled. *"Me?"* She pointed at herself.

Lauren smiled. *"Yes, you. The cure requires genetic information specific to the Comin. I don't have that information."*

"We get that." Kall'ka spoke aloud and started to stand. "I have this."

"Not so fast." Lauren held up her hands. "We understand the weapon uses a virus. A naturally occurring virus harvested from your deep deserts and then reengineered to the Terran genome. When a person is infected, the virus activates a previously benign sequence of relic DNA. The benign sequence becomes malignant, is then passed along within the cellular sexual replication process to the offspring, thus creating a terminal disease in future generations."

Kall'ka rubbed a hand through her braids, making the beads tinkle. "Like desert tribes died, now children in domes sick. Birth rate fall. Not sustain much longer. We live domes to protect from. But domes not keep virus out. G'iad'a is last."

The Empress' words tore at Lauren's heart and she glanced at G'iad'a. *No wonder they were so desperate to get her back.* This planet and her civilization were dying, just as the Terrans were before Lauren came through the nexus.

"Correct, but the treatment we created for Terran children won't work here. We must sequence the Comin genome, create a new retrovirus to overwrite the changes the desert-virus makes in your DNA. With your biomedical background, you know viruses can't replicate on their own. They appropriate proteins from inside host cells to replicate themselves, using your own proteins against you. Instead of a strategy to attack the virus head-on, we create a strategy to defeat it through its own cellular actions. Activating fossil DNA in your genome to encode modified proteins in immune cells and increase or change your base proteins to allow those cells to attack this specific viral infection." Lauren shook her head. "It's a lot of work and we don't have access to your medical databases and to do all this, we need a starting point."

"Where start? We get." Kall'ka leaned forward. Lauren felt her excitement through their open bond.

Kall'ka paused when Lauren averted her eyes, as sadness gripped her heart. "It's not that easy. We need to find someone who has never been exposed to the virus. Someone with a pristine genome."

Chapter Twelve
Aboard the Fraser Red Stag Biomedical Laboratory

Lauren sat with her head propped in one hand, the other deep in an analyzer gel pad. She stared unseeing at the data streaming across the monitor. More tired than she had ever been and knowing she could easily miss something critical; she rubbed her eyes. The days had melded together, and she really wasn't sure what day it was let alone what time. Angus was asleep on a nearby lab bench, his head resting on crossed arms. Once Kall'ka gave the go ahead, the pair had begun the process of developing a genomic therapy to counteract the native virus.

The Terran retrovirus delivery system was revised from single patient inoculation to mass population treatment. Now the Comin could spread the retrovirus across the planet with low-level atmospheric dispersal outside the domes and via the air filtration systems within the environmental domes.

That was all well and good, but now Lauren and Angus were at a standstill. They had yet to find the Comin 'Neanderthal'. Comin medical personnel were enlisted to test the populace within the domes, with the aid of the military medical corps. Outside the domes, teams of Comin guard were scouring the wilderness collecting samples from the nomadic tribes. But as the number of samples increased with no success, the chance of finding a pristine genome decreased. Lauren was so frustrated she was ready to construct a gene therapy from scratch: one which would splice a new DNA strand directly into the patient's genome, just like they did with the Terran children. The problem with this idea was its application would be patient specific. Even though they knew which genes contained the viral changes and could target those sites specifically, everyone had minor genetic mutations which would alert the spliced strand. This solution just wasn't doable on a planet-population scale.

The pneumatically sealed doors of the lab swished open and Alex entered the brightly lit space. "Dearheart, you must get some rest. You will be no help to this effort if you collapse or get sick."

"I'll have plenty of time to rest once we find our key." Lauren didn't look up from the data stream.

"At least take some time to have dinner with me and then a soak before you continue." Alex placed a hand on Lauren's shoulder to look her in the eye. "Ice and Snow miss you. I do too. On another note, we sent the communication packet off with Robert. He will travel back to the last relay beacon and send the information to Terra."

Lauren smiled at her bondmate. "Good, hopefully we'll have a solution soon, and then we can return to Terra. I miss Susan and Sharon."

Alex sat on a nearby stool and leaned an elbow on the cool black bench. She idly traced the minute crystals within the dark surface. "We should have some communication packets waiting for us in the beacon." Alex looked up at her. "It is the best I can do for now. We will have some news and I agree it will be good to hear from home."

Lauren stood and stretched her back, then reached her arms over her head allowing her injured shoulder to pop. She noticed Alex wince at the sound. "We'll find what we need; it's just a matter of time."

"Is there something I can do to help?"

Moving over to encircle Alex's broad shoulders, Lauren leaned down and whispered, "Nothing, Dearest, but thanks for offering. We just need more samples. Just being together is a huge help though, I totally appreciate that. Having you here makes this is so much easier than preparing the clans to chase after you. I don't think I've ever felt so alone as then." Alex pulled her tight against her back. Lauren felt love and strength flow through their bond, and her heart swelled. Some of her exhaustion fell away.

She looked at Lauren's monitor. "Are we looking in the correct places?" Alex swiveled on the stool, turning within Lauren's arms. "What I mean is I cannot believe those who have never lived within a dome would be uninfected. Everyone in the domes goes outside sometimes. Given this, are there other places we should be focusing your sampling efforts?"

Lauren touched her forehead to Alex's and sighed. She thought about explaining how their sampling procedures were designed, but stopped as what Alex said sank in. "What other places are you thinking about?"

"I do not know, but it seems illogical to look in places where we know the virus exists."

"Where it exists? Where else can we look?" Lauren murmured to herself, as her mind raced through other possibilities. She moved back to her analyzer and entered a request for population dispersal data. "You might be on to something, Dearest. Thank you." Lauren's weariness vanished in the wave of new ideas Alex's question created.

"But I just asked a question."

Lauren laughed loud enough to wake Angus.

"What is happening?" The young man asked groggily.

Lauren grinned at him. "I don't know yet, but Alex may've found our uninfected genome."

Angus glanced at Alex. "Alex?"

"I just asked a question." Alex shrugged, giving him a confused frown.

After several long minutes, Lauren's analyzer beeped. She cracked her knuckles and dropped her hand into the gel pad. "Let's see what we've got."

Alex leaned closer as a star chart of the Comin solar system filled the monitor. Several outlying colonies were highlighted in red. Lauren entered another data request to refine their search. The Comin net wasn't the fastest and the data transfer lag time from the surface to the *Stag* further slowed the process. But soon the star chart resolved. This time location data was overlaid with historical information.

There. Lauren selected an isolated mining colony within one of the Comin asteroid belts.

She entered another request for information and received an immediate access denial. *What the?* It seemed there was a total information blackout surrounding the colony. When she entered another request, all she received was the same basic historical information.

The colony was established long before the bioweapon was developed and the virus refined from the deserts, this would fit their search parameters. Because of their desire to maintain isolation and religious freedom, the colonists left the Homeworld and developed a mining colony within the outer asteroid belt. Since their departure, they had no direct contact with the Comin populace. The colony was fully self-sufficient using robotic go-betweens for all commerce, communications, supply acquisitions, and trade exchanges.

Lauren jumped off her stool. "Alex, would you please ask the Empress to gather some genetic samples from the Ab'strc'kl Three colony?"

Alex looked at the screen and then moved over to another workstation. She sent the message directly to Kall'ka's personal system. "This may take a bit, depending on what she is doing at this time." She walked back over to Lauren. "So, as we wait, we will eat, and you will soak your shoulder." When Lauren began to protest, Alex shook her head and simply pointed at the door.

"Fine, I give." Lauren wrapped her arm around Alex's waist. "Isn't it nice to breathe clean, moist air and not feel like you're melting from the oppressive heat?"

It took a full day for the Empress to answer Alex's request. They had no information and no Comin would volunteer to visit the colony given their isolationist history. The colony continued to ignore her request for samples. They were at an impasse again. Samples continued to be collected on the planet and Lauren hoped they would get lucky, but it wasn't likely. *We need to find a way to get samples from that colony.*

G'iad'a arrived with the next set of samples and joined Alex, Lauren, the wolves, and Angus for breakfast. She stated between mouthfuls of eggs and toast. "I want see lab. I help work."

"Once we finish eating, I'll take you down and show you around. I'm sure Angus would love a lab assistant." Lauren heard the young man splutter. "Right, Angus?"

Angus wiped his mouth on his napkin and took a slow drink of juice. Lauren raised an eyebrow in question at him, letting him know she knew he was stalling. "Of course, Majesty. I could use some help with cataloguing the samples to date."

"Good, let go." G'iad'a stood from the table.

"Not yet," Alex said from her place at the head of the dining table. "Others have yet to finish."

The heir dropped back into her chair and harrumphed.

"Has your mother had any luck reaching the mining colony?" Lauren asked to redirect the conversation.

"AI only talk now. Not pass message on. Protocol."

Lauren wiped her mouth and dropped her linen napkin on the table beside her half-finished plate. "Is that how you always communicate with them?"

G'iad'a picked a small orange out of the fruit bowl in the middle of the table. She began to peel the tiny fruit and nodded. "Only way, ever. Cause T'iik'lac and those before him. Colony no want bad influence there."

"Any idea how we can get around the AIs to contact the colonists directly?"

Tearing small pieces of peel off the fruit, the young girl sat back and seemed to consider the question. "Maybe, like ask."

Everyone looked at G'iad'a. "What?" Alex asked seeking clarification.

"Like ask, one-one" The heir continued to focus on her fruit.

Lauren sat forward. "G'iad'a, what's one-one?"

Putting the peeled fruit down on her plate, she looked put out by Lauren's questions. "AI talk AI, in AI language, explain what needed, why. What not understand? Easy do." When Lauren shook her head, G'iad'a looked at her as if she'd lost her mind.

"Sorry, I still don't understand."

The young girl rose and adjusted her kilt. "Come." She marched out of the captain's mess.

"Well, I believe we have been ordered to follow." Angus chuckled.

By the time the three, with Ice and Snow at their heels, caught up to G'iad'a, she had entered the bridge. She marched across the upper steps of the command dais and stopped in front of the Lauren's command cabin. The doors didn't open at her approach. Crossing her small arms across her chest, G'iad'a inclined her head to the door, her eaglet beads flashing in the low lighting.

"Open," she ordered the door.

Lauren stepped around her and the door swished open. "There you go." She swept her arm out, indicating the young girl should enter. G'iad'a moved into the cabin and walked around Lauren's desk, climbing onto her chair. The young girl teetered, and Lauren reached out to steady her. "Whoa, what do you need?"

"Admiral." The young girl reached up to the black cube resting on the high shelf.

"Easy there. I'll get him." *I understand now.* If the avatar speaks to the colony AI, perhaps it could find a way around their protocols and be able to contact the colonists. Lauren helped her down and then activated the avatar, placing it on her desk. She dropped into her chair.

"Good day, Majesty. How may I be of assistance?"

G'iad'a frowned. "Call colony, get sample."

The admiral's avatar looked down at the child where she stood next to Lauren. "And you are?"

"You know me. I heir to condor throne, need sample, you get." She pointed at him.

"The heir I know has better manners than you are exhibiting. A please and thank you will go far versus a demand, young one." Angus and Alex snorted in laughter. The avatar did behave exactly like the admiral. Ice and Snow whiffled from their place on Lauren's sofa.

"No laugh me." G'iad'a placed her hands on her hips and scowled.

"We're not laughing at you, but the admiral's correct. Politeness and patience are skills a future ruler needs to learn." Lauren smiled at the child. "So, ask your question again, please."

G'iad'a frowned at the holographic image. "Peese speak colony AI. Ask sample, need help Homeworld. Tank you."

"Of course, young heir. One moment please." The hologram winked at G'iad'a and disappeared with a snick.

After several minutes, G'iad'a climbed into Lauren's lap and leaned back against her chest. Lauren felt the small body relax toward sleep as they waited. Alex and Angus dropped into the two facing desk chairs and began a quiet discussion of various weapon system modifications Tavish had recommended for the clans. They waited almost an hour before the avatar snicked back into existence. Lauren started out of a nap.

A frown marred his photonic forehead. "I am afraid you will not be able to contact the colonists directly, Majesty."

Lauren looked over G'iad'a's shoulder. "And why not?"

"There are no colonists alive."

"What?" Lauren's gasp of alarm woke G'iad'a.

The avatar shook his head. "I am afraid there was a reactor accident and the resultant radiation leak killed all the colonists. The AIs continue to mine and sell the ores as mandated in their protocols, but no colonists exist."

"Well, damn. That was our best shot at getting a pristine genomic sample." *Our task just got much more difficult. Now I'll have to individualize genome sequencing at a population-wide scale.* She slumped back in her chair, defeated.

The avatar tilted his head. "I said there were no colonists, I did not say there were no medical records."

"Medical records? What records?" Angus asked.

"The colony AIs have complete medical records on each of the colonists by generation. We have selected sixteen as possible candidates for genomic analysis. We agree these have the best genetic records for your study." The monitor on Lauren's desktop rose and data filled the screen.

Oh god, sixteen samples? Lauren gasped. "Hop down, please."

G'iad'a jumped off her lap and Lauren moved her chair closer to the desk. Angus stood, leaning on the desk to peer at the Comin karyotype displayed on the screen. Lauren stared at the data, lost in thought. Neither spoke. Then Angus pointed to one of the twenty-three chromosomes.

"Avatar, please display chromosome seventeen, magnify and measure the position of the centromere," Angus requested.

Lauren leaned even closer to the monitor as the requested chromosome filled the screen.

Angus pointed. "This centromere is metacentric, not submetacentric as we have found in all the Homeworld samples. The arms of the chromosome are almost equal with the centromere in the middle."

The avatar replied, "Actually, the arms are of equal size. I believe in your samples the infected chromosome seventeen centromere is located at the twenty-four-point three mega-base pair position."

Lauren drew a deep breath, leaned back in her chair and grinned until she thought her face would split. "We've got it."

C A Farlow

Chapter Thirteen
The Comin Homeworld, Imperial Court

Over the next weeks, Lauren and Angus inoculated the planet against the desert virus. It would take time for the treatment to take full effect and mitigate the viral infection, but the Terrans were pleased with the results so far. No adverse reactions had been reported. The Ab'strc'kl Three mining colonists were heralded as posthumous heroes and afforded all honors the Comin could give. Other environmental remediation and changes to their nuclear power generation were also well on the way. Kall'ka hoped they could abandon the maintenance of their domes and route all the energy needed to sustain them to other more urgent projects, like clean water generation, improved living conditions, surface reclamation, and air purification. Release of the Terran nanites would augment these projects. Once these efforts were started, Comin terraforming processes would regenerate a viable ecosystem on the planet's surface.

Tomorrow, the Terrans would go home. Each of the companions and the crews of their magnificent clans looked forward to the journey. Empress Kall'ka was planning a large festival to thank the Terrans for their help in saving their home. In their assigned apartment, Alex and Lauren dressed in their finest formalwear.

"I can't wait to get home." Lauren buttoned the cuffs of her white silk shirt. "Tomorrow won't come soon enough."

"I agree, but our work here was worth the effort. You and Angus created a solid foundation for our continued alliance with the Comin. I look forward to a rewarding partnership, rather than always looking over my shoulder for the Comin blade to strike. Now, we can live in peace on Terra. Perhaps, even plan a reconnaissance trip to Terra Prime. I would very much like to show you the planet of my birth, even if it is from space."

Lauren felt her bond fill with sadness as Alex thought about her home planet. She pushed a burst of love into their bond and gathered Alex into her arms. "I'd love to see Terra Prime. Perhaps, with the inoculation data we've got now, we can determine when we can explore the surface together."

"Perhaps," Alex answered wistfully.

The door to their suite burst open as G'iad'a ran in, braids flying, a Comin nanny dressed in long white robes rushing to catch her. The young heir skidded to a halt in front of Alex and looked up at her with tear-streaked cheeks. "I not wear this." She indicated the flowing caftan she was swaddled in and stomped her small, slipper-covered foot. "I wear kilt."

Alex looked at the frazzled nanny who dropped to her knees and bowed her head, her black braids covering her face. "I sorry Queen. No stop."

"I would imagine no one can stop an imp when she sets her mind to something." Alex gathered the child in a hug. "Am I right?"

"You right." Came the muffled response, G'iad'a's head was buried in Alex's stomach.

Lauren laughed and poked G'iad'a in the side making her squirm away. She looked at the nanny. "We'll take care of her, but I imagine she'll wear what she pleases, not what's expected."

The nanny smiled at Lauren and rose. "You right." They all laughed.

After much struggle and argument, the heir was dressed in Terran attire, with one concession. She wore a loose open caftan shirt of shimmering silk, rather than the high-necked, white linen shirt Alex wore and she did not wear a sash. G'iad'a abandoned her silk slippers in favor of knee-high black leather boots. Her muhaddab was slung across her back. The trio met the other companions and, flanked by Ice and Snow, proceeded down to the formal dais surrounding the condor throne.

Evening descended on the gathering as food and drink flowed. The massive crowd filled the grand road all the way to the Arch of Heroes in the far distance. The air shimmered with torchlight and music surrounded the Terrans as they sat with Kall'ka. Lauren relaxed into her cushioned chair. *This is the first time since Alex's kidnapping I feel like I can relax. I've got nothing to do, nothing to figure out, nothing to invent. Time is ours to do with as we wish. What am I going to do with all of it?* Lauren chuckled and Alex looked over at her. Lauren just shook her head.

Once full dark was upon them, Empress Kall'ka rose from her chair, moved to the condor throne and sat. A servant approached carrying a large purple silk pillow. Kneeling, he placed the pillow at her feet. Then, she motioned for Alex to approach the throne.

"Queen Terra, Comin in debt always. We no able repay. You give back life and future to our people and planet. I give you gift of friendship." She stood and took up a large pectoral from the pillow. In the shape of a giant condor with outstretched wings, the large brooch was made of gold, inlaid with blue-green emeralds and red rubies. The precious stones flashed cold and hot in the torch light. A thick cord of spun gold spanned from wingtip to wingtip. Kall'ka placed it around Alex's neck. The brooch sat directly over her sternum. "We happy friends now." Kall'ka gripped Alex's upper arms, pulling her down to kiss each of her cheeks. When Empress Kall'ka turned Alex around, the crowd roared its approval. The two monarchs bowed to each other, and then to the crowd.

Alex moved back to her chair and sat, taking Lauren's hand in hers. *"I did not expect that."*

"Neither did I, but you handled it well. Perhaps our gift won't seem inappropriate now. I know you're worried about it." Alex squeezed her hand.

The party continued on into the evening, G'iad'a had fallen asleep in Lauren's lap. Alex rose and the crowd near the dais fell silent. "Terra welcomes your friendship and we look forward to a lasting relationship of mutual trust and alliance. Should you be in need, we are as near as the T'le'cac and pledge our aid and support."

The crowd roared in answer.

"To affirm our alliance, we give you this gift." Tavish presented a long narrow ironwood box to Alex. She opened the lid and withdrew a ceremonial broadsword cast in platinum and detailed with golden eagles etched down the blade. The hilt was an open-winged condor, with its beak fashioned to curve around the wielder's wrist. Alex presented the weapon to Empress Kall'ka hilt first. Tavish had worked for days on this blade.

"I lost words. This magnificent." She closed her small hand around the hilt and raised the long weapon above her head. "We one now." Kall'ka smiled at Alex and winked at Lauren.

A bolt of lightning pierced the night and struck the blade above the Kall'ka's head, driving her to the stone pavers. Kall'ka didn't have time to scream before Alex sprang forward and crouched protectively over her body, drawing her broadsword from its scabbard in a single motion. Tavish, Robert, and Angus drew their weapons and surrounded Alex. Ice and Snow dashed forward and completed the circle around Alex. The Imperial guards encircled the small group creating an impenetrable phalanx. As everyone looked for the next attack. However, that move left Lauren and G'iad'a exposed and isolated.

In the next instance, a shimmering wraith appeared before Lauren, where she sat holding G'iad'a close. Gwenhwyfach. "I have come for you. You will not defeat me this time." The witch raised her hands, fingers outstretched. Bolts of green-red lightning rained down, as she drew energy from the environmental dome over their heads. The witch began to glow with an unnatural aura. The dome shimmered and holes opened in the protective cover. "You severed me from my physical body with your energy-web, but I massed my remaining energy and occupied the nearest available vessel. Camella was a good host, but now I no longer need her physical form. Now the time was right for me to attack and I created this form." The wraith continued to draw energy from the dome overhead. She pointed a clawed finger at Lauren. "Now you will pay for your alien actions against Terra. Clan Cador will triumph." *So that's why Camella died in custody.*

Lauren tried to stand but G'iad'a tightened a frightened hold around her neck, her small body shaking in Lauren's arms. Gwenhwyfach redirected the accumulated energy from the dome toward Lauren. Lightning crackled toward her. Lauren dove to the side, knocking her chair aside and rolling over G'iad'a to protect her. Bolts struck where the chair had been, leaving charred streaks etched in the stone. A strong smell of ozone rose from the burnt stone. Lauren continued to roll away. She pushed the heir ahead of her and G'iad'a tumbled down several of the high stone steps toward the crowd. A guard sprang forward, lifting the heir up by the scruff of her neck and encircling the child in armored arms. Lauren's heart raced and her body shook as adrenalin poured into her system.

Lauren came to her feet and drew her rapier. She bounced on the balls of her feet to gain her center of balance and faced Gwenhwyfach. Swallowing down her fear, Lauren challenged. "Bring it on, bitch. I'm not afraid of you."

Alex yelled to Angus, "Protect the Empress. Tavish, Robert you are with me." The three jumped down the wide stairs toward Lauren. Brandishing their drawn broadswords before them, they moved behind the witch to block her in. Their advance was halted as they slammed into an invisible wall. They couldn't get any closer. Gwenhwyfach had erected some sort of barrier around herself and Lauren. "Move around, find the edge." Alex pointed with her sword. "We must get to Lauren!"

Gwenhwyfach and Lauren circled each other, searching for an opening. Out of the corner of her eye, Lauren saw Alex. She was so close, but their bond was diminished to nearly zero as if they were a galaxy apart again. "She will not be able to help you this time. I have cut her off. Your bond is nothing against me."

If that's true, I shouldn't be able to still feel Alex. But Lauren could and she drew strength from that. Her torque came alive in her mind. *"We are holding the bond open. You will have it in reserve, if needed. But, you must defeat her yourself, Consort. You have vowed to be the queen's protector. Now, you must do as you swore."*

"*Fine,*" Lauren answered through gritted teeth. She slid another step to her left, keeping her sword arm open and in front of her.

Suddenly more power surged through her, all the power massed from Terra herself, from the Terran people, power stored within her bond from the day she shared her rescue plans with the populace. That energy was available to her now. Her bond swelled and energy surged through her.

The shimmering wraith swept her arm down and a flaming broadsword appeared in her hand. *The bitch has found a way to create a physical construct using her psi-energy.* Lauren frowned and a trickle of doubt ran down her spine. *Great. Another leftie. With a broadsword, too. Damn.*

"*Do not defeat yourself, Consort. The witch will do that for you,*" her torque admonished. Lauren swept her rapier in front of her in a figure eight.

The witch laughed. "I saw your Investiture challenge; you did not defeat the champion. You tricked him. You are not worthy to protect a Terran queen. You are an alien." Gwenhwyfach taunted.

Lauren ground her teeth. "I earned my place at Alex's side. I am Terran!"

"You are not." The witch roared as she swept her blade down. Lauren ducked and executed a perfect quinte-parry, blocking the blade above her head. She pushed off her parry, driving into Gwenhwyfach, pushing her back toward Alex. Focused on moving the bitch away and opening her guard, Lauren missed the witch raising her other hand. A bolt struck Lauren in the chest. Lauren was tossed away, landing flat on her back. She lost her breath. Pain exploded in her chest. *I can't breathe.*

Gasping, she tried to rise, but the witch was on her in two long strides. She reversed her blade and raised it above her head in a two-handed grip, preparing to drive it down into Lauren's midsection. Lauren rolled and got her feet under her. "You will not get inside my guard with that move." The broadsword flashed down, but Lauren dove forward. The broadsword cleaved through her plaid hanging down her back. The witch shrieked as her blade pierced only fabric and became embedded in stone. Just like the Champion. "You missed, bitch."

Lauren knew she had to get away. Maintain her distance from the witch. *Gotta watch her hands, both of them are deadly.* Alex moved into her field-of-view as she continued around the barrier, hand outstretched looking for an edge or a seam. *She's frantic.* Lauren felt the drain on their bond energy as Alex pulled energy to her to find a way through.

The broadsword flashed in the torchlight a split second before it arced down toward Lauren's side. Lauren spun away, blocking the overt attack. The witch reversed her thrust. Their blades met with a shower of sparks. Agony burned hot in her shoulder and Lauren felt newly healed tendons tear. The witch drove her broadsword down to the rapier's hilt, where it caught on one of the quillons. Lauren jerked her blade toward her, pulling Gwenhwyfach off balance, causing the witch to stumble. As the witch's head fell forward, Lauren drove her fist down into the back of the witch's neck, surprised how solid the wraith's form was. *No wonder her physical body is dead. She must have pulled all its life energy into this psi-form and then all of Camella's as well.* Lauren raised her arm to deliver another blow.

As Lauren's fist came down, the witch grabbed her forearm in a death grip. Her fingertips dug deep into Lauren's flesh. Lauren's dragon torque roared; her dragon tattoo roiled beneath the witch's fingers. Fire surged through Lauren as Gwenhwyfach touch ripped into her psyche. Flames rose up her arm; her skin bubbled and melted under the witch's hand. Lauren screamed as white-hot pain lanced through her and she dropped to one knee. The witch lifted her broadsword above her head and swung it toward Lauren's immobilized form. Lauren's vision tunneled as the pain continued build.

In a move faster than the eye could follow, her dragon torque lash out. Flame spouted from its open maw and engulfed Gwenhwyfach's face. Lauren felt anger flare through her bond with her torque as the flames continued to boil around the witch's head. Lauren heard laughter.

"Really? You hide behind a relic who lost her power millennia ago?" The witch brought her right hand up and a spout of ice water slammed into her torque. Lauren watched her torque fall to the floor with a tinkle of scales against stone, her flame extinguished. Lauren lost her connection with the dragon torque. Pain lanced through her psyche due to her severed bond and her heart bled for her lost companion. From outside the barrier, Alex's torque roared in anger and pain, impotent to come to her mate's aid.

The torque's efforts distracted Gwenhwyfach. This allowed Lauren time to regain her feet and prepare an attack of her own. The witch still held her forearm in a deadly grasp. But Lauren stepped under her guard and drove the pommel of her rapier up into the witch's chin, snapping the witch's head back. The witch released her arm and Lauren spun away.

Lauren took three steps backward and gasping for breath, trying to compartmentalize her pain. She looked at her forearm, the sleeve was burned away above her elbow. An imprint of the witch's hand was etched into her skin. Lauren could see the tendons and muscles move as she flexed her hand, but the pain had stopped. Lauren staggered in relief, until she realized what this meant. *Goddamn it! The bitch destroyed the underlying nerve tissue.* Rage filled her. *I gotta end this now. Shock's next.* She moved on instinct. All the hours of sparring created ingrained muscle memory. Lauren relaxed her mind and let her body flow. She charged forward. Her scream echoed around the Imperial dais.

Lauren attacked. Her rapier sang, ripping the air open. She struck high and then twirled away, to return with a backhanded slice across the witch's knees. Gwenhwyfach staggered, but Lauren continued to press her attack. As the witch lifted the broadsword, Lauren blocked the blade with her rapier and drove her shoulder into Gwenhwyfach's chest, knocking the woman back. Lauren feinted to her blade side and then spun left through a compound attack of stroke and counterstroke. Her rapier found the witch's cheek. She sliced it open to the bone. A shimmering glow filled the wound and the gash closed.

"You'll bleed before I'm done," Lauren shouted.

Another slice raked her blade down Gwenhwyfach's right arm. Blood now dripped from the witch's fingers.

Lauren spun away laughing. "See the bitch bleeds."

"I bleed because I have traversed reality and pulled my physical life force into this one. I am a new life form, created from pure psi-energy. I can do anything now. Exist anywhere." She thrust her broadsword up, preparing to resume her attack. The witch laughed, throwing her head back. "I have you to thank. When you trapped me in your psi-energy web, my only means of escape was to coalesce into an atomic sized spec. Once done, I discovered a different existence. My body collapsed and I drew out all of its life energy." She lowered her blade and pointed it at Lauren.

So that's what happened. Lauren let the witch ramble, hoping her arrogance would distract her while she continued to press the attack. Lauren spun back to feint right as Gwenhwyfach raised her blade, pointed directly at Lauren's chest. Before Lauren could counter, the witch lunged forward. Lauren ducked under the lunge and threw her left arm up to protect her face. The tip of Gwenhwyfach's blade caught her palm and sliced the inside of her arm open from wrist to elbow. Alex screamed. Ice howled. Lauren fell back and held her arm against her chest to staunch the blood gushing from the wound. Laughter filled her ears as Gwenhwyfach raised her blade and swung it toward Lauren's neck.

"I will always love you, Alex." Lauren screamed into their bond. Fire exploded around her. Flames engulfed her. The smell of brimstone and burning flesh overwhelmed her. *I'm on fire.* And the world went black.

Consciousness returned and Lauren realized she wasn't on fire. When she opened her eyes, the carcass of the witch lay before her, nothing more than a pile of smoldering rags. A roar split the air. Lauren looked up and collapsed on her side, captured in swirling multifaceted emerald-sapphire eyes. Her bond swelled to bursting as a new psi-being burst into it. Pain forgotten; Lauren stared in disbelief.

"You will live, Consort. But you will hurt first." Her dragon tattoo stood before her; its blue scales burnished purple in the red light of the torches. The dragon dropped her large head and looked into Lauren's eyes. *"You must get up, so we can pass the barrier together."* Her dragon's mind voice rumbled, a deep contralto, which jarred her teeth. A small stream of smoke trickled from the dragon's nostrils, and Lauren sneezed at the sulphur-rich smell. *"The barrier is the last remnant of the witch. Once pierced, she will cease to exist for all time, destroyed in all planes of reality."*

"Who are you?" Lauren struggled to form the words in her mind as pain continued to rage through her body.

"I am Suil Gorm-Vaiore Dréagan Saifaere. You may call me Faere." The dragon's eyes swirled. *"I am Ddraig and swear to protect you."*

The strength of her dragon's bond overwhelmed Lauren, as the dragon settled into her soul with a contented sigh. This bond was foreign, nothing like what she shared with Alex or the companions. She tried to get to her knees, only to fall back onto her side. Shock began to crawl through her. Her vision tunneled. *"Please gather up our mentor, Lauren."*

"I don't understand." *I'm in shock. This is all be a dream.* She watched blood pool around her, soaking into the pavers beneath an arm. *Is that my arm?* Lauren struggled to remain conscious.

Faere brought one emerald-sapphire eye in line with Lauren's face. *"She fought bravely and distracted the witch allowing us to be successful. We must not leave her on the stones. Her mate can heal her. Replenish her life energy. But you must carry her through the barrier."* In a daze, Lauren looked around. Her torque lay where she fell after her attack on Gwenhwyfach. Lauren gathered the platinum scaled dragon up, cradling her to her chest.

Lauren struggled to her knees and then grabbed Faere's forepaw, pulling herself to her feet. She swayed and Faere moved to support her. *"Lean on me, Consort. Together we will move forward."*

Lauren held her wounded arm against her chest, her torque in her other hand. She could feel blood running down her chest. *"Yes, together. Always together."* Lauren took one staggering step after another until they reached the barrier.

"You must go first. It will hurt to pass this obstacle. But I am with you; I will share my strength and take some of your pain."

Lauren felt energy surge through her, and she stepped forward. Standing in front of her dragon, Lauren reached out. As her hand touched the shimmering barrier, pain lanced through her soul. Lauren cried out and began to fall.

"Step forward, Dearheart. I will catch you. I will not let you fall." Alex encouraged from the other side. Her companions gathered close; more energy surged through her bond as they poured their psi-strength into her.

Lauren pushed through the barrier. When she and her dragon were past, the barrier collapsed with a snap. Faere roared and a great cheer rose around her. Turning, Lauren saw only a stain on the pavers where the witch had been. *She's gone, vanished for good! Thank god.* Alex's strong arms gathered her close. Love blanketed her soul. *Alex caught me.* Another mighty roar filled her ears and then darkness swallowed her.

Part Four

Epilogue

*Gravitation is not responsible
for people falling in love.*
~Albert Einstein

Epilogue
Planet Terra, The Keep
Standing Stone Circle

Lauren sat on her throne at Alex's right hand, behind the stone altar within the sacred circle. They were waiting on G'iad'a to make her way up the grand approach. Once within the circle, she would swear allegiance to Alex and Lauren, and they would swear their oath to foster the young heir. Raise her, educate her, protect her, and prepare her for her future role as Empress of the Comin. She would live among the Terrans until the age of fifteen cycles. Kall'ka and Alex hoped this cross-training would reinforce their new alliance for future generations.

Lauren rested her wounded arm across her lap. She had no memories of the last weeks. All she knew after she defeated Gwenhwyfach was what others told her and memory-images Faere and her torque shared with her. She smiled as she thought about the great beast who shared the companion bond with her and the others.

Her injury was grievous, and Alex knew she didn't have the medical resources aboard the clans to heal Lauren. She had lost so much blood, the only option was to put Lauren in stasis and race back to Terra aboard the *Stag*. Then Kall'ka intervened and reminded Alex of the T'le'cac. They could transport Lauren through the nexus and have her home within a matter of hours. Ice, Snow, Faere, Alex, G'iad'a, and the admiral carried Lauren home.

Once back on Terra, Alex called to Ffrwyn and asked her horse to have Merilyn send a flitter. Due to the Empress Kall'ka's fast thinking and Alex's bond with Ffrwyn, the healing techs had saved Lauren's life and her arm. Now she only needed time for the grafts of pseudo-skin to heal and then physiotherapy would help her regain her arm's strength. The boys were flying the clans home and would be in Luna orbit within the next few weeks. They used Angus' route around the supermassive black hole without incident. Robert promoted Shamus to captain of the *Boar*, as he took command of the *Stag* in Lauren's absence.

Lauren had missed the funerals for her lost crew but once better she had visited each family. She shared her grief and in a small way this helped heal a portion of her heart. Once Merilyn learned the location of the *Orchid* crew, she sent a rescue mission to the planet. The executive officer and the other loyal Terrans were no longer alive, having been killed in a conflict with the traitorous members of the clan. The rescuers were told to leave and take the communications beacon with them. None of the traitors wanted to return to Terra. Lauren and Alex discussed this with the companions, and it was decided to keep a close eye on this planet. A passive stealth reconnaissance beacon was left in orbit about the planet. It would only activate and send a signal back to Terra if a space craft entered the traitor's solar system.

The members of Clan Cador still on Terra and Luna Keep were all interrogated under psi-examination. Those found to be aligned with the traitors were scheduled to be transported to the traitor's planet within the next week. Those loyal to Terra were allowed to form a clan. This new clan would be recognized as an equal to the other twelve Terran clans.

Drums began to beat, and the dissonant tones of a bagpipe pierced the silence. The piper stepped into the circle, leading the young heir forward. Alex smiled and placed a gentle hand on Lauren's upper arm. *"This is right for Terra and for us, Dearheart. And you made it all possible."*

"We made it possible, always we, dearest." Alex smiled at her with a lopsided grin.

Excitement surged through their bond as G'iad'a approached the altar. Both grinned at the young girl. Lady MacDonald held both hands above her head and silence fell on this sacred place.

Empress Kall'ka leaned forward and Lauren felt her excitement. The Empress sat on a carved ironwood chair before a new standing stone. Once the witch died on the Comin Homeworld, the Clan Cador stone evaporated, leaving an opening within the circle. Alex had aided the Imperial guard in quarrying a new stone on Luna and transporting it to the circle. They chose a stone of pure white anorthosite shot through with blue streaks of labradorite. The stone shone in the early morning light, its white brilliance in contrast to the darker stones of the Terran clans. This was now known as the Clan Comin stone.

Part of G'iad'a's fostering ceremony would appoint her clan chief in her mother's absence. Lady MacDonald led G'iad'a through the ceremony, helping her with the Terran words. Lauren smiled at her and Alex sent reassurance through their bond to the young girl. Alex winked when she looked up. The heir had studied hard over the weeks of Lauren's recovery and she performed the ceremony perfectly. The clan chiefs and all the Terrans bore witness to the short fostering ceremony. The Terrans were thrilled by the new alliance with the Comin.

Lauren looked around the circle. This large stone space held her family and friends, which today grew by one, as their cadre of companions welcomed G'iad'a into their rank. Sharon and Susan stood with Làireach. Boscoe sat beside the young foal, smiling a silly doggy smile. G'iad'a had bonded with the corgi immediately on her arrival in the Keep and the two went everywhere together. Ffrwyn stood beside her foal, nuzzling the young horse when she whinnied in excitement.

All the clan chiefs sat in rapt attention. They were in total agreement with the treaties Alex had forged with the Comin and accepted the heir in fostering with them. Each clan pledged to participate in her education. Ice sat beside Lauren leaning against her throne, while Snow sat beside Alex.

The other new member of their family sprawled along the edge of the stone dais, warming herself in the morning sun. Lauren smiled at her blue-scaled dragon as she raised her head and captured Lauren in her swirling eyes. *"I thank you. You freed me from the blade and the witch freed me from you. Now I walk with the companions."* Lauren's anger with Gwenhwyfach for kidnapping Alex was tempered by this gift of a new friend and bondmate. *"Anger is not a healthy emotion, Lauren. You are strengthened by what has happened, and now are truly Consort—Protector of the Queen of Terra."* Truer words had never been spoken. Lauren sent a burst of love to Faere.

Lauren's heart and soul were filled to overflowing. She had no idea how she had gone from a work-obsessed, perfectionist loner to a member of such a diverse and loving family; and a respected, contributing member of such an incredible civilization.

Ice leaned against her stone throne and whiffled. *"What is so hard to understand? You only needed to cross realities to find your heart's mate and your home with us. I am glad I found you."*

Lauren chuckled and dropped her hand into soft warm fur. *I am finally home.*

Life without love is not life at all.
~Leonardo Da Vinci

About C.A. Farlow

CA grew up amidst the verdant fields of farm country. From the age of four, she spent summers on an island in northwestern Ontario, Canada, and winters among frozen fields. Her grandfather imparted his love for the natural world.

CA earned degrees in geology and tectonics. She worked for an international petroleum company for many years and traveled the globe. Now she lives in the Rocky Mountains. Science is the focus of her writing and her ongoing research. She lives with her cats and has a passion for long-distance cycling.

List of Major Characters - The Nexus Series

Lauren Beckwith: Ph.D./M.D., pediatric oncologist and environmental scientist in Earth Reality. Nexus traveler and healing technician; adopted daughter of Clan Fraser; soulmate of Alexandra, Regain Rìoghachd Fuar Ćala, Queen of the Planet Terra; Cáraid Rioghail, Royal Consort to Alex, Co-Ruler Fuar Ćala. Considered by the people of Terra as the Savior of Terra, Terran Reality.

Alex: Alexandra Aoeron Aonwyn nighean mic Fionnaghal, Regain Rioghachd Fuar Ćala, daughter of Fionna, 14th Doouglas Ruler of Terra, Royal Ruler of Cold Harbour, soulmate of Lauren, Terran Reality.

Snow (Sneachda): White Wolf, Animal companion to Alex and Lauren, partner of Deigh (Ice).

Ice (Deigh): White Wolf, Animal companion to Alex and Lauren, partner of Sneachda (Snow).

Ffrwyn: Animal companion to Alex and Lauren, Horse, partner of Gríobhtha.

Gríobhtha: Horse companion to Chief Guardian McLaran, partner of Ffrwyn.

Merilyn: Merilyn Arrin Can Fionna Fraser Doouglas, The Seneschal of Fuar Ćala. Mentor and Guardian to Alex. Adoptive Mother to Lauren, Terran Reality.

Robert McLaran, the Elder: Chief Guardian, Leader of Alex's Black Guard; Chief of Clan McLaran; father of Robert McLaran the Younger; Terran Reality.

Angus Newkirk: Companion to Alex and Lauren, Alex's Wisdom and Skeptic, Master Technician, Terran Reality.

Robert McLaran, the Younger: Companion to Alex and Lauren, Alex's Compass and Conscious. Son of Robert McLaran, the Elder, Terran Reality.

Tavish MacDonald: Companion to Alex and Lauren, Alex's Strength and Right Arm. Son of Lady Síobhan MacDonald, Mastersmith and jeweler, Lauren's Guardian, Pilot, and Protector, Terran Reality.

Lady Síobhan MacDonald: Our Lady of the Ancients-Chief Historian of the Terrans, Chief of Clan MacDonald, Lauren's teacher, mother of Tavish MacDonald, Terran Reality.

Newkirk, the Elder: Chief, Clan Newkirk, Chief Shield Technician and Master Psi-technician of Terra Keep, father of Angus Newkirk, Terran Reality.

Iain McLeod: Chief, Luna Keep; Chief, Clan McLeod; Admiral of the Terran Intragalactic Fleet; Spacing and Engineering Technician; Terran Reality.

Hamish McLeod: Interim Chief, Clan McLeod on Terra; Inventor, Master Weaver; Terran Reality.

Stewart McGuiness: SwordMaster, Champion of Terra and the People; Member, Clan Campbell.

Suil Gorm-Vaiore Dréagan Saifaere: Faere, Lauren's blue-scaled dragon. Released from the tattoo on Lauren's arm in the battle with Gwenhwyfach.

Gwenhwyfach: Chief, Clan Cador, Traitor to Terra; in exile, Terran Reality.

Jamie Gilchrist: Co-worker and good friend of Lauren's at GeoDynamics, Earth Reality.

Susan Stanley: DVM-Veterinarian, Friend of Lauren, Partner of Susan Frasier, Earth Reality.

Sharon Frasier: Head of Steamboat Heritage Foundation, eco-environmentalist, Friend of Lauren, Partner of Susan, Earth Reality.

Boscoe: Pembrook Welsh Corgi, dog of Susan and Sharon, Earth Reality.

Altair Doouglas: Chief of Clan Doouglas in the time of The Fraser and The Doouglas (First Foremothers of Terra Prime).

The Doouglas: First Foremother, Terra Prime, Chief of Clan Doouglas, Pilot/Spacing technician, Inventor of faster-than-light pulse flight technology, Partner of The Fraser, Terran Reality.

The Fraser: First Foremother, Terra Prime, Chief of Clan Fraser, Healing technician, Partner of The Doouglas, Inventor of immersion therapy used in the Ruler's Rite, Terran Reality.

G'iad'a: Heir to the Condor Throne of the Comin. Nine cycles old. Com-panion and fosterling to Alex and Lauren.

Kall'ka: Empress of the Comin. Holder of the Condor Throne.

T'iik'lac: Past Emperor of the Comin, overthrown by Kall'ka.

L'illa'ka: Commander of the *Golden Condor*, Commander of the Comin nebular fleet, First of the Empress' Guard.

The Thirteen Clans of Terra

Clan Buchan — Master builders

Clan Cador — Chief, Gwenhwyfach, in exile, traitor to the Terran throne

Clan Cameron — Pilots and astro-navigators, Chief Pilot Sarah daughter to the Chief

Clan Doouglas — Ruling clan of Terra for fourteen generations

Clan Fraser — Seneschals to Clan Doouglas, Merilyn last clan member, adopted clan of Lauren

Clan Graham — Allies of Clan Buchan, opponents to Lauren's right-rule in Alex's absence

Clan MacBain — Animal husbandry

Clan MacDonald — Chief, The Lady MacDonald, Terran Lady of the Ancients

Clan McLaran — Chief, Lord McLaran, Head of the Black Guard

Clan McLeod — Chief, Iain McLeod Admiral of the Terran Fleet, Chief of Luna Keep

Clan Newkirk — Chief, Lord Newkirk, Master Psi-Engineer Technician, Master science and psi-technicians

Clan Stuart — Allies of Clan Cador, in exile, traitors to the Terran throne

List of Terran Clan Ships

Alexandra's *Red Dragon* — the *Y Ddraig Goch*

Clan Doouglas' *Sea Eagle* — the *Iolar Mara*

Clan Fraser's *Red Stag* — the *Ruadh làn-damh*

Clan Newkirk's *Golden Kestrel* — the *Ordha Speireag-ghlas*

Clan MacDonald's *Red Lion* — the *Ruadh Leòmhann*

Clan McLaran's *Wild Boar* — the *Faol Muc-fhiadhaich*

Clan Cador's *Black Orchid* — the *Dubh Mogairle*

Pronunciation Guide and Translations

Some of the terms, names and titles are taken loosely from Scottish Gaelic. A translation guide is included below for some of the more intricate terms. These pronunciations could then be used as a guide for pronunciation of other words in the books.

Scottish Gaelic has just eighteen letters each of which is named after a tree or shrub. The consonants all have more than one pronunciation depending on their position in a word and which vowels precede or follow them.

The orthography of Scottish Gaelic was regularized in the late 1970s. For details see: http://www.smo.uhi.ac.uk/gaidhlig/goc/

Thanks to a reviewer for suggesting this be included.

- **a' Mhaighdeann** - A mai den. Translated as "a lady"
- **Bhean chéile aquas Comh-rialóir** - Van Hail a Coo Re-al. Translated as "a Royal Lady"
- **Cáraid Rioghail** - Kar id REE-na. Translated as "Royal Consort"
- **céile** - cee lə. Translated as "partner"
- **Deigh** - dāy
- **éideadn an** - edh ən A. Translated as "Investiture"
- **Ffrwyn** - frē num
- **Fuar Ćala** - For Kăla. Translated as "Cold Harbour"
- **Gríobhtha** - Grĭf fin a
- **Gwenhwyfach** - Guine Vak
- **nighean mhic Fionnaghal** - Nee-an ic FYOON uh gaul. Translated as "daughter of Fiona"
- **Rigain Rioghachd** - Rīoga REE-nah. Translated as "Royal Ruler"
- **Sneachda** - snau
- **Subhachas** - su exes. Translated as "a celebration"
- **Y Ddraig Goch** - ə ðraig gox. Translated as "the Red Dragon

NOTE: The Comin names and terms are pronounced with an accent on the consonant. And a guttural pause at each apostrophe.

Reading List - Book Three
A Quantum Singularity

Carroll, Sean. *The Particle at the End of the Universe: How the Hunt for the Higgs Boson Leads Us to the Edge of a New World*. New York, Dutton, 2012.

Gott, J. Richard. *Time Travel in Einstein's Universe: The Physical Possibilities of Travel Through Time*. Boston, Houghton Mifflin Harcourt, 2001.

Holt, Jim. *When Einstein Walked with Gödel*: Excursions to the Edge of Thought. New York, Farrar, Straus and Giroux, 2018.

Isaacson, Walter. *Einstein: His Life and Universe*. New York, Simon and Schuster, 2007.

Kumar, Manjit. *Quantum: Einstein, Bohr, and the Great Debate About the Nature of Reality*. New York, W.W. Norton, 2008.

NOVA. *Einstein's Quantum Riddle*: Season 46-Episode 2. Directed by Jamie Lochhead. January 9, 2019. Boston, MA: PBS Broadcast.

NOVA. *Inside Einstein's Mind*: Season 42-Episode 23. Directed by Jamie Lochhead. November 25, 2015. Boston, MA: PBS Broadcast.

NOVA. *Einstein's Big Idea*: Season 33-Episode 3. Directed by Gary Johnstone. December 6, 2005. Boston, MA: PBS Broadcast.

Schrödinger, Erwin. *What is Life?: The Physical Aspect of the Living Cell*, Cambridge, UK, Cambridge University Press, 1944.

Reading List - Book Two
A Quantum Uncertainty

Guerrier, Simon, editor. *Short Trips: The History of Christmas (Doctor Who Series Anthology)*. Berkshire, UK, Big Finish Productions, 2005.

Lindley, David. *Uncertainty: Einstein, Heisenberg, Bohr and the Struggle for the Soul of Science*. New York, Doubleday, 2007.

Rovelli, Carlo. *Reality is Not What It Seems: The Journey to Quantum Gravity*. New York, Riverhead Books/Penguin Random House, 2017.

Rovelli, Carlo. *Seven Brief Lessons on Physics*. New York, Riverhead Books/Penguin Random House, 2016.

Rovelli, Carlo. *The First Scientist: Anaximander and His Legacy*. Pennsylvania, Westholme Publishing, 2011.

Sobel, Dava. *The Glass Universe-How the Ladies of Harvard Observatory Took the Measure of the Stars*. New York, Viking Press/Penguin Random House, 2016.

Stewart, Ian. *Calculating the Cosmos-How Mathematics Unveils the Universe*. New York, Basic Books/Hachette, 2016.

Tegmark, Max. *Our Mathematical Universe: My Quest for the Ultimate Nature of Reality*. New York, Alfred P. Knopf, 2015.

Reading List – Book One
A Quantum Convergence

Crease, Robert P. and Alfred Scharff Goldhaber. *The Quantum Moment: How Planck, Bohr, Einstein, and Heisenberg Taught Us to Love Uncertainty.* New York, W.W. Norton, 2015.

Greene, Brian. *The Fabric of the Cosmos: Space, Time, and the Texture of Reality.* New York, Alfred P. Knopf, 2003.

Greene, Brian. *The Elegant Universe: Superstrings, Hidden Dimensions, and the Quest for the Ultimate Theory.* New York, W.W. Norton, 1999.

Greene, Brian. *The Hidden Reality: Parallel Universes and the Deep Laws of the Cosmos.* New York, Alfred P. Knopf, 2011.

Gribbin, John. *In Search of Schrödinger's Cat: Quantum Physics and Reality.* New York, Bantam Books, 1984.

Gribbin, John. *Schrödinger's Kittens and the Search for Reality: Solving the Quantum Mysteries.* Boston, Little Brown & Co, 1995.

Gribbin, John. *In Search of the Multiverse.* Hoboken, Wiley, 2009

Kaku, Michio. *Parallel Worlds: A Journey Through Creation, Higher Dimensions, and the Future of the Cosmos.* New York, Doubleday, 2004.

Randall, Lisa. *Warped Passages: Unraveling the Mysteries of the Universe's Hidden Dimensions.* New York City, HarperCollins, 2005.

Smolin, Lee. *Time Reborn: From the Crisis in Physics to the Future of the Universe.* Boston, Houghton Mifflin Harcourt, 2013.